Women's Weird 2

Also published by Handheld Press

Women's Weird 2

More Strange Stories by Women,

1891–1937

edited by Melissa Edmundson

Handheld Classic 18

This edition published in 2020 by Handheld Press
72 Warminster Road, Bath BA2 6RU, United Kingdom.
www.handheldpress.co.uk

ISBN 978-1-912766-44-4

1 2 3 4 5 6 7 8 9 0

Series design by Nadja Guggi and typeset in Adobe Caslon Pro
and Open Sans.

Printed and bound in Great Britain by Short Run Press, Exeter.

MIX
Paper from
responsible sources
FSC® C014540

Contents

Acknowledgments

I would like to express my gratitude to Kate Macdonald of Handheld Press, for commissioning me to curate the stories in this book.

My thanks go as well to Stefan Dziemianowicz and Mike Ashley for providing information on the status of the estate of Mary Elizabeth Counselman.

For securing the republication rights to stories still in copyright, I appreciate the help of Sharon Eden for permission to reprint Marjorie Bowen's 'Florence Flannery', as well as Becky Brown of Curtis Brown and the Estate of Stella Gibbons for permission to reprint Gibbons' 'Roaring Tower'.

Finally, I wish to thank Jeff Makala for his feedback on the introduction, his editorial assistance, and for helping to secure a first edition copy of Bessie Kyffin-Taylor's *From Out of the Silence*.

Melissa Edmundson

Melissa Edmundson is a Lecturer in English Literature at Clemson University, South Carolina, and works on nineteenth and early twentieth-century British women writers, with a particular interest in women's supernatural fiction. She is the editor of a 2011 critical edition of Alice Perrin's *East of Suez* (1901), and author of *Women's Ghost Literature in Nineteenth-Century Britain* (2013) and *Women's Colonial Gothic Writing, 1850–1930: Haunted Empire* (2018). She edited *Avenging Angels: Ghost Stories by Victorian Women Writers* (2018), and *Women's Weird: Strange Stories by Women, 1890–1940* (2019).

Introduction

BY MELISSA EDMUNDSON

In her introduction to *The Supernatural in Modern English Fiction* (1917), Dorothy Scarborough discusses the lasting popularity of the supernatural tale. Mentioning Lafcadio Hearn's comment in *Interpretations of Literature* (1916) that the supernatural 'touches something within us that relates to infinity', Scarborough considers how interest in the paranormal is connected to fundamental emotions shared by all humanity:

> This continuing presence of the weird in literature shows the popular demand for it and must have some basis in human psychosis. The night side of the soul attracts us all. The spirit feeds on mystery. It lives not by fact alone but by the unknowable, and there is no highest mystery without the supernatural. Man loves the frozen touch of fear, and realizes pure terror only when touched by the unmortal [...] Man's varying moods create heaven, hell, and faery wonder-lands for him, and people them with strange beings. (Scarborough 1917, 2)

This is integral to the continuance and the evolution of the supernatural in fiction. Our ghosts change as we change; like us, they must adapt, and in so doing, reflect modern sensibilities and complexities. As Scarborough says, 'Primitive times produced a primitive supernaturalism and the gradual advance in intellectual development has brought about a heightening and complexity of the weird story. 'Tis in ourselves that ghosts are thus and so!' (Scarborough 1917, 126).

Scarborough continued this analysis in the introduction to her edited anthology *Famous Modern Ghost Stories* (1921), in which she examines how supernatural literature evolved in the early decades of the twentieth century: 'Modern ghosts are less simple and primitive than their ancestors, and are developing complexes of various kinds. They are more democratic than of old, and have more of a diversity of interests, so that mortals have scarcely the ghost of a chance with them' (Scarborough 1921, xi). Yet these supernatural beings always retain a connection with the living and the power of the writer to create new worlds of terror: 'Man's imagination, always bigger than his environment, overleaps the barriers of time and space and claims all worlds as eminent domain, so that literature, which he has the power to create [...] possesses a dramatic intensity, an epic sweep, unknown in actuality. In the last analysis, man is as great as his daydreams – or his nightmares!' (Scarborough 1921, viii–ix).

In her Preface to the collection *Kecksies and Other Twilight Tales* (published posthumously by Arkham House in 1976), Marjorie Bowen echoes Scarborough as she comments on the ability of the ghost story to adapt and to retain a sense of vitality for the reader. These stories are rooted in universal fears that have existed since the first supernatural stories were written. She observes, 'The old-fashioned emphasis on evil, the malice of the dead, the unholy power of fiend and phantom, the miasma, shuddering into palpable shakes of secret crime, is what arouses that thrill of emotion that is the tribute to the most satisfactory kind of ghost story' (Bowen 1976, x). The 'old ghost stories' continue to be meaningful in their many reimaginings because they retain the emphasis on doubt, and '[n]one can be "explained", made credible, or wholly destroyed' (Bowen 1976, x). These stories remain 'expressions of the desire to relate the terrible, the monstrous, or the incredible that some story-tellers ardently feel' (Bowen 1976, ix). Bowen is speaking from personal experience. In her autobiography *The Debate Continues* (1939), she recalls feeling a continued sense of fear and unease while staying in her grandmother's house in Hampstead: 'the rooms above were the worst of all. Someone must have told me about ghosts, devils and demons, for I soon peopled those top rooms with every imaginable terror' (Campbell 1939, 14). She continues:

> My sufferings were acute; night after night I lay awake listening to what I supposed were footsteps overhead, crouching under the bedclothes in terror of the ghosts and demons that I believed would at any moment descend upon me. All these terrors were a secret that I kept to myself, so no one was to be blamed for this mental anguish, which became so acute that I would have destroyed myself had I known how. (Campbell 1939, 14)

As a professional writer, Bowen would put her experiences to good use, channeling these childhood terrors and crafting some of the best Weird fiction ever written.

With Scarborough and Bowen's ideas in mind, we can contemplate what exactly it is about the supernatural, the Weird, the unexplained that continues to fascinate us. What is it about these stories that attracts us and keeps us coming back for more? Why are we drawn to the unknown, the dark corners of our subconscious? One major appeal is the escapism and entertainment value these stories provide and the fact that we can vicariously experience fear and danger in the safety of our favourite reading nook. However, Weird stories give us something else, something not as easily defined. They help us come to terms with our shared sense of fear at what we cannot control or explain. And through written descriptions of someone's encounters with the unknown – whether in a work of fiction or in a personal account such as Bowen's – we begin to see that the supernatural does not alienate us, but instead it connects us. By reading these stories, we see that we are not alone in our own struggles. For all its ghosts, ghouls, demons, and monsters, a continuing interest in human relationships and individual character – with all their flaws and weaknesses, their strength and resilience – is at the heart of these scary stories.

Women's Weird 2 showcases how supernatural fiction written by women developed in ways similar to Scarborough and Bowen's descriptions of the progression of the modern supernatural tale. These stories, covering roughly fifty years from the early 1890s to the late 1930s, complicate and expand more traditional notions of the Victorian supernatural, and while the reader can still find ghosts within the pages of this volume, the spectres themselves have become more varied as a result of 'living' in the modern world. They have become more complex and carry more cultural baggage. For writers who had witnessed world war, the devastating effects of imperialism, first-wave feminism, and economic depression, the supernatural story could never be the same.

Terror Incognita: Widening the Possibilities for Women's Weird Fiction

Women's Weird 2 develops the premise of the original *Women's Weird* volume of 2019 by extending into new territories. Perhaps most notably, there is wider geographical coverage. In addition to British and US writers, this volume includes writers from Australia, Canada, Ireland, and New Zealand, and the stories themselves take readers into remote and uncanny Australian bush landscapes, secluded islands, Anglo-Indian hill stations, and South American jungles. With this regional diversity comes more variety within the stories themselves. Some tales expand on traditional tropes of the ghost story. Lucy Maud Montgomery's 'The House Party at Smoky Island', comes closest to what would be termed a 'proper' ghostly tale, while Katherine Mansfield's 'The House' and Bessie Kyffin-Taylor's 'Outside the House' present apparitions in significantly new and inventive ways. Other stories concern themselves with ideas of haunting, even when no ghosts are present. By including such stories, this volume will hopefully challenge the already blurred boundaries between the Weird, the Gothic, and the ghostly. In *The*

Weird (2011), Ann and Jeff VanderMeer comment on the melding of genres and modes that is inherent within so-called Weird literature:

> As a twentieth and twenty-first century art form the story of The Weird is the story of the refinement (and de-stabilization) of supernatural fiction within an established framework but also of the welcome contamination of that fiction by the influence of other traditions, some only peripherally connected to the fantastic. (VanderMeer & VanderMeer 2011, xv–xvi)

Sean Moreland likewise notes that 'rather than a fixed literary form or genre, weird fiction is best understood as a series of mutations and hybridizations of other literary forms' (Moreland 2017, 166). With these parameters (or lack thereof?) in mind, the stories included in *Women's Weird 2* intentionally push the boundaries of what Weird fiction can be. One story in this current volume has no supernatural element at all but is nonetheless quintessentially 'weird' in setting and atmosphere. Other stories have happy endings, yet again, those endings come about through decidedly weird events.

While it is useful to see a blending of modes and genres within the Weird, it is also helpful in our understanding of the evolution of the Weird tale written by women to recognise a broader, more long-standing tradition of women's supernatural writing in general, a tradition that critics tend to limit to the Victorian era. However, expanding our horizons with regard to women's involvement in the Gothic and Weird shows us that they were integral to early depictions of the supernatural. Scholars of the early Gothic have been guilty at times of having tunnel vision when it comes to appreciating the vast role women played in the development of the genre at the turn of the nineteenth century. Making the work of Ann Radcliffe as a Gothic novelist most prominent at the expense of other women writers and other literary forms has resulted in the often-restrictive concept of the 'female Gothic'. While this term has allowed us to appreciate different writing styles and authorial attitudes within the Gothic, it has also become a definition that tends to leave out a number of women who were writing subversive, innovative supernatural short fiction and poetry in the opening decades of the 1800s. In these works, particularly in the Gothic ballads of writers such as Anne Bannerman, Charlotte Dacre, and Elizabeth Harcourt Rolls, happy endings and fainting heroines were absent. Instead we find unexplained endings, nightmarish landscapes, biting social commentary, and encounters with dangerous otherworldly beings. Women's supernatural fiction in the latter half of the nineteenth century and early twentieth century has more in common with these writers than with the work of Ann Radcliffe. By connecting women's more recent strange fiction with fiction and poetry of this earlier era, we can begin to see the Victorian ghost story not as a beginning and end of women's involvement with the supernatural, but as a continuation in the ongoing development of the supernatural tale written by women, a tradition that encompasses the Gothic, the Weird, the ghost story, the macabre, and the horror story. So while classification systems are important in helping us recognise the nuances in the 'ghost story' and the 'weird story', we also need to appreciate how these borders frequently break down and transgress easily defined categories.

Like the first volume of *Women's Weird* (2019), the strange elements in the present volume take many forms. In addition to geographic locations, this volume highlights weird places, evidenced by the many stories with 'room' and 'house' in the title. Anthony Vidler, in his study of the 'architectural uncanny', says that buildings give a sense of 'estrangement', 'alienation', and a 'feeling of unease' (Vidler 1999, ix, 3). He claims that 'the house provided an especially favored site for uncanny disturbances: its apparent domesticity, its residue of family history and nostalgia, its role as the last and most intimate shelter of private comfort sharpened by contrast the terror of invasion by alien spirits' (Vidler

1999, 17). There are several stories that reinvent how we read and understand the preternatural and focus on how a haunted self can exist within a weird landscape. For instance, Katherine Mansfield's 'The House' is a picture of domestic bliss that becomes too good to be true because it is haunted by unlived futures. The young colonial family in Bithia Mary Croker's 'The Red Bungalow' is haunted by a troubled past that aggressively 'lives' within what otherwise should be a contented domestic space. The demonic terror in Lettice Galbraith's 'The Blue Room' seems to be of the past, present, and future. In the story, the evil force represented by the otherworldly entity is not destroyed, only displaced, waiting to be summoned again. And the alternative dimension in Mary E Wilkins Freeman's 'The Hall Bedroom' symbolises both the unfulfilled lives of people who inhabit the space as well as the desperation of those who choose to enter an uncertain future in order to escape the confines of the 'regular' world.[1] As the spiritualist Violet Tweedale observes, 'Wherever some great mental disturbance has taken place, wherever overwhelming sorrow, hatred, pain, terror, or any kind of violent passion has been felt, an impression of a very marked character has been imprinted on the astral light' (Tweedale 1919, 221). These physical spaces are indeed 'marked' by a traumatic event that occurs within them as the stories show how our surroundings can control us and shape behavior. The traumatic – the feeling of being altered by some inescapable event, memory, or feeling – can also be weird, and several stories included in the volume explore these connections and similarities.

Barbara Baynton's 'A Dreamer', while presenting no actual supernatural elements, nonetheless describes a weird, uncanny, and hostile landscape. The story concerns both outer and inner worlds: the Australian bush setting that seemingly prohibits the progress of the woman, as well as the woman's own emotional upheaval as she desperately tries to return to a home (and an idea of home) that is forever changed, alien, unattainable. Emily Carr, in her study of the Gothic and ecofeminism, has discussed how 'the real and the unreal, the domestic and the grotesque, the alluring and the terrible coexist. The everyday is collapsed with the nightmarish; distortion, dislocation and disruption become the norm' (Carr 2913, 164). Baynton's story shows us these collapses while presenting readers with an example of how the realist mode can also be weird and unsettling. The 'dreamer' can only imagine a home that is now lost, as she battles with a familiar yet strange landscape that resists her efforts to find that lost home. In the end, the dream becomes nightmare.

These stories engage directly with historical events and use the Weird to comment on the lingering trauma caused by those events. Anne Whitehead has claimed that our connection with the past is a consistently troubled one, saying that our inability to completely know history makes it something that 'perpetually escapes or eludes our understanding' (Whitehead 2004, 13). Shadows of the First World War appear in Bessie Kyffin-Taylor's 'Outside the House', a story that reflects women's involvement in WWI writing. While most women remained on the home front during the war, they saw the tragic after-effects of soldiers returning home and wrote about it in their fiction. Kyffin-Taylor's story is representative of numerous other supernatural WWI stories written by women throughout the 1920s and 1930s, including war-tinged collections by Elizabeth Bowen, H D Everett, and Naomi Royde-Smith. The soldier-protagonist in 'Outside the House' is doubly haunted. He has seen horrific human destruction on the battlefield, but when he visits a family home in the English countryside, his supposedly peaceful recuperation from a leg injury becomes yet another battlefield. When initially confronted with the supernatural mystery in the story, he remarks,

> Some of us out in 'No-Man's-Land' were not unknowing of
> other forms being present as well as our comrades in the
> flesh. There are those of us, who, in spite of the jeerings
> of scoffers, still say, that the Angels of Mons were *not* the

phantasy of unhinged minds [...] Therefore, I, among many others, have learned to be less sceptical and not to take non-understandable things as impossibilities. (143)

Kyffin-Taylor, by combining the supernatural with explorations of traumatic memory, anticipates modern descriptions of trauma as a form of possession or haunting.

Cathy Caruth has stated that '[t]o be traumatized is precisely to be possessed by an image or event' (Caruth 1995, 4–5). Roger Luckhurst has discussed trauma and its relation to representations of psychical disorder within a supernatural framework: 'Trauma is a piercing or breach of a border that puts inside and outside into strange communion. Trauma violently opens passageways between systems that were once discrete, making unforeseen connections that distress or confound' (Luckhurst 2008, 3). The concepts of 'inside' and 'outside' appear in innovative ways within Kyffin-Taylor's story: the 'outside' is a dangerous place, but so is the 'inside' of a mind that has seen too much. Trauma often resists precise representation and becomes that which is inexpressible or unreachable, returning over and over again to haunt its object. This resistance is symbolised in the figure of the ghost or other supernatural event as a force which seeks to relay a message or to expose a hidden truth, and in 'Outside the House' this truth is about the return of haunted memory from the recesses of the human mind and from the bowels of the earth.

Tensions over the British colonisation of India surface in Bithia Mary Croker's 'The Red Bungalow'. On an even more ominous level, the supernatural presence in the story specifically targets children, the most vulnerable members of the Anglo-Indian community. Fiction about the occult and supernatural and fiction about empire are both concerned with what lies beyond the margins of the everyday world. According to Simon Hay, because 'the only-marginally-visible is precisely the central concern of ghost stories in general', these stories are thus 'insistently about

Empire' (Hay 2011, 10). There is a double anxiety in these narratives: one concerned with the tenuous presence of the British as an occupying power, and another with the disruption of everyday life by strange, unexplained events. Likewise, the importance of personal encounters – natural ones between the living as well as supernatural ones between the living and the dead – are the central concern of the supernaturally-themed story and are also at the heart of colonial narratives. However, Croker's story also merges into the Weird in how she refuses to let us 'see' the malign presence in the story. The juxtaposition of normality and abnormality is heightened by the fact that '[i]t was a beautiful afternoon, the sun streamed in upon them', and yet the seemingly empty room is 'not empty to the trembling little creatures on the table, for with wide, mad eyes they seemed to follow the motion of a something that was creeping round the room close to the wall' (110). Croker never describes the supernatural being in detail, leaving it up to the reader's imagination just what it is that preys on the family. This refusal to reveal the true nature of the entity serves to amplify the horror latent in these lines of the story. She leaves us in an uncertain space, not knowing exactly of what it is we should be frightened. Just as with the Weird in general, we cannot precisely describe it, but we know it is there, and it unsettles us.

Supernatural creatures return in *Women's Weird 2*, from incubi, grotesque fish beings, and slugs, to glowing blobs, giant rat-like monsters, and predatory fairies. The meaning latent in such creatures is directly tied to the English word 'monster', from the Latin 'monstrum', a combination of 'to reveal' and 'to portend'. The monstrous creatures in these stories indeed do both. They threaten the natural world and our place within it, while they also highlight that which is lacking in the people who summon or interact with such beings. These otherworldly creatures show us what can happen when we lose control of an otherwise regulated world. This world seemingly operates under a series of 'rules', but as these stories reveal, the rules are often illusory and easily broken. Whether it is a deal with a demonic force, a betrayed lover, or a desire for fame, the protagonists must reckon with the consequences of their decisions. These creatures constantly remind us that everything comes with a cost, and past mistakes must be paid for.

Crime and mystery are closely linked to the Weird tale, and these themes are central to several stories, including Edith Stewart Drewry's 'A Twin-Identity', Mary Elizabeth Counselman's 'The Black Stone Statue', and Lucy Maud Montgomery's 'The House Party at Smoky Island'. Significantly, however, the detective in 'A Twin-Identity' cannot rationalise the supernatural event that leads to the solving of the crime. The crime in Counselman's story is directly tied to greed and frustrated ambition, while the rumoured murder in Montgomery's narrative is explained by an apparition whose appearance remains unexpected and mysterious.

Women are a continuing subject of interest to these authors, and it is perhaps not surprising that it would take female authors to establish women characters as central protagonists in these types of stories. Versions of female power can be seen in Sarah Orne Jewett's 'The Green Bowl' with its exploration of witchcraft. Jewett's story is double-edged: the power of second sight is passed down from woman to woman, but that power – seeing into people's futures that brings happiness and tragedy – is also a burden.[2] Elizabeth Ammons claims that Jewett 'seems to have believed that there existed a type of therapeutic female psychic energy which could be communicated telepathically and which could operate both to bond individuals and to create a spiritual community – or occult sisterhood – among women in general' (Ammons 1984, 168). According to Ammons, this 'energy' is passed down from one generation to the next in order to keep traditions alive within the female community: 'A key pattern in Jewett is the initiation of one woman, usually younger and sometimes a girl, into the powerful, extrasensory, and usually ultraterrestrial female knowledge possessed by another' (Ammons 1984, 168). In Jewett's story, the green bowl itself takes on a weird, unexplained quality as the conduit for the continuance of this 'female knowledge'. As Monika Elbert and Wendy Ryden note, the 'exotic object' which 'seem[s] to be inhabited by an unseen presence via a mysterious provenance' creates 'a disjunction, rendered at times as horrifying, grotesque, and *unheimlich*', between the ill-defined boundaries of the natural and the supernatural (Elbert & Ryden 2017, 499). In Jewett's story, this object becomes 'both familiar and strange; a commodity and yet a source of spiritual and communal connection; part of the homey New England farm interior and yet arrived from foreign shores under perhaps sketchy circumstances' (Elbert & Ryden 2017, 499). In this way, '[t]he secret of the bowls themselves hovers in the liminal space between the natural and the supernatural as well as the exotic and domestic realms' (Elbert & Ryden 2017, 502). Thus, the mystery of the bowls and their placement within the household, along with the strange effect they have on the women who come into contact with them, become yet another example of the 'less easily mapped spaces' that appear so often in Jewett's weird fiction (Downey 2014, 141).[3]

The extrasensory perceptions and psychic powers of Viola in Helen Simpson's 'Young Magic' likewise turn from something empowering, something that gives her an imaginative release from an otherwise dull life, into something she cannot control. In the story, Viola's uncle tells her mother, 'You suppose that your daughter must be lonely and dull if she is left alone with her imagination, because, similarly left, you would yourself be lonely and dull. And why? Because you, in common with most fully developed persons, physically, are in the habit of restraining your imagination' (190). Simpson's coming-of-age story explores a darker side to imagination, of letting things inside. Viola's childhood fairytale worlds, where she becomes a heroic prince, change into something more intense and violent with adolescence. As a young woman, she attempts to use her ESP to establish an emotional connection with her would-be fiancé when the two are physically apart, but soon learns that her powers have even greater, more troubling consequences. It turns out that some imaginary friends – who are not so imaginary after all – refuse to go away.

The New Woman becomes a major character in two stories from the 1890s: 'A Twin-Identity' and 'The Blue Room'. Patricia Murphy has noted how the New Woman Gothic incorporates elements of Victorian Gothic, a sub-genre that has typically been discussed 'from a masculinist perspective whereby the female somehow deserves disapprobation for creating chaos and danger' (Murphy 2016, 6). In 'The Blue Room' one woman from a past century creates the chaos that resides in the room over several generations, but it is a modern woman who is integral to solving the mystery. The narrator herself admits, 'If Miss Erristoun, now, hadn't been the clever, strong-minded young lady she is, she'd never have cleared the Blue Room of its terrible secret' (22). The protagonist in 'A Twin-Identity' is even more unconventional for her time. As a woman detective with the Paris police, Marie Lacroix describes herself as having 'a woman's wits and a man's courage' (1), and she must use both to solve the murder mystery at the heart of the story.

Other stories navigate the fine line between woman as victimiser and woman as victim. This is a central concern in Marjorie Bowen's 'Florence Flannery', as well as 'The House Party at Smoky Island', which tells a tale reminiscent of Daphne du Maurier's *Rebecca*, though Montgomery's story was published a year before du Maurier's novel. Both stories revel in the pull of the past. In 'Florence Flannery' two unconventional, opportunistic women merge as the present-day Florence must reckon with the choices made by her predecessor. In the story's opening line, 'She who had been Florence Flannery...' (156), Bowen gives her readers a hint to the chilling conclusion of the tale. The old and the modern blend together in both stories as we see that what is done in the past continues to influence the present and future. Likewise, the women depicted show us that the *femme fatale* is an effective plot device for the Weird tale.

In Stella Gibbons' 'Roaring Tower' a young woman who has suffered the forced end to a love affair must learn to live again. Told from the perspective of the woman near the end of her life, the story centres on themes of forgiveness and acceptance and how grief and loneliness can be unifying emotions that lead us to a greater understanding of the pain of others. The protagonist's encounter with the monstrous creature and the story's ultimate outcome represent an exception to most weird narratives. Despite its difference from other weird stories – and also because of this difference – 'Roaring Tower' is a quintessential example of what women's Weird can be.

Women's Weird 2 also spotlights women's involvement in *Weird Tales*. Eric Leif Davin notes that there were at least 127 known women writers who published 365 stories in that magazine from 1923–1954 (Davin 2006, 68). He describes the pivotal role women played within the pages of *Weird Tales* during its years of publication:

> [The magazine] published women from the very beginning of its existence, in which all editors published women writers during their tenures, a magazine with a long-time female editor [Dorothy McIlwraith], with a female artist [Margaret Brundage] sometimes called 'The First Lady of pulp magazine illustration' as the most famous of its cover artists, with a readership which may have been over a quarter female, with a membership in the magazine's fan club which may have been between a quarter and almost a third female, with over 17 percent of its fiction authors female, and with over 40 percent of its poets female. (Davin 2006, 68)

Mary Elizabeth Counselman, who is probably most well-known among connoisseurs of the Weird for her frequent and popular contributions to the magazine over several years, specialised in stories that incorporated strange happenings in order to highlight the darker side of the human psyche. She eventually published thirty stories in *Weird Tales*, including 'The Three Marked Pennies' (August 1934), which was voted by readers as one of the most popular tales ever published in the magazine. Another *Weird Tales* contributor will most likely come as a surprise: Lucy Maud Montgomery. Her supernatural tales were written over the span of forty years and show a very different side to the author of the beloved *Anne of Green Gables* series.[4]

(Re)Defining Boundaries, Expanding Voices

The difficulty that has consistently met critics who try to apply a set, all-encompassing definition to the Weird, to the ghost story, and to the Gothic in general, is just as evident when we try to summarise women's involvement in these literary modes and genres. Their contributions are traditional and innovative, conservative and subversive, simplistic and complex. Often these dichotomies occur within the same story. But one thing is certain: from the late nineteenth century and into the first half of the twentieth, women were integral to the development of the Weird tale. The stories collected in *Women's Weird 2* will hopefully continue to show the vast creative output within the wider tradition of supernatural writing and place these women's names alongside those of M R James, Arthur Machen, Algernon Blackwood, William Hope Hodgson, Lafcadio Hearn, and H P Lovecraft. *Women's Weird 2* includes ghost stories in order to show the continuities in the ghost story tradition – which had its beginning before the Victorian era – as well as the developments, expansions, and innovations that occur in supernatural literature and Weird fiction during the first half of the twentieth century. These stories have something to tell us of our never-ending relationship to uncertainty, doubt, fear, and the things which lurk in the shadows. These 'things' take different forms: the ghost, the grotesque creature, the stranger on the street, the person in the mirror.

The stories span continents and centuries, are told from a multitude of voices, and present entities that both intrigue and repel. They show us humanity at its best and worst and challenge us with meanings and messages that always fall somewhere between the explained and unexplained. As a group, women's Weird, like the Weird and Gothic, refuses to be contained and controlled. Just when we think we have it figured out, it escapes our grasp in order to return in newer, scarier, and more imaginative forms.

Notes

1   Unlike many writers included in *Women's Weird 2*, Mary E Wilkins Freeman's supernatural fiction was recognised and admired by contemporary critics. In *The Development of the American Short Story* (1923), Fred Lewis Pattee praised Freeman for her ability to craft such effective supernatural narratives, noting that her literary fame allowed Freeman to delve into the commercially 'riskier' areas of speculative short fiction: 'In later years, after her fame was secure enough to dominate to a degree her market, she attempted often pure symbolism [...] and once, at least, the area of ghostly mysticism. Her ghost stories in *The Wind in the Rose Bush* are among the best New England has ever produced – unconventional, unexplained, unreduced, yet seemingly natural and wholly convincing' (Pattee 1923, 322). Freeman herself had a complicated attitude towards her supernatural fiction. After her contemporary Sarah Orne Jewett wrote to Freeman on 12 August 1889 commending the latter's story 'A Gentle Ghost' (1889), Freeman responded by saying, 'You don't know how glad I am that you do like my Gentle Ghost, for I have felt somewhat uncertain as to how it would be liked. It is in some respects a departure from my usual vein, and I have made a little lapse into the mystical and romantic one for which I have strong inclination, but do not generally yield to' (Freeman 1985, 97). On 5 September 1919, writing to Pattee, Freeman was even more honest in her description of having to write for public taste: 'Most of my own work, is not really the kind I myself like. I want more symbolism, more mysticism. I left that out, because it struck me people did not want it, and I was forced to consider selling qualities' (Freeman 1985, 382).

2   Sarah Orne Jewett's recurring focus on witchcraft and versions of female psychical power within her short fiction (as well as in her 1896 work *The*

Country of the Pointed Firs) is also evidenced by her continuing interest in Spiritualist and occult practices. She visited Spiritualist mediums on a few occasions and spoke about them favourably. On 4 April 1882 she wrote to her friend and fellow author John Greenleaf Whittier:

> She [the spirit medium Rose Darrah] told me wonderful things about my father and about his death and our relation to each other, and what he said to me was amazing. [...]

> There was no 'mind reading'. I have not thought of her for months, but it all needed no proof, and it gives me such a pleasant glimpse of father's life. It was a very long talk and it was very pleasant. There was much about my writing, and about my taking care of myself, that showed on someone's part a complete knowledge of 'the situation'.

> I do not think I care to go again, though it was said Father wished to say one or two other things before I went away. I can't tell you how much good it did me, for it made me certain of some things which had puzzled me. I should like to go to another 'medium' someday, to see what was common to the two, for I still have 'an eye out' for tricks of the trade and yet I can't help being ashamed as I write this, for it was all so real and so perfectly sensible and straightforward, and free from silliness. (quoted in Blanchard 181, 182)

3   The masculine club setting that provides the frame story for so many supernatural tales is made a distinctly female space in Jewett's story, something Elbert and Ryden call 'a kind of feminised club tale that relays the story to a parlor assemblage' (Elbert & Ryden 2017, 499). This idea becomes even more meaningful when we also consider that the story appeared in *A House Party: An Account of Stories Told at a Gathering of Famous American Authors*, and Jewett was invited to contribute a story to a literary 'gathering' that contained stories by mostly male authors.

4   According to Rea Wilmshurst, Montgomery wrote in her journals about her disbelief in Spiritualism, though she did take part in a few 'table rapping' sessions (Wilmshurst 1992, 11). Yet in 1919, after the death of her friend Frederica Campbell, Montgomery wrote in her journal that animals 'are aware of presences which human beings cannot sense', and felt that Campbell had tried to reach her through Daffy, her cat (quoted in Wilmshurst 1992, 12; Montgomery 1985, 320). Montgomery returned to the Gothic and supernatural in several of her short stories and later novels. For Wilmshurst, these represent a 'less acknowledged aspect of Canada's favourite author' (Wilmshurst 1992, 7).

Works Cited

Ammons, Elizabeth, 'Jewett's Witches,' in *Critical Essays on Sarah Orne Jewett*, Gwen L Nagel (ed.) (Boston 1984), 165–183.

Blanchard, Paula, *Sarah Orne Jewett: Her World and Her Work* (Reading MA 1994).

Bowen, Marjorie, 'Preface,' in *Kecksies and Other Twilight Tales* (Sauk City WI 1976), ix–xiii.

— [as Margaret Campbell], *The Debate Continues, Being the Autobiography of Marjorie Bowen* (London 1939).

Carr, Emily, 'The Riddle Was the Angel in the House: Towards an American Ecofeminist Gothic,' in *Ecogothic*, Andrew Smith and William Hughes (eds.) (Manchester 2013), 160–176.

Caruth, Cathy, 'Introduction,' *Trauma: Explorations in Memory* (Baltimore 1995), 3–12.

Davin, Eric Leif, *Partners in Wonder: Women and the Birth of Science Fiction, 1926–1965* (Lanham MD 2006).

Downey, Dara, *American Women's Ghost Stories in the Gilded Age* (Basingstoke and New York 2014).

Elbert, Monika, and Wendy Ryden, 'EcoGothic Disjunctions: Natural and Supernatural Liminality in Sarah Orne Jewett's Haunted Landscapes,' *ISLE: Interdisciplinary Studies in Literature and Environment*, 24.3 (Summer 2017), 496–513.

Freeman, Mary E Wilkins, *The Infant Sphinx: Collected Letters of Mary E. Wilkins Freeman*, Brent L. Kendrick (ed.) (Metuchen NJ 1985).

Hay, Simon, *A History of the Modern British Ghost Story* (Basingstoke and New York 2011).

Luckhurst, Roger, *The Trauma Question* (London and New York 2008).

Montgomery, L M, *The Selected Journals of L M Montgomery: 1910–1921*, vol 2, Mary Rubio and Elizabeth Waterston (eds.) (Oxford 1985).

Moreland, Sean, 'Weird and Cosmic Horror Fiction,' in *Horror Literature through History: An Encyclopedia of the Stories that Speak to Our Deepest Fears*, vol. 1, Matt Cardin (ed.), (Santa Barbara CA 2017), 163–168.

Murphy, Patricia, *The New Woman Gothic: Reconfigurations of Distress* (Columbia MO 2016).

Pattee, Fred Lewis, *The Development of the American Short Story: An Historical Survey* (New York and London 1923).

Scarborough, Dorothy, *The Supernatural in Modern English Fiction* (New York and London 1917).

— , 'The Imperishable Ghost: Introduction,' in *Famous Modern Ghost Stories* (New York and London 1921), vii–xix.

Tweedale, Violet, *Ghosts I Have Seen and Other Psychic Experiences* (New York 1919).

VanderMeer, Ann and Jeff, 'Introduction,' *The Weird: A Compendium of Strange and Dark Stories*, Ann and Jeff VanderMeer (eds.) (New York 2011), xv–xx.

Vidler, Anthony, *The Architectural Uncanny: Essays in the Modern Unhomely* (Cambridge MA 1999).

Whitehead, Anne, *Trauma Fiction* (Edinburgh 2004).

Wilmshurst, Rea, 'Introduction,' *Among the Shadows* (1990) (Toronto ON 1992), 7–15.

Biographical notes

Barbara Baynton (1857–1929) was born in Scone, New South Wales, to John Lawrence and Elizabeth Ewart Lawrence, who had immigrated to Australia from Londonderry, Ireland. Baynton and her siblings endured the physical and mental harshness of Australian bush life from an early age. Baynton accepted a position as governess to the Frater family living in Liverpool Plains, New South Wales. When she decided to marry one of the older Frater sons (against the wishes of the father), she and her husband moved to an even more remote location, near Coonamble. By 1889, Alex Frater had abandoned his wife and their three small children for a younger woman. For a time, Barbara was forced to sell bibles door-to-door until she found a position as a housekeeper in the Woollahra residence of Dr Thomas Baynton. In 1890, after being granted a divorce and custody of her children, Barbara married Thomas Baynton. Achieving a steadier life with a more supportive and financially stable husband allowed Barbara the leisure time she needed to begin her writing career. Baynton resided in London during the First World War, where she had lived since Thomas Baynton's death in 1904, and both her London home and her country home near Cambridge were used as open houses for soldiers. She married Rowland George Allanson Allanson-Winn, 5th Baron Headley, in 1921, but after his bankruptcy, she returned to Australia, living in Melbourne until her death. As well as newspaper articles, Baynton published two collections of short stories, *Bush Studies* (1902) and *Cobbers* (1917), and one short novel, *Human Toll* (1907).

Marjorie Bowen (1885–1952) is the pseudonym of Margaret Gabrielle Vere Long (née Campbell). She was born on Hayling Island in Hampshire, England, to Vere Douglas Campbell and Josephine Elisabeth Bowen Ellis Campbell. Her parents separated when she was four, and Bowen disliked her mother's bohemian lifestyle which meant that the family often lived in poverty. She studied at the Slade School of Fine Art and worked as a research assistant at the British Museum. Bowen published numerous historical novels, and her sensational first novel, *The Viper of Milan* (1906), set in medieval Italy, went on to become a bestseller and provided Bowen with financial security. In 1912, Bowen married Zeffirino Emilio Constanzo, and the couple had one surviving son. After Constanzo's death, she married Arthur L Long, with whom she had two sons. Throughout her career, Bowen used many pseudonyms, including Robert Paye, George R Preedy, and John Winch. She wrote mystery novels as 'Joseph Shearing'. Her supernatural novels include *Black Magic: A Tale of the Rise and Fall of Antichrist* (1909), *The Haunted Vintage* (1921), *Julia Roseingrave* (1933), and *The Fetch* (1942). Bowen's supernatural fiction appears in *The Last Bouquet* (1933), *The Bishop of Hell* (1949), and *Kecksies*, a posthumous collection assembled by Arkham House in the late 1940s and published in 1976. She published her autobiography, *The Debate Continues, Being the Autobiography of Marjorie Bowen*, in 1939.

Mary Elizabeth Counselman (1911–1995) was born in Birmingham, Alabama, to John Sanders Counselman and Nettie Yonque McCrorey Counselman. She attended the University of Alabama and Montevallo University and later became a reporter for the *Birmingham News*. In 1941, Counselman married Horace Benton Vinyard and the couple settled in Gadsden, Alabama. In addition to her own writing, Counselman also taught creative writing at Gadsden State Junior College. In the early 1930s, her work began to appear in national publications, including *Collier's*, *Good Housekeeping*, *Ladies' Home Journal*, and *The Saturday Evening Post*. In 1933, she began publishing stories in *Weird Tales* and quickly became one of the magazine's most popular writers with thirty stories appearing from the 1930s to the 1950s. Counselman's most famous story, 'The Three Marked Pennies', was published in the August 1934 issue of *Weird Tales*. It was later adapted for radio for *General Electric Theater* in the 1950s and for an episode of the television series *The Unforeseen* in 1959. Her supernatural fiction was collected in *Half in Shadow*, published by Arkham House in 1964.

Bithia Mary Croker (c1850–1920) was born in Kilgefin, County Roscommon, Ireland, to William Sheppard, the Rector of Kilgefin, and Bithia Watson Sheppard. She was educated at Rockferry, Cheshire, and at Tours, France. As a young girl, Croker excelled at horse riding and developed an early talent for writing. As a schoolgirl, reading and writing were Croker's favourite subjects, and she would often trade her maths assignments, something she disliked very much, in return for doing someone else's writing assignments. On 16 November 1871, she married Lt Col John Stokes Croker, an Anglo-Irish descendent of the Crokers of County Limerick. Their only child, Gertrude Eileen, was born the following year. Colonel Croker served in the Royal Scots Fusiliers, and later in the Royal Munster Fusiliers. In 1877, the couple moved to Madras, where Croker was stationed before moving to Burma, and then to Bengal, prior to his retirement in 1892. It was during these years in India that Bithia Croker began writing. She followed the success of her first two novels, *Proper Pride* (1882) and *Pretty Miss Neville* (1883), with several collections of short stories, including *To Let* (1893), *Village Tales and Jungle Tragedies* (1895), *In the Kingdom of Kerry* (1896), *Jason* (1899), *A State Secret* (1901), *The Old Cantonment* (1905), and *Odds and Ends* (1919), with the first two collections containing most of her Anglo-Indian supernatural fiction. By the time of her death in 1920, she had written over forty novels in addition to her collections of short stories.

Edith Stewart Drewry (1841–1925) was born in London to the barrister Charles Stewart Drewry and Laurentia Buschman Drewry. She published her first novel, *Baptized with a Curse*, in 1870. This was followed by *A Death Ring* (1881), *On Dangerous Ground* (1883), *Only an Actress* (1883), and *For Somebody's Sake* (1890). Drewry was also a frequent contributor to many periodicals, including *Belgravia*, *The Family Herald*, and *The London Journal*. From 1874–1880, she was a classical concert reviewer with the *Musical Standard*. She never married and lived for most of her life with her sisters.

Mary Eleanor Wilkins Freeman (1852–1930) was born in Randolph, Massachusetts, to Warren E Wilkins and Eleanor Lothrop Wilkins. The family moved to Brattleboro, Vermont, where Mary graduated from high school in 1870 and later attended the Mount Holyoke Female Seminary in South Hadley, Massachusetts, from 1870–1871, and the Glenwood Seminary in West Brattleboro from 1871–1872. After her mother's death in 1880 and her father's death in 1883, she returned to the family farm in Randolph and remained there for the next twenty years with her longtime friend Mary Wales. During this time, Mary was free to spend much of her time writing and established herself as a preeminent regionalist writer with the collections *A Humble Romance and Other Stories* (1887) and *A New England Nun and Other Stories* (1891). In 1902, she married Dr Charles M Freeman and subsequently moved to Metuchen, New Jersey. The marriage was not a success as Dr Freeman suffered from the effects of alcoholism. In order to financially support both herself and her husband (and his drinking habit), Mary began writing and publishing. After Freeman was institutionalised, Mary obtained a legal separation. In 1926, she was awarded the William Dean Howells Gold Medal for Fiction and was also elected to the National Institute of Arts and Letters. Her literary output includes fourteen novels, fifteen volumes of short stories, three volumes of poetry, three plays, eight children's books, as well as several prose essays and uncollected short stories. Her most well-known volume of supernatural fiction, *The Wind in the Rose-Bush*, was published in 1903.

Little is known of the life of **Lettice Galbraith**. Throughout the 1890s, Galbraith published her work in popular fiction magazines, and in addition to her supernatural fiction collected in *New Ghost*

Stories (1893), she published another short story collection, *Pretty Miss Allington and Other Tales* (1893). Her short fiction frequently features unconventional women protagonists.

Stella Gibbons (1902–1989) was born in London to Telford Gibbons and Maude Phoebe Standish Williams Gibbons. Gibbons attended the North London Collegiate School for Girls and went on to complete a two-year journalism course at University College, London. In 1923, Gibbons became a cable decoder for British United Press and later worked as a journalist for publications such as the *Evening Standard* and *The Lady*. She gained fame after the publication of her best-known work, *Cold Comfort Farm* (1932), for which she was awarded the Femina Vie Heureuse prize in 1933. That same year, she married Allan Bourne Webb, an actor and singer, and the couple had one daughter. Gibbons continued to write novels, poetry, and short stories at the rate of about one book a year until 1970, but none of her works achieved the same level of success as *Cold Comfort Farm*.

Sarah Orne Jewett (1849–1909) was born in South Berwick, Maine, to Theodore Herman Jewett and Caroline Frances Perry Jewett. Considered one of the best American regional writers of the period, Jewett wrote novels, poems and short fiction. She began publishing in magazines in the 1860s and several of these early sketches of life in a fictional town in Maine were collected in *Deephaven* (1877). Her novels include *A Country Doctor* (1884), *A Marsh Island* (1885), *Betty Leicester* (1890), and *The Tory Lover* (1901). She also published several short story collections, such as *A White Heron* (1886), *The King of Folly Island* (1888), *A Native of Winby* (1893), and *The Life of Nancy* (1895). Jewett is best known for *The Country of the Pointed Firs* (1896), a collection of stories about life in a village along the Maine coast. She never married and lived with the widowed Annie Adams Fields, wife of the Boston publisher James T Fields, for many years. The pair traveled to Europe and hosted American and European writers. Jewett's writing career was cut short when she was injured after a carriage accident in 1902. Although she is regarded as a virtuoso of local colour, Jewett occasionally invoked the Gothic and macabre in her stories, most notably 'Lady Ferry' (1879), 'The Gray Man' (1886), 'The Landscape Chamber' (1887), 'In Dark New England Days' (1890), and 'The Green Bowl' (1901).

Bessie Kyffin-Taylor (1869–1922) was born in Liverpool, the daughter of Thomas Cope and Sarah Davies Cope of Huyton. After her father's death in 1884, her mother married John A Willox, journalist and later proprietor of the *Liverpool Courier*, in 1888. In 1892, Bessie married Gerald Kyffin-Taylor, who became a Member of Parliament in 1910. He resigned his seat in order to serve in the First World War, where he became a Brigadier-General, and later served as Director of Housing for Lancashire. The couple lived in Heswall from their marriage until Bessie's death in 1922. According to a brief obituary in the *Hull Daily Mail* on 29 August 1922, she was 'well known in literary circles as a writer of articles and stories' and was 'a keen sportswoman ... fond of angling and motoring' (4). The obituary references *From Out of the Silence* (1920), her one known collection of supernatural fiction, as well as a play titled *Rosemary*.

Katherine Mansfield (1888–1923) was born Kathleen Beauchamp in Wellington, New Zealand, to Harold Beauchamp and Annie Burnell Dyer Beauchamp. The family moved to a country house at Karori in 1893, and Kathleen began attending primary school. Mansfield became increasingly unhappy in New Zealand and in 1903 moved to London where she attended Queen's College. She returned to New Zealand in 1906 and published some of her first stories in the *Native Companion*. In 1908, Mansfield convinced her parents to allow her to return to England, and she never returned to New Zealand. After an affair with the musician Garnet Trowell (a relationship that resulted in a miscarriage), Mansfield married the singing teacher George Bowden in 1909. These relationships, including a lifelong friendship with Ida Baker, resulted in an estrangement between Mansfield and her mother. After the publication of her first story collection *In a German Pension* (1911), Mansfield met her future husband, John Middleton Murry, and the two worked together as editors on *Rhythm* (later called the *Blue Review*). In December 1917, Mansfield was diagnosed with tuberculosis and travelled to France for her health. The following year, *Prelude* was published by the Hogarth Press. Mansfield continued to travel between Britain and Europe in an effort to prolong her life. In 1920, *Bliss and Other Stories* was published, followed by *The Garden Party and Other Stories* in 1922.

Lucy Maud Montgomery (1874-1942) was born in Clifton (New London) on Prince Edward Island, Canada, to Hugh John Montgomery and Clara Woolner Macneill Montgomery. In 1911, she married the Reverend Ewen (Ewan) Macdonald, and the couple had three sons. Prince Edward Island inspired the fictional town of Avonlea, the setting for her most famous novel, *Anne of Green Gables* (1908). Her early attempts at writing were discouraged by her family. From 1893-1894, she completed a teacher training course at Prince of Wales College in Charlottetown and, with her grandmother's financial assistance, studied English literature at Dalhousie College in Halifax from 1895-1896. In 1894, she began working with twenty children ranging in age from 6 to 13, teaching as many as sixty students, while devoting each day to writing fiction and poetry for newspapers and magazines. From 1901-1902, she worked as a proofreader for the *Daily Echo* in Halifax. From 1898-1911, Montgomery published hundreds of short stories. In 1934, she collaborated with Marian Keith and Mabel Burns McKinley on *Courageous Women*, a collection of twenty-one biographical essays on women who made contributions to the arts, politics, missionary work, nursing, and war relief efforts. Her later novels, including *The Blue Castle* (1926) and *Magic for Marigold* (1929), feature modern, professional women. Montgomery's supernatural fiction was collected in *Among the Shadows* (1990).

Helen Simpson (1897–1940) was born in Sydney, New South Wales, to Edward Percy Simpson and Anne de Lauret Simpson. Helen de Guerry Simpson was educated at the Convent of the Sacred Heart in Rose Bay and at Abbotsleigh, Wahroonga. In 1914, she traveled to France to continue her studies. After her arrival in England, she attended the University of Oxford, reading French from 1916–1917. In 1918, she joined the Women's Royal Naval Service (popularly known as the Wrens) and worked as a senior section officer specialising in decoding. In 1919, Simpson returned to Oxford to study music and while there also became interested in theatre, eventually founding the Oxford Women's Dramatic Society, as well as publishing several plays. Her studies ended in 1921 when she broke university regulations which prohibited male and female students from acting together. In 1927, she married the surgeon Sir Denis John Browne. Her first novel, *Acquittal*, was published in 1925. One of her most successful works, *Boomerang*, an historical fiction novel, was published in 1932 and won the James Tait Black Memorial Prize. Simpson published two historical biographies, *The Spanish Marriage* (1933) and *Henry VIII* (1934), and a book on household management, *The Happy Housewife* (1934). She collaborated with Clemence Dane on the novels, *Enter Sir John* (1929), *Printer's Devil* (1930) and *Re-enter Sir John* (1932). Another novel, *Under Capricorn* (1937), was adapted into a 1949 British thriller directed by Alfred Hitchcock. In 1939, Simpson was chosen as a parliamentary candidate by the Isle of Wight Liberal Association but her political career was cut short by illness and her death the following year.

Bibliographical details

Unless stated otherwise, the texts reproduced in this volume are based on the following editions.

'A Twin-Identity' was published in the Christmas issue of *Belgravia* in 1891.

'The Blue Room' was published in *Macmillan's Magazine* in October 1897.

'The Green Bowl' was published in *A House Party: An Account of Stories Told at a Gathering of Famous American Authors* (Boston 1901).

'A Dreamer' was published as the opening story in Barbara Baynton's collection *Bush Studies* (London 1902).

'The Hall Bedroom' was published in Volume IV of *Short Story Classics (American)* (New York 1905).

'The House' was published in *Hearth and Home* on 28 November 1912.

'The Red Bungalow' was published in Bithia Mary Croker's collection *Odds and Ends* (London 1919).

'Outside the House' was published in Bessie Kyffin-Taylor's collection *From Out of the Silence: Seven Strange Stories* (London 1920).

'Florence Flannery' was first published in the December 1924 issue of *Regent Magazine* and appeared in Marjorie Bowen's collection *The Last Bouquet: Some Twilight Tales* (London 1933). The text in this volume is based on the 1933 publication.

'Young Magic' was published in Helen Simpson's collection *The Baseless Fabric* (London 1925). The current text is based on the 1925 American edition, published in New York by Alfred A. Knopf.

'The House Party at Smoky Island' appeared in the August 1935 issue of *Weird Tales*.

'The Black Stone Statue' appeared in the December 1937 issue of *Weird Tales*.

'Roaring Tower' was published in Stella Gibbons' collection *Roaring Tower and Other Short Stories* (London 1937).

Obvious typographical errors and inconsistencies have been silently corrected, and some punctuation has been modernised where it would not affect meaning. American spellings have been rendered into British English.

1 A Twin-Identity

BY EDITH STEWART DREWRY (1891)

'What am I?' you ask, because I say I have had – though I am only thirty – a stranger experience than any with which you five gentlemen have favoured us to beguile the weary time we are snowed up in the train; and as it seems it will be quite an hour before we can get on to London, I will tell you – if you care to hear the story – why I say so, and what I am; only I hope those two ladies will not be shocked to find themselves in my company? No? – thanks – well then, I am an *agent-de-police*, and have just come over from Paris to spend Christmas with some English friends. Even we poor police-agents get a little holiday sometimes – *hein!* And the life has its attractions too, as well as its dangers and repulsions. Personally I had little choice, for I was born in the service, brought up in it, for my father was a very clever officer of the Paris Secret Police. I married in the force, widowed in it, and being one of their best women detectives, I was sure of retaining my position. Nature has favoured me, for, as you see, I am a tall but very slight made woman, with a face which lends itself well to masculine disguise. *Pardons*, madame, what did you say? – Oh! I make a handsome young fellow too – ha, ha! I have often been told so, and that I have a woman's wits and a man's courage. One needs both in my profession too, I can tell you; and steady nerves, too, as you will see.

Well, about this time five years ago, all Paris was suddenly startled into horror by the discovery of one of those revoltingly brutal crimes in which, I must confess, France is only occasionally rivalled by the wildest deeds of the Far West.

Some few months previously a wealthy banker, named Folcade, had married a very pretty American girl, one of twins, who in all but personal resemblance were so absolutely as one being, and so deeply attached, as to be singular even for twins. Remember that I knew nothing of all this till nearly the termination of my connection with the case. All that the police knew was the bare fact that Madame Folcade had a sister who after the former's marriage had returned to Virginia, US, and was there when the tragedy took place, the news of it completely prostrating her health for months. Remember that also, please.

M Folcade had a villa in large grounds some way out of Paris, in a lonely place, and that fatal evening the banker, having a violent headache, retired about ten o'clock, leaving his wife down in the *salon* reading, with her pet dog, a Scotch terrier, in the room, and that was the last the poor fellow saw of his wife and her faithful would-be defender alive. M Folcade awoke at two in the morning, and finding himself still alone, got up, partially dressed, and went downstairs, thinking his wife had dropped asleep over her book. The *salon* was empty, the window open, and blood was on the floor near the wife's chair!

Monsieur was frantic, called up the household, sent for the nearest police, and every inch of the grounds was searched. As a result Paris soon blazed with the horrible discovery that Madame Folcade had been stabbed to the heart (from behind, the doctor said), probably in the room, then the body carried out to a remote corner of the grounds, and literally cut up piecemeal, for the head, trunk, hands and limbs were found by degrees in different parts of the grounds – also a long sharp-pointed knife, blood-stained, was found, and the *sergent-de-police* himself discovered, in a remote spot, under a bush, the body of the poor terrier all bloody from a ghastly stab, but close to its mouth, as if the teeth in the death agony had unclenched and dropped it, was a man's right hand *fourth finger* with a ring upon it. The faithful animal had evidently flown at the murderer and bitten off that little finger; then, doubtless, mortally wounded itself, fled to the bushes and died before it could reach the house with its prize. Of the assassin there was no trace whatsoever, not even a foot-print, for the ground was dry under a hard black frost.

Well, the finger was, of course, at once preserved in spirits. The signet-ring we found had a monogram on the stone in it, of 'L S'. On that finger, and ring, and knife, we had to rely primarily to identify the murderer.

Of course, M Folcade himself was questioned as under possible suspicion; but it was soon clear that he was guiltless. The marriage had been one of love. He was a fond and unjealous husband and one worthy of true trust; but that some savage hate and jealousy was the motive of the crime was tolerably clear. Nothing was stolen nor touched. The devilish deliberation and sequence to the murder betrayed a bloodthirsty revenge – but for what? – by whom done? A lover scorned, perhaps, but when and where? No trace, no sign of any one to suspect, present or missing, whom she had known; could be found, although M Folcade made it understood that no expense or time should be bounded, and that the arrest of the murderer would be well recognised. You know that in France we do not allow any reward, officially or openly offered, as you do here for such things. It is done, of course, but – *sub-rosa*.

The case was in my especial *chef's* hands, but I was not in it then, for my hands were full, as that week I went off to Vienna on a matter of political crime which took me six months to run my men to earth and have them arrested. I only learned the details of the Folcade tragedy on my return – learned of necessity from my *chef*, M Dupré.

'Madame Marie Lacroix,' said he grimly, 'I must have your aid now in this Folcade mystery.'

'*Eh bien! M le Chef*,' I answered, 'tell me all details and I obey the order.'

This he did, therefore, and concluded emphatically: 'Now, although I shall not relax my efforts, it is on you, Marie, that your old *chef* relies to maintain his repute. We want the assassin; the evidence is clear. We have the man who a month before the murder sold the knife to a gentleman who he says he shall know again but cannot describe enough to be of much use – these common people are so stupid, so unobservant – *hein!* "Rather tall, sallow, good-looking, about thirty or forty!" – bah, see there! – that would do for hundreds. Last Christmas, whilst still unmarried Madame Folcade (then Miss Grey) was in the Riviera with a lady since dead, but we could find no trace of anyone to whom suspicions would attach. Do your best, Marie, money is not to be spared – a great thing.'

I was then well supplied, and withdrew. I will not trouble you with details here, but I threw myself heart and soul into this mysterious case, which had so baffled my *confrères*. I do not know when I have been so intensely absorbed in a case, so passionately set on success, all my faculties so entirely concentrated on that end. This almost abnormal enfolding of my whole being in the interests of those who had so loved the ill-fated lady, may perhaps account for the strange sequel.

I set to work my own way. I visited the Villa Folcade, saw the place, the picture of Madame Folcade there, and the knife, ring and finger in our possession, and all the people connected with the case. Then I went off to the Riviera, taking a photo of Madame, of course; went to Nice, Monte Carlo, and, after weeks of patient research I discovered that a certain Polish lady had said that at a rather mixed *bal masqué* last autumn she had noticed a very pretty American who was rather annoyed by the notice of a blue domino. Following up that slender chance I traced out the Pole – a work of time – and she recognised the photo, laughed at the freedom of American girls, said this one appeared to be alone and to have come in bravado, but had got frightened at the attentions or persecutions of the blue domino, had hastily resumed her mask (the Pole added), and vanished.

Here, then, was surely the root of the subsequent tragedy. A reckless 'lark' – as you English say – in ignorance of the world; an encounter, probably followed by secret persecution; the girl, afraid to betray her mad escapade to her friends lest a worse construction should be put on it; the man, doubtless in love, in a fashion, jealousy, revenge – *voilà tout!* I returned hopefully to Monte Carlo, and, after some time, obtained the slightest clue to that blue domino, which led me to suspect that (if he were the murderer) he would have made his way to London several months after the crime, as the safest hiding-place, *ma parole!* – so it is – so vast – so many millions to be lost amongst.

Well, I came straight over to London, it being then the October after the murder, and at once went to Scotland Yard to put the authorities there on the *qui vive* for a man such as I described, lacking a finger and the hand probably marked still by the wound of the dog's teeth. Why did I not advertise, you ask, monsieur? – *Ciel!* because my bird was clearly wary, clever and I wanted him to be lulled into false security and think the police had given up in despair, after nearly a year.

I was unremitting in my cautious inquiries and watchful search, continually changing my disguises (mostly masculine, of necessity), and invariably armed with a loaded revolver for self-defence or to prevent the bird's escape. I am a dead shot and can hit where I will, I may assert. Day and night until quite late I was abroad, here, there and everywhere – in public resorts, public vehicles, great thoroughfares, east, west, north and south. I haunted the gambling resorts, from the West End proprietary club to the low 'hell' – all *en garçon*, of course. How could I get the entré of some of these, you say, madame? Ha, ha, that was easily enough managed with money, and I am an accomplished gambler – to be *au fait* in that line was part of my training.

But day after day, week after week, passed, and I was still baffled. I got not one clue, and at last, just before Christmas, I wrote to my *chef*: 'Even I am almost in despair that 'L S' is either dead, or at the Antipodes. If I learn nothing by December 31st, I fear I must resort to the desperate measure of advertising; I am mad at failing, and more, my whole soul and brain are wrapped up in this case.'

That letter reached Paris a few days before Christmas.

On the 24th of December, all day, I had detectives watching the great stations for any man answering to such description as I had, as the assassin might possibly spend the festive season out of town. I myself was about the West End in the evening, dressed much as I am now, in black, with a dark fur toque.

I gave a look over Paddington Terminus, and about ten o'clock I thought I would return to my lodging in Bloomsbury, and there decide on my further action to-night, or whether I should rest – that is, if I could. It was the very anniversary of the tragedy I was to unravel – Christmas Eve. I was beginning to feel the long heavy strain on mental and physical powers, I suppose, and every nerve was strung up to a high nervous tension. I felt in a curious unaccountable manner that would not be shaken off. I stepped into a City-going omnibus, sitting down by the door and instinctively taking notice of the other passengers – only two stout old men at the far end – for it was a bitterly cold night, with a heavy snow-laden sky, dreary enough to make one lonely and miserable under any circumstances. I was both. Yet, withal, as we started eastwards, there began to steal over me, an odd internal excitement, as of a vague expectancy, a restlessness, and intensified desire to gain my end, which became almost agony in its passionate vividness. It seemed to grip me, thrall my very soul, like a visible force. God of Justice! was there nothing above or below that knew the dread secret I sought? No power – seen or unseen – from whence my inmost being could draw the knowledge of that one man's hiding-place?

What, too, was my *chef* thinking of his trusted agent, on whose success he had flung his whole credit? What on this dread night were the feelings of *her* relations, that their beloved dead was still unavenged? In those moments I felt half maddened with longing, and then in and through that longing there grew a strange sensation, as if something – I knew not what – went out from me, taking my life from me, then seeming to draw back with it in returning something that I could not grasp or define – that I never shall be able to define – but made me, with a sort of sudden mental wrench, look up, impelled by a force quite outside myself, to see sitting opposite to me a lady, young and lovely, dressed in handsome mourning.

How and when had she got in? Had the omnibus stopped or even slackened, unnoticed by me, in my strange absorption? No, no, how could it? yet there the stranger sat. And what a singular face it was! What deathly pallor and painful melancholy in every line! What sad, wistful eyes, that seemed full of unshed tears, and kept looking, looking at me, through me, into my soul, with an intense strained gaze that never wavered, and seemed every moment to grow deeper in its dumb agony of appeal as of one struggling for the speech of which God had bereft her tongue.

I looked away, aside, out of the doorway, conscious that my blood was creeping dull and heavily, like half-frozen water, through my veins; but a strange, weird fascination compelled me to again meet that gaze. Did she know me? Impossible! I had certainly never seen her before. My heart throbbed up into my throat, my blood began to beat fast and warm again, and as we rolled onwards I was aware of a curious subtle change in my sensations. Every nerve, every fibre was still strung up to a painful tension; but there stole over me, into me, body and spirit, a sense of steel-like strength – a strange settling down of my faculties into cool, steadfast power, and more than that, a sense that grew slowly to impelling conviction that that fellow passenger knew what I did not – whosoever or *whatsoever* she was, and that my movements must follow hers, blindly. As that odd feeling deepened and possessed me, my eyes again went to the woman's face – to meet a look of intense restfulness and content that dominated all other expression of anguish or strained eagerness as, if after something unreached. Did she – or – *It* – read my soul and find there all its tortured, trammelled spirit sought?

It gave me almost a shock to suddenly see the stalwart, prosaic conductor at the doorway asking for 'fares to Tottenham Court Road', which I had named when I got in. I noticed at once that he did not even glance at my strange neighbour – seemed not to see her – but I saw her shake her head to me.

'No,' I said to the man, 'I am going further. I'll stop you when I want to get out.'

Under this curious calm that had settled on me, I was not at all surprised at the man's evident obliviousness of that passenger. I should have been surprised if he had evinced any knowledge of her presence, and it seemed to me quite in the order of things when, on reaching Gray's Inn Road, she raised her white hand to me, and glided out on to the pavement unnoticed by the conductor. I paid him and stepped to the stranger's side, thrilled right through with a weird feeling that should ordinarily unnerve one; yet I had never felt more strong, cool, ready for the most desperate danger or emergency; and as my guide – I following – moved swiftly along northwards I drew off my gloves and felt in my bosom to be sure the revolver was ready to hand. There was grim work, I knew. She led on straight up past the shops, still ablaze at past eleven in that neighbourhood on this eve, and at last turned down a street which I knew to be mostly filled with third-rate, shady lodging-houses, where doors are on the latch all night, and never a question is asked of 'whence, whither or what?' This class of houses have the commonest latch-locks that are easily fitted, and, of course, I was well provided with such appliances of noiseless entrance.

Before one of these houses my mysterious guide stopped. Save a light in the first floor window all was darkness – either the inmates were asleep or out. To that window my guide eagerly pointed, with a look and gesture that vehemently urged instant action, as if a minute's delay were fatal; so I drew out and fitted a key. She was close, her lips moved, but there was no sound, not a whisper; yet into my mind, as if I had heard it, came a name – *Louis Saumarez* – and at that moment I opened the door and entered, leaving the door just ajar for her to follow. But she did not. What I meant to do or felt I never could put into words. My mind was concentrated on one great fact – that the murderer was in that lighted room, about to escape, and that I – a woman, alone must stop him and arrest him.

Terror, danger, were not present to me then – I was too strung up – grimly cool. It was I who was dangerous. I stole up quietly, easily, as if I had a right there, opened that door and paused.

One glance took in the *mise-en-scène*. A shabby room, scantily furnished, a fire nearly out, wine and food on the table, a valise packed up, and just drinking a glass of wine, using the left hand, was a rather tall, good-looking, but sallow-faced man. Mon Dieu! I must see that other hand by some *ruse*.

'*Que Diable*,' said I, with a bitter but abandoned kind of manner, 'but you are a cruel enough lover to me, M Saumarez.'

He swung round, so startled that he staggered and caught at a chair with the right hand, to which it was nearest. I saw it full under the lamplight; a dark scar across it; the *fourth finger gone!* The assassin at last!

'Who the devil are you?' he demanded savagely, recovering himself a little. 'I never saw you before, and you are too damned handsome to be forgotten. Leave my room! I have to catch a train, and my name is Mercier.'

'*Pardons*, Monsieur,' said I coolly, my right hand on the butt of my weapon, my eyes on his ready for his attack, 'you are Louis Saumarez, and you – are – my prisoner for murder.'

I stood near the door, he at the far end of the large room. At the last awful word, he snatched a knife from the table with a fierce '*Sacre–r*,' and sprang towards me; but at that second I fired, and the fellow reeled back with a yell like a wounded wild beast, and fell heavily, partially stunned by the blow to his head, on the floor, the blood coming from his side. I knew where to hit safely. I was turning quickly to get police help before my prisoner regained consciousness, when men's steps came quickly along from below, up the stairs, and two constables came into the room, one exclaiming:

'Hulloa! What's this – murder? Are you hurt too, ma'am?'

Shaken now a little, I had leaned against the wall, as the other man knelt beside Saumarez.

'*Non, non*,' I said. 'I fired in self-defence. I am here to arrest that man for the murder of Madame Folcade. I am a French police agent. It is all right.'

One was a sergeant, and whilst the other bound up the slight wound, I briefly explained matters and gave my captive in charge. The sergeant sent for the divisional surgeon, who had Saumarez removed to the hospital – in custody, of course – and said in two or three days he would be able to be taken to Bow Street for the necessary formalities of extradition. After we had left him at the hospital, with the constable in charge,

I asked the sergeant, as we walked back westward, how they arrived so opportunely – had they heard the shot and cry?

'Yes – just outside,' he said; 'but they had come from the station near at the summons of a lady in black, who was as white as a ghost, and was dumb, for she could only beckon – beckon like mad, and when we followed led us to that house – just as the shot was fired – and was gone before we could look round. Awful queer, ma'am,' he added. 'Who was she?'

'I do not know,' I answered in a choked voice. 'Good-night, I am dead tired now.'

I was shaken to the centre now that the terrible, long strain was so far over, and the murderer secured; but next day, Christmas Day, I wired to my *chef*, and received a reply that he would send over a responsible official with a *mandat d'arrêt* to receive the prisoner from the English authorities and bring him over to Paris. Meanwhile, I of course had to obtain at Bow Street a warrant under the Extraditions Act, and two days later Saumarez was pronounced quite able to be removed. As a result – well, within five or six days of his arrest he was safely lodged in the Parisian prison. I had travelled with my French comrades (two of course) and their captive, who had maintained a sulky silence save once – to savagely curse that 'diablesse of an agent.'

I went the same day of our arrival to report myself to my delighted *chef*, who asked how I had trapped the bird at last? I felt too shattered then to tell him the actual truth, I shrank in sensitive dread from the possible smile of incredulity, so I said that a person I met by chance had spoken of a Frenchman named Saumarez who had one finger gone, and this person had shown me his lodgings, which he was on the point of leaving when I entered.

'So I had to be summary in my actions,' I added, as I rose to go.

'Quite right, Marie, you are invaluable and have well

redeemed my confidence in you. You have earned a rest truly, and a reward from M Folcade. By the way, I have made a promise there for you.'

'*Comment, Monsieur?*' – I was surprised – 'my existence is unknown to him and his.'

'Individually, yes, but professionally, not so. I went myself to tell M Folcade of the daring arrest of the assassin by my clever agent – a woman, I added, and he made me promise to send you to his house here in Paris directly you arrived. He and his sister-in-law, the wife's twin-sister, especially wish to see the lady of whom I spoke.'

I started, but said quietly:

'The twin-sister, Monsieur, is she then over here?' For though outwardly not a muscle of mine moved, I was startled right through by his words, by the wildly extraordinary fancy that flashed across me as I recalled all that had taken place on Christmas Eve.

'Yes,' Dupré replied, 'Mademoiselle Clarice Grey came over here to her bereaved brother-in-law just before Christmas; she was too ill to bear the voyage earlier. Will you have a *fiacre* and go at once, *mon agent?*'

'Yes, assuredly,' I said. I felt that I must go at once and solve this mystery, which was surely on the borderland of the real and unreal, the seen and the wondrous unseen, of which our finite humanity, the soul's prison, knows so little and conjectures so much. I went then to the banker's house, but found that he himself was not yet returned from the bank, though momentarily expected. 'Would I see Mademoiselle Clarice?' I said yes, gave my name, and was shown into an elegant *salon*.

In three minutes a young lady came in, and in that moment as we faced each other we both stood transfixed, dazed – as if pulsation itself were arrested – each had seen the other, each knew where, but not how – not how; – my strange silent, fellow-passenger and guide of Christmas Eve, no flesh and blood, as this was who now came slowly forward and held my hands tightly – but, the same identity – only that other was in the spirit.

'We know each other,' she said, in a hushed, awed way, 'not in the flesh but in the soul, and yet a reality, not a dream, though they say I lay like one dead asleep, and when I came back to sentient life knew nothing of where we – she and I – had been.'

'*We* – you and she!' I repeated, feeling my flesh creep and my heart stand still. 'There – there were not two but one guide with me.'

'We, twain but always one,' Clarice said in the same way, her wistful eyes looking into mine – 'dead and living, our twinborn souls are one identity for ever, and so the dread secret with which her soul was oppressed, passed with it into mine, but densely trammelled by my mortality till your despair and strength of purpose and desire drew us from our mortal prison to your aid. l felt the mighty spell of your agony enfolding itself with my own maddened thirst for justice, felt a strange oblivion stealing my physical senses, and knew no more, save when I awoke, a deep joy, gratitude, triumph – a restfulness. I knew before your *chef* spoke that the murderer was arrested by the agent he named, it all came back to me then, and I – we twain knew all.'

I stood looking at her as her mystic presence that night had looked at me. What awesome secret of the unknown was indeed half unfolded it seemed, in these twin-born sisters whom even the mystery of death could not part from their entwined coexistence? Had, in truth, the dead sister's soul passed as it were into its twin soul yet encompassed by its mortal body, and so through its own beyond death, knowledge, God-given yet only 'through a glass darkly', had a mystic power as the one spirit of the Twin-Identity to guide me, the mortal agent who was the material instrument of God's justice? It might be so. Could I – could any mortal in his bounded finiteness say it could not be? So there must it rest as mystery till all mysteries shall be seen face to face …

You ask me 'What was the end of that grim tragedy?' Well – I traced out Saumarez's antecedents and my suspicions of his motive proved to be true. His guilt was undeniable by the proofs we had – the ring, the finger and knife and many other collateral links of evidence, and Louis Saumarez was condemned and guillotined.

It was months before I could work again, and indeed M Folcade and Clarice Grey would have had me retire on the competence they insisted on settling on me, but I could not settle to a quiet, useless life whilst I was young and strong. So I am still *agent-de-police*, and I am going to visit Clarice in London, where she is married to an Englishman. Ah, see, the train is going on again and we shall soon reach London. Clarice likes her *chère* Marie Lacroix 'to be with her on Christmas Eve'.

2 The Blue Room

BY LETTICE GALBRAITH (1897)

It happened twice in my time. It will never happen again, they say, since Miss Erristoun (Mrs Arthur, that is now,) and Mr Calder-Maxwell between them found out the secret of the haunted room, and laid the ghost; for ghost it was, though at the time Mr Maxwell gave it another name, Latin, I fancy, but all I can remember about it now is that it somehow reminded me of poultry-rearing. I am the housekeeper at Mertoun Towers, as my aunt was before me, and her aunt before her, and first of all my great-grandmother, who was a distant cousin of the Laird, and had married the chaplain, but being left penniless at her husband's death, was thankful to accept the post which has ever since been occupied by one of her descendants. It gives us a sort of standing with the servants, being, as it were, related to the family; and Sir Archibald and my Lady have always acknowledged the connection, and treated us with more freedom than would be accorded to ordinary dependants.

Mertoun has been my home from the time I was eighteen. Something occurred then of which, since it has nothing to do with this story, I need only say that it wiped out for ever any idea of marriage on my part, and I came to the Towers to be trained under my aunt's vigilant eye for the duties in which I was one day to succeed her.

Of course I knew there was a story about the blue tapestry room. Everyone knew that, though the old Laird had given strict orders that the subject should not be discussed among the servants, and always discouraged any allusion to it on the part of his family and guests. But there is a strange fascination about everything connected with the supernatural, and orders or no orders, people, whether gentle or simple, will try to gratify their curiosity; so a good deal of surreptitious talk went on both in the drawing-room and the servants' hall, and hardly a guest came to the house but would pay a visit to the Blue Room and ask all manner of questions about the ghost. The odd part of the business was that no one knew what the ghost was supposed to be, or even if there were any ghost at all. I tried hard to get my aunt to tell me some details of the legend, but she always reminded me of Sir Archibald's orders, and added that the tale most likely started with the superstitious fancy of people who lived long ago and were very ignorant, because a certain Lady Barbara Mertoun had died in that room.

I reminded her that people must have died, at some time or other, in pretty nearly every room in the house, and no one had thought of calling them haunted, or hinting that it was unsafe to sleep there.

She answered that Sir Archibald himself had used the Blue Room, and one or two other gentlemen, who had passed the night there for a wager, and they had neither seen nor heard anything unusual. For her part, she added, she did not hold with people wasting their time thinking of such folly, when they had much better be giving their minds to their proper business.

Somehow her professions of incredulity did not ring true, and I wasn't satisfied, though I gave up asking questions. But if I said nothing, I thought the more, and often when my duties took me to the Blue Room I would wonder why, if nothing had happened there, and there was no real mystery, the room was never used; it had not even a mattress on the fine carved bedstead, which was only covered by a sheet to keep it from the dust. And then I would steal into the portrait gallery to look at the great picture of the Lady Barbara, who had died in the full bloom of her youth, no one knew why, for she was just found one morning stiff and cold, stretched across that fine bed under the blue tapestried canopy.

She must have been a beautiful woman, with her great black eyes and splendid auburn hair, though I doubt her beauty was all on the outside, for she had belonged to the gayest set of the Court, which was none too respectable in those days, if half the tales one hears of it are true; and indeed a modest lady would hardly have been painted in such a dress, all slipping off her shoulders, and so thin that one can see right through the stuff. There must have been something queer about her too, for they do say her father-in-law, who was known as the wicked Lord Mertoun, would not have her buried with the rest of the family; but that might have been his spite, because he was angry that she had no child, and her husband, who was but a sickly sort of man, dying of consumption but a month later, there was no direct heir; so that with the old Lord the title became extinct, and the estates passed to the Protestant branch of the family, of which the present Sir Archibald Mertoun is the head. Be that as it may, Lady Barbara lies by herself in the churchyard, near the lych-gate, under a grand marble tomb indeed, but all alone, while her husband's coffin has its place beside those of his brothers who died before him, among their ancestors and descendants in the great vault under the chancel.

I often used to think about her, and wonder why she died, and how; and then It happened and the mystery grew deeper than ever.

There was a family gathering that Christmas, I remember, the first Christmas for many years that had been kept at Mertoun, and we had been very busy arranging the rooms for the different guests, for on New Year's Eve there was a ball in the neighbourhood, to which Lady Mertoun was taking a large party, and for that night, at least, the house was as full as it would hold.

I was in the linen-room, helping to sort the sheets and pillow-covers for the different beds, when my Lady came in with an open letter in her hand.

She began to talk to my aunt in a low voice, explaining something which seemed to have put her out, for when I returned from carrying a pile of linen to the head-housemaid, I heard her say: 'It is too annoying to upset all one's arrangements at the last moment. Why couldn't she have left the girl at home and brought another maid, who could be squeezed in somewhere without any trouble?'

I gathered that one of the visitors, Lady Grayburn, had written that she was bringing her companion, and as she had left her maid, who was ill, at home, she wanted the young lady to have a bedroom adjoining hers, so that she might be at hand to give any help that was required. The request seemed a trifling matter enough in itself, but it just so happened that there really was no room at liberty. Every bedroom on the first corridor was occupied, with the exception of the Blue Room, which, as ill-luck would have it, chanced to be next to that arranged for Lady Grayburn.

My aunt made several suggestions, but none of them seemed quite practicable, and at last my Lady broke out: 'Well, it cannot be helped; you must put Miss Wood in the Blue Room. It is only for one night, and she won't know anything about that silly story.'

'Oh, my Lady!' my aunt cried, and I knew by her tone that she had not spoken the truth when she professed to think so lightly of the ghost.

'I can't help it,' her Ladyship answered: 'beside I don't believe there is anything really wrong with the room. Sir Archibald has slept there, and he found no cause for complaint.'

'But a woman, a young woman,' my aunt urged; 'indeed I wouldn't run such a risk, my Lady; let me put one of the gentlemen in there, and Miss Wood can have the first room in the west corridor.'

'And what use would she be to Lady Grayburn out there?' said her Ladyship. 'Don't be foolish, my good Marris. Unlock the door between the two rooms; Miss Wood can leave it open if she feels nervous; but I shall not say a word about that foolish superstition, and I shall be very much annoyed if anyone else does so.'

She spoke as if that settled the question, but my aunt wasn't easy. 'The Laird,' she murmured; 'what will he say to a lady being put to sleep there?'

'Sir Archibald does not interfere in household arrangements. Have the Blue Room made ready for Miss Wood at once. *I* will take the responsibility – if there is any.'

On that her Ladyship went away, and there was nothing for it but to carry out her orders. The Blue Room was prepared, a great fire lighted, and when I went round last thing to see all was in order for the visitor's arrival, I couldn't but think how handsome and comfortable it looked. There were candles burning brightly on the toilet-table and chimney-piece, and a fine blaze of logs on the wide hearth. I saw nothing had been overlooked, and was closing the door when my eyes fell on the bed. It was crumpled just as if someone had thrown themselves across it, and I was vexed that the housemaids should have been so careless, especially with the smart new quilt. I went round, and patted up the feathers, and smoothed the counterpane, just as the carriages drove under the window.

By and by Lady Grayburn and Miss Wood came upstairs, and knowing they had brought no maid, I went to assist in the unpacking. I was a long time in her Ladyship's room, and when I'd settled her I tapped at the next door and offered to help Miss Wood. Lady Grayburn followed me almost immediately to inquire the whereabouts of some keys. She spoke very sharply, I thought, to her companion, who seemed a timid, delicate slip of a girl, with nothing noticeable about her except her hair, which was lovely, pale golden, and heaped in thick coils all round her small head.

'You will certainly be late,' Lady Grayburn said. 'What an age you have been, and you have not half finished unpacking yet.' The young lady murmured something about there being so little time. 'You have had time to sprawl on the bed instead of getting ready,' was the retort, and as Miss Wood meekly denied the imputation, I looked over my shoulder at the bed, and saw there the same strange indentation I had noticed before. It made my heart beat faster, for without any reason at all I felt certain that crease must have something to do with Lady Barbara.

Miss Wood didn't go to the ball. She had supper in the schoolroom with the young ladies' governess, and as I heard from one of the maids that she was to sit up for Lady Grayburn, I took her some wine and sandwiches about twelve o'clock. She stayed in the schoolroom, with a book, till the first party came home soon after two. I'd been round the rooms with the housemaid to see the fires were kept up, and I wasn't surprised to find that queer crease back on the bed again; indeed, I sort of expected it. I said nothing to the maid, who didn't seem to have noticed anything out of the way, but I told my aunt, and though she answered sharply that I was talking nonsense, she turned quite pale, and I heard her mutter something under breath that sounded like 'God help her!'

I slept badly that night, for, do what I would, the thought of that poor young lady alone in the Blue Room kept me awake and restless. I was nervous, I suppose, and once, just as I was dropping off, I started up, fancying I'd heard a scream. I opened my door and listened, but there wasn't a sound, and after waiting a bit I crept back to bed, and lay there shivering till I fell asleep.

The household wasn't astir as early as usual. Everyone was tired after the late night, and tea wasn't to be sent to the ladies till half-past nine. My aunt said nothing about the ghost, but I noticed she was fidgety, and asked almost first thing if anyone had been to Miss Wood's room. I was telling her that Martha, one of the housemaids, had just taken up the tray, when the girl came running in with a scared, white face. 'For pity's sake, Mrs Marris,' she cried, 'come to the Blue Room; something awful has happened!'

My aunt stopped to ask no questions. She ran straight upstairs, and as I followed I heard her muttering to herself, 'I knew it, I knew it. Oh Lord! what will my Lady feel like now?'

If I live to be a hundred I shall never forget that poor girl's face. It was just as if she'd been frozen with terror. Her eyes were wide open and fixed, and her little hands clenched in the coverlet on each side of her as she lay across the bed in the very place where that crease had been.

Of course the whole house was aroused. Sir Archibald sent one of the grooms post-haste for the doctor, but he could do nothing when he came; Miss Wood had been dead for at least five hours.

It was a sad business. All the visitors went away as soon as possible, except Lady Grayburn, who was obliged to stay for the inquest.

In his evidence, the doctor stated death was due to failure of heart's action, occasioned possibly by some sudden shock; and though the jury did not say so in their verdict, it was an open secret that they blamed her Ladyship for permitting Miss Wood to sleep in the haunted room. No one could have reproached her more bitterly than she did herself, poor lady; and if she had done wrong she certainly suffered for it, for she never recovered from the shock of that dreadful morning, and became more or less of an invalid till her death five years later.

All this happened in 184–. It was fifty years before another woman slept in the Blue Room, and fifty years had brought with them many changes. The old Laird was gathered to his fathers, and his son, the present Sir Archibald, reigned in his stead; his sons were grown men, and Mr Charles, the eldest, married, with a fine little boy of his own. My aunt had been dead many a year, and I was an old woman, though active and able as ever to keep the maids up to their work. They take more looking after now, I think, than in the old days before there was so much talk of education, and when young women who took service thought less of dress and more of dusting. Not but what education is a fine thing in its proper place, that is, for gentlefolk. If Miss Erristoun, now, hadn't been the clever, strong-minded young lady she is, she'd never have cleared the Blue Room of its terrible secret, and lived to make Mr Arthur the happiest man alive.

He'd taken a great deal of notice of her when she first came in the summer to visit Mrs Charles, and I wasn't surprised to find she was one of the guests for the opening of the shooting-season. It wasn't a regular house-party (for Sir Archibald and Lady Mertoun were away), but just half-a-dozen young ladies, friends of Mrs Charles, who was but a girl herself, and as many gentlemen that Mr Charles and Mr Arthur had invited. And very gay they were, what with lunches at the covert-side, and tennis-parties, and little dances got up at a few hours' notice, and sometimes of an evening they'd play hide-and-seek all over the house just as if they'd been so many children.

It surprised me at first to see Miss Erristoun, who was said to be so learned, and had held her own with all the gentlemen at Cambridge, playing with the rest like any ordinary young lady; but she seemed to enjoy the fun as much as anyone, and was always first in any amusement that was planned. I didn't wonder at Mr Arthur's fancying her, for she was a handsome girl, tall and finely made, and carried herself like a princess. She had a wonderful head of hair, too, so long, her maid told me, it touched the ground as she sat on a chair to have it brushed. Everybody seemed to take to her, but I soon noticed it was Mr Arthur or Mr Calder-Maxwell she liked best to be with.

Mr Maxwell is a Professor now, and a great man at Oxford; but then he was just an undergraduate the same as Mr Arthur, though more studious, for he'd spend hours in the library poring over those old books full of queer black characters, that they say the wicked Lord Mertoun collected in the time of King Charles the Second. Now and then Miss Erristoun would stay indoors to help him, and it was something they found out in their studies that gave them the clue to the secret of the Blue Room.

For a long time after Miss Wood's death all mention of the ghost was strictly forbidden. Neither the Laird nor her Ladyship could bear the slightest allusion to the subject, and the Blue Room was kept locked, except when it had to be cleaned and aired. But as the years went by the edge of the tragedy wore off, and by degrees it grew to be just a story that people talked about in much the same way as they had done when I first came to the Towers; and if many believed in the mystery and speculated as to what the ghost could be, there were others who didn't hesitate to declare Miss Wood's dying in that room was a mere coincidence, and had nothing to do with supernatural agency. Miss Erristoun was one of those who held most strongly to this theory. She didn't believe a bit in ghosts, and said straight out that there wasn't any of the tales told of haunted houses which could not be traced to natural causes, if people had courage and science enough to investigate them thoroughly.

It had been very wet all that day, and the gentlemen had stayed indoors, and nothing would serve Mrs Charles but they should all have an old-fashioned tea in my room and 'talk ghosts', as she called it. They made me tell them all I knew about the Blue Room, and it was then, when everyone was discussing the story and speculating as to what the ghost could be, that Miss Erristoun spoke up. 'The poor girl had heart-complaint,' she finished by saying, 'and she would have died the same way in any other room.'

'But what about the other people who have slept there?' someone objected.

'They did not die. Old Sir Archibald came to no harm, neither did Mr Hawksworth, nor the other man. They were healthy, and had plenty of pluck, so they saw nothing.'

'They were not women,' put in Mrs Charles; 'you see the ghost only appears to the weaker sex.'

'That proves the story to be a mere legend,' Miss Erristoun said with decision. 'First it was reported that everyone who slept in the room died. Then one or two men did sleep there, and remained alive; so the tale had to be modified, and since one woman could be proved to have died suddenly there, the fatality was represented as attaching to women only. If a girl with a sound constitution and good nerve were once to spend the night in that room, your charming family-spectre would be discredited forever.'

There was a perfect chorus of dissent. None of the ladies could agree, and most of the gentlemen doubted whether any woman's nerve would stand the ordeal. The more they argued the more Miss Erristoun persisted in her view, till at last Mrs Charles got vexed, and cried: 'Well, it is one thing to talk about it, and another to do it. Confess now, Edith, you daren't sleep in that room yourself.'

'I dare and I will,' she answered directly. 'I don't believe in ghosts, and I am ready to stand the test. I will sleep in the Blue Room to-night, if you like, and tomorrow morning you will have to confess that whatever there may be against the haunted chamber, it is not a ghost.'

I think Mrs Charles was sorry she'd spoken then, for they all took Miss Erristoun up, and the gentlemen were for laying wagers as to whether she'd see anything or not. When it was too late she tried to laugh aside her challenge as absurd, but Miss Erristoun wouldn't be put off. She said she meant to see the thing through, and if she wasn't allowed to have a bed made up, she'd carry in her blankets and pillows, and camp out on the floor.

The others were all laughing and disputing together, but I saw Mr Maxwell look at her very curiously. Then he drew Mr Arthur aside, and began to talk in an undertone. I couldn't hear what he said, but Mr Arthur answered quite short:

'It's the maddest thing I ever heard of, and I won't allow it for a moment.'

'She will not ask your permission perhaps,' Mr Maxwell retorted. Then he turned to Mrs Charles, and inquired how long it was since the Blue Room had been used, and if it was kept aired. I could speak to that, and when he'd heard that there was no bedding there, but that fires were kept up regularly, he said he meant to have the first refusal of the ghost, and if he saw nothing it would be time enough for Miss Erristoun to take her turn.

Mr Maxwell had a kind of knack of settling things, and somehow with his quiet manner always seemed to get his own way. Just before dinner he came to me with Mrs Charles, and said it was all right, I was to get the room made ready quietly, not for all the servants to know, and he was going to sleep there.

I heard next morning that he came down to breakfast as usual. He'd had an excellent night, he said, and never slept better.

It was wet again that morning, raining 'cats and dogs', but Mr Arthur went out in it all. He'd almost quarrelled with Miss Erristoun, and was furious with Mr Maxwell for encouraging her in her idea of testing the ghost-theory, as they called it. Those two were together in the library most of the day, and Mrs Charles was chaffing Miss Erristoun as they went upstairs to dress, and asking her if she found the demons interesting. Yes, she said, but there was a page missing in the most exciting part of the book. They could not make head or tail of the context for some time, and then Mr Maxwell discovered that a leaf had been cut out. They talked of nothing else all through dinner, the butler told me, and Miss Erristoun seemed so taken up with her studies, I hoped she'd forgotten about the haunted room. But she wasn't one of the sort to forget. Later in the evening I came across her standing with Mr Arthur in the corridor. He was talking very earnestly, and I saw her shrug her shoulders and just look up at him and smile, in a sort of way that meant she wasn't going to give in. I was slipping quietly by, for I didn't want to disturb them, when Mr Maxwell came out of the billiard-room. 'It's our game,' he said; 'won't you come and play the tie?'

'I'm quite ready,' Miss Erristoun answered, and was turning away, when Mr Arthur laid his hand on her arm. 'Promise me first,' he urged, 'promise me that much, at least.'

'How tiresome you are!' she said quite pettishly. 'Very well then, I promise; and now please, don't worry me anymore.'

Mr Arthur watched her go back to the billiard-room with his friend, and he gave a sort of groan. Then he caught sight of me and came along the passage. 'She won't give it up,' he said, and his face was quite white. 'I've done all I can; I'd have telegraphed to my father, but I don't know where they'll stay in Paris, and anyway there'd be no time to get an answer. Mrs Marris, she's going to sleep in that d − − room, and if anything happens to her – I – – ' he broke off short, and threw himself on to the window-seat, hiding his face on his folded arms.

I could have cried for sympathy with his trouble. Mr Arthur has always been a favourite of mine, and I felt downright angry with Miss Erristoun for making him so miserable just out of a bit of bravado.

'I think they are all mad,' he went on presently. 'Charley ought to have stopped the whole thing at once, but Kate and the others have talked him round. He professes to believe there's no danger, and Maxwell has got his head full of some rubbish he has found in those beastly books on Demonology, and he's backing her up. She won't listen to a word I say. She told me point-blank she'd never speak to me again if I interfered. She doesn't care a hang for me; I know that now, but I can't help it; I – I'd give my life for her.'

I did my best to comfort him, saying Miss Erristoun wouldn't come to any harm; but it wasn't a bit of use, for I didn't believe in my own assurances. I felt nothing but ill could come of such tempting of Providence, and I seemed to see that other poor girl's terrible face as it had looked when we found her dead in that wicked room. However, it is a true saying that 'a wilful woman will have her way', and we could do nothing to prevent Miss Erristoun's risking her life; but I made up my mind, to one thing, whatever other people might do, *I* wasn't going to bed that night.

I'd been getting the winter-hangings into order, and the upholstress had used the little boudoir at the end of the long corridor for her work. I made up the fire, brought in a fresh lamp, and when the house was quiet, I crept down and settled myself there to watch. It wasn't ten yards from the door of the Blue Room, and over the thick carpet I could pass without making a sound, and listen at the keyhole. Miss Erristoun had promised Mr Arthur she would not lock her door; it was the one concession he'd been able to obtain from her. The ladies went to their rooms about eleven, but Miss Erristoun stayed talking to Mrs Charles for nearly an hour while her maid was brushing her hair. I saw her go to the Blue Room, and by and by Louise left her, and all was quiet. It must have been half-past one before I thought I heard something moving outside. I opened the door and looked out, and there was Mr Arthur standing in the passage. He gave a start when he saw me. 'You are sitting up,' he said, coming into the room; 'then you do believe there is evil work on hand to-night? The others have gone to bed, but I can't rest; it's no use my trying to sleep. I meant to stay in the smoking-room, but it is so far away; I couldn't hear there even if she called for help. I've listened at the door; there isn't a sound. Can't you go in and see if it's all right? Oh, Marris, if she should – – '

I knew what he meant, but I wasn't going to admit *that* possible – yet. 'I can't go into a lady's room without any reason,' I said; 'but I've been to the door every few minutes for the last hour and more. It wasn't till half-past twelve that Miss Erristoun stopped moving about, and I don't believe, Mr Arthur, that God will let harm come to her, without giving those that care for her some warning. I mean to keep on listening, and if there's the least hint of anything wrong, why I'll go to her at once, and you are at hand here to help.'

I talked to him a bit more till he seemed more reasonable, and then we sat there waiting, hardly speaking a word except when, from time to time, I went outside to listen. The house was deathly quiet; there was something terrible, I thought, in the stillness; not a sign of life anywhere save just in the little boudoir, where Mr Arthur paced up and down, or sat with a strained look on his face, watching the door.

As three o'clock struck, I went out again. There is a window in the corridor, angle for angle with the boudoir-door. As I passed, someone stepped from behind the curtains and a voice whispered: 'Don't be frightened Mrs Marris; it is only me, Calder-Maxwell. Mr Arthur is there, isn't he?' He pushed open the boudoir door. 'May I come in?' he said softly. 'I guessed you'd be about, Mertoun. I'm not at all afraid myself, but if there *is* anything in that little legend, it is as well for some of us to be on hand. It was a good idea of yours to get Mrs Marris to keep watch with you.'

Mr Arthur looked at him as black as thunder. 'If you didn't *know* there was something in it,' he said, 'you wouldn't be here now; and knowing that, you're nothing less than a blackguard for egging that girl on to risk her life, for the sake of trying to prove your insane theories. You are no friend of mine after this, and I'll never willingly see you or speak to you again.'

I was fairly frightened at his words, and for how Mr Maxwell might take them; but he just smiled, and lighted a cigarette, quite cool and quiet.

'I'm not going to quarrel with you, old chap,' he said. 'You're a bit on the strain to-night, and when a man has nerves he mustn't be held responsible for all his words.' Then he turned to me. 'You're a sensible woman, Mrs Marris, and a brave one too, I fancy. If I stay here with Mr Arthur, will you keep close outside Miss Erristoun's door? She may talk in her sleep quietly; that's of no consequence; but if she should cry out, go in at once, *at once*, you understand; we shall hear you, and follow immediately.'

At that Mr Arthur was on his feet. 'You know more than you pretend,' he cried. 'You slept in that room last night. By Heaven, if you've played any trick on her I'll – – '

Mr Maxwell held the door open. 'Will you go, please, Mrs Marris?' he said in his quiet way. 'Mertoun, don't be a d – fool.'

I went as he told me, and I give you my word I was all ears, for I felt certain Mr Maxwell knew more than we did, and that he expected something to happen.

It seemed like hours, though I know now it could not have been more than a quarter of that time, before I could be positive someone was moving behind that closed door.

At first I thought it was only my own heart, which was beating against my ribs like a hammer; but soon I could distinguish footsteps, and a sort of murmur like someone speaking continuously, but very low. Then a voice (it was Miss Erristoun's this time) said, 'No, it is impossible; I am dreaming, I must be dreaming.' There was a kind of rustling as though she were moving quickly across the floor. I had my fingers on the handle, but I seemed as if I'd lost power to stir; I could only wait for what might come next.

Suddenly she began to say something out loud. I could not make out the words, which didn't sound like English, but almost directly she stopped short. 'I can't remember any more,' she cried in a troubled tone. 'What shall I do? I can't – – ' There was a pause. Then – 'No, *no*!' she shrieked. 'Oh, Arthur, Arthur!'

At that my strength came back to me, and I flung open the door.

There was a night-lamp burning on the table, and the room was quite light. Miss Erristoun was standing by the bed; she seemed to have backed up against it; her hands were down at her sides, her fingers clutching at the quilt. Her face was white as a sheet, and her eyes staring wide with terror, as well they might – I know I never had such a shock in my life, for if it was my last word, I swear there was a man standing close in front of her. He turned and looked at me as I opened the door, and I saw his face as plain as I did hers. He was young and very handsome, and his eyes shone like an animal's when you see them in the dark.

'Arthur!' Miss Erristoun gasped again, and I saw she was fainting. I sprang forward, and caught her by the shoulders just as she was falling back on to the bed.

It was all over in a second. Mr Arthur had her in his arms, and when I looked up there were only us four in the room, for Mr Maxwell had followed on Mr Arthur's heels, and was kneeling beside me with his fingers on Miss Erristoun's pulse. 'It's only a faint,' he said, 'she'll come round directly. Better take her out of this at once; here's a dressing-gown.' He threw the wrapper round her, and would have helped to raise her, but Mr Arthur needed no assistance. He lifted Miss Erristoun as if she'd been a baby, and carried her straight to the boudoir. He laid her on the couch and knelt beside her, chafing her hands. 'Get the brandy out of the smoking room, Maxwell,' he said. 'Mrs Marris, have you any salts handy?'

I always carry a bottle in my pocket, so I gave it to him, before I ran after Mr Maxwell, who had lighted a candle, and was going for the brandy. 'Shall I wake Mr Charles and the servants?' I cried. 'He'll be hiding somewhere, but he hasn't had time to get out of the house yet.'

He looked as if he thought I was crazed. 'He – who?' he asked.

'The man,' I said; 'there was a man in Miss Erristoun's room. I'll call up Soames and Robert.'

'You'll do nothing of the sort,' he said sharply. 'There was no man in that room.'

'There was,' I retorted, 'for I saw him; and a great powerful man too. Someone ought to go for the police before he has time to get off.'

Mr Maxwell was always an odd sort of gentleman, but I didn't know what to make of the way he behaved then. He just leaned against the wall, and laughed till the tears came into his eyes.

'It is no laughing matter that I can see,' I told him quite short, for I was angry at his treating the matter so lightly; 'and I consider it no more than my duty to let Mr Charles know that there's a burglar on the premises.'

He grew grave at once then. 'I beg your pardon, Mrs Marris,' he said seriously; 'but I couldn't help smiling at the idea of the police. The vicar would be more to the point, all things considered. You really must not think of rousing the household; it might do Miss Erristoun a great injury, and could in no case be of the slightest use. Don't you understand? It was not a man at all you saw, it was an – well, it was what haunts the Blue Room.'

Then he ran downstairs leaving me fairly dazed, for I'd made so sure what I'd seen was a real man, that I'd clean forgotten all about the ghost.

Miss Erristoun wasn't long regaining consciousness. She swallowed the brandy we gave her like a lamb, and sat up bravely, though she started at every sound, and kept her hand in Mr Arthur's like a frightened child. It was strange, seeing how independent and stand-off she'd been with him before, but she seemed all the sweeter for the change. It was as if they'd come to an understanding without any words; and, indeed, he must have known she had cared for him all along, when she called out his name in her terror.

As soon as she'd recovered herself a little, Mr Maxwell began asking questions. Mr Arthur would have stopped him, but he insisted that it was of the greatest importance to hear everything while the impression was fresh; and when she had got over the first effort, Miss Erristoun seemed to find relief in telling her experience. She sat there with one hand in Mr Arthur's while she spoke, and Mr Maxwell wrote down what she said in his pocket-book.

She told us she went to bed quite easy, for she wasn't the least nervous, and being tired she soon dropped off to sleep. Then she had a sort of dream, I suppose, for she thought she was in the same room, only differently furnished, all but the bed. She described exactly how everything was arranged. She had the strangest feeling too, that she was not herself but someone else, and that she was going to do something – something that must be done, though she was frightened to death all the time, and kept stopping to listen at the inner door, expecting someone would hear her moving about and call out for her to go to them. That in itself was queer, for there was nobody sleeping in the adjoining room. In her dream, she went on to say, she saw a curious little silver brazier, one that stands in a cabinet in the picture-gallery (a fine example of *cinque cento* work, I think I've heard my Lady call it), and this she remembered holding in her hands a long time, before she set it on a little table beside the bed. Now the bed in the Blue Room is very handsome, richly carved on the cornice and frame, and especially on the posts, which are a foot square at the base and covered with relief-work in a design of fruit and flowers. Miss Erristoun said she went to the left-hand post at the foot, and after passing her hand over the carving, she seemed to touch a spring in one of the centre flowers, and the panel fell outwards like a lid, disclosing a secret cupboard out of which she took some papers and a box. She seemed to know what to do with the papers, though she couldn't tell us what was written on them; and she had a distinct recollection of taking a pastille from the box, and lighting it in the silver brazier. The smoke curled up and seemed to fill the whole room with a heavy perfume, and the next thing she remembered was that she awoke to find herself standing in the middle of the floor, and – what I had seen when I opened the door was there.

She turned quite white when she came to that part of the story, and shuddered. 'I couldn't believe it,' she said; 'I tried to think I was still dreaming, but I wasn't, I wasn't. It was real, and it was there, and – oh, it was horrible!'

She hid her face against Mr Arthur's shoulder. Mr Maxwell sat, pencil in hand, staring at her. 'I was right then,' he said. 'I felt sure I was; but it seemed incredible.'

'It is incredible,' said Miss Erristoun; 'but it is true, frightfully true. When I realised that I was awake, that it was actually real, I tried to remember the charge, you know, out of the office of exorcism, but I couldn't get through it. The words went out of my head; I felt my will-power failing; I was paralysed, as though I could make no effort to help myself and then – then I –' she looked at Mr Arthur and blushed all over her face and neck. 'I thought of you, and I called – I had a feeling that you would save me.'

Mr Arthur made no more ado about us than if we'd been a couple of dummies. He just put his arms round her and kissed her, while Mr Maxwell and I looked the other way.

After a bit, Mr Maxwell said: 'One more question, please; what was it like?'

She answered after thinking for a minute. 'It was like a man, tall and very handsome. I have an impression that its eyes were blue and very bright.' Mr Maxwell looked at me inquiringly, and I nodded. 'And dressed?' he asked. She began to laugh almost hysterically. 'It sounds too insane for words, but I think – I am almost positive it wore ordinary evening dress.'

'It is impossible,' Mr Arthur cried. 'You were dreaming the whole time, that proves it.'

'It doesn't,' Mr Maxwell contradicted. 'They usually appeared in the costume of the day. You'll find that stated particularly both by Scott and Glanvil; Sprenger gives an instance too. Besides, Mrs Marris thought it was a burglar, which argues that the – the manifestation was objective, and presented no striking peculiarity in the way of clothing.'

'What?' Miss Erristoun exclaimed. 'You saw it too?' I told her exactly what I had seen. My description tallied with hers in everything, but the white shirt and tie, which from my position at the door I naturally should not be able to see.

Mr Maxwell snapped the elastic round his note-book. For

a long time he sat silently staring at the fire. 'It is almost past belief,' he said at last, speaking half to himself, 'that such a thing could happen at the end of the nineteenth century, in these scientific rationalistic times that we think such a lot about, we, who look down from our superior intellectual height on the benighted superstitions of the Middle Ages.' He gave an odd little laugh. 'I'd like to get to the bottom of this business. I have a theory, and in the interest of psychical research and common humanity, I'd like to work it out. Miss Erristoun, you ought, I know, to have rest and quiet, and it is almost morning; but will you grant me one request. Before you are overwhelmed with questions, before you are made to relate your experience till the impression of to-night's adventure loses edge and clearness, will you go with Mertoun and myself to the Blue Room, and try to find the secret panel?'

'She shall never set foot inside that door again,' Mr Arthur began hotly, but Miss Erristoun laid a restraining hand on his arm.

'Wait a moment, dear,' she said gently; 'let us hear Mr Maxwell's reasons. Do you think,' she went on, 'that my dream had a foundation in fact; that something connected with that dreadful thing is really concealed about the room?'

'I think,' he answered, 'that you hold the clue to the mystery, and I believe, could you repeat the action of your dream, and open the secret panel, you might remove forever the legacy of one woman's reckless folly. Only if it is to be done at all, it must be soon, before the impression has had time to fade.'

'It shall be done now,' she answered; 'I am quite myself again. Feel my pulse; my nerves are perfectly steady.'

Mr Arthur broke out into angry protestations. She had gone through more than enough for one night, he said, and he wouldn't have her health sacrificed to Maxwell's whims.

I have always thought Miss Erristoun handsome, but never, not even on her wedding-day, did she look so beautiful as then when she stood up in her heavy white wrapper, with all her splendid hair loose on her shoulders.

'Listen,' she said; 'if God gives us a plain work to do, we must do it at any cost. Last night I didn't believe in anything I could not understand. I was so full of pride in my own courage and common sense, that I wasn't afraid to sleep in that room and prove the ghost was all superstitious nonsense. I have learned there are forces of which I know nothing, and against which my strength was utter weakness. God took care of me, and sent help in time; and if He has opened a way by which I may save other women from the danger I escaped, I should be worse than ungrateful were I to shirk the task. Bring the lamp, Mr Maxwell, and let us do what we can.' Then she put both hands on Mr Arthur's shoulders. 'Why are you troubled?' she said sweetly. 'You will be with me, and how can I be afraid?'

It never strikes me as strange now that burglaries and things can go on in a big house at night, and not a soul one whit the wiser. There were five people sleeping in the rooms on that corridor while we tramped up and down without disturbing one of them. Not but what we went as quietly as we could, for Mr Maxwell made it clear that the less was known about the actual facts, the better. He went first, carrying the lamp, and we followed. Miss Erristoun shivered as her eyes fell on the bed, across which that dreadful crease showed plain, and I knew she was thinking of what might have been, had help not been at hand.

Just for a minute she faltered, then she went bravely on, and began feeling over the carved woodwork for the spring of the secret panel. Mr Maxwell held the lamp close, but there was nothing to show any difference between that bit of carving and the other three posts. For full ten minutes she tried, and so did the gentlemen, and it seemed as though the dream would turn out a delusion after all, when all at once Miss

Erristoun cried, 'I have found it,' and with a little jerk, the square of wood fell forward, and there was the cupboard just as she had described it to us.

It was Mr Maxwell who took out the things, for Mr Arthur wouldn't let Miss Erristoun touch them. There were a roll of papers and a little silver box. At the sight of the box she gave a sort of cry; 'That is it,' she said, and covered her face with her hands.

Mr Maxwell lifted the lid, and emptied out two or three pastilles. Then he unfolded the papers, and before he had fairly glanced at the sheet of parchment covered with queer black characters, he cried, 'I knew it, I knew it! It *is* the missing leaf.' He seemed quite wild with excitement. 'Come along,' he said. 'Bring the light, Mertoun; I always said it was no ghost, and now the whole thing is as clear as daylight. You see,' he went on, as we gathered round the table in the boudoir, 'so much depended on there being an heir. That was the chief cause of the endless quarrels between old Lord Mertoun and Barbara. He had never approved of the marriage, and was forever reproaching the poor woman with having failed in the first duty of an only son's wife. His will shows that he did not leave her a farthing in event of her husband dying without issue. Then the feud with the Protestant branch of the family was very bitter, and the Sir Archibald of that day had three boys, he having married (about the same time as his cousin) Lady Mary Sarum, who had been Barbara's rival at Court and whom Barbara very naturally hated. So when the doctors pronounced Dennis Mertoun to be dying of consumption, his wife got desperate, and had recourse to black magic. It is well known that the old man's collection of works on Demonology was the most complete in Europe. Lady Barbara must have had access to the books, and it was she who cut out this leaf. Probably Lord Mertoun discovered the theft and drew his own conclusions. That would account for his refusal to admit her body to the family vault. The Mertouns were staunch Romanists, and it is one of the deadly sins, you know, meddling with sorcery. Well, Barbara contrived to procure the pastilles, and she worked out the spell according to the directions given here, and then – Good God! Mertoun, what have you done?'

For before anyone could interfere to check him, Mr Arthur had swept papers, box, pastilles, and all off the table and flung them into the fire. The thick parchment curled and shrivelled on the hot coals, and a queer, faint smell like incense spread heavily through the room. Mr Arthur stepped to the window and threw the casement wide open. Day was breaking, and a sweet fresh wind swept in from the east which was all rosy with the glow of the rising sun.

'It is a nasty story,' he said; 'and if there be any truth in it, for the credit of the family and the name of a dead woman, let it rest for ever. We will keep our own counsel about to-night's work. It is enough for others to know that the spell of the Blue Room is broken, since a brave, pure-minded girl has dared to face its unknown mystery and has laid the ghost.'

Mr Calder-Maxwell considered a moment. 'I believe you are right,' he said, presently, with an air of resignation. 'I agree to your preposition, and I surrender my chance of world-wide celebrity among the votaries of Psychical Research; but I *do* wish, Mertoun, you would call things by their proper names. It was *not* a ghost. It was an —'

But as I said, all I can remember now of the word he used is, that it somehow put me in mind of poultry-rearing.

Note – The reader will observe that the worthy Mrs Marris, though no student of Sprenger, unconsciously discerned the root-affinity of the *incubator* of the hen-yard and the *incubus* of the MALLEUS MALEFICARUM.

3 The Green Bowl

BY SARAH ORNE JEWETT (1901)

'I am a person who has always cherished a prejudice against crossing the sea, and I have made up for it handsomely by taking many journeys on land here at home. Some of the dearest of these have also been the shortest. I have had an unbroken custom these many years, of going away for a week's driving up the country in late September or early October, and just before I came here I had an adventure for the first time. And that little green bowl on the table there is to me a dear and valued memento of it.'

'Do you mean that you go through the country quite, quite alone,' asked Mrs Crosdyck, a majestic-looking elderly lady, with some reproach in her voice.

'A coachman and a footman would spoil my joys altogether,' acknowledged Miss Montague with decision. 'There is only one way to do it; one must have a good companion and an excellent horse, a light buggy, and almost no baggage at all. One must wear a shirt-waist and a corduroy skirt and jacket, she must have a dressing kit of the most frugal sort, no silver boxes or dressing-table tools or any tea gowns allowed! One may provide a very little good tea for emergencies, and a small box of biscuit, and a nubbin of chocolate or some decent raisins. Yes, and one needs a good golf cape in case of rain,' the traveller insisted eagerly, as if the serious duty of selection had suddenly arrived. 'But the most important things are the horse and companion!'

'And then, my dear child,' asked the disapproving lady, 'do you mean to say that you really go driving off to strange places, quite, quite alone? Have you no fear of tramps?'

'None whatever,' answered the story-teller with a fire of enthusiasm for which the guests were unprepared. 'I might be the only living descendant of Robin Hood himself: besides, I don't go alone; Miss Kent always almost goes with me. My only sorrow is that I can't go gypsying afoot and be a tramp myself. Should you really like to know about our last year's excursion?'

'You would hardly think, to look at my companion now, that she was fit for adventuring,' resumed the speaker after a warm response. 'You see Miss Frances Kent sitting there, gowned in white, with rare old pink topaz ornaments? (I speak as the society newspaper.) I now show you the celebrated Miss Frances Kent, ladies and gentlemen, known as the best of companions for such a journey. She is ever thankful for "the key of the fields" like myself, and we are going again this year, gowned in well-worn corduroy, and with happy hearts, to see what else we can of the world. The only thing that troubles us is that we have to take so many clumsy things for the horse, and they make the buggy quite uncomfortable, but we mind nothing when we are really out upon the road.'

'Where do you go?' asked an awestricken voice.

'Oh anywhere,' replied Miss Montague with the utmost cheerfulness. 'Sometimes northeast and sometimes north-west, as the case may be. The country taverns are much better since the days of bicycling came in. We start off boldly and just say that we are going up the country and then let fate or fortune choose the way. Last year we had been to see an old village, high on the shoulders of the mountains, which I had always wished to visit. We were on our way home, as safe as dolls in a nursery when we had our little adventure and got the green bowl.'

The audience politely waited for the story.

'Rain is a great enemy to the primitive traveller and to lose one's way is exciting, but not really dangerous,' the speaker explained. 'We also wish that there was a useful society for the maintenance of sign-boards. We were hurrying toward home that day, and lost our way because we could find no sign-boards at all, though we poked about with a stick in the raspberry bushes at the fork of the roads and thought we had found what was left of the sign-post, and then were obliged to let the horse himself select the way home, and he struck into a road that carried us many miles through the woods. Instead of leading us the way we expected, this road at last seemed to take a turn back toward the hills again. The bushes grew closer against the wheels, and after we had passed some rough wood-roads by which timber had been hauled out in the winter, the signs of travel were so slight that we feared that we were for the first time likely to spend a night in an impromptu camp. I confess that it was a little too late in the season for that, and it was so near the end of the day that we were sorry to think of going all the way back. Frances, there, began to be timid and even reproachful, she had insisted from the first that we should have taken the other road, and was pleased to blame me when our mistake was all the fault of the horse.'

'You haven't said that it was already growing dark and that the clouds were of a threatening hue,' broke in Miss Kent. 'It looked like a black rainy night; I expected every minute that we should come to a deserted clearing or a ruined logging camp; for at last the road itself seemed hard to find, there were bushes in it by that time as well as alongside and your ignorant horse stopped still in his tracks!'

'Yes, and then we heard a cock crowing,' Miss Montague interrupted her scornfully, 'and we went on again directly; we should have been all right if it hadn't been for the rain. I like that horse myself and I think that I shall take him again this year. Then we hurried on toward the farm which could not be far away. The voice of poultry usually means not only a hen-coop but a barn and a house, and we began to laugh at each other and I whipped the horse because it was just beginning to rain. It was not long before we were out of the woods but there was no hen-coop to be seen, much less a house or barn. There was indeed a piece of open country but it was all pasture land, and we thought that the cock's crow was only a ghost of a bird and sat and looked at each other. Beyond the empty pastures the road plunged into the woods again.'

'And then you said, "This is what we have always wanted, Frances; this is really an adventure!"' said Miss Kent laughing, but one of the elder ladies gave a groan of dismay.

'It was raining fast and the light was fast going. I began to wonder if there was anything better to do than to drive under a thick pine tree and pull out the rubber lap-robe and put it over our knees and sit still all night in the buggy,' continued the narrator, making the most of the situation. 'But we really had heard the encouraging rooster; I suppose now that some track led through that pasture to a farmhouse hidden behind the woods. The horse knew more than we did, perhaps he heard some sounds of life that we couldn't hear, for he began to trot along cheerfully as fast as he could go and pretty soon we had passed through those black hemlock woods that lay beyond the pastures and came out to the open world where we saw a funny little church steeple not far away.

'Now, the very morning before this, we had passed another church and I had told Frances, when I saw the long row of open sheds where the horses were left during service time, that ever since I could remember I had thought what fun it would be to drive under such a shelter and keep oneself dry and safe if a shower came up, and that never yet had the shower and the sheds and I all been in the same place at the same time. That was enough to say, the interfering fates had listened to me; my opportunity had arrived; and I fairly whirled in out of the steady rain, thankful enough to get under cover.'

'Isn't it the strangest thing in the world!' interrupted Mrs Crosdyck with enthusiasm, 'if you say that you haven't had a headache for a year, you simply do remind the fates to send you one; the careful Germans knock under the table to drive such evil spirits away, but we take no proper precautions here in America, we really are too self-sufficient!'

The hostess looked relieved and even triumphant.

'Go on my dear Katie!' Mrs Goddard urged the traveller with a contented smile.

'Oh yes, the fates had not only taken heed of me, but they seemed to have provided rain and sheds enough to make up for all lacks of either in my whole history,' said Miss Montague. 'The only trouble was that there was so little of me. It must have been a large parish, though one could see no houses the line of sheds looked as long as a cavalry barrack, and the rain was a drowning rain. Frances was now more sulky than can be described, though she had been complaining through the whole week's drive of too much dust, and I looked across the road at the church spire and the vane pointed northeast in the most determined fashion, by this time it was quite half-past five o'clock. We had passed one little dark low-storied house that looked quite deserted, but I had seen no barn beside it, it was no use to go back, we should be wet through. We sat there in the buggy and looked at each other in despair. You were very decent in your behaviour Frances! though very glum indeed!' she exclaimed, at which tribute of respect the company laughed aloud.

'What *did* you do?' demanded Mrs Crosdyck. 'What an awful situation for two young ladies!'

'And a hungry horse!' added a merciful masculine with an amused smile. 'I should have advised driving as fast as you could through the rain until you found shelter, there must have been good farmhouses not far beyond.'

Miss Montague laughed a little. 'If you had only seen how it poured and how dark it was growing!' she answered modestly, 'and we might have gone a mile or even two, and Frances here was already wet and shivering. "Get out my dear!" said I affectionately "and jump up and down a little to warm you, I'll run across to the church!" and I did not wait for argument but caught up my skirts and ran. I was ready to pound in the door by the time I got to it, but it quietly opened as if it had heard good preaching, and knew its duty; and in the entry I saw that there was a nice pile of pine wood, and I even observed in my extremity, a tin match-box on the ledge of the rough wainscotting. All I wanted was the stove, and that was just beyond, at the back of the pews. I hadn't consciously thought about the cold while we were driving, but I now knew that I was shivering myself. So I just stopped and made a fire in that good old box-stove, then and there. I may have used a few leaves of a tattered hymn-book for kindling, I really can't say, and the smoke puffed out at me so that I thought I should be forever blind, but in two minutes I had a good fire going.'

There was a murmur of admiration from the audience.

'Then I ran across the road again, meaning to send Frances over to the church to get dry and warm while I drove on alone to find a good place where we could be housed for the night; you must know that Frances had been ill the winter before, and her lungs were still considered to be delicate. I was going to run no risks; but when I got back she was fairly beaming with joy, I could see her eyes shine though it was almost dark under the sheds. "Look here," said she, "here's a fine pile of hay in the next cubby but one! I suppose some farmer has a horse that won't stand quietly without refreshments, or someone may have been at work about the church and brought it." "Don't let's search for reasons," said I; the dear child had already brought an armful of hay, though I had always thought she knew nothing about horses, and had even let the check rein down, and old Bob was munching away as comfortably as possible. So I told Frances about the fire in the church and sent her across to sit beside it, and made up my mind to stay all night just where we were. I unharnessed old Bob and put on his blanket and halter, and led him through to the stall where the hay was, and pulled the buggy farther in out of the wet, and spread out the rug we had had over us and put all our things into it, and then I splashed over again to the little church. You certainly never heard such a rain, it drummed louder than ever on the roof, and I was as wet as I could be.'

'We thought it must be the equinoctial storm,' said Miss Frances Kent laughing a little. 'Your poor hat, Katie! It had been trimmed with nice ostrich feathers, and when I saw you coming in at the door with your great load, and those feathers dripping into your eyes, you were truly a most forlorn object.'

'Of what importance were our looks!' demanded Miss Montague with royal scorn. 'You may not believe it, any of you who are listening to me, but we had a most charming evening together, Frances and I, after we got dry. The church was not cold, it had been sunshiny weather, rather hot for the season, all that week, and the pine-wood fire soon made us only too warm. We had a little of our luncheon left and we ate it thankfully, with the aforesaid nubbin of chocolate for dessert. Of course there were plenty of kerosene lamps in the meeting-house, and we lighted two or three of them and made our corner quite gay. There was a little organ in the singing seats that wasn't half bad; a very nice tone it had; and Frances played upon it (contented, sober things), that she remembered, and sang a good deal, dear girl, and made it very pleasant for me, though I don't know much about music; then we got sleepy and looked about for two pews with good cushions. It was a nice old church with decent wide pews that made us very comfortable. We just locked the church door to keep out burglars, and laid ourselves down in our two pews and went to sleep!'

'It was a great bit of fun,' insisted Miss Kent, protesting a little at the mingled amusement and horror of the company. 'We really had a delightful evening, but you must tell them now about our breakfast, Katie dear.'

'I was just waking up in wonder,' said the story-teller. 'I did really feel a little stiff and lame that next morning, but it was not an equinoctial rain at all; the sunshine was pouring in through the big windows, and I always did like to sleep in a bright room. It was half-past five by the church clock; old Bob was whinnying and there was somebody knocking very loud at the meeting-house door. I was not startled, but I was half provoked, because whoever it was kept up such an incessant knocking and calling. I got there as quick as I could, but Frances was still sound asleep, like a stupid baby, in her pew. I opened the door and there stood the most dear kind-looking old woman that you ever saw, with a face of such anxiety that I couldn't help laughing as I looked at her.'

'"You poor dear young creatur's!"' she said, '"be you alive this morning? I see you drive by in that drowning rain, and I run out and called after you to come in, but I couldn't make you hear. I expected you'd go right on to Duffy's folks, but 'tis a mile an' a quarter further, and then I watched an' I didn't see ye pass up the hill right out beyond here, and so I knowed you'd been discreet and drove into the sheds. It was pourin' so I couldn't do nothin'; my health ain't sufficient to risk a wetting, but I did feel anxious, and 'twant half an hour afore I see you'd got safe into the meetin'-house, an' lit the lamps, an' I set down then an' felt easy, an' says to myself the Lord will provide; they looked like very competent girls an' they can easy make 'em a nice fire. I'd been over early in the morning,

a-sweeping out the pews, an' 'twas I that had left the door
unlocked, meanin' to go back if it hadn't come on to rain so.
I keep the keys; they call me the deacon, some on 'em in the
parish! Now I want you to come right along home with me; I
laid awake in the night considerable and I see when you put
the lights out nice an' careful, an' I says; now what I can do for
them strangers is to give 'em a nice hot breakfast!"

'Frances had got herself well waked up and put together by
that time, and came out with her most cordial manners, and
we all three helped to put the church to rights. Mrs Patton
looked anxiously about to see if we had done any mischief,
but we hadn't, and she found the church broom, and swept
neatly about the stove for us as I had meant to do myself. We
put some money into the contribution box, and then we went
off up the road with the good little old soul. It was a perfectly
enchanting morning, old Bob was still munching away at his
pile of hay, and he called after us most sociably. Mrs Patton
said that we could bring him a pail of water when we came
back from breakfast.'

'Well, and how did you fare, my dear?' asked Mrs Crosdyck
again, a little incredulous.

'It was the very best breakfast we had ever eaten in our lives,
you know that we hadn't in the least over-eaten at supper,'
said Miss Kent, eagerly taking up the thread of discourse.
'By this time it was only six o'clock, but Mrs Patton had
made everything ready that she could before she came over.
We ate and ate, and we laughed and laughed, the dear little
old woman was so droll and her house was one of those
warm little brown country houses that are full of welcome
and homely comfort. I believe there wasn't a bit of paint in
it except on her pretty green kitchen chairs. She had some
good old pictures on the wall too, prints of Bible subjects
mostly, and a splendid, coloured one of the Pirate's Bride.
Her garden was full of phlox and tiger-lilies then, but it had

been a lovely garden all the season; she said that she always put the Sunday flowers on the pulpit desk in summer. As for the green bowl, it was standing on a side-table between the windows in the kitchen, with three yellow apples in it, and I said what a beauty it was, and Katie praised it too, you can see it for yourselves!'

Miss Montague had stopped suddenly in mid-course. She had been gayly recounting this simple adventure of a rainy day, but almost with the first entrance of a figure with so wet a rustic landscape, her manner had entirely changed.

'One always knows when one sees a real friend for the first time,' she said gravely. 'Frances and I took Mrs Patton to our lonely hearts at that first moment.'

'You ought to call this "The Tale of a Lonely Parish", only Mr Marion Crawford thought of the title first, laughed Mrs Goddard. 'I can imagine your two faces in the doorway; I am sure that you looked apprehensive, both of you, and tired and hungry too!'

'I shall never forget how Mrs Patton trotted ahead of us down the road towards her house,' laughed Miss Kent. 'She was talking as fast as she could over her shoulder all the way, and her cat had come with her and kept close by her skirts. The horse was whinnying after us like a whole circus, poor old Bob feared that he might be forgotten, and altogether we made a great excitement.'

'I should have rung the church bell for help,' announced Mrs Crosdyck, with an air of being the only resourceful member of the company.

'There wasn't any bell,' retorted the girl, 'and nobody who listens to me need think that we were frightened for one moment. I should like to know what there was to frighten one in such a peaceful, honest, little corner of the world as that.'

'And then you saw the bowl,' Mrs Crosdyck suggested impatiently.

'Yes, all the time we were at the table I kept stealing glances at the green bowl. It was on the other table between the front windows. It was behind Frances and so she couldn't see it as well as I.'

'I had seen it,' answered Miss Kent, 'and I knew very well what you were looking at.'

'It is not an unusual thing to see so good a piece of china in a little house like that,' explained Mrs Goddard. 'Nearly all the best things in my collection have come out of just such houses. There was a time when they were not much valued, but twenty years have made an entire change. After those of us who began to make collections, came a deluge of mercenary collectors, who canvassed the neighbourhood of all the old seaport towns. There is little to be found now, but the former owners of old china, and French and English pottery, have become well educated in the real values of old plates and bowls, that they once gladly sold for a quarter of a dollar.'

'Mrs Patton was begging us to eat more of everything on her dear little square table,' Miss Montague went on. 'Somebody asked me if we had pie a few minutes ago, and I would not answer him because the question was not asked in the right spirit, but I now say that we did have an apple pie such as I have never eaten before or since. It made a sort of dessert to our breakfast, instead of berries or any other stewed fruit. For my own part,' and she challenged the whole company with great spirit, 'I never had any sympathy with those who can accept an inelegant, dull English tart without protest, and then smile at a New England pie. They do not see that the pie is a highly developed English tart made fit for Christian food and attractive to the epicure. Imagination has worked upon it, the higher education of women has spiritualised its grosser form. The English tart is nothing but a pie without a soul. If I described the creation that we ate for breakfast at Mrs Patton's! – '

'Oh, but we aren't as hungry as you were then!' cried someone. The listeners were in the best of humour now, especially Mrs Crosdyck, but she proved to have at least one wish still unsatisfied.

'Your travels are very interesting, my dear,' she said loftily, 'but I should like to hear a real story. I am really curious about that green bowl.'

'So were we!' agreed Katie pleasantly. 'Presently, when there was a pause, I asked a question: you see that we first had to tell all about ourselves, and hear all about each other, and give proper time to the preliminaries of so true a friendship; then I frankly asked Mrs Patton where she got that beautiful little green bowl.'

'She laughed aloud in the oddest way before she answered me. "Funny how everybody that comes to this house asks me that question!" she said. "Won't you have just one more piece of pie, dears?" and then she laughed again!

'"There's two of them little green bowls! My great aunt gave them to me. She said she must have owned 'em full fifty years; they were given to her just after she was married, by a brother of her husband's that was a sailor, a wild sort of fellow that fetched 'em home from China. They look as if they were plain green from here, but when you hold 'em in the light you see a pattern underneath."

'"'Twan't the aunt that brought me up; 'twas still another. I was left an orphan when I was a baby, and I'd every reason to be a lonesome person, but 'twan't my nature.'"

'That's just the way she talked – oh Katie, you've got it exactly!' interrupted Frances Kent, with delight.

'"No dears, 'twas my other aunt,"' Miss Montague went on reporting, as if she had not been interrupted at all. '"My Aunt Mally, that was the doctor's wife's mother over to Jopham Corners. They went off down to Meriden where he thought he saw a great opening for practice, but aunt said she was too old to change, I don't know but they were glad; 'twas her own house at the Corners and there were times when she made 'em feel it. One o' them two green bowls was always on the mantlepiece in her own room, and folks were always proposing that she should put it on the parlour mantlepiece where 'twould show, but she never consented. She had that bowl and a little Samuel, and a bunch of feather flowers under a bell-glass, between them. When I was a little girl and went to see her, she used to take a cent out of one of them bowls and give it to me, real pleasant, and when I was grown up she used to offer me a hoarhound drop. Aunt and me was always good friends!'" and Katie and Mrs Goddard were seen by all the company to smile at each other.

'I asked Mrs Patton if her aunt had been dead a good while, and she said it was forty years.'

Said Frances Kent, 'Somehow one feels as if so few things had ever happened and as if everything were so tremendously interesting.'

'I began to have a strange feeling about the little green bowl myself,' acknowledged Katie, speaking in a low voice. 'You see that when we had got up from the table I noticed that Mrs Patton kept looking at it as if it was somehow in her mind. We helped her clear away the breakfast things, and when we had been in the house an hour one felt as if it had been a week. After awhile she took me by the sleeve when Frances was putting away some plates in the cupboard (somehow one always knew just where everything went), and she whispered to me, "I expect there's some sort of charm about that bowl!"

'I wasn't going to have dear Frances left out of any pleasure!' said the speaker, 'and I called to her at once and asked her. "Did you hear what Mrs Patton says? There is a charm about the green bowl!" But Mrs Patton looked a little disturbed.

'"I can't tell it to but one, dear," she said, and her cheeks grew quite scarlet. "Aunt never told it to anybody but me."

Oh I assure you it was quite exciting!'

'I knew there must be a story!' said Mrs Crosdyck complacently, and she smoothed down her satin dress as if she wore an invisible apron.

'Somehow the whole thing was mysterious,' said Frances Kent, slowly. 'First we lost the road and then we heard the rooster crowing and could see no house, and then we spent the night in the church, and this strange little old woman came to the door in the morning, and we seemed to know all about each other before we had been together for five minutes, and now we had had that wonderful breakfast, and it was all exactly as if the green bowl had something to do with it; we were all thinking of it from the first minute we had entered her door! I was ready to burst with curiosity, and I said: Oh do tell us! But she grew still more scarlet and confused and caught up a water pail from its little bench, and ran away to the well to fill it.'

'Did you say there were two bowls?' asked Mrs Goddard, smiling a little in spite of herself.

'We never saw but one,' answered Katie. 'Now don't interrupt me anymore, Frances, if you please! You know that –'

'I don't know anything,' retorted Miss Kent, with some spirit. 'I begin to believe that I never shall! I have always insisted that you might tell me what Mrs Patton told you!'

All this time the green bowl stood in plain sight. There was a handful of pansies in it which did not hide its lovely outlines or its deep rich colour. All the members of the house party were looking at the strange old piece of eastern ware with constantly increasing curiosity. The fire had sprung afresh on the hearth and a reflection of it twirled and glowed on the bowl. Everybody's attention was centred upon this thing of which hardly anyone had been in the least conscious an hour before. It had taken on a strange importance.

'You see it was the one really valuable and beautiful thing in that little house. It shone like a jewel on its table between the windows in the sun that morning,' Katie went on. 'You can't help wondering about the past experiences of a thing like that,' and she looked at the bowl with a sort of apprehensive interest. 'The sailor and the old aunt and Mrs Patton make but a short chapter of its long history; it is a very old bowl indeed!'

'But the charm?' asked someone eagerly. 'Did Mrs Patton tell you the secret? Were there really two bowls – and one held a curse and the other a blessing?'

'They were for the cents and the hoarhound drops?' suggested an eager listener. But the young narrators looked at each other with odd intentness across the room and did not laugh at all.

'We had to wait there for a while,' Miss Montague went on. 'Mrs Patton had been watching all breakfast time for a messenger and finally saw a boy from the nearest house, the one behind the woods where we had heard the cock crow, and sent him for old Bob with orders for plenty of oats and water and to rub him down and keep him until called for. This was at about half-past eight so that Bob was not really suffering. We kept thinking that he would come, but it proved later that the wheels had wanted oiling and that the good woman had dried our blankets and everything. Mrs Patton looked more and more cheerful and said that she wished that we had no choice but to spend the day with her and our loss of time was her gain. We said that she must let us help her if we stayed, and what was she going to do if we had not been there? Finally she confessed that she had some beans that she was in a hurry to pick over for market, and send off, that day or the next, whenever they were called for, and we sat down together as if we had always been work-mates.'

'Wasn't it the cosiest thing you ever did? I am always thinking of it when things are tiresome,' exclaimed Miss Kent.

'Picking beans, how odd!' said a scornful voice, but nobody

seconded the scoffer, while Mrs Crosdyck asked with great interest if there were a cat.

'Oh, yes, two enchanting kittens!' cried the teller with enthusiasm. 'But now I must really tell you about the bowl! Only as Frances says there is a secret.'

She got up from her chair and went and stood by the table and lifted the beautiful old thing in her hand so that all the company could see it.

'It looks too distinguished to have wasted its beauty in such a house as that,' said Mrs Crosdyck who was nearest. 'Look out, my dear, that you don't break it.'

'Mrs Patton said that her old aunt used to have the gift of telling fortunes,' said Miss Montague solemnly as she still stood there looking very eager and handsome. 'And we asked if she couldn't tell fortunes, too, as we sat round the bushel-basket of beans. She seemed a little confused, and then told us that she didn't know why she shouldn't admit it, the gift had brought her more pain than pleasure, but anybody might use the good of any gift, and she had warned some folks of what was coming so that they had been thankful to her afterward. "And keeping my mind on that," she said impressively, "has made me learn to read folks' faces easier than most people can. One of our ministers went so far as to say 'twas a gift that would lead me and other folks straight to the pit if I continued its exercise, but I made bold to say it had heretofore seemed to lead the other way if I wasn't mistaken." She reached forward then and rolled out the three yellow apples, and took the green bowl and looked at it and into it as I have seen other people looking into crystals, the dear old thing was quite lost in it and I saw her eyelids quiver strangely once or twice. Frances and I stopped clicking the beans and watched her. "One o' you's been in danger lately," she whispered, "and the other's been living in the shadows. Yes, I can read it plain!" You who know us both will know that she spoke the truth. "And you're going from here to a house near a river, and there'll be lots of folks there," so she went on and told us nothing that was important, but everything she said was true. Then she told me about my uncle's death in a southern country where the sun was too bright, and that his head would suffer, and that I would have much more money, but wish for the one who had loved me back again and count myself poor without him instead of rich: there were enough remarkable things to make one respect Mrs Patton as a seer, but she sat there quite simply and used her plain country words while she revealed us, to ourselves and to each other. Then suddenly she gave herself a queer little shake and seemed to wake up into the commonplace world again. You see that there wasn't anything startling about it that she could tell, but we saw plainly that she had the gift.'

'Oh, I wish that we had her here!' said one of the listeners, 'she would tell all our fortunes!'

'But Miss Montague has been given the power to tell fortunes; didn't you tell us so?' urged another.

'Not on Sunday, my dear,' commanded Mrs Goddard impressively. 'No, I should never consent to it!'

'I can only tell you about the two bowls, that is really the most interesting thing of all,' said Katie blushing, and looking a little confused. 'It seems that the two bowls, the "sister bowls" she called them, must be kept by two different persons, and the other, which she had kept for many years was put away in the closet, only the day before this one had come back to her from the other owner who had just died. And when she saw me standing in the meeting-house door that morning she said that she knew; she had a certain sign that made it plain to her that she must give this other green bowl to me. She stood them together on the table and they looked just alike. We asked her how she understood about them, and she said that her old aunt taught her and she would teach me; the sailor who brought them home to her had been a roving man and had gone into some far province of China, and got his strange learning there. He had meant to settle down and be a fortune-teller, and expected to make a great deal of money, but after he had told the aunt about the bowls and made her his companion in their mysteries, he went away, only for a day's journey, and was killed by an accident. Now I am Mrs Patton's "*companion*", as she calls it; she said that if there were not two of us *companions* the life of the bowls would soon be gone. She said one very strange thing – the friend who had kept it for her had been dead two days but she said she could have waited another day if I had not appeared, that as long as the other "*companion's*" soul was in her body or near it, there was no danger. But she was glad when she saw me and got the sign. She said that our souls always stayed with our bodies a little while after we die.'

'How very strange,' said Frances Kent. 'But somehow she did not seem half so strange to me at the time when we were there. I sat picking over the beans, not at all excited, even when Mrs Patton took Katie into the little bedroom and shut the door, and divulged the principles of magic. You certainly did look a little pale when you came out, Katie!'

'Can you see things in it, in the bowl, I mean?' one of the guests asked hurriedly. 'Do you try very often, Miss Montague? Oh, please throw out those pansies and tell us something!'

'Aren't you afraid that it will be broken?' some careful soul inquired.

'No, it is the most wonderful thing, like some precious stone or dull crystal – I don't think it is any sort of pottery,' said its owner. 'It made me a little fidgety to see it in my room and I brought it here. You see that there isn't any story at all. I only promised to give you a plain account of our travels,' she added hastily, for everyone began to ask questions.

'I don't like this revelation very much,' protested Mrs Goddard. 'Katie, my dear, you never told me so much before. I have been enchanted at having such an exquisite thing in the house, but I begin to be a little afraid of the green bowl.'

'Mrs Patton said that it was like any other bowl except for those who could master it. She was very matter of fact, after all,' said Frances Kent. 'There we sat together nearly all that long morning, and grew to be the best of friends. I tried to make her talk about the bowl to me, but she put on such a droll look and said that I was the joking sort like herself and perhaps she could find some sort of charm that would be fit for me before we came again. We were quite at home together, I assure you. She did not talk much with Katie after they had their secret session. I asked her all about her housekeeping.'

Miss Kent was glancing at her friend as she spoke who was standing by the table with the bowl in her hand looking into it as if she had forgotten everything else.

'What is it, dear?' whispered Frances Kent, as she rose and stood beside her.

'I just saw something very strange like a living picture!' answered the holder of the bowl softly. She was turning it to the light and gazing at it with a half-frightened look on her face. 'It is just as Mrs Patton said: she told me that some day I should find that the gift had come.'

'Tell me what it is that you see,' persisted her friend.

'Oh, don't ask me out loud, don't say anything now!' begged Katie, 'I saw two of the people who are sitting here, they were saying farewell to each other like the figures on a Greek vase; one of them is going to die. I knew them at once, Frances! I could not go on looking – Take it away! put it on the table for me, and don't let any one suspect anything!'

Miss Kent crossed the broad hearth rug a little unsteadily and there was a queer look on her face as she put the green bowl down on the table. Miss Montague, by the fire, had stood still for a moment and then turned to the great china jar and lifting the cover took out some of Mrs Goddard's treasured bits of lightwood to fling them on the bright coals.

'She writes us the most quaint, delightful letters, does Mrs Patton,' said Miss Kent, taking up the story, for someone asked if anything were the matter. 'She likes to have us send her magazines and stories to read. Oh, I assure you that by the time we took the road again late that morning we were the very best of friends!'

'It certainly did turn out very well,' pronounced Mrs Crosdyck with great amiability, 'but I should feel very anxious about you if you were girls of mine, driving about in this way in these lonely places!'

'Where are you going for your driving journey this year, young ladies?' inquired an old gentleman who had just waked up from a good nap.

'Oh, first to Mrs Patton's again!' answered Katie Montague gallantly. 'We have promised to spend a night at her dear little house.'

The bright firelight shone upon Katie's face, but she spoke with cheerful determination and instant decision, though more than one of the guests noticed that she looked strangely pale. Then she rose quickly and stood facing them.

'You know,' she said, 'that I shall have to tell my *companion* all that has happened about the green bowl!' But though everyone, even the sleepy old gentleman, begged to know what had really happened, Katie could not be persuaded to tell anything more.

4 A Dreamer

BY BARBARA BAYNTON (1902)

A swirl of wet leaves from the night-hidden trees decorating the little station beat against the closed doors of the carriages. The porter hurried along holding his blear-eyed lantern to the different windows, and calling the name of the township in language peculiar to porters. There was only one ticket to collect.

Passengers from far up-country towns have importance from their rarity. He turned his lantern full on this one, as he took her ticket. She looked at him too, and listened to the sound of his voice, as he spoke to the guard. Once she had known every hand at the station. The porter knew everyone in the district. This traveller was a stranger to him.

If her letter had been received, someone would have been waiting with a buggy. She passed through the station. She saw nothing but an ownerless dog, huddled, wet and shivering, in a corner. More for sound she turned to look up the straggling street of the township. Among the she-oaks, bordering the river she knew so well, the wind made ghostly music, unheeded by the sleeping town. There was no other sound, and she turned to the dog with a feeling of kinship. But perhaps the porter had a message! She went back to the platform. He was locking the office door, but paused as though expecting her to speak.

'Wet night!' he said at length, breaking the silence.

Her question resolved itself into a request for the time, though this she already knew. She hastily left him.

She drew her cloak tightly round her. The wind made her umbrella useless for shelter. Wind and rain and darkness lay before her on the walk of three bush miles to her mother's home. Still it was the home of her girlhood, and she knew every inch of the way.

As she passed along the sleeping street, she saw no sign of life till near the end. A light burned in a small shop, and the sound of swift tapping came to her. They work late to-night, she thought, and, remembering their gruesome task, hesitated, half-minded to ask these night workers, for whom they laboured. Was it someone she had known? The long dark walk – she could not – and hastened to lose the sound.

The zigzag course of the railway brought the train again near to her, and this wayfarer stood and watched it tunnelling in the teeth of the wind. Whoof! whoof! its steaming breath hissed at her. She saw the rain spitting viciously at its red mouth. Its speed, as it passed, made her realise the tedious difficulties of her journey, and she quickened her pace. There was the silent tenseness that precedes a storm. From the branch of a tree overhead she heard a watchful mother-bird's warning call, and the twitter of the disturbed nestlings. The tender care of this bird-mother awoke memories of her childhood. What mattered the lonely darkness, when it led to mother. Her forebodings fled, and she faced the old track unheedingly, and ever and ever she smiled, as she foretasted their meeting.

'Daughter!'

'Mother!'

She could feel loving arms around her, and a mother's sacred kisses. She thrilled, and in her impatience ran, but the wind was angry and took her breath. Then the child near her heart stirred for the first time. The instincts of motherhood awakened in her. Her elated body quivered, she fell on her knees, lifted her hands, and turned her face to God. A vivid flash of lightning flamed above her head. It dulled her rapture. The lightning was very near.

She went on, then paused. Was she on the right track? Back, near the bird's nest, were two roads. One led to home, the other was the old bullock-dray road, that the railway had almost usurped. When she should have been careful in her choice, she had been absorbed. It was a long way back to the cross-roads, and she dug in her mind for landmarks. Foremost she recalled the 'Bendy Tree', then the 'Sisters', whose entwined arms talked, when the wind was from the south. The apple trees on the creek-split flat, where the cows and calves were always to be found. The wrong track, being nearer the river, had clumps of she-oaks and groups of pines in places. An angled line of lightning illuminated everything, but the violence of the thunder distracted her.

She stood in uncertainty, near-sighted, with all the horror of the unknown that this infirmity could bring. Irresolute, she waited for another flash. It served to convince her, she was wrong. Through the bush she turned.

The sky seemed to crack with the lightning; the thunder's suddenness shook her. Among some tall pines she stood awed, while the storm raged.

Then again that indefinite fear struck at her. Restlessly she pushed on till she stumbled, and, with hands outstretched, met some object that moved beneath them as she fell. The lightning showed a group of terrified cattle. Tripping and falling, she ran, she knew not where, but keeping her eyes turned towards the cattle. Aimlessly she pushed on, and unconsciously retraced her steps.

She struck the track she was on when her first doubt came. If this were the right way, the wheel ruts would show. She groped, but the rain had levelled them. There was nothing to guide her. Suddenly she remembered that the little clump of pines, where the cattle were, lay between the two roads. She had gathered mistletoe berries there in the old days.

She believed, she hoped, she prayed that she was right. If

so, a little further on, she would come to the 'Bendy Tree'. There long ago a runaway horse had crushed its drunken rider against the bent, distorted trunk. She could recall how in her young years that tree had ever after had a weird fascination for her.

She saw its crooked body in the lightning's glare. She was on the right track, yet dreaded to go on. Her childhood's fear came back. In a transient flash she thought she saw a horseman galloping furiously towards her. She placed both her hands protectingly over her heart, and waited. In the dark interval, above the shriek of the wind, she thought she heard a cry, then crash came the thunder, drowning her call of warning. In the next flash she saw nothing but the tree. 'Oh, God, protect me!' she prayed, and diverging, with a shrinking heart passed on.

The road dipped to the creek. Louder and louder came the roar of its flooded waters. Even little Dog-trap Gully was proudly foaming itself hoarse. It emptied below where she must cross. But there were others that swelled it above.

The noise of the rushing creek was borne to her by the wind, still fierce, though the rain had lessened. Perhaps there would be someone to meet her at the bank! Last time she had come, the night had been fine, and though she had been met at the station by a neighbour's son, mother had come to the creek with a lantern and waited for her. She looked eagerly, but there was no light.

The creek was a banker, but the track led to a plank, which, lashed to the willows on either bank, was usually above flood-level. A churning sound showed that the water was over the plank, and she must wade along it. She turned to the sullen sky. There was no gleam of light save in her resolute, white face.

Her mouth grew tender, as she thought of the husband she loved, and of their child. Must she dare! She thought of the grey-haired mother, who was waiting on the other side. This dwarfed every tie that had parted them. There was atonement in these difficulties and dangers.

Again her face turned heavenward! 'Bless, pardon, protect and guide, strengthen and comfort!' Her mother's prayer.

Steadying herself by the long willow branches, ankle deep she began. With every step the water deepened.

Malignantly the wind fought her, driving her back, or snapping the brittle stems from her skinned hands. The water was knee-deep now, and every step more hazardous.

She held with her teeth to a thin limb, while she unfastened her hat and gave it to the greedy wind. From the cloak, a greater danger, she could not in her haste free herself; her numbed fingers had lost their cunning.

Soon the water would be deeper, and the support from the branches less secure. Even if they did reach across, she could not hope for much support from their wind-driven, fragile ends.

Still she would not go back. Though the roar of that rushing water was making her giddy, though the deafening wind fought her for every inch, she would not turn back.

Long ago she should have come to her old mother, and her heart gave a bound of savage rapture in thus giving the sweat of her body for the sin of her soul.

Midway the current strengthened. Perhaps if she, deprived of the willows, were swept down, her clothes would keep her afloat. She took firm hold and drew a deep breath to call her child-cry, 'Mother!'

The water was deeper and swifter, and from the sparsity of the branches she knew she was nearing the middle. The wind unopposed by the willows was more powerful. Strain as she would, she could reach only the tips of the opposite trees, not hold them.

Despair shook her. With one hand she gripped those, that

had served her so far, and cautiously drew as many as she could grasp with the other. The wind savagely snapped them, and they lashed her unprotected face. Round and round her bare neck they coiled their stripped fingers. Her mother had planted these willows, and she herself had watched them grow. How could they be so hostile to her!

The creek deepened with every moment she waited. But more dreadful than the giddying water was the distracting noise of the mighty wind, nurtured by the hollows.

The frail twigs of the opposite tree snapped again and again in her hands. She must release her hold of those behind her. If she could make two steps independently, the thicker branches would then be her stay.

'Will you?' yelled the wind. A sudden gust caught her, and, hurling her backwards, swept her down the stream with her cloak for a sail.

She battled instinctively, and her first thought was of the letter-kiss she had left for the husband she loved. Was it to be his last?

She clutched a floating branch, and was swept down with it. Vainly she fought for either bank. She opened her lips to call. The wind made a funnel of her mouth and throat, and a wave of muddy water choked her cry. She struggled desperately, but after a few mouthfuls she ceased. The weird cry from the 'Bendy Tree' pierced and conquered the deep throated wind. Then a sweet dream voice whispered 'Little Woman!'

Soft, strong arms carried her on. Weakness aroused the melting idea that all had been a mistake, and she had been fighting with friends. The wind even crooned a lullaby. Above the angry waters her face rose untroubled.

A giant tree's fallen body said, 'Thus far!' and in vain the athletic furious water rushed and strove to throw her over the barrier. Driven back, it tried to take her with it. But a jagged arm of the tree snagged her cloak and held her.

Bruised and half-conscious she was left to her deliverer, and the back-broken water crept tamed under its old foe. The hammer of hope awoke her heart. Along the friendly back of the tree she crawled, and among its bared roots rested. But it was only to get her breath, for this was mother's side.

She breasted the rise. Then every horror was of the past and forgotten, for there in the hollow was home.

And there was the light shining its welcome to her.

She quickened her pace, but did not run – motherhood is instinct in woman. The rain had come again, and the wind buffeted her. To breathe was a battle, yet she went on swiftly, for at the sight of the light her nameless fear had left her.

She would tell mother how she had heard her call in the night, and mother would smile her grave smile and stroke her wet hair, call her 'Little woman! My little woman!' and tell her she had been dreaming, just dreaming. Ah, but mother herself was a dreamer!

The gate was swollen with rain and difficult to open. It had been opened by mother last time. But plainly her letter had not reached home. Perhaps the bad weather had delayed the mail boy.

There was the light. She was not daunted when the bark of the old dog brought no one to the door. It might not be heard inside, for there was such a torrent of water falling somewhere close. Mechanically her mind located it. The tank near the house, fed by the spouts, was running over, cutting channels through the flower beds, and flooding the paths. Why had not mother diverted the spout to the other tank!

Something indefinite held her. Her mind went back to the many times long ago when she had kept alive the light while mother fixed the spout to save the water that the dry summer months made precious. It was not like mother, for such carelessness meant carrying from the creek.

Suddenly she grew cold and her heart trembled. After she

had seen mother, she would come out and fix it, but just now she could not wait.

She tapped gently, and called 'Mother!'

While she waited she tried to make friends with the dog. Her heart smote her, in that there had been so long an interval since she saw her old home that the dog had forgotten her voice.

Her teeth chattered as she again tapped softly. The sudden light dazzled her when a stranger opened the door for her. Steadying herself by the wall, with wild eyes she looked around. Another strange woman stood by the fire, and a child slept on the couch. The child's mother raised it, and the other led the now panting creature to the child's bed. Not a word was spoken, and the movements of these women were like those who fear to awaken a sleeper.

Something warm was held to her lips, for through it all she was conscious of everything, even that the numbing horror in her eyes met answering awe in theirs.

In the light the dog knew her and gave her welcome. But she had none for him now.

When she rose one of the women lighted a candle. She noticed how, if the blazing wood cracked, the women started nervously, how the disturbed child pointed to her bruised face, and whispered softly to its mother, how she who lighted the candle did not strike the match but held it to the fire, and how the light bearer led the way so noiselessly.

She reached her mother's room. Aloft the woman held the candle and turned away her head.

The daughter parted the curtains, and the light fell on the face of the sleeper who would dream no dreams that night.

5 The Hall Bedroom

BY MARY E WILKINS FREEMAN (1905)

My name is Mrs Elizabeth Jennings. I am a highly respectable woman. I may style myself a gentlewoman, for in my youth I enjoyed advantages. I was well brought up, and I graduated at a young ladies' seminary. I also married well. My husband was that most genteel of all merchants, an apothecary. His shop was on the corner of the main street in Rockton, the town where I was born, and where I lived until the death of my husband. My parents had died when I had been married a short time, so I was left quite alone in the world. I was not competent to carry on the apothecary business by myself, for I had no knowledge of drugs, and had a mortal terror of giving poisons instead of medicines. Therefore I was obliged to sell at a considerable sacrifice, and the proceeds, some five thousand dollars, were all I had in the world. The income was not enough to support me in any kind of comfort, and I saw that I must in some way earn money. I thought at first of teaching, but I was no longer young, and methods had changed since my school days. What I was able to teach, nobody wished to know. I could think of only one thing to do: take boarders. But the same objection to that business as to teaching held good in Rockton. Nobody wished to board. My husband had rented a house with a number of bedrooms, and I advertised, but nobody applied. Finally my cash was running very low, and I became desperate. I packed up my furniture, rented a large house in this town and moved here. It was a venture attended with many risks. In the first place the rent was exorbitant, in the next I was entirely unknown. However, I am a person of considerable ingenuity, and have inventive power, and much enterprise when the occasion presses. I advertised in a very original manner, although that actually took my last penny, that is, the last penny of my ready money, and I was forced to draw on my principal to purchase my first supplies, a thing which I had resolved never on any account to do. But the great risk met with a reward, for I had several applicants within two days after my advertisement appeared in the paper. Within two weeks my boarding-house was well established, I became very successful, and my success would have been uninterrupted had it not been for the mysterious and bewildering occurrences which I am about to relate. I am now forced to leave the house and rent another. Some of my old boarders accompany me, some, with the most unreasonable nervousness, refuse to be longer associated in any way, however indirectly, with the terrible and uncanny happenings which I have to relate. It remains to be seen whether my ill luck in this house will follow me into another, and whether my whole prosperity in life will be forever shadowed by the Mystery of the Hall Bedroom. Instead of telling the strange story myself in my own words, I shall present the Journal of Mr George H Wheatcroft. I shall show you the portions beginning on January 18 of the present year, the date when he took up his residence with me. Here it is:

※

'January 18, 1883. Here I am established in my new boarding-house. I have, as befits my humble means, the hall bedroom, even the hall bedroom on the third floor. I have heard all my life of hall bedrooms, I have seen hall bedrooms, I have been in them, but never until now, when I am actually established in one, did I comprehend what, at once, an ignominious and sternly uncompromising thing a hall bedroom is. It proves the ignominy of the dweller therein. No man at thirty-six (my age) would be domiciled in a hall bedroom, unless he were himself ignominious, at least comparatively speaking. I am proved by this means incontrovertibly to have been left far behind in the race. I see no reason why I should not live in this hall bedroom for the rest of my life, that is, if I have money enough to pay the landlady, and that seems probable, since my small funds are invested as safely as if I were an orphan-ward in charge of a pillar of a sanctuary. After the valuables have been stolen, I have most carefully locked the stable door. I have experienced the revulsion which comes sooner or later to the adventurous soul who experiences nothing but defeat and so-called ill luck. I have swung to the opposite extreme. I have lost in everything – I have lost in love, I have lost in money, I have lost in the struggle for preferment, I have lost in health and strength. I am now settled down in a hall bedroom to live upon my small income, and regain my health by mild potations of the mineral waters here, if possible; if not, to live here without my health – for mine is not a necessarily fatal malady – until Providence shall take me out of my hall bedroom. There is no one place more than another where I care to live. There is not sufficient motive to take me away, even if the mineral waters do not benefit me. So I am here and to stay in the hall bedroom. The landlady is civil, and even kind, as kind as a woman who has to keep her poor womanly eye upon the main chance can be. The struggle for money always injures the fine grain of a woman; she is too fine a thing to do it; she does not by nature belong with the gold grubbers, and it therefore lowers her; she steps from heights to claw and scrape and dig. But she cannot help it oftentimes, poor thing, and her deterioration thereby is to be condoned. The landlady is all she can be, taking her strain of adverse circumstances into consideration, and the table is good, even conscientiously so. It looks to me as if she were foolish enough to strive to give the boarders their money's worth, with the due regard for the main chance which is inevitable. However, that is of minor importance to me, since my diet is restricted.'

'It is curious what an annoyance a restriction in diet can be even to a man who has considered himself somewhat indifferent to gastronomic delights. There was to-day a pudding for dinner, which I could not taste without penalty, but which I longed for. It was only because it looked unlike any other pudding that I had ever seen, and assumed a mental and spiritual significance. It seemed to me, whimsically no doubt, as if tasting it might give me a new sensation, and consequently a new outlook. Trivial things may lead to large results: why should I not get a new outlook by means of a pudding? Life here stretches before me most monotonously, and I feel like clutching at alleviations, though paradoxically, since I have settled down with the utmost acquiescence. Still one cannot immediately overcome and change radically all one's nature. Now I look at myself critically and search for the keynote to my whole self, and my actions, I have always been conscious of a reaching out, an overweening desire for the new, the untried, for the broadness of further horizons, the seas beyond seas, the thought beyond thought. This characteristic has been the primary cause of all my misfortunes. I have the soul of an explorer, and in nine out of ten cases this leads to destruction. If I had possessed capital and sufficient push, I should have been one of the searchers after the North Pole. I have been an eager student of astronomy. I have studied botany with avidity, and have dreamed of new flora in unexplored parts of the world, and the same with animal life and geology. I longed for riches in order to discover the power and sense of possession of the rich. I longed for love in order to discover the possibilities of the emotions. I longed for all that the mind of man could conceive as desirable for man, not so much for purely selfish ends, as from an insatiable thirst for knowledge of a universal trend. But I have limitations, I do not quite understand of what nature – for what mortal ever did quite understand his own limitations, since a knowledge of them would preclude their existence? – but they have prevented my progress to any extent. Therefore behold me in my hall bedroom, settled at last into a groove of fate so deep that I have lost the sight of even my horizons. Just at present, as I write here, my horizon on the left, that is my physical horizon, is a wall covered with cheap paper. The paper is an indeterminate pattern in white and gilt. There are a few photographs of my own hung about, and on the large wall space beside the bed there is a large oil painting which belongs to my landlady. It has a massive tarnished gold frame, and, curiously enough, the painting itself is rather good. I have no idea who the artist could have been. It is of the conventional landscape type in vogue some fifty years since, the type so fondly reproduced in chromos – the winding river with the little boat occupied by a pair of lovers, the cottage nestled among trees on the right shore, the gentle slope of the hills and the church spire in the background – but still it is well done. It gives me the impression of an artist without the slightest originality of design, but much of technique. But for some inexplicable reason the picture frets me. I find myself gazing at it when I do not wish to do so. It seems to compel my attention like some intent face in the room. I shall ask Mrs Jennings to have it removed. I will hang in its place some photographs which I have in a trunk.'

'January 26. I do not write regularly in my journal. I never did. I see no reason why I should. I see no reason why anyone should have the slightest sense of duty in such a matter. Some days I have nothing which interests me sufficiently to write out, some days I feel either too ill or too indolent. For four days I have not written, from a mixture of all three reasons. Now, to-day I both feel like it and I have something to write.

Also I am distinctly better than I have been. Perhaps the waters are benefiting me, or the change of air. Or possibly it is something else more subtle. Possibly my mind has seized upon something new, a discovery which causes it to react upon my failing body and serves as a stimulant. All I know is, I feel distinctly better, and am conscious of an acute interest in doing so, which is of late strange to me. I have been rather indifferent, and sometimes have wondered if that were not the cause rather than the result of my state of health. I have been so continually balked that I have settled into a state of inertia. I lean rather comfortably against my obstacles. After all, the worst of the pain always lies in the struggle. Give up and it is rather pleasant than otherwise. If one did not kick, the pricks would not in the least matter. However, for some reason, for the last few days, I seem to have awakened from my state of quiescence. It means future trouble for me, no doubt, but in the meantime I am not sorry. It began with the picture – the large oil painting. I went to Mrs Jennings about it yesterday, and she, to my surprise – for I thought it a matter that could be easily arranged – objected to having it removed. Her reasons were two; both simple, both sufficient, especially since I, after all, had no very strong desire either way. It seems that the picture does not belong to her. It hung here when she rented the house. She says if it is removed, a very large and unsightly discolouration of the wall-paper will be exposed, and she does not like to ask for new paper. The owner, an old man, is traveling abroad, the agent is curt, and she has only been in the house a very short time. Then it would mean a sad upheaval of my room, which would disturb me. She also says that there is no place in the house where she can store the picture, and there is not a vacant space in another room for one so large. So I let the picture remain. It really, when I came to think of it, was very immaterial after all. But I got my photographs out of my trunk, and

I hung them around the large picture. The wall is almost completely covered. I hung them yesterday afternoon, and last night I repeated a strange experience which I have had in some degree every night since I have been here, but was not sure whether it deserved the name of experience, but was not rather one of those dreams in which one dreams one is awake. But last night it came again, and now I know. There is something very singular about this room. I am very much interested. I will write down for future reference the events of last night. Concerning those of the preceding nights since I have slept in this room, I will simply say that they have been of a similar nature, but, as it were, only the preliminary stages, the prologue to what happened last night.'

'I am not depending upon the mineral waters here as the one remedy for my malady, which is sometimes of an acute nature, and indeed constantly threatens me with considerable suffering unless by medicine I can keep it in check. I will say that the medicine which I employ is not of the class commonly known as drugs. It is impossible that it can be held responsible for what I am about to transcribe. My mind last night and every night since I have slept in this room was in an absolutely normal state. I take this medicine, prescribed by the specialist in whose charge I was before coming here, regularly every four hours while awake. As I am never a good sleeper, it follows that I am enabled with no inconvenience to take any medicine during the night with the same regularity as during the day. It is my habit, therefore, to place my bottle and spoon where I can put my hand upon them easily without lighting the gas. Since I have been in this room, I have placed the bottle of medicine upon my dresser at the side of the room opposite the bed. I have done this rather than place it nearer, as once I jostled the bottle and spilled most of the contents, and it is not easy for me to replace it, as it is expensive. Therefore I placed it in security on the dresser, and, indeed, that is but three or four steps from my bed, the room being so small. Last night I wakened as usual, and I knew, since I had fallen asleep about eleven, that it must be in the neighborhood of three. I wake with almost clock-like regularity and it is never necessary for me to consult my watch.'

'I had slept unusually well and without dreams, and I awoke fully at once, with a feeling of refreshment to which I am not accustomed. I immediately got out of bed and began stepping across the room in the direction of my dresser, on which I had set my medicine-bottle and spoon.'

'To my utter amazement, the steps which had hitherto sufficed to take me across my room did not suffice to do so. I advanced several paces, and my outstretched hands touched nothing. I stopped and went on again. I was sure that I was moving in a straight direction, and even if I had not been I knew it was impossible to advance in any direction in my tiny apartment without coming into collision either with a wall or a piece of furniture. I continued to walk falteringly, as I have seen people on the stage: a step, then a long falter, then a sliding step. I kept my hands extended; they touched nothing. I stopped again. I had not the least sentiment of fear or consternation. It was rather the very stupefaction of surprise. "How is this?" seemed thundering in my ears. "What is this?"'

'The room was perfectly dark. There was nowhere any glimmer, as is usually the case, even in a so-called dark room, from the walls, picture-frames, looking-glass or white objects. It was absolute gloom. The house stood in a quiet part of the town. There were many trees about; the electric streetlights were extinguished at midnight; there was no moon and the sky was cloudy. I could not distinguish my one window, which I thought strange, even on such a dark night. Finally I changed my plan of motion and turned, as nearly as I could estimate, at right angles. Now, I thought, I must reach soon, if I kept on, my writing-table underneath the window; or, if I am going in the opposite direction, the hall door. I reached neither. I am telling the unvarnished truth when I say that I began to count my steps and carefully measure my paces after that, and I traversed a space clear of furniture at least twenty feet by thirty – a very large apartment. And as I walked I was conscious that my naked feet were pressing something which gave rise to sensations the like of which I had never experienced before. As nearly as I can express it, it was as if my feet pressed something as elastic as air or water, which was in this case unyielding to my weight. It gave me a curious sensation of buoyancy and stimulation. At the same time this surface, if surface be the right name, which I trod, felt cool to my feet with the coolness of vapor or fluidity, seeming to overlap the soles. Finally I stood still; my surprise was at last merging into a measure of consternation. "Where am I?" I thought. "What am I going to do?" Stories that I had heard of travelers being taken from their beds and conveyed into strange and dangerous places, Middle Age stories of the Inquisition flashed through my brain. I knew all the time that for a man who had gone to bed in a commonplace hall bedroom in a very commonplace little town such surmises were highly ridiculous, but it is hard for the human mind to grasp anything but a human explanation of phenomena. Almost anything seemed then, and seems now, more rational than an explanation bordering upon the supernatural, as we understand the supernatural. At last I called, though rather softly, "What does this mean?" I said quite aloud, "Where am I? Who is here? Who is doing this? I tell you I will have no such nonsense. Speak, if there is anybody here." But all was dead silence. Then suddenly a light flashed through the open transom of my door. Somebody had heard me – a man who rooms next door, a decent kind of man, also here for his health. He turned on the gas in the hall and called to me.

"What's the matter?" he asked, in an agitated, trembling voice. He is a nervous fellow.'

'Directly, when the light flashed through my transom, I saw that I was in my familiar hall bedroom. I could see everything quite distinctly – my tumbled bed, my writing-table, my dresser, my chair, my little wash-stand, my clothes hanging on a row of pegs, the old picture on the wall. The picture gleamed out with singular distinctness in the light from the transom. The river seemed actually to run and ripple, and the boat to be gliding with the current. I gazed fascinated at it, as I replied to the anxious voice:

"Nothing is the matter with me," said I. "Why?"

"I thought I heard you speak," said the man outside. "I thought maybe you were sick."

"No," I called back. "I am all right. I am trying to find my medicine in the dark, that's all. I can see now you have lighted the gas."

"Nothing is the matter?"

"No; sorry I disturbed you. Good-night."

"Good-night." Then I heard the man's door shut after a minute's pause. He was evidently not quite satisfied. I took a pull at my medicine-bottle, and got into bed. He had left the hall-gas burning. I did not go to sleep again for some time. Just before I did so, some one, probably Mrs Jennings, came out in the hall and extinguished the gas. This morning when I awoke everything was as usual in my room. I wonder if I shall have any such experience to-night.'

'January 27. I shall write in my journal every day until this draws to some definite issue. Last night my strange experience deepened, as something tells me it will continue to do. I retired quite early, at half-past ten. I took the precaution, on retiring, to place beside my bed, on a chair, a box of safety matches, that I might not be in the dilemma of the night before. I took my medicine on retiring; that made me due to wake at half-past two. I had not fallen asleep directly, but had had certainly three hours of sound, dreamless slumber when I awoke. I lay a few minutes hesitating whether or not to strike a safety match and light my way to the dresser, whereon stood my medicine-bottle. I hesitated, not because I had the least sensation of fear, but because of the same shrinking from a nerve shock that leads one at times to dread the plunge into an icy bath. It seemed much easier to me to strike that match and cross my hall bedroom to my dresser, take my dose, then return quietly to my bed, than to risk the chance of floundering about in some unknown limbo either of fancy or reality.'

'At last, however, the spirit of adventure, which has always been such a ruling one for me, conquered. I rose. I took the box of safety matches in my hand, and started on, as I conceived, the straight course for my dresser, about five feet across from my bed. As before, I traveled and traveled and did not reach it. I advanced with groping hands extended, setting one foot cautiously before the other, but I touched nothing except the indefinite, unnameable surface which my feet pressed. All of a sudden, though, I became aware of something. One of my senses was saluted, nay, more than that, hailed, with imperiousness, and that was, strangely enough, my sense of smell, but in a hitherto unknown fashion. It seemed as if the odour reached my mentality first. I reversed the usual process, which is, as I understand it, like this: the odour when encountered strikes first the olfactory nerve, which transmits the intelligence to the brain. It is as if, to put it rudely, my nose met a rose, and then the nerve belonging to the sense said to my brain, "Here is a rose." This time my brain said, "Here is a rose," and my sense then recognized it. I say rose, but it was not a rose, that is, not the fragrance of any rose which I had ever known. It was undoubtedly a flower-odour, and rose came perhaps the nearest to it. My mind realized it first with what seemed a leap of rapture. "What is this delight?" I asked myself. And then the ravishing fragrance smote my sense. I breathed it in and it seemed to feed my thoughts, satisfying some hitherto unknown hunger. Then I took a step further and another fragrance appeared, which I liken to lilies for lack of something better, and then came violets, then mignonette. I cannot describe the experience, but it was a sheer delight, a rapture of sublimated sense. I groped further and further, and always into new waves of fragrance. I seemed to be wading breast-high through flower-beds of Paradise, but all the time I touched nothing with my groping hands. At last a sudden giddiness as of surfeit overcame me. I realized that I might be in some unknown peril. I was distinctly afraid. I struck one of my safety matches, and I was in my hall bedroom, midway between my bed and my dresser. I took my dose of medicine and went to bed, and after a while fell asleep and did not wake till morning.'

'January 28. Last night I did not take my usual dose of medicine. In these days of new remedies and mysterious results upon certain organizations, it occurred to me to wonder if possibly the drug might have, after all, something to do with my strange experience.'

'I did not take my medicine. I put the bottle as usual on my dresser, since I feared if I interrupted further the customary sequence of affairs I might fail to wake. I placed my box of matches on the chair beside the bed. I fell asleep about quarter past eleven o'clock, and I waked when the clock was striking two – a little earlier than my wont. I did not hesitate this time. I rose at once, took my box of matches and proceeded as formerly. I walked what seemed a great space without coming into collision with anything. I kept sniffing for the wonderful fragrances of the night before, but they did not recur. Instead, I was suddenly aware that I was tasting something, some morsel of sweetness hitherto unknown, and, as in the case of the odour, the usual order seemed reversed, and it was as if I tasted it first in my mental consciousness. Then the sweetness rolled under my tongue. I thought involuntarily of "Sweeter than honey or the honeycomb" of the Scripture. I thought of the Old Testament manna. An ineffable content as of satisfied hunger seized me. I stepped further, and a new savour was upon my palate. And so on. It was never cloying, though of such sharp sweetness that it fairly stung. It was the merging of a material sense into a spiritual one. I said to myself, "I have lived my life and always have I gone hungry until now." I could feel my brain act swiftly under the influence of this heavenly food as under a stimulant. Then suddenly I repeated the experience of the night before. I grew dizzy, and an indefinite fear and shrinking were upon me. I struck my safety match and was back in my hall bedroom. I returned to bed, and soon fell asleep. I did not take my medicine. I am resolved not to do so longer. I am feeling much better.'

'January 29. Last night to bed as usual, matches in place; fell asleep about eleven and waked at half-past one. I heard the half-hour strike; I am waking earlier and earlier every night. I had not taken my medicine, though it was on the dresser as usual. I again took my match-box in hand and started to cross the room, and, as always, traversed strange spaces, but this night, as seems fated to be the case every night, my experience was different. Last night I neither smelled nor tasted, but I heard – my Lord, I heard! The first sound of which I was conscious was one like the constantly gathering and receding murmur of a river, and it seemed to come from the wall behind my bed where the old picture hangs. Nothing in nature except a river gives that impression of at once advance and retreat. I could not mistake it. On, ever on, came the swelling murmur of the waves, past and ever past they died in the distance. Then I heard above the murmur of the river a song in an unknown tongue which I recognized as being unknown, yet which I understood; but the understanding was in my brain, with no words of interpretation. The song had to do with me, but with me in unknown futures for which I had no images of comparison in the past; yet a sort of ecstasy as of a prophecy of bliss filled my whole consciousness. The song never ceased, but as I moved on I came into new sound-waves. There was the pealing of bells which might have been made of crystal, and might have summoned to the gates of heaven. There was music of strange instruments, great harmonies pierced now and then by small whispers as of love, and it all filled me with a certainty of a future of bliss.'

'At last I seemed the centre of a mighty orchestra which constantly deepened and increased until I seemed to feel myself being lifted gently but mightily upon the waves of sound as upon the waves of a sea. Then again the terror and the impulse to flee to my own familiar scenes was upon me. I struck my match and was back in my hall bedroom. I do not see how I sleep at all after such wonders, but sleep I do. I slept dreamlessly until daylight this morning.'

'January 30. I heard yesterday something with regard to my hall bedroom which affected me strangely. I cannot for the life of me say whether it intimidated me, filled me with the horror of the abnormal, or rather roused to a greater degree my spirit of adventure and discovery. I was down at the Cure, and was sitting on the veranda sipping idly my mineral water, when somebody spoke my name. "Mr Wheatcroft?" said the voice politely, interrogatively, somewhat apologetically, as if to provide for a possible mistake in my identity. I turned and saw a gentleman whom I recognized at once. I seldom forget names or faces. He was a Mr Addison whom I had seen considerable of three years ago at a little summer hotel in the mountains. It was one of those passing acquaintances which signify little one way or the other. If never renewed, you have no regret; if renewed, you accept the renewal with no hesitation. It is in every way negative. But just now, in my feeble, friendless state, the sight of a face which beams with pleased remembrance is rather grateful. I felt distinctly glad to see the man. He sat down beside me. He also had a glass of the water. His health, while not as bad as mine, leaves much to be desired.'

'Addison had often been in this town before. He had in fact lived here at one time. He had remained at the Cure three years, taking the waters daily. He therefore knows about all there is to be known about the town, which is not very large. He asked me where I was staying, and when I told him the street, rather excitedly inquired the number. When I told him the number, which is 240, he gave a manifest start, and after one sharp glance at me sipped his water in silence for a moment. He had so evidently betrayed some ulterior knowledge with regard to my residence that I questioned him.'

"What do you know about 240 Pleasant Street?" said I.

"Oh, nothing," he replied, evasively, sipping his water.

'After a little while, however, he inquired, in what he evidently tried to render a casual tone, what room I occupied. "I once lived a few weeks at 240 Pleasant Street myself," he said. "That house always was a boarding-house, I guess."

"It had stood vacant for a term of years before the present occupant rented it, I believe," I remarked. Then I answered his question. "I have the hall bedroom on the third floor," said I. "The quarters are pretty straitened, but comfortable enough as hall bedrooms go."

'But Mr Addison had showed such unmistakable consternation at my reply that then I persisted in my questioning as to the cause, and at last he yielded and told me what he knew. He had hesitated both because he shrank from displaying what I might consider an unmanly superstition, and because he did not wish to influence me beyond what the facts of the case warranted. "Well, I will tell you, Wheatcroft," he said. "Briefly all I know is this: When last I heard of 240 Pleasant Street it was not rented because of foul play which was supposed to have taken place there, though nothing was ever proved. There were two disappearances, and – in each case – of an occupant of the hall bedroom which you now have. The first disappearance was of a very beautiful girl who had come here for her health and was said to be the victim of a profound melancholy, induced by a love disappointment. She obtained board at 240 and occupied the hall bedroom about two weeks; then one morning she was gone, having seemingly vanished into thin air. Her relatives were communicated with; she had not many, nor friends either, poor girl, and a thorough search was made, but the last I knew she had never come to light. There were two or three arrests, but nothing ever came of them. Well, that was before my day here, but the second disappearance took place when I was in the house – a fine young fellow who had overworked in college. He had to pay his own way. He had taken cold, had the grip, and that and the overwork about finished him, and he came on here for a month's rest and recuperation. He had been in that room about two weeks, a little less, when one morning he wasn't there. Then there was a great hullabaloo. It seems that he had let fall some hints to the effect that there was something queer about the room, but, of course, the police did not think much of that. They made arrests right and left, but they never found him, and the arrested were discharged, though some of them are probably under a cloud of suspicion to this day. Then the boarding-house was shut up. Six years ago nobody would have boarded there, much less occupied that hall bedroom, but now I suppose new people have come in and the story has died out. I dare say your landlady will not thank me for reviving it."

'I assured him that it would make no possible difference to me. He looked at me sharply, and asked bluntly if I had seen anything wrong or unusual about the room. I replied, guarding

myself from falsehood with a quibble, that I had seen nothing
in the least unusual about the room, as indeed I had not, and
have not now, but that may come. I feel that that will come
in due time. Last night I neither saw, nor heard, nor smelled,
nor tasted, but I – felt. Last night, having started again on
my exploration of, God knows what, I had not advanced a
step before I touched something. My first sensation was one
of disappointment. "It is the dresser, and I am at the end of
it now," I thought. But I soon discovered that it was not the
old painted dresser which I touched, but something carved, as
nearly as I could discover with my unskilled finger-tips, with
winged things. There were certainly long keen curves of wings
which seemed to overlay an arabesque of fine leaf and flower
work. I do not know what the object was that I touched. It
may have been a chest. I may seem to be exaggerating when
I say that it somehow failed or exceeded in some mysterious
respect of being the shape of anything I had ever touched. I do
not know what the material was. It was as smooth as ivory, but
it did not feel like ivory; there was a singular warmth about
it, as if it had stood long in hot sunlight. I continued, and I
encountered other objects I am inclined to think were pieces
of furniture of fashions and possibly of uses unknown to me,
and about them all was the strange mystery as to shape. At last
I came to what was evidently an open window of large area. I
distinctly felt a soft, warm wind, yet with a crystal freshness,
blow on my face. It was not the window of my hall bedroom,
that I know. Looking out, I could see nothing. I only felt the
wind blowing on my face.'

'Then suddenly, without any warning, my groping hands to
the right and left touched living beings, beings in the likeness
of men and women, palpable creatures in palpable attire. I
could feel the soft silken texture of their garments which swept
around me, seeming to half infold me in clinging meshes like
cobwebs. I was in a crowd of these people, whatever they were,

and whoever they were, but, curiously enough, without seeing one of them I had a strong sense of recognition as I passed among them. Now and then a hand that I knew closed softly over mine; once an arm passed around me. Then I began to feel myself gently swept on and impelled by this softly moving throng; their floating garments seemed to fairly wind me about, and again a swift terror overcame me. I struck my match, and was back in my hall bedroom. I wonder if I had not better keep my gas burning to-night? I wonder if it be possible that this is going too far? I wonder what became of those other people, the man and the woman who occupied this room? I wonder if I had better not stop where I am?'

'January 31. Last night I saw – I saw more than I can describe, more than is lawful to describe. Something which nature has rightly hidden has been revealed to me, but it is not for me to disclose too much of her secret. This much I will say, that doors and windows open into an out-of-doors to which the outdoors which we know is but a vestibule. And there is a river; there is something strange with respect to that picture. There is a river upon which one could sail away. It was flowing silently, for to-night I could only see. I saw that I was right in thinking I recognized some of the people whom I encountered the night before, though some were strange to me. It is true that the girl who disappeared from the hall bedroom was very beautiful. Everything which I saw last night was very beautiful to my one sense that could grasp it. I wonder what it would all be if all my senses together were to grasp it? I wonder if I had better not keep my gas burning to-night? I wonder –'

✕

This finishes the journal which Mr Wheatcroft left in his hall bedroom. The morning after the last entry he was gone. His friend, Mr Addison, came here, and a search was made. They even tore down the wall behind the picture, and they did find something rather queer for a house that had been used for boarders, where you would think no room would have been let run to waste. They found another room, a long narrow one, the length of the hall bedroom, but narrower, hardly more than a closet. There was no window, nor door, and all there was in it was a sheet of paper covered with figures, as if somebody had been doing sums. They made a lot of talk about those figures, and they tried to make out that the fifth dimension, whatever that is, was proved, but they said afterward they didn't prove anything. They tried to make out then that somebody had murdered poor Mr Wheatcroft and hid the body, and they arrested poor Mr Addison, but they couldn't make out anything against him. They proved he was in the Cure all that night and couldn't have done it. They don't know what became of Mr Wheatcroft, and now they say two more disappeared from that same room before I rented the house.

The agent came and promised to put the new room they discovered into the hall bedroom and have everything new – papered and painted. He took away the picture; folks hinted there was something queer about that, I don't know what. It looked innocent enough, and I guess he burned it up. He said if I would stay he would arrange it with the owner, who everybody says is a very queer man, so I should not have to pay much if any rent. But I told him I couldn't stay if he was to give me the rent. That I wasn't afraid of anything myself, though I must say I wouldn't want to put anybody in that hall bedroom without telling him all about it; but my boarders would leave, and I knew I couldn't get any more. I told him I would rather have had a regular ghost than what seemed to be a way of going out of the house to nowhere and never coming back again. I moved, and, as I said before, it remains to be seen whether my ill luck follows me to this house or not. Anyway, it has no hall bedroom.

6 The House

BY KATHERINE MANSFIELD (1912)

Rain came suddenly from a swollen sky and with it a cold, whipping wind blowing in her face. She buttoned her coat collar, thrust her hands into her pockets, and head bent, battled on.

Another day ended! Darkness was pouring into the world like grey fluid into a greyer cup – no amethyst twilight this, no dropping of a chiffon scarf – no trailing of a starbroidered mantle … a sense of smudging over – that was all. Fallen leaves spattered the pavement. Still over wall and house-front the Virginia creeper draggled her tousled tresses. And the cold wind was full of the shuddering breath of winter.

Rain fell faster – a downpour now. She had no umbrella … remembered leaving it behind the office door … so stupid – careless. With a hat, too, that 'spotted'!

And then, looking up, she saw an iron gate swinging idly on its hinges leading to a stone house placarded 'To be Let or Sold', with a wide, empty porch covered in by a creeping plant and a little glass partition. She decided to wait there a moment to see if the weather showed any signs of passing over. Also she was suddenly and unaccountably tired … to sit on that top step just a moment … the wind seemed to take all your breath – and so cold, to eat into your bones.

What a piece of luck! An old basket chair in one corner of the porch! She sat down, felt the bottom of her skirt, soaked already, lifted up her foot and made a little grimace at the burst shoe, half laughing. Her veil was sticking to her face – there was no more abominable sensation – and this parcel was *pretty* – madeira cake sodging through the brown paper – oh, very pretty indeed.

She stripped off her gloves and sat, hands folded in her lap, looking up at the green blistered door, and a little octagonal lamp hanging over the doorway. Found herself staring at the lamp ... now where had she seen it before? What trick of memory ... *had* she seen it? She remembered so well hearing a girl saying 'An octagonal lamp over the doorway – that settles the question!' ...

Too tired to remember. Rain seemed to be falling now so violently that it must wear itself out in a moment, she decided, leaning her head against the wall. ...

Quick, light steps down the street, the iron gate swung open, a man strode up the gravel walk, up the steps, taking a key from his pocket. A tall thin man in a fur coat, with an immense umbrella hooked over one arm, flowers in his hand, and a long oddly shaped box.

She sat up hastily, the basket chair creaking. What could he be doing there at this hour – a House Agent – a purchaser? And at the sound of the basket chair he wheeled round.

'Good heavens, you ridiculous child,' he said, peering through the gloom. 'Marion, we're too old to play "hide and seek" – no, not too old, darling, but too cold. Or have you lost the last key and Alice has gone stone-deaf, or ...' his laughing voice ended in real laughter; he caught hold of her hand, 'Ups-a-daisy, Honey, and I want my tea.' A rose colour sweetened her tired face into bloom.

'I was just waiting,' she faltered, 'such a strange effect in the darkness – and autumn rain and falling leaves in the hollow darkness – you know?'

He put his arm round her, together they crossed the threshold.

The hall was full of firelight with a lovely scent of logs burning. The flames seemed to leap up to meet them – to show them again that fascinating hall – to light the pictures – the pottery – old oak settles – their "Bruges" brass and the standard rose-tree and its green tub.

The grandfather clock struck six.

'We're late,' said the man laconically, taking up a pile of visiting-cards, handing them to her, 'Testifying to your youth and beauty, my child. Do ask Alice to hurry tea; I've got *caverns* and wet feet and all sorts of horrors. Will you take long to change?'

She was unbuttoning her coat when she suddenly remembered with thankfulness that she had left the 'madeira' cake on the veranda.

'Five minutes,' she said, pushing a bell, then, as the maid appeared, 'tea in the library, please, and we would like some toasted buns.'

'Yes, Madam.'

The maid stepped forward, taking their wet coats. Marion sat down and the girl removed her rubbers. 'I lighted the fire in your bedroom at five o'clock, Madam.'

When she had gone Marion stood up and looked across at the man who stood before the fire kicking a piece of wood into place with his boot, sending up a little shower of sparks.

'Don't do that, darling,' she said, 'be good and go and take off your wet things' – she caught him by the arm – 'this coat's quite damp, and, my child, *look* at the mud on your trousers.'

He looked down.

'Do you mean to say I've to change before tea,' he protested.

'Right away, now,' she slipped her arm through his. Together they slowly walked up the broad stairs. How beautiful the faded tones of the Japanese prints lining the staircase wall, in this faded light! And how mysterious the great Buddha on the half-landing, set about the creeping plant they called 'orchidaceous'.

A fire, too, on the landing, showing on warm rugs, low couch and little flat Persian pillows; from their room she saw a reflected brightness.

She paused just a moment – her lip quivering – John led her in.

'What a fire,' he cried, 'if Alice wasn't such an angel you'd be bound to think she had an intimate acquaintance with the place where angels do *truly* fear to tread.'

Marion went on to the oval mirror, unpinning her hat and veil, threw them down on a chair and looked around, smiling.

'Do run away like a good boy and get ready!'

'Oh, I feel I haven't seen you for a thousand years,' he came up behind her, drawing her head on to his shoulder, putting his arms round her neck, and catching her hands.

'*Look* at yourself, you beautiful woman,' and then, suddenly whispering, 'When I look in the mirror, so, and see you – know that this is no dream, that through the years, I have but to look to find you, always there, my darling, and every time it seems to me, more beautiful – more adorable, I wonder what I can have done … why this is *my* portion – this life with you. *Baby*,' he cried, suddenly laughing, and pulling the pins from her hair, 'you don't look more than sixteen! You ought to be ashamed of yourself and you – the …'

She turned round, slipped her arms round his neck and buried her face on his shoulder.

'Oh, John, when I am away from you, my body aches for this, its resting place – for the pillow of your heart. I never feel safe further from you than this; you hold the anchor to this drifting being. In the security of your arms, dearest, I am – ' her voice suddenly broke a little, 'such a willing prisoner.'

He held her to him, trembling.

'I cannot hold you close enough,' he said, 'I shall never make you feel my love which grows in the giving – a Faery purse, the more I give – the more I *have* to give – and all that is mine so all yours – just mine that it may the more truly belong to you.'

'Oh, husband,' she suddenly laughed, releasing herself, 'and people question miracles ... fly along, dear.'

'Well,' he said, reluctantly, 'can I leave the door open?'

'Yes of course. *Do* go.'

His dressing-room led from their bedroom. When he was gone she pushed back the loosened masses of her hair, and looked round her. At the great bed, the heavy rugs, and curtains drawn across the windows and patterned with pomegranate trees. The low mantlepiece was covered in photographs – Roger, Frank, Virginia, Otto, Valerie with her new baby.

She glanced at the shelf of books just above their bed, bound in white leather, with the 'Crane' design, and everywhere flowers and a confusion of fascinating perfumes – jars and little odd-shaped cases on her dressing-table.

'Marion,' John's voice from the next room – she heard him pouring water into a basin. 'I've had such a day.'

'Have you, dear,' brushing her long hair, and gazing tremulously at the flushed girlish face that smiled back at her.

'Yes. Do you know the sort of day when everybody seems a bore, and yourself the greatest.'

'Oh, I know ... horrid.'

'And then I had no lunch ... just tore round the corner and bolted something.'

'I do wish you would not over-work like that.'

He was speaking between splashes.

'But two new people came in this evening, darling, and asked for the benefit of your humble servant's genius.'

'Goody-o – that's fine, John. Did you see anything of Roger?'

'No; he 'phoned me, though; he's coming round this evening to play with ...'

'Oh, I'm glad,' she cried, quickly interrupting; her fingers trembled with the fastenings of her grey chiffon gown.

'And, Marion – Oh, the Lord! I've lost a slipper again; the brute's hiding under the bed – darling, we must ask two more people to that dinner; we'd forgotten – *the Simpsons*!'

'My *dear* – so we had.'

Mechanically she opened a little box and took out a long silver chain set with opals.

'What a blessing you remembered; we'd have been in their black books for ever.'

'I know – how about the work today?'

'Finished, finished – I'll read you some after dinner. Don't ask my opinion; I'm still at the cackling stage, the successfully-laid-for-all-the-world-to-see stage. Are you ready?'

'Yes. May I come in?'

'Do, Boy dear.'

He had changed into a lounge coat, and on his feet he wore extraordinary Japanese stork-embroidered slippers. He sat on the edge of the bed, swinging one foot and whistling. A low clear note struck from downstairs.

Standing on the landing this time she noticed a little gate at the foot of the next flight of stairs, and the walls were covered in brilliant posters – French, Belgian, English, Italian, and, too, a little picture of a boy in blue trousers standing in a daisy field.

John paused.

'Shall we go up a minute,' he said.

'Oh, afterwards,' she answered, hurriedly.

Each time he mentioned the … each time she felt he was going to speak of their … she had a terrible, suffocating sensation of fear. If that should prove untrue, if that should prove its dream origin – and at the thought something within her cried out and trembled.

'Oh, well' he said, 'later. Perhaps it's better not to disturb …'

'Much better,' said Marion.

In the library a rose-coloured lamp lighted the round table holding the tray with its delicate china and silver. The soft sound of the kettle, the great leather chairs – yes even the smell of the toasted buns – every moment created in her a greater happiness.

'One small lump of sugar,' carefully selecting it for his cup. 'Did you remember to bring home cigarettes?'

'In the hall with my flowers for you. I brought a surprise for ...'

'Bring the flowers, dear. I'm just greedy for them this weather. Um – how good the tea is.'

They sat almost silently, one on either side of the table, drinking their tea – eating – occasionally looking up, smiling, and then looking into the fire – each occupied with thoughts, perfectly content – rested after the long day.

'Why does lamplight shed such peace?' he said, in a low tone: 'it so shuts us in together; I love a lamp.'

And again, as she leaned forward to light her cigarette at the little silver fire-breathing 'Devil's Head' – 'Marion.'

'Yes, John.'

'What makes me almost laugh, times, is that the novelty never ceases. I feel each day is our first day together.'

'Oh, it is the sense of "home" which is so precious to me – it is the wonderful sense of peace – of the rooms sanctified – of the quiet permanence – it is that which is so precious after –'

In the silence she heard the sweet sound of the rain against the window.

John put down his cup and lighted a cigarette.

'Let's go up. I'll race you to the top of the house.'

'I can't run in this long gown.'

'Well, wait a minute – my parcel.'

He brought from the hall the oddly shaped box.

'I won't undo the string – half the excitement gone –'

So again they went up the stairs, and together, and this time through the little gate.

Her heart was beating in her throat – her hands were cold – a curious sensation in her breast and arms – but the fear vanished when she saw the old nurse at the top of the stairs putting away linen into a green cupboard.

'Yes, sir, he's in the day nursery.'

John opened the door and Marion, swaying forward, saw the child banging the wooden head of a Dutch doll on the floor, and singing to himself. He wore a blue pinafore, tan socks and black patent leather slippers fastened with a strap and button.

'Darling,' she cried, swooping down upon him. 'Little son!'

The child cried 'Mummy, Mummy,' and clung to her dress. She sat in a low rocking-chair and held him on her lap. Oh, the comfortable feeling of the child in her arms, against her breast! John was explaining something marvellous about the odd-shaped box. She twined one of his curls round her finger – felt the little neck-band of his pinafore – a tiny frown between her brows – to see if it were too tight – he moved his head as though it was not quite comfortable, and then, out of the box came *another* bear, a black one with a white nose! The child slipped off her lap, and went over to the toy-cupboard to show his treasure to the rest of the 'Teddy family.'

'An' you've got to shake hands, an' you've got to give him a nice kiss, an' you've got to say "thank you, dear Daddy", I never *did* see such a nice daddy.'

The man looked over at the woman, she was rocking to and fro, a sweet brightness in her eyes.

'Sometimes,' she whispered, 'I think my heart will break for joy.'

'Oh, Daddy – *do* be a gallopin' pony.'

John went down on hands and knees – the child clambered on to his back.

'I don't know which is the younger of you,' she cried. 'John, I'll have to knit you a little pair of kneecaps ...'

Suddenly as she watched them, she heard her name being called from the lower part of the house. Whose voice was that? *What*, what was *he* doing there – yes, it was he. Something within her seemed to crash and give way – she went white to the lips. Oh, please God, they would not hear until she had silenced that voice.

'I'll be back in a minute.'

But they were almost too gay to notice.

'Marion ... Marion ... Marion!'

Please God, she could stop that voice.

Down the stairs she ran into the hall. Where was it coming from – calling and calling she wrung her hands. Once listening, she heard the high, laughing voice of the child.

'Marion ... Marion ... Marion!'

From the porch. Yes, it came from the porch. She pulled the heavy door open – wind and rain rushed in upon her – out into the porch she stepped – and the door banged to behind her. It was dark and cold ... and ... silent ... cold.

✳

'I seen 'er come up 'ere last evening – thinkin' she was a friend of your missus.'

'What she come to front door for then – with the airy steps. Look out, wot's in that bag, Take care, you leave that bag alone ... there'll be a clue there ... Bags and things, they always let the cat out.'

'Go on; it's a madeiry cake and all sodgin' through the paper ... Why don't they 'urry-up?'

'They'll be here soon ... ain't she young, too ... Look 'ere, 'er veil's slipping off.'

'You leave 'er alone – you'll ketch it when they know.'

'Oh, Lord, it's fallen off ... Oh, Lord, I seen 'er before. I remember 'er face as pline as yestiday. She come with a young feller to look over this 'ouse. I'll bet you anythink yer like it's 'er. It's 'er alright – Thet's 'er face; she gave me 'arf a crown and they stayed foolin' round and me 'anging on their 'eels and listening to them fixin' up nurseries and rose-trees and turkeys carpets, 'er 'anging on 'is arm.'

'You'd better look out what yer say. It'll go *down*.'

'I can't 'elp it; people ain't got no right to go round dyin' as if they owned the 'ole plice. It'll be called 'aunted now. Oh, Lord, it's 'er, straight, the names they called me too. St Peter and H'Eros and 'Yman – it's like yestiday. And when 'e'd gone, she comes back, laughin', and says – "We ain't got enough money to furnish a cottage," she says, "we're just dreamin' true," she says, "and 'eres half a crown, Peter dear." I never 'eard people laugh the way they did – and she, so set on this 'ere lamp ...'

'It'll always be empty now.'

'Yes, always empty now ... 'ere They come!'

7 The Red Bungalow

BY BITHIA MARY CROKER (1919)

It is a considerable time since my husband's regiment ('The Snapshots') was stationed in Kulu, yet it seems as if it were but yesterday, when I look back on the days we spent in India. As I sit by the fire, or in the sunny corner of the garden, sometimes when my eyes are dim with reading I close them upon the outer world, and see, with vivid distinctness, events which happened years ago. Among various mental pictures, there is not one which stands forth with the same weird and lurid effect as the episode of 'The Red Bungalow.'

Robert was commanding his regiment, and we were established in a pretty spacious house at Kulu, and liked the station. It was a little off the beaten track, healthy and sociable. Memories of John Company and traces of ancient Empires still clung to the neighbourhood. Pig-sticking and rose-growing, Badminton and polo, helped the residents of the place to dispose of the long, long Indian day – never too long for me!

One morning I experienced an agreeable surprise, when, in reading the Gazette, I saw that my cousin, Tom Fellowes, had been appointed Quartermaster-General of the district, and was to take up the billet at once.

Tom had a wife and two dear little children (our nursery was empty), and as soon as I had put down the paper I wired to Netta to congratulate and beg them to come to us immediately. Indian moves are rapid. Within a week our small party had increased to six, Tom, Netta, little Guy, aged four, and Baba, a dark-eyed coquette of nearly two. They also brought with them an invaluable ayah – a Madrassi. She spoke English with a pretty foreign accent, and was entirely devoted to the children.

Netta was a slight young woman with brilliant eyes, jet black hair, and a firm mouth. She was lively, clever, and a capital helpmate for an army man, with marvellous energy, and enviable taste.

Tom, an easy-going individual in private life, was a red-hot soldier. All financial and domestic affairs were left in the hands of his wife, and she managed him and them with conspicuous success.

Before Netta had been with us three days she began, in spite of my protestations, to clamour about 'getting a house'.

'Why, you have only just arrived,' I remonstrated. 'You are not even half unpacked. Wait here a few weeks, and make acquaintance with the place and people. It is such a pleasure to me to have you and the children.'

'You spoil them – especially Guy!' she answered with a laugh. 'The sooner they are removed the better, and, seriously, I want to settle in. I am longing to do up my new house, and make it pretty, and have a garden – a humble imitation of yours – a Badminton court, and a couple of ponies. I'm like a child looking forward to a new toy, for, cooped up in Fort William in Calcutta, I never felt that I had a real home.'

'Even so,' I answered, 'there is plenty of time, and I think you might remain here till after Christmas.'

'Christmas!' she screamed. 'I shall be having Christmas parties myself, and a tree for the kids; and you, dear Liz, shall come and help me. I want to get into a house next week.'

'Then pray don't look to me for any assistance. If you make such a hasty exit the station will think we have quarrelled.'

'The station could not be so detestable, and no one could quarrel with *you*, you dear old thing,' and as she stooped down and patted my cheek, I realised that she was fully resolved to have her own way.

'I have yards and yards of the most lovely cretonne for cushions, and chairs, and curtains,' she continued, 'brought out from home, and never yet made up. Your Dirzee is bringing me two men tomorrow. When I was out riding this morning, I went to an auction-room – John Mahomed, they call the man – and inspected some sofas and chairs. Do let us drive there this afternoon on our way to the club, and I also wish to have a look round. I hear that nearly all the good bungalows are occupied.'

'Yes, they are,' I answered triumphantly. 'At present there is not *one* in the place to suit you! I have been running over them with my mind's eye, and either they are near the river, or too small, or – not healthy. After Christmas the Watsons are going home; there will be their bungalow – it is nice and large, and has a capital office, which would suit Tom.'

We drove down to John Mahomed's that afternoon, and selected some furniture – Netta exhibiting her usual taste and business capacity. On our way to the club I pointed out several vacant houses, and, among them, the Watsons' charming abode – with its celebrated gardens, beds of brilliant green lucerne, and verandah curtained in yellow roses.

'Oh yes,' she admitted, 'it is a fine, roomy sort of abode, but I hate a thatched roof – I want one with tiles – red tiles. They make such a nice bit of colour among trees.'

'I'm afraid you won't find many tiled roofs in Kulu,' I answered; 'this will limit you a good deal.'

For several mornings, together, we explored bungalows – and I was by no means sorry to find that, in the eyes of Netta, they were all more or less found wanting – too small, too damp, too near the river, too stuffy – and I had made up my mind that the Watsons' residence (despite its thatch) was to be Netta's fate, when one afternoon she hurried in, a little breathless and dusty, and announced, with a wild wave of her sunshade, 'I've found it!'

'Where? Do you mean a house?' I exclaimed.

'Yes. What moles we've been! At the back of this, down the

next turn, at the cross roads! Most central and suitable. They call it the Red Bungalow.'

'The Red Bungalow,' I repeated reflectively. I had never cast a thought to it – what is always before one is frequently unnoticed. Also it had been unoccupied ever since we had come to the station, and as entirely overlooked as if it had no existence! I had a sort of recollection that there was some drawback – it was either too large, or too expensive, or too out of repair.

'It is strange that I never mentioned it,' I said. 'But it has had no tenant for years.'

'Unless I am greatly mistaken, it will have one before long,' rejoined Netta, with her most definite air. 'It looks as if it were just waiting for us – and had been marked "reserved".'

'Then you have been over it?'

'No, I could not get in, the doors are all bolted, and there seems to be no chokedar. I wandered round the verandahs, and took stock of the size and proportions – it stands in an imposing compound. There are the ruins at the back, mixed up with the remains of a garden – old guava trees, lemon trees, a vine, and a well. There is a capital place at one side for two Badminton courts, and I have mentally laid out a rose-garden in front of the portico.'

'How quickly your mind travels!'

'Everything *must* travel quickly in these days,' she retorted. 'We all have to put on the pace. Just as I was leaving, I met a venerable coolie person, who informed me that John Mahomed had the keys, so I despatched him to bring them at once, and promised a rupee for his trouble. Now do, like a good soul, let us have tea, and start off immediately after to inspect my treasure-trove!'

'I can promise you a cup of tea in five minutes,' I replied, 'but I am not so certain of your treasure-trove.'

'I am. I generally can tell what suits me at first sight. The only thing I am afraid of is the rent. Still, in Tommy's position one must not consider that. He is obliged to live in a suitable style.'

'The Watsons' house has often had a staff-tenant. I believe it would answer all your requirements.'

'Too near the road, and too near the *General*,' she objected, with a gesture of impatience. 'Ah, here comes tea at last!'

It came, but before I had time to swallow my second cup, I found myself hustled out of the house by my energetic cousin and *en route* to her wonderful discovery – the Red Bungalow.

We had but a short distance to walk, and, often as I had passed the house, I now gazed at it for the first time with an air of critical interest. In Kulu, for some unexplained reason, this particular bungalow had never counted; it was boycotted – no, that is not the word – *ignored*, as if, like some undesirable character, it had no place in the station's thoughts. Nevertheless, its position was sufficiently prominent – it stood at a point where four ways met. Two gateless entrances opened into different roads, as if determined to obtrude upon public attention. Standing aloof between the approaches was the house – large, red-tiled, and built back in the shape of the letter 'T' from an enormous pillared porch, which, with some tall adjacent trees, gave it an air of reserve and dignity.

'The coolie with the keys has not arrived,' said Netta, 'so I will just take you round and show you its capabilities myself. Here' – as we stumbled over some rough grass – 'is where I should make a couple of Badminton courts, and this' – as we came to the back of the bungalow – 'is the garden.'

Yes, here were old choked-up stone water-channels, the traces of walks, hoary guava and apricot trees, a stone pergola and a dead vine, also a well, with elaborate tracery, and odd, shapeless mounds of ancient masonry. As we stood we faced the back verandah of the house. To our right hand lay tall cork trees, a wide expanse of compound, and the road; to our left, at a distance, more trees, a high wall, and clustered beneath it the servants' quarters, the cookhouse, and a long range of stables.

It was a fine, important-looking residence, although the stables where almost roofless and the garden and compound a wilderness, given over to stray goats and tame lizards.

'Yes, there is only one thing I am afraid of,' exclaimed Netta.

'Snakes?' I suggested. 'It looks rather snaky.'

'No, the rent; and here comes the key at last,' and as she spoke a fat young clerk, on a small yellow pony, trotted quickly under the porch – a voluble person, who wore spotless white garments, and spoke English with much fluency.

'I am abject. Please excuse being so tardy. I could not excavate the key; but at last I got it, and now I will hasten to exhibit premises. First of all, I go and open doors and windows, and call in the atmosphere – ladies kindly excuse.' Leaving his tame steed on its honour, the baboo hurried to the back, and presently we heard the grinding of locks, banging of shutters, and grating of bolts. Then the door was flung open and we entered, walked (as is usual) straight into the drawing-room, a fine, lofty, half-circular room, twice as large and well-proportioned as mine. The drawing-room led into an equally excellent dining-room. I saw Netta measuring it with her eye, and she said, 'One could easily seat thirty people here, and what a place for a Christmas-tree!'

The dining-room opened into an immense bedroom which gave directly on the back verandah, with a flight of shallow steps leading into the garden.

'The nursery,' she whispered; 'capital!'

At either side were two other rooms, with bath and dressing-rooms complete. Undoubtedly it was an exceedingly commodious and well-planned house.

As we stood once more in the nursery – all the wide doors being open – we could see directly through the bungalow out into the porch, as the three large apartments were *en suite*.

'A draught right through, you see!' she said. 'So cool in the hot weather.'

Then we returned to the drawing-room, where I noticed that Netta was already arranging the furniture with her mental eye. At last she turned to the baboo and said, 'And what is the rent?'

After a moment's palpable hesitation he replied, 'Ninety rupees a month. If you take it for some time it will be all put in repair and done up.'

'Ninety!' I mentally echoed – and we paid one hundred and forty!

'Does it belong to John Mahomed?' I asked.

'No – to a client.'

'Does he live here?'

'No – he lives far away, in another region; we have never seen him.'

'How long is it since this was occupied?'

'Oh, a good while –'

'Some years?'

'Perhaps,' with a wag of his head.

'Why has it stood empty? Is it unhealthy?' asked Netta.

'Oh no, no. I think it is too majestic, too gigantic for insignificant people. They like something more altogether and *cosy*; it is not cosy – it is suitable to persons like a lady on the General's staff,' and he bowed himself to Netta.

I believe she was secretly of his opinion, for already she had assumed the air of the mistress of the house, and said briskly, 'Now I wish to see the kitchen, and servants' quarters,' and, picking up her dainty skirts, she led the way thither through loose stones and hard yellow grass. As I have a rooted antipathy to dark and uninhabited places, possibly the haunt of snakes and scorpions, I failed to attend her, but, leaving the baboo to continue his duty, turned back into the house alone.

I paced the drawing-room, dining-room, the nursery, and as I stood surveying the long vista of apartments, with the sun pouring into the porch on one hand, and on the green foliage and baked yellow earth of the garden on the other, I confessed to myself that Netta was a miracle!

She, a new arrival, had hit upon this excellent and suitable residence; and a bargain. But, then, she always found bargains; their discovery was her *métier*!

As I stood reflecting thus, gazing absently into the outer glare, a dark and mysterious cloud seemed to fall upon the place, the sun was suddenly obscured, and from the portico came a sharp little gust of wind that gradually increased into a long-drawn wailing cry – surely the cry of some lost soul! What could have put such a hideous idea in my head? But the cry rang in my ears with such piercing distinctness that I felt myself trembling from head to foot; in a second the voice had, as it were, passed forth into the garden and was stifled among the tamarind trees in an agonised wail. I roused myself from a condition of frightful obsession, and endeavoured to summon my common sense and self-command. Here was I, a middle-aged Scotchwoman, standing in this empty bungalow, clutching my garden umbrella, and imagining horrors!

Such thoughts I must keep exclusively to myself, lest I become the laughing-stock of a station with a keen sense of the ridiculous.

Yes, I was an imaginative old goose, but I walked rather quickly back into the porch, and stepped into the open air, with a secret but invincible prejudice against the Red Bungalow. This antipathy was not shared by Netta, who had returned from her quest all animation and satisfaction.

'The stables require repair, and some of the go-downs,' she

said, 'and the whole house must be recoloured inside, and matted. I will bring my husband round tomorrow morning,' she announced, dismissing the baboo. 'We will be here at eight o'clock sharp.'

By this I knew – and so did the baboo – that the Red Bungalow was let at last!

'Well, what do you think of it?' asked Netta triumphantly, as we were walking home together.

'It is a roomy house,' I admitted, 'but there is no office for Tom.'

'Oh, he has the Brigade Office. Any more objections?'

'A bungalow so long vacant, so entirely overlooked, must have *something* against it – and it is not the rent –'

'Nor is it unhealthy,' she argued. 'It is quite high, higher than your bungalow – no water near it, and the trees not too close. I can see that you don't like it. Can you give me a good reason?'

'I really wish I could. No, I do not like it – there is something about it that repels me. You know I'm a Highlander, and am sensitive to impressions.'

'My dear Liz,' and here she came to a dead halt, 'you don't mean me to suppose that you think it is haunted? Why, this is the twentieth century!'

'I did not say it was haunted' – (I dared not voice my fears) – 'but I declare that I do not like it, and I wish you'd wait; wait only a couple of days, and I'll take you to see the Watsons' bungalow – so sunny, so lived in – always so cheerful, with a lovely garden, and an office for Tom.'

'I'm not sure that *that* is an advantage!' she exclaimed with a smile. 'It is not always agreeable to have a man on the premises for twenty-four hours out of the twenty-four hours!'

'But the Watsons –'

'My dear Liz, if you say another word about the Watsons' bungalow I shall have a bad attack of the sulks, and go straight to bed!'

It is needless to mention that Tom was delighted with the bungalow selected by his ever-clever little wife, and for the next week our own abode was the resort of tailors, hawkers, butchers, milkmen, furniture-makers, ponies and cows on sale, and troops of servants in quest of places.

Every day Netta went over to the house to inspect, and to give directions, to see how the mallees were laying out the garden and Badminton courts, and the matting people and whitewashers were progressing indoors.

Many hands make light work, and within a week the transformation of the Red Bungalow was astonishing. Within a fortnight it was complete; the stables were again occupied – also the new spick-and-span servants' quarters; Badminton courts were ready to be played upon; the verandah and porch were gay with palms and plants and parrots, and the drawing-room was the admiration of all Kulu. Netta introduced plants in pots – pots actually dressed up in pongee silk! – to the station ladies; her sofa cushions were frilled, she had quantities of pretty pictures and photos, silver knick-knacks, and gay rugs.

But before Netta had had the usual name-board – 'Major Fellowes, AQMG' – attached to the gate piers of the Red Bungalow, there had been some demur and remonstrance. My ayah, an old Madrassi, long in my service, had ventured one day, as she held my hair in her hand, 'That new missus never taking the old Red Bungalow?'

'Yes.'

'My missus then telling her, *please*, that plenty bad place – oh, so bad! No one living there this many years.'

'Why – what is it?'

'I not never knowing, only the one word – *bad*. Oh, my missus! you speak, never letting these pretty little children go there –'

'But other people have lived there, Mary –'

'Never long – so people telling – the house man paint bungalow all so nice – same like now – they make great bargain – so pleased. One day they go away, away, away, never coming back. Please, please,' and she stooped and kissed my hand, 'speak that master, tell him – *bad* bungalow.'

Of course I pooh-poohed the subject to Mary, who actually wept, good kind creature, and as she did my hair had constantly to dry her eyes on her saree.

And, knowing how futile a word to Tom would prove, I once more attacked Netta. I said, 'Netta, I'm sure you think I'm an ignorant, superstitious imbecile, but I believe in presentiments. I have a presentiment, dear, about that Bungalow – *do* give it up to please and, yes, comfort me –'

'What! my beautiful find – the best house in Kulu – my *bargain?*'

'You may find it a dear bargain!'

'Not even to oblige you, dear Liz, can I break off my agreement, and I have really set my heart on your *bête noire*. I am so, so sorry,' and she came over and caressed me.

I wonder if Netta in her secret heart suspected that I, the Colonel's wife, might be a little jealous that the new arrival had secured a far more impressive looking abode than her own, and for this mean reason I endeavoured to persuade her to 'move on'.

However, her mind must have been entirely disabused of this by a lady on whom we were calling, who said:

'Oh, Mrs Fellowes, have you got a house yet, or will you wait for the Watsons'? Such a –'

'I am already suited,' interrupted Netta. 'We have found just the thing – not far from my cousin's, too – a fine, roomy, cheerful place, with a huge compound; we are already making the garden.'

'Roomy – large compound; near Mrs Drummond,' she

repeated with knitted brow. 'No – oh, surely you do not mean the Red Bungalow?'

'Yes, that is its name; I am charmed with it, and so lucky to find it.'

'No difficulty in finding it, dear Mrs Fellowes, but I believe the difficulty is in remaining there.'

'Do you mean that it's haunted?' enquired Netta with a rather superior air.

'Something of that sort – the natives call it "the devil's house". A terrible tragedy happened there long ago – so long ago that it is forgotten; but you will find it almost impossible to keep servants!'

'You are certainly most discouraging, but I hope some day you will come and dine with us, and see how comfortable we are!'

There was a note of challenge in this invitation, and I could see with the traditional 'half-eye' that Mrs Dodd and Mrs Fellowes would scarcely be bosom friends.

Nor was this the sole warning.

At the club a very old resident, wife of a Government employé, who had spent twenty years in Kulu, came and seated herself by me one morning with the air of a person who desired to fulfil a disagreeable duty.

'I am afraid you will think me presuming, Mrs Drummond, but I feel that I *ought* to speak. Do you know that the house your cousin has taken is said to be unlucky? The last people only remained a month, though they got it for next to nothing – a mere song.'

'Yes, I've heard of these places, and read of them, too,' I replied, 'but it generally turns out that someone has an interest in keeping it empty; possibly natives live there.'

'*Any*where but there!' she exclaimed. 'Not a soul will go near it after night-fall – there is not even the usual chokedar – '

'What is it? What is the tale?'

'Something connected with those old mounds of brickwork, and the well. I think a palace or a temple stood on the spot thousands of years ago, when Kulu was a great native city.

Do try and dissuade your cousin from going there; she will find her mistake sooner or later. I hope you won't think me very officious, but she is young and happy, and has two such dear children, especially the little boy.'

Yes, especially the little boy! I was devoted to Guy – my husband, too. We had bought him a pony and a tiny monkey, and were only too glad to keep him and Baba for a few days when their parents took the great step and moved into the Red Bungalow.

In a short time all was in readiness; the big end room made a delightful nursery; the children had also the run of the back verandah and the garden, and were soon completely and happily at home.

An inhabited house seems so different to the same when it stands silent, with closed doors – afar from the sound of voices and footsteps. I could scarcely recognise Netta's new home. It was the centre of half the station gaieties – Badminton parties twice a week, dinners, 'Chotah Hazra' gatherings on the great verandah, and rehearsals for a forthcoming play; the pattering of little feet, servants, horses, cows, goats, dogs, parrots, all contributed their share to the general life and stir. I went over to the Bungalow almost daily: I dined, I breakfasted, I had tea, and I never saw anything but the expected and the common-place, yet I failed to eradicate my first instinct, my secret apprehension and aversion. Christmas was over, the parties, dinners and teas were among memories of the past; we were well advanced in the month of February, when Netta, the triumphant, breathed her first complaint. The servants – excellent servants, with long and *bonâ fide* characters – arrived, stayed one week, or perhaps two, and then came and said, 'Please I go!'

None of them remained in the compound at night, except the horsekeepers and an orderly; they retired to more congenial quarters in an adjoining bazaar, and the maddening part was that they would give no definite name or shape to their fears – they spoke of 'It' and a 'Thing' – a fearsome object, that dwelt within and around the Bungalow.

The children's ayah, a Madras woman, remained loyal and staunch; she laughed at the Bazaar tales and their reciters; and, as her husband was the cook, Netta was fairly independent of the cowardly crew who nightly fled to the Bazaar.

Suddenly the ayah, the treasure, fell ill of fever – the really virulent fever that occasionally seizes on natives of the country, and seems to lick up their very life. As my servants' quarters were more comfortable – and I am something of a nurse – I took the invalid home, and Netta promoted her understudy (a local woman) temporarily into her place. She was a chattering, gay, gaudy creature, that I had never approved, but Netta would not listen to any advice, whether with respect to medicines, servants, or bungalows. Her choice in the latter had undoubtedly turned out well, and she was not a little exultant, and bragged to me that *she* never left it in anyone's power to say, 'There – I told you so!'

It was Baba's birthday – she was two – a pretty, healthy child, but for her age backward: beyond 'Dadda', 'Mamma', and 'Ayah', she could not say one word. However, as Tom cynically remarked, 'she was bound to make up for it by and by!'

It was twelve o'clock on this very warm morning when I took my umbrella and topee and started off to help Netta with her preparations for the afternoon. The chief feature of the entertainment was to be a bran pie.

I found my cousin hard at work when I arrived. In the verandah a great bath-tub full of bran had been placed on a table, and she was draping the said tub with elegant festoons of pink glazed calico – her implement a hammer and tacks – while I burrowed into the bran, and there interred the bodies of dolls and cats and horses, and all manner of pleasant surprises. We were making a dreadful litter, and a considerable noise, when suddenly above the hammering I heard a single sharp cry.

'Listen!' I said.

'Oh, Baba is awake – naughty child – and she will disturb her brother,' replied the mother, selecting a fresh tack. 'The ayah is there. Don't go.'

'But it had such an odd, uncanny sound,' I protested.

'Dear old Liz! how nervous you are! Baba's scream is something between a whistle of an express and a fog-horn. She has abnormal lung power – and to-day she is restless and upset by her birthday – and her teeth. Your fears –'

Then she stopped abruptly, for a loud, frantic shriek, the shriek of extreme mortal terror, now rose high above her voice, and, throwing the hammer from her, Netta fled into the drawing-room, overturning chairs in her route, dashed across the drawing-room, and burst into the nursery, from whence came these most appalling cries. There, huddled together, we discovered the two children on the table which stood in the middle of the apartment. Guy had evidently climbed up by a chair, and dragged his sister along with him. It was a beautiful afternoon, the sun streamed in upon them, and the room, as far as we could see, was empty. Yes, but not empty to the trembling little creatures on the table, for with wide, mad eyes they seemed to follow the motion of a something that was creeping round the room close to the wall, and I noticed that their gaze went up and down, as they accompanied its progress with starting pupils and gasping breaths.

'Oh! *what* is it, my darling?' cried Netta, seizing Guy, whilst I snatched at Baba.

He stretched himself stiffly in her arms, and, pointing with a trembling finger to a certain spot, gasped, 'Oh, Mummy! look, look, *look!*' and with the last word, which was a shriek of horror, he fell into violent convulsions.

But look as we might, we could see nothing, save the bare matting and the bare wall. What frightful object had made itself visible to these innocent children has never been discovered to the present day.

Little Guy, in spite of superhuman efforts to save him, died of brain fever, unintelligible to the last; the only words we could distinguish among his ravings were, 'Look, look, look! Oh, Mummy! look, look, look!' and as for Baba, whatever was seen by her is locked within her lips, for she remains dumb to the present day.

The ayah had nothing to disclose; she could only beat her head upon the ground and scream, and declare that she had just left the children for a moment to speak to the milkman.

But other servants confessed that the ayah had been gossiping in the cook-house for more than half an hour. The sole living creature that had been with the children when 'It' had appeared to them, was Guy's little pet monkey, which was subsequently found under the table quite dead.

At first I was afraid that after the shock of Guy's death poor Netta would lose her reason. Of course they all came to us, that same dreadful afternoon, leaving the birthday feast already spread, the bran pie in the verandah, the music on the piano; never had there been such a hasty flight, such a domestic earthquake. We endeavoured to keep the mysterious tragedy to ourselves. Little Guy had brain fever; surely it was natural that relations should be together in their trouble, and I declared that I, being a noted nurse, had bodily carried off the child, who was followed by the whole family.

People talked of 'a stroke of the sun', but I believe something of the truth filtered into the Bazaar – where all things are known. Shortly after little Guy's death Netta took Baba home, declaring she would never, never return to India, and Tom applied for and obtained a transfer to another station. He sold off the household furniture, the pretty knick-knacks, the pictures, all that had gone to make Netta's house so attractive, for she could not endure to look on them again. They had been in *that* house. As for the Red Bungalow, it is once more closed, and silent. The squirrels and hoo-poos share the garden, the stables are given over to scorpions, the house to white ants. On application to John Mahomed, anyone desirous of becoming a tenant will certainly find that it is still to be had for a mere song!

8 Outside the House

BY BESSIE KYFFIN-TAYLOR (1920)

If I say I was just engaged to be married, you will forgive my thus intruding my own affairs for a moment, because, through being engaged, I was landed into the most curious happening of my life.

I had been in France some two and a half years before the bit of shell met me, which landed me back in Blighty, with a leg that was not going to be of much more service to me. I had had many and varied experiences in France – horrors, of course – but of these we do not often speak, much of deep interest, and much which goes to the furthering of knowledge of many kinds – knowledge which has led thousands of men to get down to realities – and to shun for evermore the superficial shams which made up their existences before 1914 – but this is not a war story, except in so far that it transformed me, an officer in a well-known regiment, into a very ordinary civilian, with a game leg, and fathoms deep in love with the sweet child who nursed me – Elsie Falconer was my nurse – in the stately Home of England in which I and my mangled leg found ourselves after a long, troublesome journey. It was a home – there are many such, especially in the south of England – given up by their owners to needs of 'woundeds'. Homes, where, in many cases gallant young heirs have laid down their lives for King and Country, leaving none to inherit the stately bourne which for so many generations had belonged to their honoured name – so it comes to pass, that the old house is metamorphosed into a well-equipped hospital, strict routine taking the place of former gay hunting, shooting, and careless living.

It was a wonderfully beautiful old grey stone house, with an old-world garden; no money was spared, no labour was withheld to make it what it was now, a well-worked comfortable happy hospital.

I had been there some six weeks in the hands of an austere but clever elderly nurse, before Elsie was given charge of me. She was a joy to look at, to talk to, to joke with – but, she was *not* a nurse – Some women are born nurses – some have nursing thrust upon them – and some achieve nursing – Elsie was none of these, but she was very sweet, very sympathetic, and it was a delight to watch her little fingers bandage my poor leg, though I would not for worlds have let her guess the agonies I endured until, in her time off, I could capture the Sister, and beg a little relief, saying my bandages were not quite tight enough. Sister would smile, and being a sport, keep her own counsel.

It was an easy matter to step from sympathetic companionship into love-making – lots of us men have done it – perhaps some will find, to their sorrow, though each man says: 'That will not be me.' Not the least pleasurable part of it was a friendship I formed in hospital with a man whom chance placed in the bed next to mine.

It was one of those friendships which come into some lives at the first meeting of the eyes, without a word spoken – something that makes one's innermost mind think the words, 'At last!' – as if one knew that into one's life had come something hitherto wholly lacking. In this way came my friendship with Percy Hesketh, and as the weeks of our hospital life passed on, we drew even closer, making a compact that, if either should fall on the battlefield, he would endeavour to communicate with the other. The end of my third month in that stately home found me, with my discharge papers, a stiff leg, and a dear little girl, my promised wife.

Elsie did not wish to give up her nursing, so I agreed to wait patiently a while, and when she met me one morning armed with an invitation from her people to spend a month with them to convalesce – adding that she would take her holidays at home during the month – I felt that my lines had fallen in pleasant places.

It was the morning of my departure from the hospital that I noticed the first shadow I had ever seen on my little girl's face. I asked her what was the trouble, and her reply was somewhat vague. 'I was wondering,' she said, 'how you will feel at my home.'

'How I will feel?' I queried. 'Why, how should I feel, except happy to be there.'

'I hope so,' was her somewhat vague response, as she walked away almost as if she didn't wish to say any more.

Later in the day, just before I started, she came to me, saying:

'John, you will try and like it all, won't you, for my sake, don't let anything worry you, will you. Nothing can really do you any harm.'

In the rush of getting away, her few words had not much effect – indeed it was not until some hours later, when my train slowed down at a little wayside station, and an elderly man in livery met me, that I remembered them, and driving along between high hedges of wild roses, honeysuckle and sweetness of many kinds, I failed to attach the least importance to those little words 'nothing can *really* do you any harm'. Did the little girl mean the jolting of rough roads for my poor leg, or what, I wondered. Then a sudden thought struck me. Perhaps her people were not well off and she feared a little roughing it for my shattered health, but this thought was speedily banished, as we pulled up at a charming little black and white lodge, where a smiling woman opened a massive iron gate bearing a coat of arms in blue and gold. Elsie had not told me much of her home, or people, beyond that they were an old family and owned all the coalfields round about them. I had paid little or no attention at the time, for the girl – and not her people or position – was before all in my mind.

A long sheltered drive, between giant trees, presently brought us to a broad gravel sweep in front of a beautiful half-timbered house. I had scarcely time to see it, however, before I was hailed by a regular chorus of voices from a deep sunk lawn on the right of the house – it was curiously deep sunken. One is accustomed, I suppose, to see a lawn stretching away level with the house or almost, but this one, which I later learnt was always spoken of as the low lawn, was at least five or six feet below the drive; it almost gave one a feeling that if it had been a lake – it would have looked prettier that way – one seemed to have to look too far below for it – the walks and flower-beds surrounding it were so high above it.

At one end of the lawn was a glorious copper beech, beneath which were grouped some seven or eight people near a tea-table, lavishly spread – for war days.

Two people detached themselves from the group and came to meet me – an elderly man with iron grey hair and slightly bent back, and a slim dark-haired girl, perhaps three or four years older than my Elsie. My welcome was warm, as warm as man could desire from the father of the girl he loved, though, man-like, few words were spoken, a firm hand-grip, a keen look, and then –

'I am very glad John to welcome the man our little girl has given her heart to. This is Maude, Elsie's sister.'

Maude favoured me with a quick scrutinising glance, shook hands and turned away to a school-boy brother, who had followed close on her heels.

My ears, keenly sensitive through long nights on O P duties, caught the few words she murmured to him, as she met him.

'*He'll* never stand it, Bob, he isn't the sort, but mum's the word.'

Bob glanced back at me, and then shook off the sisterly hand on his shoulder, and came up to me with a boyish grin.

'Game leg, sir? Sorry, lean on me, and come down the steps to Mater and some tea.'

'Right! many thanks,' was my reply in the same spirit. 'I'll be glad of some tea; it's been my first journey since the horrible one back to Blighty.'

'Rotten luck, sir,' went on the young voice, 'you'll tell me about it sometime, won't you?'

'Not much honour and glory about it, Bob,' I replied.

'But you've got a ribbon, sir, a purple and white ribbon; I know that wasn't got with sitting still in a funk-hole!'

'No, not exactly,' I replied laughing, 'but lots of chaps who will never get it, have earned that bit of ribbon better than I did. I'll tell you some other time, if you like.'

He nodded his head and said –

'Mater, this is Elsie's John, dying for some tea.'

'Mater' made the usual little fuss mothers do make, when something in khaki steals into her flock, and wants one of her lambs, and I was soon in a comfortable chair, my game leg on another, while I was refreshed with tea, war scones, honey, and strawberries as I surveyed the rest of the group – Mr and Mrs Falconer, Maude, Bob, a Captain McKlean and his sister Nora, staying in the house, a fair-haired girl in a dark severe-looking frock, whom I subsequently learned had charge of the three boisterous younger members of the family; the Rev L Roberts, a middle-aged man, who had evidently dropped in for a cup of tea, and the three young members, who lay sprawled on the grass beside their mother – Lottie, a cherub, aged six, with red-gold hair and impish blue eyes, Alec and Ken, twins, just at the knickerbocker stage and brimming over with every conceivable mischief – composed the group, of which, for the moment, I found myself the centre.

Talk drifted along from War to Rations, and back again;

from battles to the keeping of pigs, and the price of eggs; from the scarcity of jam; to my purple and white ribbon; and so on, from grave to gay, until the sun, hitherto blazing in glory on lawn and flower beds, gradually began to sink behind the trees, in a pink glow, that lit up the house as if a pink limelight were thrown upon it. I was intently watching it, enjoying the beauty of it, when my attention was arrested by a sudden move among the group of people, as if with one accord they were seized with the same idea at the same moment.

Mrs Falconer got up, and trailed away with her knitting in her hand, her ball of wool dragging behind her, I made a move to retrieve it, but was stopped by Bob saying –

'Don't worry, sir, if you begin, you'll never stop. Mother's things always trail after her, they arrive at the house in time; we never bother.' He softly kicked the ball of wool on its way, with a sly wink at me, adding –

'That's how they get there, unless the Twins walk off with them in another direction, among the trees; it's a wonder they didn't spot it; oh! they've cleared, I might have known; it's getting late.'

'Late!' I said. 'Why it's only just after five!'

'I mean late for the garden,' he said.

'Late for the garden?' I asked. 'Why, it's the loveliest time in a garden now, when the heat dies down, and the air is all perfume.'

'Maybe in most gardens,' he replied, 'but this isn't one of them.'

'Why it's perfect,' I said.

'That's all right, sir, but I wouldn't stay too long, it gets – er – damp and – er – well damp,' he said, stuffing his hands in his pockets, as he strolled away whistling.

'It seems an interesting place, Mr Roberts,' I said, turning to face the parson. 'I do not know this part of the country at all, perhaps you'll light a pipe, and tell me about my surroundings.'

The parson got to his feet – hurriedly, awkwardly – blew his nose violently, and said – 'Yes, yes, my dear Major, I shall be most delighted, any time – er – that is, any *other* time, but now I must hurry away, my parish, you see, my work, er – my duties – you'll come and see my library, yes, yes, a fine collection. Good-bye, come very soon, – er – good-bye.' And his long lean figure was scuttling over the lawn ere I had managed to gasp a reply.

A circle of empty chairs, a tableful of empty plates, myself, and little Miss Dorcas, the governess, only remained. She was sewing 'Comforts bags' for wounded men – the joy of the Tommys' hearts. If *only* more people who can sew, would get on and make thousands more!

I lit a cigarette and then said –

'Are you vanishing also, Miss Dorcas?'

'I suppose so,' she answered.

'Won't you stay and talk a bit?' I asked. 'You see I have to sit still most of my time.'

'You will be more comfortable in the smoke-room, or billiard-room,' she said, still intent upon her sewing.

'I couldn't be,' I said. 'A garden like this, a comfy chair, my pipe, and a warm July evening; it doesn't appeal to me to leave it for a billiard-room.'

'No,' she said, 'not yet, but it will.'

'Oh! I must go,' rising as she spoke, and hurriedly folding her work. 'You will come in when you've had enough, I suppose.'

'Enough what?' I asked, smiling.

'Enough garden,' she answered, as she hurried away, leaving me the now sole survivor of the cheery group I had come into, not two hours ago.

Idly I lay back in my chair, puffing away at my war-worn pipe, the drowsy hum of insects lulled me, the scent of flowers soothed, the silence rested my tired nerves and body. I didn't particularly want to think, but my mind kept wondering what was the need of all these good folks to hurry away to other occupations, one and all leaving their rather crippled guest, without apparently a thought as to how I should get my lame leg up the deep grass steps and into the house later. I wished Elsie had been here, but she had decided to come in a few days, leaving me to get to know her family without her helpful influence.

Well! I must make the best of it; at least, I could rest and enjoy the peace of it all. I did my best to go to sleep, but signally failed, though nothing could be more perfect than my surroundings for such a mode of passing a little of the time I seemed destined to spend alone. It was gloriously warm, and I was pleased to find no trace of damp, such as I had feared, and which would certainly necessitate my moving. No, it certainly was *not* damp, of that I was sure, *then what was it?* For it *was* something, though what I meant by *it*, I haven't the remotest idea. I felt confused, surely I must be sleepy, for my mind, usually alert, seemed dulled, almost as if I were once again under the noxious influence of morphia, as I lay in my chair endeavouring to collect wits that appeared to have a tendency to become scattered, I saw coming across the lawn an elderly man-servant. He approached the tea-table, and with one eye on me, stolidly began to clear away the tea-things. Then he coughed, and hesitatingly said to me –

'Are you thinking of going in, sir? Can I help you?'

'Well, I wasn't,' I replied, 'but perhaps I will, if you will give me an arm, when you have cleared away. I am not in any hurry.'

'Very good, sir, but I'll help you first if you wish, though it is getting a bit late.'

'Late!' The same word, and again I asked –

'Late – for what?'

'Late – er – for the teacups, sir,' he replied.

'For the teacups!' I said, astonished.

'Yes, sir, I mustn't be late.' Saying which, he gathered them up on his large tray, and set off with his load. He hadn't gone more than five or six yards when he appeared to stumble or slip, staggered to recover himself, and the tray and china crashed to the ground.

'There,' he gasped, amidst the wreckage, 'I knew it was late.'

I regret to say my first feeling was one of idiotic merriment, something about the old man, amidst the debris of china and odds and ends of food, struck a latent sense of humour in me, and I laughed unrestrainedly. Not so the worthy butler – he, with an expression that baffles description, slowly rose and stood staring at the broken china for the space of a full minute, before turning to me, as if to reprove my merriment. I frustrated him, by saying –

'I am sorry to laugh at you, but "over there" we somehow learnt to laugh at calamities, and it seemed to help.'

'Very good, sir,' he answered, stiffly, 'I understand, but it isn't *funny*, sir, not leastways what *I* call funny.'

'No,' I said, 'I can see your point of view. I suppose it means censure for breaking good china.'

'No, sir, it isn't that, for it isn't good china, it's cheap – because any delay means a smash, and we're late to-day, as I said.'

'I fail to understand you, my good man,' I answered, 'I've seen many queer incidents lately, but I can't see why the clearing of a few tea-things from a garden table should mean they will be smashed if left late, though it is but 5.30 now.'

'Quite true, sir. May I help you in now?' he said.

'Won't you remove the smash first?' I asked.

'No, sir,' was his emphatic reply. 'I will not, *they* wait till morning, they do.'

I shrugged my shoulders, feeling the hopelessness of it

– the old man must surely have a slate off. I would perhaps hear further of the smash later. Meantime, I was conscious of a wish for a more cheery spot, so turning to the old butler, remarked –

'I will try the steps now if you will give me an arm, but I cannot go quickly.'

'No, sir,' he replied, 'you certainly cannot, leastways not here, and we'll maybe get there sooner by going slower.'

As an Irishman, that speech appealed to me, and I chuckled as we started our crawl towards the steps. True, I was compelled to move slowly, but I certainly had every intention of moving at least as quickly as I had been able to do during the last few weeks. This, however, was far from the case, some inexplicable 'Something' retarded my every step! I found myself trying to put into words my inability to get along, in a joking way. I said to the worthy butler –

'I must have grown stiff sitting still so long, I feel as if my feet were unable to carry me.'

'Quite so, sir,' he answered, imperturbably, 'lean on me, sir.'

I did, but speedily found I was trusting to a broken reed, for the man stumbled at every other step. To an onlooker we must have had every appearance of a couple of very drunken reprobates struggling home after a wildly dissipated night, and not, as we were, a worn soldier with a game leg, leaning for support on the shoulder of a worthy grey-haired family retainer, crossing a little space of smooth green turf, leaving behind us a heap of smashed china! If I had been asked to describe that march, I should have said –

'Oh yes! I am aware that I was said to be walking across a smooth expanse of velvety lawn, without so much as a croquet hoop to trip me up, but seemingly I was struggling through a close tangle of strong briars, which entwined themselves round me as if they were endowed with sense, and each successive one was struggling to twist and pull harder than the other. That was my impression; yet, on that expanse of smooth green, there was not a single item to suggest such a state of affairs. Slowly, slowly, inch by inch, with the perspiration streaming from us, we reached at last the steps, mounted the first, and were confronted by a heavy pressure, as if to force us back.

'Stick to it, sir,' whispered the old man. And we did, but it took all my limited strength and his combined, to press through that invisible barrier, and finally reach the top. The presence relaxed then suddenly, and I breathed more freely, nor did it need the butler's muttered 'Hurry in, now, sir,' to urge me to the greatest speed my exhausted frame was capable of.

I entered the hall, with a word of thanks to my worthy friend, who disappeared in haste through a baize door, mopping his face.

I dropped into the nearest chair, feeling far more done than I ever remembered feeling after long hours in the trenches, and was content to lie back with my eyes shut, until I heard a mocking voice say –

'Drink this, John, you'll be all square in a minute.'

I wearily drank what was offered to me, opening my eyes to see the slightly quizzical face of Maude looking at me.

'Thanks!' I murmured, 'it's a trying day.'

'Very,' she responded, 'in the garden. I watched you coming in. Rest a few minutes, and then I will take you to the others. They are in our *indoor* garden; we prefer it.' Then she went away, leaving me to rest. I must have dozed for a few brief moments for again I did not hear her until she spoke, in a voice that, to my sensitive ears, still had a mocking note –

'Come along, John, you are quite alive, you know, come to the others.'

She helped me up, with a good strong pull – the kind of pull our young women are beginning to acquire since they metaphorically took their coats off, and gave up fancy work and crochet for making shells, milking cows, and tilling the land – and having got me on to my feet, she calmly tucked my arm through hers, saying, laughing –

'Elsie won't mind, you know.' And led me down a long stone corridor with a broad crimson carpet running down the centre, a few old coaching scenes on the walls, one or two heavy oak chairs on either side, and in each of the two windows an old-fashioned flower-stand filled with flowering plants.

'What a ripping corridor!' I said.

'Yes,' she answered, 'it's rather nice, but this is nicer,' she added, throwing open a big glass door and drawing me forward into what I can best describe as a gigantic greenhouse, though Maude's words of 'our indoor garden', more aptly describes it. It was immense, having a dome-shaped roof, painted a clear pale blue. Three sides of the place were of glass, through which lovely views were seen, the fourth side was an exquisitely painted landscape of a hayfield and trees stretching away into the distance. For a moment one scarcely realised whether one was looking at real scenes or painted ones, or where one began and the other ended. Clumps of shrubs here and there made secluded corners, where cosy chairs and couches were placed. A hammock was slung under another tree – one side of the place was trellis-work, with glorious roses rambling over it, and everywhere were flowers or flowering plants. The ground was dull green, like a solid linoleum; in one corner clock golf was marked out; Badminton occupied another place, and under an orange tree was a large round table, with writing materials and many magazines; the dome top could be worked by pulleys and rolled back, the whole idea giving one the atmosphere of a lovely foreign garden.

All the family were present, though each seemed intent on

his or her occupation and no one seemed to have the remotest thought of leaving it for a stroll in the garden *outside*, though a most perfect summer evening was vainly calling.

An hour ago I should unhesitatingly have said they were cranks, or had bees in their bonnets, but now – well – I was not sure what I truly thought.

'Won't you come and sit down, John?' called Mrs Falconer.

'Thanks!' I said, 'I was feeling rather struck in a heap, this is such an unusual greenhouse.'

'It isn't a greenhouse,' chimed in a little shrill voice, 'it's a 'ninside garding, come and see 'noranges,' and a moist chubby hand was thrust into my hand.

'I'm very tired, Lottie,' I said, 'may I come in a minute?'

'That's just like grown-ups,' lisped the little kiddie, 'vey always say, "in a minute" – they forgets.'

Mrs Falconer smiled, and patted the chair at her side saying – 'Run away, Lottie, John's tired.'

'John is,' I answered, gladly sinking into the cushioned chair. 'Why am I tired, Mrs Falconer?' I asked. 'What is the meaning of it all?'

'All what?' she asked blankly.

'The garden,' I said, 'the difficulty of coming in.'

'You've been asleep,' she said, 'and got stiff.'

'And the broken tea-things,' I went on.

'Oh! that's Jacobs, he's always having smashes.' And the good lady went on placidly knitting her soldier's socks.

Nothing to be learnt there, I thought, as I started chatting about the lovely 'garden' in which we sat.

'It's like a wonderful Winter Garden,' I said.

'It is,' she smiled, 'only it's a summer garden as well, after five o'clock.'

'Maude!' she called suddenly, as if remembering, 'you haven't fed the birds. I'll do it myself.' And she moved away, wool as usual trailing in her wake.

I was left to my own devices once more. What an unconventional crowd they were, or is it, they don't want to talk, I was wondering idly as I smoked a cigarette, when Bob sidled up to the vacant chair and perched himself upon its arm.

'You'll come in earlier tomorrow, sir, won't you?' he asked half-shyly, 'it kind of knocks one about to stay late.'

But I was going to play the same game as others, so answered casually –

'Oh! does it? It didn't knock me about.'

'Didn't it, sir? It did Jacobs,' he added slyly, 'he's what he calls "all of a dither".'

'I saw nothing to "dither" about,' I said.

'No, sir, I daresay you didn't, but it isn't what you *see* that does it.'

'And I most certainly didn't *hear* anything odd,' I went on.

'I hope you won't, sir, I did once, and (lowering his voice) I had brain fever afterwards. You won't catch me out after five.'

'Bob, come here, I want you,' rang out Maude's compelling voice.

'Oh! blow!' muttered the boy, 'they are dead scared for fear I tell you, and you cut off and leave Elsie.' With which cryptic 'give away' of his relations he strolled off, hands in pockets.

Once more I was alone, and content to be so, to light another cigarette and have a review of the rapid sequence of events – my arrival, tea, the sudden scattering of the group beneath the trees, the broken china and my desperate attempt to cross a few yards of turf. I could not make 'head nor tail' of any of it – sufficient for me I was in love and prepared to put up with a good deal to await the coming of the little girl I loved. My musings were interrupted by the sound of a bell in the distance.

'Dressing-bell, John,' shouted someone. 'I'll take you to your room,' called Bob.

'Many thanks, I'll be glad,' I said, 'I – I'm not very good at stairs alone.'

'You aren't upstairs, you're on this floor, Pater thought you'd like it, though I'm blessed if I should – too near the garden for this child to – hang on, sir, I'm pretty tough.'

Together we traversed again the long stone corridor, through the hall, along a similar corridor, but of more recent date, being of polished pine, instead of grey stones.

Bob opened a door about half-way down, saying – 'There you are, I hope you'll like it – shout, I mean ring, if you want things. Neither Mum nor Dad ever remember visitors.'

'Right,' I said, 'but I'll manage,' turning as I spoke to open the window.

'I wouldn't, sir,' said the lad, 'it's beastly – er – damp – '

There were three windows in my spacious bedroom, two on one side, one at a queer angle, in a built-out corner, this latter was heavily shuttered, barred up and padlocked.

'Great guns!' I cried, 'Who on earth are you expecting to get in – it's like being walled in – where does it look out? If it's ever opened!'

'It's opened till five pm,' said the lad, 'and it looks on to the low lawn. I'd leave it at that, sir, if I were you.' And he edged himself through the door.

'Alone again!' I thought, lighting the inevitable cigarette. What an extraordinary family they seemed to be, so detached, as it were, so self-absorbed, but above all, so skilful at playing into each other's hands – even the smallest of them aiding in the now apparent determination of each one not to remain alone with their wounded guest, and future relative! Why? I wondered. What did they fear? This last thought was a sub-conscious one, for I had not hitherto consciously thought of *fear* in any form. Well, time would reveal perhaps, meantime, it was a fresh interest – an unusual interest to find myself a guest in a unique house, full of unique people, all doing their best to keep me from finding out 'Something' – well – 'Something' that so far hadn't a name – it would amuse me to circumvent them, and help to pass the days until my girl came. And now to dress for another scene; the scenes were certainly following one another in rather rapid succession – perhaps too rapidly for a 'convalescent' and yet, I have a firm and fixed belief that the quickest way for a sick person to become a well one, is to keep the mind occupied, busy, interested, to fill up the days and hours, leaving no time for brooding, or speculation as to the why or wherefore of one's apparent slow healing; thoughts of health bring health, just as quickly as brooding melancholy brings depression, and subsequent ills in its train. It has been truthfully said, that the wounded lads who have recovered best are those whose outlook has been buoyant and cheery, those of whom 'even a swamp did not depress them', as Mark Tapley would have said. My days certainly gave promise of being full enough.

I had finished my leisurely dressing to the running accompaniment of this train of thought, just as a silver chime of low notes rang through the house. 'Pretty' I thought, 'and much better than the dull boom of the orthodox family gong, which always suggested to me the dullest of meals.'

No one seemed to be passing my way, no cheery voice called out to me their offer of escort. Very well, I would find my own way, since it did not appear to have struck anyone that so far I had not been in any room other than the 'Indoor Garden' – if it could be called a room, or that I had not any idea of my bearings.

I switched off the light in my room, and started to locate the dining room. I need not have hesitated, for the whole family were gathered in the Hall, talking, laughing, and in high spirits.

There were not any other guests, simply a family party. The Hall was beautifully lighted from above by reflected lights – I mean the actual lights were not visible. The windows – there were three – were heavily draped in a light shade of gold, almost giving the idea of sunlight, as they caught the light from above. I am not a great hand at describing these things, sufficient to say the place gave one a feeling of brightness and comfort, without glare or striking colour.

I was nodded to as if I were one of them, as with one accord, we moved away to the dining-room.

Probably I was expecting the usual sombre dining-room of an ancient family mansion – oak furniture, sideboard like a silver-smith's window, family portraits in gilt frames – but whatever I expected, it certainly was not the gay room in which I now found myself. There were not any pictures, nor did one miss them, for the walls were painted a shade of deep cream, with exquisite flowers, in groups, and sprays upon them; the chairs were of some highly-polished light wood – in appearance like a bird's eye maple – in place of the usual dado round the room, was a curved-in recess, filled with plants and flowers with tiny electric lights among them here and there, deftly shaded by foliage and flowers. The dinner-table was a blaze of wild flowers, spotless linen, and shining glass.

I was slightly breathless as I took my seat. Mrs Falconer smiled, and I explained my rather gasping condition, by saying – 'Your rooms do take a man's breath away, Mrs Falconer, they seem to transport one into a fairyland of flowers.'

'Yes,' she said, 'I hope they do. You see –' and she hesitated a second – 'we cannot enjoy them outside the house, as most people can, so we have them and a gardener inside.'

'I should miss a garden,' I said bluntly.

'You wouldn't miss *ours*,' she said, as she turned away to speak to Bob on her other side.

I enjoyed my dinner, which was perfect in a simple way,

and in the glory of that room of flowers, I did not notice, not until when next I found myself in my own room, that, on an August evening, I had dined in a room hermetically sealed, as far as an open window or fresh air was concerned. Later we gathered again in the Indoor Garden for smokes, games and music. There was not any drawing-room, which also delighted me, as I have a wholesome horror of those abominable apartments with their set chairs, cushions of silk only to be looked at. Silver table – neither use nor ornament – and corners filled with framed photographs of friends, so-called, for whom you care nothing at all, do not miss, and whose pictures you often keep in a drawer until a day when they come to call, when you at once put the right set out, trusting to luck that no one will give you away, though occasionally they have been known to do so!

It was about 9.40 when the sudden need of some fresh air seized me with uncontrollable longing. I had lived in the air so long, it was impossible for me I felt to remain shut up indoors, especially as there seemed an unwritten law forbidding the opening of windows anywhere.

I was idly wondering how I could best escape to smoke a quiet pipe in the fresh air, before turning in, when my worthy father-in-law to be dropped into a chair beside me.

'Getting tired, John?' he asked. 'I should turn in early if I were you, we are all early-to-bed folks here.'

'No thanks,' I replied, 'I'm not tired, I was admiring that painted view of the far end of this lovely place, though I should have thought glass on all sides would have better carried out your idea. What would the view be if that end were also glass?'

'It all depends upon the time of day,' was his reply. 'In the morning it would show you the garden, the Low Lawn,' he said, 'but – now for instance – well, it wouldn't, or if it did, you would rather not see it.'

He left me no chance to comment on his explanation, merely stated the fact, leaving me to make of it what I chose.

I didn't make much, needless to say, except to make up my mind more firmly to fathom what they were fast leading me to look upon as a 'Mystery', and as I have the healthy Englishman's dislike of mysteries, I did not intend it to be one for longer than I could manage.

'Very well,' I thought, 'independence is my attitude henceforth, for when I came to think of it, I had been led, influenced, ringed about, as it were in an unobtrusive kind of way ever since my arrival a few hours ago. We would see!'

I rose, shook out my pipe, strolling away as I did so, to where the piano stood under a bank of roses. Maude was playing soft snatches of rag-times. Bob was lounging by her side, Mrs Falconer nodding over her knitting close beside Mr Falconer, who was reading, while Captain McKlean and his sister Nora, with whom I had not so far had any conversation, were idly knocking the clock golf ball about.

'Come along, John, and sing,' said Maude, breaking into the old familiar 'Long, long trail'. 'All soldiers sing this, so begin.'

'I'm not just in singing form at the moment,' I replied, 'and I'm a little tired. I'm just going to smoke a pipe out of doors, before I turn in,' was my calm announcement. But, had I dropped a bomb in the midst of them, the effect of my few words could not have been more startling. Mr Falconer dropped his paper, with a muttered 'God bless my soul!'; Maude crashed into a jumble of wrong notes; Bob said but one word – 'Golly!'; and Captain McKlean and his sister dropped their putters, joining the little circle hurriedly. Mrs Falconer woke – I don't mean she merely opened her eyes – she seemed suddenly galvanised, as she rose, saying –

'John, as my future son-in-law, I ask you *not* to leave the house to-night!' There was a tense silence for a brief second, but I was determined.

'I'm sorry, Mrs Falconer, but I see no reason to comply with such a curious request. I am a soldier accustomed to be out and about in all weathers. I am *not* a hot-house plant, and if I do not breathe some fresh air, I shall neither rest nor sleep; my little evening walk is my best sedative, and I must ask your kind indulgence of my whim – Fresh air I must have.'

Bob's was the sole reply –

'If you could get it fresh, sir, it would be all right.'

Mrs Falconer seated herself again, without further words. Mr Falconer had disappeared.

I bowed, wished them all 'Good-night', moving away feeling like anything but an *honoured!* guest. I wended my way back to the hall; it was empty, so, slipping on a coat and my hat, I made for the front door, beneath the golden curtains. I pulled one back and stared idiotically at the solid wall beneath it; there wasn't the faintest suggestion of a door, yet I had entered by one – that, I knew. I walked all round. An unbroken carved cedar wood panelling ran right round to a depth of four feet. There wasn't a chink nor an opening, except the way to my sleeping corridor and the stone passage I had just come along. I felt as if I should lose my temper in a minute, but determined as I was, I retraced my steps to the Indoor Garden, meaning to ask where was the door, or any door. I reached the place only to find it dark, silent, empty; one and all must have gone to their rooms by some other way, probably suspecting exactly what *had* happened, *would* happen. Annoyed and irritated at being thus foiled in my desire, I had no choice but to go to my bedroom. The whole house seemed sunk in the silence of sleep, though it was but 10.30, and I shut my door with a rather vicious slam that echoed and reechoed along the corridor.

'Now for my windows,' I murmured, 'for a breath of fresh air I must and will have –'

Futile wish! unattainable longing! my windows were thick plate glass, minus fastening of any description – 'Foiled again!'

I murmured, as I began a minute inspection of the iron-shuttered window, which was some three or four feet above the floor, with a broad window-sill. A bit of a risk to get on to that I thought, with a lame leg. I'd best leave it for to-night, but it worried me to be beaten – so with a good deal of pain, I dragged myself up on to a chair, from whence I could at least feel and inspect the shutter. My inspection brought forth a prolonged whistle! I had discovered a weak point – true it was padlocked – but the hasp through which the padlock passed was thin, and needed only a good file and a steady hour's work to cut it through, when, so far as I could see, the shutter could be rolled back to its socket.

'Right-o!' I said gaily, 'that is for tomorrow. Tomorrow, I will buy or steal a file, and then –'

Feeling more settled in my mind now, I got into my bed, determined on two points – tomorrow would see that window open, and that I would to all intents, play the game, nor appear conscious of what was an actual fact, that after 5 pm, I, an able-bodied – or fairly so – member of HM Forces, was a prisoner.

I did not expect to sleep, lacking fresh air, but as I got into bed, the coolest breeze blew round me, and I noticed for the first time, that at either end of the room, high up, were steel electric fans, moving silently and rapidly.

'Then the "Prisoner" isn't to smother,' I thought, as I dropped into a profound sleep.

I awoke feeling rested, refreshed and fit, in spite of a night of closed windows, to which I was quite unaccustomed; tea was brought to me at 7.30 and I rose, feeling ready for whatever the day might bring; it was not going to bring my little girl, alas! though she hoped to be with me within the next day or two. In my heart was a lingering feeling that it was just as well, for she might, probably would have, interfered with my plans.

I joined the family party in the hall a little before nine.

All were in the best of form, the hall door stood wide open though I carefully refrained from taking any apparent notice of the fact.

Breakfast was served in the dining-room, which had undergone a slight change – there were fewer plants, fewer flowers, and two large windows were thrown wide open to the sun and air. The same detached spirit was plainly seen, as last night, all were intent upon their own devices. It struck me as unusual that the three guests – one of them a cripple – should not be consulted in the smallest degree, as to their tastes, ideas or wishes for the day. Not a single comment was made as to the previous day, its doings, or the evening of it. It gave one a feeling that 'sufficient for the day' was a saying ably carried out. I waited for a kindly suggestion, such as – 'Would I care to drive? Would I prefer a lounge in the garden?' *Nothing*, however, was forthcoming, so I asked blandly –

'McKlean, are you coming to smoke a pipe in the garden?'

'Captain McKlean is coming with me,' answered Maude. 'I have to go to town for some things.'

'Town', I might mention, was a small market town, called Singletown, consisting of a main Street, a Bank, and in the high Street, varied shops of a small mixed kind, and boasting quite a good ironmonger's, a lending library and hospital, up to date.

Now this began to look awkward, obviously *I* should be *de trop*, yet reach that ironmonger's I must and will.

'I wonder if you would take a passenger to town, as well?' I asked. 'I have a little shopping to do, and cannot walk far.'

'We are only going to be an hour,' replied Maude. 'Can't I shop for you?'

'Sorry!' I said, 'I am afraid not.'

I knew in her heart Maude was hating me for a spoil sport, but I had to get that file, so at the risk of being voted a nuisance, I smilingly asked again to be taken.

I was taken, but I knew in every fibre of my being I was all that I feared, a spoil sport. I had to put my feelings in my pocket, and when duly dropped at the best stationers, slipped from there into the ironmonger's without delay, the moment their backs were turned. Joyfully I selected three good files, stowing them away in an inner pocket, while ostentatiously carrying a library book and packet of stationery as well as a box of toffee – of a war kind – as a peace offering for the huffy lady. We reached the house again, well before lunch-time.

As before, I was struck with the total lack of exchange of news, none seemed to know or care what the other had been doing; it was perhaps as well, for I might now spend my time as best suited me, irrespective of anyone else.

I was deep in thought when Mrs Falconer made the only remark as to any arrangement.

'Tea will be on the Low Lawn, John, at four o'clock. We all come in at five.'

'Oh! do we?' I thought. 'Well I for one don't. I'm not being imprisoned a second time, from five until bedtime, if I can help it.' So I just murmured – 'Thanks, I will have a rest first and join you there for tea.'

Then I sought my room, ostensibly to rest, in reality to study the lie of the land, and the iron shutter. I carefully made a mental study of the position of the house, its windows, their outlook, and so on, as I went to my room. I hated my room, hated its big shut-up windows, hated its ugly iron one, above all hated the imprisoned atmosphere of it. I studied the view from those windows. They overlooked a walled fruit garden, beyond which stretched a belt of trees. I craned my neck, squirming violently in my endeavour to locate the part of the grounds the iron window would overlook; finding by my memorized plan of house and grounds that as it was a jutting out angle of the house, it would, as I more than half expected, command an uninterrupted view of the Low Lawn.

'What a pity I could not begin my work now,' I thought, 'and have a view of that lawn about 5.30.' But alas! that could not be. Very well, I would endeavour to possess my soul in patience, meaning to retire early on a plea of tiredness. I spent an hour on the couch in my room, dozing lightly under the pretence of reading, and 3.30 found me wending my steps to the Low Lawn but with a dire thought in my mind –

'Suppose my iron window should be barricaded outside as well!'

I had not long joined the group on the lawn before my misgivings were put to rest. I had spotted the iron windows, also immediately above it a similar one, it was an odd angle in a house, though, if left *as* windows, might have made an attractive corner in the rooms. I would for once, question, but whom? Mrs Falconer would rise grandiloquently to the occasion flooring me with a single terse reply, that was a foregone conclusion. Maude, not yet having forgiven my intrusion in the morning, would probably loftily disdain to reply at all. Bob was most accessible, so I rose stiffly from my chair, saying –

'Come and be kind, Bob, my leg is worrying me and needs a little gentle exercise. Will you lend me that strong shoulder of yours, in return for a war yarn?'

'Won't I just,' he answered, springing to his feet, and placing himself ready for my encircling arm to rest along his shoulders. I kept my promise, during three turns slowly up and down the lawn I spun out my yarn a little, making it end about the centre of the lawn as we faced the house.

'Half a second, old man,' I then said. 'I must have a breath.' We stood, and I gazed at the house.

'Jolly old place,' I said.

'Yes,' he answered. 'Are you ready, sir?'

'In a jiff,' I replied. 'I'm trying if I am clever enough to spot my room. I'll bet you a bob I can.'

'Right!' said the lad, all eagerness now. 'Try, sir.'

I made one or two feeble shots, which were received with yells of derision.

'I give it up,' I said at length. 'You've won your bob, so tell me.'

'Why, there,' he cried, pointing, there with the blank window looking this way, with another window like it higher up.

'Of course,' I said, 'how dense of me. I remember now – that dull window spoils the pretty room.'

'Might spoil it more, sir, if it wasn't dull,' he replied.

'Oh, I don't think so, Bob,' I went on, 'look what a picture the lawn would be from it.'

'A pretty picture – I *don't* think! I guess you'd jolly quick pack up your traps and quit, if you saw the pretty picture, sir.'

'Look here, Bob,' I began, in wheedling tones, 'let's be chums, and you tell me all about that picture in return for my yarn.'

Scornfully the young voice answered me. 'I didn't think you were a rotter, sir. I thought you were a sport, but a *real* sport would see this old shop is dad's nightmare and play the game. I'm a boy scout, sir, and I try to play the game, it isn't the game for a soldier to try and make a scout fail to be a sport.'

Humbly, I begged his pardon, feeling about three inches high as I did so, and wondering what his opinion would be of me if it transpired that I had broken open the window – though I hoped to defy detection. In silence we retraced our steps, but I had fallen from my high estate in Bob's eyes, and could feel I was not any longer a hero, even with a purple and white ribbon – so do our youthful judges censure and condemn!

Tea was somewhat more of a rag than previous meals, possibly because little Miss Dorcas, with her three charges, joined us at tea, though their other meals were taken in the seclusion of the schoolroom.

I was keeping a furtive eye on my wristwatch, and wondering which of the party would make the first move, when I saw Mrs Falconer nod to Miss Dorcas, who promptly rose, calling the children to come as she went. I wondered by what means such obedience had been taught and enforced since nine out of every ten children would have begged for 'just ten more minutes'.

'The kiddies trot in early,' I remarked, to no one in particular.

'You bet,' answered Bob, 'they always go through the fruit garden to the schoolroom, and if they get there before the sun leaves the apricot wall, they can pick one – you bet they don't miss!'

I smiled, thinking to myself how apt it all was – seemingly so natural – though every move was planned.

Maude and the McKleans were the next to go – Maude talking volubly about finishing the Badminton set begun last evening.

They had barely gone before old Jacobs hurried up – this time with a trim maid in attendance – the two cleared the tea things, and departed without loss of time. There was not to be any delay this evening, that was plain.

Mr and Mrs Falconer only remained, they were going to sit me out, so to speak!

I would alter that plan. I rose, saying –

'Might I, too, venture in search of an apricot.'

Mrs Falconer – a barely perceptible shade of relief flashing over her face – answered – 'Yes, surely, and go in by the schoolroom door, from there you can join us in the Indoor Garden.'

Mr Falconer rose, as if to accompany me, but his wife's glance restrained him, evidently it was a little further than even they could, with courtesy, go – to accompany a guest to the fruit garden, as if fearing wholesale robbing of fruit trees. So I was permitted to go alone.

My idea was, of course, to visit the fruit garden, but *not* to enter the schoolroom door, joining the caged-up company, from then onwards, until bedtime. Oh! no, I was merely going to get an apricot – dawdle a while until the coast was clear and retrace my steps, almost to the Low Lawn, but instead of descending to it, skirt right round the top of it, and so indoors, when I felt disposed.

I reached the fruit garden, took my apricot, waved gaily to little Lottie in the window – disregarded the beckoning hand of little Miss Dorcas, who was gazing at me through the long window, with almost a look of fear in her dark eyes, and retraced my steps to the path which led right round the sunk lawn.

I walked along it on the far side from the steps leading down into it, half-way along past the group of fine trees, where the tea was usually put. I paused – paused because I *had* to – I knew that, but tried not to think it. I wasn't exactly held up, nor was I conscious of briars tripping me up as last night – I had merely stopped – stopped to breathe. Yes, that was it, only I wasn't out of breath – there just wasn't anything *to* breathe; foolishly I found myself saying this idiotic sentence over and over again 'not out of breath, but nothing *to* breathe.'

I had been once in a gas-cloud in France, but this wasn't like that. *This* was like nothing; I struggled a few more yards, and gazed. The house seemed to have receded, the lawn seemed further below me, and appeared veiled in a bluish haze, thicker and thicker it seemed to get, and as I gazed, I fancied I could discern swiftly, hurrying forms moving to and fro. I struggled on again, intent only on reaching the house. As I advanced, the bluish fog closed round me, shutting me in, in an impenetrable wall. In vain I struggled, in vain I peered; at last, even beating the fog with my hands, as if to force a passage through. Nothing availed me, and ever and anon I could see the hurrying forms below me. Terror struck me! Would that I were safely in the Indoor Garden with its warmth and light and beauty, instead of here, enveloped in fog with other forms of which I dared not think, hurrying below me. Would that I had been guided instead of going my own obstinate way. Vain were such repinings now. The shapes seemed more defined, the atmosphere more dense. Feebly, I struggled to see the time by my luminous watch – Eight o'clock! Have I been wandering here so long – it seemed incredible! I must, and will, reach the house, but now I seemed to have lost the house, all trace of it had vanished.

Last night I grumbled that I was a prisoner – indoors. To-night I was to be kept 'Outside the House.'

Denser and denser grew the appalling thickness of the air. I feared to move a yard in advance. 'If only it would lift a little, just enough to enable me to go forward in safety.' Even as I spoke, the atmosphere grew perceptibly clearer. I took one step forward, to find myself standing on the edge of a precipice or what seemed like one. I was now facing the sunk lawn – sunk indeed! – for it seemed far, far below me, with a drop from where I was standing of I dare not contemplate what depth, where shapes were ever hurrying to and fro. Cautiously I bent nearer, in a way almost glad to gaze on some movement, rather than into the impenetrable wall before me. As I gazed, a figure seemed to come close up to me out of the void, stretching its arms towards me as if to drag me with it. I saw no face, no definite shape, beyond the shadowy outline, and the arms. I shrank back, and back, to find myself pressing against the shrubs. 'Could I keep in that position without losing my bearings?' I wondered, for if I could, I was then backing away from lawn and house. How far the fog extended, I could not guess, but to press back from the lawn seemed the only thing to attempt. I was weak, spent, almost done, but I threw my last ounce of strength into this move. Crash! crash! went branches behind me, my weak leg was failing me, and I found myself feebly trying to pray for help. And now the shadowy forms seemed to follow me, closer, closer, they pressed forward, as I pressed back. Suddenly, I fancied I *heard* a faint shout, then another. I tried to answer, but was powerless, terror had made me dumb. Another shout –

'John, where are you?'

I could not answer, but gave one last push, and fell.

I opened my eyes to find not a search party, not a feverish gang of people, fussing over me, but merely Mrs Falconer, with a flash of brandy in one hand, a light rug over her arm, leading a magnificent hound by a long chain. His acquaintance I had not made; he was licking my face and hands, when with a long shudder I sat up.

'Mrs Falconer,' I said.

'Yes, John, Gelert and I. Do you feel able to walk? We have some way to go, before you can rest.'

'Are we far from the house?' I asked.

'The house, as far as we are concerned, has ceased to exist until daylight,' she answered.

'I do not understand,' I said.

'Of course you don't,' she replied, 'and were not content to be guided.'

'No,' I said ruefully, 'but how topping of you to come.'

'No one else can,' she said, 'only Gelert and I can come. But now you must try to move.'

I took a little of the brandy, and struggled to my feet, to find I was on the extreme edge of the shrubberies, beyond which appeared to be meadows. With my final twist back, I had landed on my back into the meadow, nothing resisting my strength, and, of course, fell.

'How deep is the shrubbery I backed through, Mrs Falconer?' I asked.

'A matter of perhaps thirty or forty yards,' she said. 'Fortunately it occurred to you to back.'

'Why?' I said.

'Never mind why, just now,' she replied, 'we must hurry. Look.'

I looked, and saw the fog creeping after us. Gelert growled menacingly, ever and anon turning to face the way we were leaving, once, springing as if to grasp something, his eyes like fire, saliva dripping from his massive jaws. A few moments passed, and Mrs Falconer breathed – 'Hurry John, you must.'

'I can't,' I gasped.

'You must,' she said. But even as she spoke, I felt the impress of a hand heavily on my shoulder. The hound growled, prepared for a spring, I thought, at my throat, as with a quick word and sudden jerk, Mrs Falconer dragged me through a gate, sinking down on the roadside with a whispered 'Thank God!'

I suppose I lost consciousness for a few moments, for when next I opened my eyes, I was covered with the rug, my head on Mrs Falconer's knee, Gelert beside her, with his great paws close to her.

A faint, grey light, as of coming dawn, was visible, the atmosphere was clear and balmy, and very silent.

Mrs Falconer rose, and her voice was once again the cold, unemotional tones of my hostess. I vaguely wondered if it had been all part of a horrible nightmare, and had I dreamed that across it I heard her voice, anguished, distressed, calling, calling.

There was nothing now, in either her voice or bearing, other than the lady I had hitherto known.

'If you are rested, John, we will go home,' she said, in slightly ironical tones, 'you will no doubt be glad of a bath and sleep.'

'Thank you,' I answered, in the same off-hand way. 'I shall.'

I was deadly tired, sick with pain, and now, in the quickly-coming dawn, felt, and I should not hesitate to say, looked, like a truant schoolboy, caught out of bounds, and conveyed home to receive due chastisement. I felt cowed – no other word describes it, yet deep in my heart lay a feeling of annoyance, that I had been found. I was quite conscious of *not* feeling nearly as grateful as I ought, and of being still a long way from discovering the why and wherefore of strange and terrifying happenings.

That I had seen things, not of this world, in the ordinary meaning of the word, I was well aware. Nor was I unduly fearful of them, the horror lay in the suffocating fog, and in the apparent wish to haul me into some abyss. I was *not* afraid of mere forms. Some of us out in 'No-Man's-Land' were not unknowing of other forms being present as well as our comrades in the flesh. There are those of us, who, in spite of the jeerings of scoffers, still say, that the Angels of Mons were *not* the phantasy of unhinged minds, nor even a mirage due to a tot of rum. Therefore, I, among many others, have learned to be less sceptical and not to take non-understandable things as impossibilities.

The truant school-boy feeling clung to me all the way home. I shouldn't have felt surprised had Mrs Falconer taken me by the hand and bidden me trot along. As we neared the house, I observed smoke from one or two chimneys. What time it was I did not know, nor greatly care. In silence we entered the hall, hearing a large clock boom five as we did so.

A small round table was drawn near a blazing freshly kindled fire, a kettle steamed on the hob, toast, and bread and butter were there, but not a sign of any person.

Still in silence, Mrs Falconer threw off her fur coat and cap, and warming her hands at the blaze, she uttered one of her usual terse remarks – 'When you have had food, John,

I advise a bath, bed, and a still tongue. The household are aware you remained outside when you had better have been in. Details of your experience are not desirable, and for Elsie's sake, I do not advise a repetition of foolhardiness, I also ask you to conform to the house rules, which are made as little irksome as possible.'

I did not reply beyond a mild bow and she went on – 'I am going to lock Gelert up now. I counsel bed for you, and the Doctor to see your leg in the morning. Good-bye.'

I had prepared an elaborate speech of thanks for her timely help, but she cut me short, saying – 'Your best thanks, John, will be to conform to rules; no one else has ever tried to kick them over quite so deliberately before.'

She left me then, and I dragged my throbbing limb to bath and bed, too weary to think or conjecture further.

When next I awakened it was 10 am. No one apparently had been near me, so I rang my bell. Old Jacob answered it, looking at me reproachfully, as he asked if he might bring breakfast because "Madam has 'phoned the doctor to call."'

'There was no need,' I said – 'he may even order me to lie still.'

'Yes, sir,' said Jacobs, his tone implying 'that's it.'

A plentiful breakfast tray speedily arrived, and with it Bob, who perched himself on the foot of my bed, eyeing me as one who wished to know without inquiring. I vouchsafed no information, so he started off.

'Rotten luck, sir, but only your own fault – quite instructive and very thrilling – Hurt your leg, sir?'

'A bit,' I answered.

Then lowering his voice he whispered – 'Anything touch you? Fog, I suppose, and people.'

'Oh, no,' I said, 'at least I don't think so.'

'Think so!' he ejaculated, 'there would not be any *think* about it.'

'What's it all about, Bob?' I asked.

'Better ask the Gov'nor, sir, not me.'

'P'raps so – clear now, Bob – I'm going to dress.'

'Right-o, sir,' said he as he lounged away.

Fearing a doctor's visit to maul me about, I dressed and tubbed quickly, and was just about to put my jacket on, when I noticed a long tear in the shoulder, also the shoulder strap was missing.

'Then someone did touch me,' I said aloud, staring aghast at the ripped shoulder, dismayed to think what a giveaway it was to the household as it was my only available coat for day. I had better concoct a yarn to account for it, and get a maid to mend it, while I dressed.

I rang the bell and a plain-looking person with glasses and a long nose answered it.

'Did you ring, sir?' she asked, in rasping tones.

'Eh, yes,' I said, 'I've had an accident and torn my coat, I shall be obliged if someone will mend it.'

She took it without answering, and I continued dressing until she re-appeared saying –

'I've done what I could, sir, it's a tailor's job, but may do until you leave.'

'Until I leave?' I said, somewhat startled.

'Yes, sir,' she replied. 'You'll be leaving I expect. It's no use staying, sir, when things like that begin to happen,' pointing to my coat as she spoke.

I was about to try a question, softened by a half-crown, when there was a sharp knock at the door, and another maid entered with a salver on which lay a wire. With a murmured 'Thanks' I ripped it open, reading –

'Coming to-day, why don't you do as you are told. Elsie.'

Forgotten were the horrors of last night, forgotten torn coats, rules, regulations, everything, in the delight of my little girl's coming. I thanked the two women, flung on my coat, whistling like a schoolboy, as I tramped to the hall on my way to breakfast.

A curious restraint met me – something indefinable, a kind of lack of genuineness in the 'Good-mornings' I received, which gave me a feeling of being in disgrace, but no amount of that was going to damp my spirits, so I ignored it, though don't mind admitting the chill rather spoilt the morning, and I was not sorry to escape with a pipe to have a look at a time-table.

Mrs Falconer did not appear during the morning which did not unduly worry me, but when Mr Falconer asked me to be good enough to follow him to his study, I had visions of the birch-rod, and my footsteps lagged as befitted my part, when I obeyed his request. He asked me to be seated, but instead of a whipping, he mildly said –

'John, Elsie will arrive at 12.40, will you drive to meet her?'

'Thanks very much, I was hoping to,' I answered.

'She knows,' he went on, 'that you – er – that you – had an unpleasant night. I regret that you do not seem able to take us as we are obliged to be, and I admit it is difficult to make one's guests understand and respect our arrangements for their welfare, without explanations, which we are not permitted to give; for Elsie's sake, I warn you, less worse befall, to conform to rule.'

This was a whipping without a doubt; and I felt a qualm of conscience as he spoke, knowing, as I did, my pig-headed temperament and determination to know more.

I thanked him, offered him a cigarette, but evaded any promises, though he eyed me questioningly as if he awaited something of the kind.

The next few hours I passed aimlessly, wandering about alone, since one and all of the party seemed bent on avoiding me. I had a stroll to the Low Lawn; though, bathed in sunshine, it looked peaceful and serene, making me wonder vaguely had I dreamed the horrid fantasy. I was glad when the hour came to meet my little girl. I enjoyed the swift run. I was glad beyond measure to see her bright face at the railway carriage window.

'You are looking fit, old boy,' she said; adding, without any hesitancy, 'in spite of your silly tricks last night.'

'How did you know?' I asked.

'Mother wired me to come,' she replied, 'and take charge of you, as you had been out too late. I knew all *that* meant,' she said, with a shudder.

'Will you tell me about it, Kiddie?' I coaxed, but her little face took a graver look, as she answered:

'No, John, I can't; you must just trust us and do as we do. Stay with me, dear, this evening; never mind trying to fathom things, others have tried before you. Promise me you will not think of it anymore.'

'Dear child, I'm a man with a thinking machine. I can't promise not to think,' I said.

'Well, promise you won't stay out after time,' she said.

'Very well,' I assented, 'I'll promise that.'

She nestled to my side in dear content at that, and our drive back was a happy one.

Elsie was greeted with happy comradeship on our arrival, so lunch was a more cheery meal, and the afternoon was passed as usual, in a rest, a stroll, and tea beneath the old trees on the Low Lawn. At five, as usual, a general move was made to the house. Elsie held out her hand to me, merely saying:

'Come, John'; but, man-like, I wanted to remain, and was reluctant to obey that little outstretched hand, but gave in with a good grace, consenting to be imprisoned for the rest of the summer evening within the glassed garden. To a man accustomed to be out of doors, the enforced imprisonment palled, despite the games, music, gay talk, and general attempt to keep things cheery.

Little Miss Dorcas and her charges joined us for a while; and I had an idea, that if I could get her alone, she would perhaps give me some information. I would try; so invited her to a putting match, leaving Elsie to chat to her mother.

'You are playing wildly, Major,' said my partner, in a few moments.

'Yes,' I answered, 'I'm afraid my thoughts were "outside", and not in. I had a strange evening last evening, you know.'

'Yes,' she said. 'I hope it is one that will not be repeated.'

'Oh no,' I answered, 'I'm not likely to repeat it.'

'I suppose not,' she replied, 'at least not in *that* way.'

'That way?' I asked. 'What do you mean, is there any other way?'

'Unfortunately, yes,' she answered, gravely. 'Oh! Mrs Falconer is watching us,' she said, suddenly – 'play, oh, do play! I'll try and say something while we play. I don't think it is right to keep you in ignorance of your danger; they do, and no one will warn you.'

'Tell me,' I muttered, as I played.

'I can't,' she whispered. 'She is coming across, look in the books on your shelf to-night. There! I've won,' she said, in the same breath, as she waved her putter in triumph, just as Mrs Falconer came up.

'Don't overdo it, John,' she said. 'Elsie is waiting for you, and the children are getting tired, Miss Dorcas.'

So our game and little talk came to an abrupt end. From then on, I was given no chance for talks, except with Elsie; but when we separated to dress for dinner, and I found myself alone, I pondered deeply over a quiet pipe. 'Warn me of my danger' Miss Dorcas had said, then was there danger, whether I ventured outside or not? And the bookshelf, that probably meant a note. Surely I was safe inside, I thought, for I was fully determined to get the iron shutter out of my way. Well, I would leave it now, and, as they say, 'wait and see.'

Dinner was cheery, but I was rapidly beginning to detest the Indoor Garden, with its continual constraint, and made up my mind to press for an early wedding and take my little girl to more congenial surroundings.

The evening drew to a close at last! though I was happy with Elsie, and, in a secluded corner, had asked and carried my point of an early wedding.

By 10.30 all had dispersed; indeed, I am certain all hated the enforced seclusion as much in their hearts as I did. I bid them all 'Good night!' and, with a sigh of relief, flung myself into the armchair in my cosy bedroom. My eyes suddenly fell on to a book, slightly awry on the shelf, and I sprang up as quickly as my lame leg permitted, and took it down; a tiny note which lay between the pages read thus:

'You have given a loop-hole and are waited for, take care you are not taken "outside the house". Keep from your windows. – J D'

'Ho! ho!' I said; "keep from my windows". 'That little warning gives me a clue, but surely, if I do not open them, all will be well. I only desire to *see* through them, and what's more, I will.'

I took my coat off, mounted a chair with difficulty, managing to seat myself sideways on the broad window-ledge, armed with my files, and a soft cloth, to dull the sound as much as possible. Luckily the file was sharp, and the metal soft, and in a short time I had made a deep dent. It was now 11.30, all was silent, presumably the whole house was wrapt in slumber. Steadily I worked for another half-hour; the hasp was almost through. I paused for a brief rest. As I paused, there sprang into being, probably from my subconscience, the thought: 'Suppose real danger did lie in wait for me, suppose some horror undreamed of should cost me my life, or, worse, my reason, and none knew of this attempt of mine to lay bare a secret so carefully guarded.' I prolonged my rest sufficiently to climb from my window-sill, add a few lines to my carefully kept notes of events since I came here, put the bundle of papers in a long envelope, sealed it, and addressed it to Captain Percy Hesketh. Having done which, I remounted the window-sill and endeavoured to complete my task. There seemed some slight hesitancy in my movements, probably because I was now nearing the goal I had set out to win. I braced myself and started again.

How still it was, though the wind seemed to have risen a little. I could hear it moaning round the corner of the house, fitfully, as if a sudden summer storm was coming up. The hasp bent, gave way, and came in two in my fingers. Gently I moved the heavy shutter, an inch – it creaked – creaked, it seemed to me, loudly enough to wake the 'seven sleepers'. Did I imagine it, or did I hear a step overhead? I must hurry. I scrambled down, switched off all lights, climbed up again, and waited breathlessly. All was silent. Carefully I slid down on to the chair below me, and cautiously drew the shutter back a couple of inches more, then waited, – still all quiet – swung it wide – **CRACK!**

I dimly remember calling Percy, calling with my soul more than with my voice.

※

When next I remembered anything, it was to become conscious that I was in a bed in a bright, lofty room, a white-capped nurse was by my bed, holding a glass. Percy Hesketh was sitting by my side – a fact which gave me joy without an atom of surprise. It was as if I had expected him to be there.

'If you swallow this, you may say a few words,' said the nurse.

I swallowed it, and gave my hand into the warm grasp of my friend.

'John,' he said, 'I have your papers. Try to tell me what followed the cracking of the pane of glass.'

Feebly, haltingly, I tried, as I stumblingly, shudderingly, told him:

'Following the crack, the window splintered before my eyes, from top to bottom. I bent back, expecting to be covered with falling glass. It did not fall, but a pale, unearthly light illuminated it, lighting up to my horrified gaze, faces pressed against the window peering in upon me, but faces such as I never in life beheld. They were dark, almost black, with sunken, fiercely gleaming eyes, the cheekbones protruding, flesh sunken, looking almost like living skeletons, save for the skin which stretched tightly over the bones; anger, despair, ferocity, hunger, terror – all were depicted upon those awful faces. Through the cracked glass, deadly fumes began to steal, my room seemed cloudy, I was as if transfixed, unable to move, to call, to reach the lights, to do aught but stand staring, tremblingly. The faces pressed closer and yet closer; they reached the glass, it cracked again, and more fumes poured in; long arms (there seemed hundreds of them) reached wildly up, skinny hands, like those of skeletons, were held out as if to grasp. I tried to step back to get away from the window, as with a terrific crash, the glass fell in. Arms and hands stretched through, faces came nearer, nearer – I felt myself seized, held, lifted, drawn upwards.

I was on the window-sill again, held in an inexorable grip. I felt myself lifted through, felt the cold air on my face, was just able to discern the hurrying figures in the thick mist, and to know, beyond all doubt, that I was being borne swiftly, by claw-like hands, towards the Low Lawn.'

※

(Continued by Captain Percy Hesketh):

As my poor friend uttered his final words, he sank back into my arms in a state of unconsciousness, from which he never fully recovered, though in the many hours of watching over him, which were permitted by the Hospital Staff, I witnessed again and again the agony of mind and horror he passed through.

My painful task it was to bring the girl he loved to his bedside, to witness her grief, as he failed to remember her name, or face, all my life I shall remember that afternoon.

The sun was shining on the floor of the Ward – lighting up stray corners and patches, as I gently led Elsie Falconer to my friend's bedside. He was sitting up, laughingly pointing to the sunny patches, babbling about the funny light. He took no notice of the girl, beyond asking me: 'Why does that girl cry?'

'Do you know her, John?' I asked.

'No,' he replied, 'but she is pretty, tell her to look at the funny patches, then she will laugh. Take her away,' he added, 'she cries.'

Nurse led the weeping girl away, and I was thankful she had gone. One or another came to see him, it was always the same, no glimmer of memory seemed to return, though at times he would make a little more sensible remark.

One day he spoke to me, saying:

'Who was the old man who called me "John"? I'm not "John". I wish my brains wouldn't keep running round and round like a glass ball full of colours. I could listen to people if the glass ball would keep still,' he rambled on, and, uneasy and fearful, I called the Nurse. I saw by her face, it was the end, as, with sudden strength, he flung himself against the pillows, shouting as loudly as he could:

'Hark! there are the guns, at it again, are they – give me my rifle, I'll show them. Now boys, come on – over the top, and at 'em.' They were his last words, and the day after the following notice appeared in the papers: –

'On September 30th, at the Hospital, Singleton, Major John Longworth, MC, after four years' service, from shock, following an accident, aged 39.'

※

Some years later, I ventured to read through my late friend's notes of the experience which cost him his life, and to re-write them to the best of my ability, for this, I believe, was what he wished done.

It cost me an effort to re-visit the scenes of such horror, even after a lapse of years, but I desired also to learn, if I could, what really was the story of the place which my friend – bravely, though foolishly – gave his life to discover.

The landlord of the Village Inn gave me the story, as told to him by his grandfather, who knew the former tenants of the house. It seems the family had owned all the coal mines round, for generations, growing more and more wealthy as the years passed. The former owner, grandfather of my friend Francis, was an avaricious man, hard and grasping.

There was warning given, one day, of danger in the mine nearest to the house, warning that it was unsafe to permit the men to descend. Old Falconer, with his greed for money, preferred to risk men's lives rather than lose by delay, and ignored the warning – in fact had it contradicted – and the men went down – to their death – some four hundred of them. Old Falconer added to his crime, by refusing to spend money for rescue work, saying it was useless, that the earth had closed the mine completely. Apparently it had, though there were those who told of groans and shrieks coming from the bowels of the earth.

Falconer went on his way, disregarding all that was said, and in time the ground above the buried mine was cultivated, and turned into a lawn, below the level of the house.

When the old man died, he passed on the dire legacy to his sons, leaving them the whole of his fortune on condition that they lived in the house, making them promise that none on the premises would be out of the house after five in the evening, stating that the entombed men haunted the place.

None ever knew what the old man had seen or heard, but it is said that the miners had slowly starved to death, and could have been rescued at the time, but now haunted the place, intent upon finding victims to drag below with them. There had, said the landlord, been one or two sad happenings, but the worst trouble was the most recent, when a Major Longworth, MC, who was engaged to Miss Falconer, and who had been severely wounded in France, came to stay with the family, and did not rest until he had witnessed the whole of the awful happenings.

Mr Falconer was awakened in the night, it is said, by the sound of shattering glass, and rushed into Major Longworth's room in time to see him borne away towards the ill-fated lawn.

The big hound, kept on the place, was loosed, and dashed across the lawn, in which a vast crack had appeared. Mr Falconer described a furious fight for the body of Major Longworth, between the hound and something unseen, but that the hound succeeded in hauling the body out of the crack in the ground, into which it appeared to be slipping, dragging it, mauled and bleeding, back to the house.

'Major Longworth died in the hospital, here, sir,' went on my garrulous host, 'and Miss Falconer entered a nursing sisterhood.

'People say the house will collapse some day – have a look at it, sir, if you've time, before it gets late.'

I thanked him, and went my way. I found the house, desolate and dilapidated. The vast glass-house on one side of it, full of dead plants and broken chairs – dirty beyond description.

The gardens were a tangle of briars and weeds, the paths had become mere grass tracks. The Low Lawn, grown rank and rough, its greenness marred by a vast blackened crack right across it, as if a subsidence had taken place.

A brooding sense of mystery and disaster hangs over the place; nor do I hesitate to believe when I hear on all sides how the place is shunned, still less can I doubt my friend's written words of all that befell him in spite of all warnings to conform to orders, and not venture 'Outside the House.'

9 Florence Flannery

BY MARJORIE BOWEN (1924)

She who had been Florence Flannery noted with a careless eye the stains of wet on the dusty stairs, and with a glance ill used to observance of domesticities looked up for damp or dripping ceilings. The dim-walled staircase revealed nothing but more dust, yet this would serve as a peg for ill-humour to hang on, so Florence pouted.

'An ill, muddy place,' said she, who loved gilding and gimcracks and mirrors reflecting velvet chairs, and flounced away to the upper chamber, lifting frilled skirts contemptuously high.

Her husband followed; they had been married a week and there had never been any happiness in their wilful passion. Daniel Shute did not now look for any; in the disgust of this draggled homecoming he wondered what had induced him to marry the woman and how soon he would come to hate her.

As she stood in the big bedroom he watched her with dislike; her tawdry charms of vulgar prettiness had once been delightful to his dazed senses and muddled wits, but here, in his old home, washed by the fine Devon air, his sight was clearer and she appeared coarse as a poppy at the far end of August.

'Of course you hate it,' he said cynically, lounging with his big shoulders against one of the bedposts, his big hands in the pockets of his tight nankeen trousers, and his fair hair, tousled from the journey, hanging over his mottled face.

'It is not the place you boasted to have,' replied Florence, but idly, for she stood by the window and looked at the tiny leaded panes; the autumn sun gleaming sideways on this glass, picked out a name scratched there:

Florence Flannerye. Born 1500.

'Look here,' cried the woman, excited, 'this should be my ancestress!'

She slipped off a huge diamond ring she wore and scratched underneath the writing the present year, '1800.'

Daniel Shute came and looked over her shoulder.

'That reads strange – "Born 1500" – as if you would say died 1800,' he remarked. 'Well, I don't suppose she had anything to do with you, my charmer, yet she brought you luck, for it was remembering this name here made me notice you when I heard what you were called.'

He spoke uncivilly, and she responded in the same tone.

'Undervalue what is your own, Mr Shute. There was enough for me to choose from, I can swear!'

'Enough likely gallants,' he grinned, 'not so many likely husbands, eh?'

He slouched away, for, fallen as he was, it stung him that he had married a corybante of the opera, an unplaced, homeless, nameless creature for all he knew, for he could never quite believe that 'Florence Flannery' was her real name.

Yet that name had always attracted him; it was so queer that he should meet a real woman called Florence Flannery when one of the earliest of his recollections was tracing that name over with a curious finger in the old diamond pane.

'You have never told me who she was,' said Mrs Shute.

'Who knows? Three hundred years ago, m'dear. There are some old wives' tales, of course.'

He left the great bedroom and she followed him doggedly downstairs.

'Is this your fine manor, Mr Shute? And these your noble grounds? And how am I to live here, Mr Shute, who left the gaieties of London for you?'

Her voice, shrill and edged, followed him down the stairs

and into the vast dismantled drawing-room where they paused, facing each other like things caught in a trap, which is what they were.

For he had married her because he was a ruined man, driven from London by duns, and a drunken man who dreaded lonely hours and needed a boon companion to pledge him glass for glass, and a man of coarse desires who had bought with marriage what he was not rich enough to buy with money, and she had married him because she was past her meridian and saw no more conquests ahead and also was in love with the idea of being a gentlewoman and ruling in the great grand house by the sea – which was how she had thought of Shute Manor.

And a great grand house it had been, but for twenty years it had been abandoned by Daniel Shute, and stripped and mortgaged to pay for his vices, so that now it stood barren and desolate, empty and tarnished, and only a woman with love in her heart could have made a home of it; never had there been love in Florence Flanncry's heart, only greed and meanness.

Thus these two faced each other in the gaunt room with the monstrous chandelier hanging above them wrapped in a dusty brown holland bag, the walls festooned with cobwebs, the pale wintry sunshine showing the thick dust on the unpolished boards.

'I can never live here!' cried Mrs Shute. There was a touch of panic in her voice and she lifted her hands to her heart with a womanly gesture of grief.

The man was touched by a throb of pity; he did not himself expect the place to be so dilapidated. Some kind of a rascally agent had been looking after it for him, and he supposed some effort would have been made for his reception.

Florence saw his look of half-sullen shame and urged her point.

'We can go back, cannot we?' she said, with the rich drop in her voice, so useful for coaxing; 'back to London and the house in Baker Street? All the old friends and old pleasures, Mr Shute, and a dashing little cabriolet to go round the park?'

'Curse it!' he answered, chagrined. 'I haven't the money, Flo; I haven't the damned money!' She heard the ring of bitter truth in his voice and the atrocious nature of the deception he had practiced on her overwhelmed her shallow understanding.

'You mean you've got no money, Mr Shute?' she screamed.

'Not enough for London, m'dear.'

'And I've to live in this filthy barn?'

'It has been good enough for my people, Mrs Shute,' he answered grimly. 'For all the women of my family, gentlewomen, all of 'em with quarterings, and it will be good enough for you, m'dear, so none of your Bartholomew Fair airs and graces.'

She was cornered, and a little afraid of him; he had been drinking at the last place where they stopped to water the horses and she knew how he could be when he was drunk; she remembered that she was alone with him and what a huge man he was.

So she crept away and went down into the vast kitchens where an old woman and a girl were preparing a meal.

The sight of this a little heartened Mrs Shute; in her frilled taffetas and long ringlets she sat down by the great open hearth, moving her hands to show the firelight flashing in her rings and shifting her petticoats so that the girl might admire her kid shoes.

'I'll take a cordial to stay my strength,' she said, 'for I've come a long way and find a sour welcome at the end of it, and that'll turn any woman's blood.'

The old dame smiled, knowing her type well enough; for even in a village you may find women like this.

So she brought Mrs Shute some damson wine and a plate of biscuits, and the two women became friendly enough and gossiped in the dim candle-lit kitchen while Daniel Shute wandered about his old home, even his corrupt heart feeling many a pang to see the places of his childhood desolate, the walks overgrown, the trees felled, the arbours closed, the fountains dried, and all the spreading fields about fenced by strangers.

The November moon was high in a misted space of open heaven by the time he reached the old carp pond.

Dead weeds tangled over the crumbling, moss-grown stone, trumpery and slime coated the dark waters.

'I suppose the carp are all dead?' said Mr Shute.

He had not been aware that he spoke aloud, and was surprised to hear himself answered.

'I believe there are some left, esquire.'

Mr Shute turned sharply and could faintly discern the figure of a man sitting on the edge of the pond so that it seemed as if his legs half dangled in the black water.

'Who are you?' asked Daniel Shute quickly.

'I'm Paley, sir, who looks after the grounds.'

'You do your work damned badly,' replied the other, irritated.

'It is a big place, esquire, for one man to work.'

He seemed to stoop lower and lower as if at any moment he would slip into the pond; indeed, in the half dark, it seemed to Mr Shute as if he was already half in the water; yet, on this speech, he moved and showed that he was but bending over the sombre depths of the carp pond.

The moonlight displayed him as a drab man of middling proportions with slow movements and a large languid eye which glittered feebly in the pale light; Mr Shute had an impression that this eye looked at him sideways as if it was set at the side of the man's head, but soon saw that this was an illusion.

'Who engaged you?' he asked acidly, hating the creature.

'Mr Tregaskis, the agent,' replied the man in what appeared to be a thick foreign accent or with some defect of speech, and walked away into the wintry undergrowth.

Mr Shute returned home grumbling; in the grim parlour Mr Tregaskis was waiting for him – a red Cornishman, who grinned at his employer's railings. He knew the vices of Mr Shute, and the difficulties of Mr Shute, and he had seen Mrs Shute in the kitchen deep in maudlin gossip with old Dame Chase and the idiot-faced girl, drinking the alcoholic country wine till it spilled from her shaking fingers on to her taffeta skirt.

So he assumed a tone of noisy familiarity that Mr Shute was too sunken to resent; the last of the old squire's Oporto was sent for and the men drank themselves on to terms of easy good-fellowship.

At the last, when the candles were guttering, the bottles empty, and the last log's ashes on the hearth, Mr Shute asked who was the creature Paley he had found hanging over the carp pond.

Mr Tregaskis told him, but the next morning Mr Shute could not recollect what he had said; the whole evening had, in his recollection, an atmosphere of phantasmagoria; but he thought that the agent had said that Paley was a deserted sailor who had wandered up from Plymouth and taken the work without pay, a peculiar individual who lived in a wattled hut that he had made himself, and on food he caught with his own hands.

His sole explanation of himself was that he had waited for something a long time and was still waiting for it; useful he was, Mr Tregaskis had said, and it was better to leave him alone.

All this Mr Shute remembered vaguely, lying in the great

bed staring at the pale sun glittering on the name 'Florence Flannery' scratched on the window with the two dates.

It was late in the autumnal morning, but his wife still lay beside him, heavily asleep, with her thick heavy chestnut hair tossed over the pillow and her full bosom panting, the carnation of her rounded face flushed and stained, the coarse diamonds glowing on her plump hands, the false pearls slipping round her curved throat.

Daniel Shute sat up in bed and looked down at her prone sleep.

'Who is she? And where does she come from?' he wondered. He had never cared to find out, but now his ignorance of all appertaining to his wife annoyed him.

He shook her bare shoulder till she yawned out of her heavy sleep.

'Who are you, Flo?' he asked. 'You must know something about yourself.'

The woman blinked up at him, drawing her satin bedgown round her breast.

'I was in the opera, wasn't I?' she answered lazily. 'I never knew my people.'

'Came out of an orphanage or the gutter, I suppose?' he returned bitterly.

'Maybe.'

'But your name?' he insisted. 'That is never your name, "Florence Flannery"?'

'I've never known another,' she responded indifferently.

'You're not Irish.'

'I don't know, Mr Shute. I've been in many countries and seen many strange things.'

He laughed; he had heard some of her experiences.

'You've seen so much and been in so many places I don't know how you've ever got it all into one life.'

'I don't know myself. It's all rather like a dream and the most dreamlike of all is to be lying here looking at my own name written three hundred years ago.'

She moved restlessly and slipped from the bed, a handsome woman with troubled eyes.

"Tis the drink brings the dreams, m'dear,' said Mr Shute. 'I had some dreams last night of a fellow named Paley I met by the carp pond.'

'You were drinking in the parlour,' she retorted scornfully.

'And you in the kitchen, m'dear.'

Mrs Shute flung a fringed silk shawl, the gift of an Indian nabob, round her warm body and dropped, shivering and yawning, into one of the warm tapestry chairs.

'Who was this Florence Flannery?' she asked idly.

'I told you no one knows. An Irish girl born in Florence, they said, when I was a child and listened to beldam's gossip. Her mother a Medici, m'dear, and he a groom! And she came here, the trollop, with some young Shute who had been travelling in Italy – picked her up and brought her home, like I've brought you!'

'He didn't marry her?' asked Mrs Shute indifferently.

'More sense,' said her husband coarsely. 'I'm the first fool of me family. She was a proper vixen. John Shute took her on his voyages; he'd a ship and went discovering. They talk yet at Plymouth of how she would sit among the parrots and the spices and the silks when the ship came into Plymouth Hoe.'

'Ah, the good times!' sighed Mrs Shute, 'when men were men and paid a good price for their pleasures!'

'You've fetched your full market value, Mrs Shute,' he answered, yawning in the big bed.

'I'd rather be John Shute's woman than your wife,' she returned.

'What do you know of him?'

'I saw his portrait on the back stairs last night. Goody Chase showed me. A noble man with a clear eye and great arms to fight and love with.'

'He used 'em to push Florence Flannery out with,' grinned Mr Shute, 'if half the tales are true. On one of their voyages they picked up a young Portuguese who took the lady's fancy and she brought him back to Shute Court.'

'And what was the end of it?'

'I know no more, save that she was flung out, as I'd like to fling you out, my beauty!' foamed Mr Shute with gusty violence.

His wife laughed and got up discordantly.

'I'll tell the rest of the tale. She got tired of her new love, and he wasn't a Portuguese, but an Indian, or partly, and his name was D'Ailey, Daly the people called it here. On one voyage she told John Shute about him, and he was marooned on a lonely island in the South Seas – tied up to a great, great stone image of a god, burning hot in the tropic sun. He must have been a god of fishes for there was nothing else near that island but monstrous fish.'

'Who told you this?' demanded Mr Shute. 'Old Dame Chase, with her lies? I never heard of this before.'

"Tis the story,' resumed his wife. 'The last she saw of him was his bound figure tied tight, tight, to the gaping, grinning idol while she sat on the poop as the ship – the *Phoenix* – sailed away. He cursed her and called on the idol to let her live till he was avenged on her – he was of the breed, or partly of the breed, that these gods love, and Florence Flannery was afraid, afraid, as she sailed away – '

'Goody Chase in her cups!' sneered Mr Shute. 'And what's the end of your story?'

'There's no end,' said the woman sullenly. 'John Shute cast her off, for the bad luck that dogged him, and what became of her I don't know.'

'It's an ugly tale and a stupid tale,' grumbled Daniel Shute with a groan as he surveyed the bleak chill weather beyond the lattice panes. 'Get down and see what's to eat in the house and what's to drink in the cellar, and if that rogue Tregaskis is there send him up to me.'

Mrs Shute rose and pulled fiercely at the long wool-embroidered bell-rope so that the rusty bell jangled violently.

'What'll you do when the wine is all drunk and the boon companions have cleared out your pockets?' she asked wildly. 'Do your own errands, Mr Shute.'

He flung out of bed with a pretty London oath, and she remained huddled in the chair while he dressed and after he had left her, wringing her hands now and then and wailing under her breath, till Dame Chase came up with a posset and helped her to dress. The sight of her dishevelled trunks restored some of Mrs Shute's spirits; she pulled out with relish her furbelows and flounces, displaying to Goody Chase's amazed admiration the last fashions of Paris and London, mingling her display with fond reminiscences of gilded triumphs.

'Maybe you'd be surprised to learn that Mr Shute isn't my first husband,' she said, tossing her head.

The fat old woman winked.

'I'd be more surprised, m'lady, to learn he was your last.'

Mrs Shute laughed grossly, but her spirits soon fell; kneeling on the floor with her tumbled finery in her lap, she stared out through the window on which her name was written at the tossing bare boughs, the chill sky, the dry flutter of the last leaves.

'I'll never get away,' she said mournfully, 'the place bodes me no good. I've had the malaria in me time, Mrs Chase, in one of those cursed Italian swamps and it affected me memory; there's much I can't place together and much I recall brokenly – dreams and fevers, Mrs Chase.'

'The drink, m'lady.'

'No,' returned the kneeling woman fiercely. 'Wasn't the drink taken to drown those dreams and fevers? I wish I could tell you half I know – there's many a fine tale in me head, but when I begin to speak it goes!'

She began to rock to and fro, lamenting.

'To think of the fine times I've had with likely young men drinking me health in me slipper and the little cabriolet in Paris and the walks in the Prater outside Vienna. So pleasant you would hardly believe!'

'You'll settle down, m'lady, like women do.'

Indeed, Mrs Shute seemed to make some attempt at 'settling down'; there was something piteous in the despairing energy with which she set to work to make her life tolerable; there was a suite of rooms lined with faded watered green silk that she took for her own and had cleaned and furnished with what she could gather from the rest of the house – old gilt commodes and rococo chairs and threadbare panels of tapestries and chipped vases of Saxe or Lunéville, one or two pastel portraits that the damp had stained, together with some tawdry trifles she had brought in her own baggage.

She employed Mr Tregaskis to sell her big diamond in Plymouth and bought pale blue satin hangings for her bedroom and spotted muslin for her bed, a carpet wreathed with roses, a gaudy dressing-table and phials of perfume, opopanax, frangipane, musk, potent, searing, to dissipate, she said, the odours of must and mildew.

Arranging these crude splendours was her sole occupation. There were no neighbours in the lonely valley and Mr Shute fell into melancholy and solitary drinking; he hung on to his existence as just more tolerable than a debtor's prison, but the fury with which he met his fate expressed itself in curses awful to hear. Such part of the estate as still belonged to him he treated with complex contempt; Mr Tregaskis continued to supervise some rough farming and the man Paley worked in the garden; taciturn, solitary and sullen, he made an ill impression on Mr Shute, yet he cost nothing and did some labour, as carrying up the firewood to the house and clearing away some of the thickets and dying weeds and vast clumps of nettles and docks.

Mrs Shute met him for the first time by the carp pond; she was tricked out in a white satin pelisse edged with fur and a big bonnet, and wandered forlornly in the neglected paths. Paley was sitting on the edge of the carp pond, looking intently into the murky depths.

'I'm the new mistress,' said Mrs Shute, 'and I'll thank you to keep better order in the place.'

Paley looked up at her with his pale eyes.

'Shute Court isn't what it was,' he said, 'there is a lot of work to do.'

'You seem to spend a power of time by the pond,' she replied. 'What are you here for?'

'I'm waiting for something,' he said. 'I'm putting in time, Mrs Shute.'

'A sailor, I hear?' she said curiously, for the draggled nondescript man in his greenish-black clothes was difficult to place; he had a peculiar look of being boneless, without shoulders or hips, one slope slipping into another as if there was no framework under his flabby flesh.

'I've been at sea,' he answered, 'like yourself, Mrs Shute.'

She laughed coarsely.

'I would I were at sea again,' she replied; 'this is horror to me.'

'Why do you stay?'

'I'm wondering. It seems that I can't get away, the same as I couldn't help coming,' a wail came into her voice. 'Must I wait till Mr Shute has drunk himself to death?'

The wind blew sharp across the pond, cutting little waves in the placid surface, and she who had been Florence Flannery shuddered in the bite of it and turned away and went muttering up the path to the desolate house.

Her husband was in the dirty parlour playing at bezique with Mr Tregaskis and she flared in upon them.

'Why don't you get rid of that man Paley? I hate him. He does no work – Mrs Chase told me that he always sits by the carp pond and to-day I saw him – ugh!'

'Paley's all right, Mrs Shute,' replied Tregaskis, 'he does more work than you think.'

'Why does he stay?'

'He's waiting for a ship that's soon due in Plymouth.'

'Send him off,' insisted Mrs Shute. 'Isn't the place melancholic enough without you having that sitting about?'

Her distaste and disgust of the man seemed to amount to a panic, and her husband, whose courage was snapped by the drink, was infected by her fear.

'When did this fellow come?' he demanded.

'About a week before you did. He'd tramped up from Plymouth.'

'We've only his word for that,' replied Mr Shute with drunken cunning; 'maybe he's a Bow Street runner sent by one of those damned creditors! You're right, Flo, I don't like the wretch – he's watching me, split him! I'll send him off.'

Mr Tregaskis shrugged as Daniel Shute staggered from his chair.

'The man's harmless, sir; half-witted if you like, but useful.'

Still Mr Shute dragged on his greatcoat with the capes and followed his wife out into the grey garden.

The carp pond was not near the house, and by the time that they had reached it a dull twilight had fallen in the cold and heavy air.

The great trees were quite bare now and flung a black tracing of forlorn branches against the bleak evening sky;

patches and clumps of dead weeds obstructed every path and alley; by the carp pond showed the faint outline of a blind statue crumbling beneath the weight of dead mosses.

Paley was not there.

'He'll be in his hut,' said Mr Shute, 'sleeping or spying – the ugly old devil. I'll send him off.'

The dead oyster white of Mrs Shute's pelisse gleamed oddly as she followed her husband through the crackling undergrowth.

There, in the thickening twilight, they found the hut, a queer arrangement of wattles cunningly interwoven in which there was no furniture whatever, nothing but a bare protection from the wind and weather.

Paley was not there.

'I'll find him,' muttered Mr Shute, 'if I have to stay out all night.'

For his half-intoxicated mind had fixed on this stranger as the symbol of all his misfortunes and perhaps the avenger of all his vices.

His wife turned back, for her pelisse was being caught on the undergrowth; she went moodily towards the carp pond.

A moment later a sharp shriek from her brought Mr Shute plunging back to her side. She was standing in a queer bent attitude, pointing with a shaking plump hand to the murky depths of the pond.

'The wretch! He's drowned himself!' she screamed.

Mr Shute's worn-out nerves reacted to her ignoble panic; he clutched her arm as he gazed in the direction of her finger; there was something dark in the shallower side of the pond, something large and dark, with pale flat eyes that glittered malevolently.

'Paley!' gasped Mr Shute.

He bent closer in amazed horror, then broke into tremulous laughter.

"Tis a fish,' he declared; 'one of the old carp.'

Mrs Shute indeed now perceived that the monstrous creature in the water was a fish; she could make out the wide gaping jaw, tall spines shadowing in the murk, and a mottled skin of deadly yellow and dingy white.

'It's looking at me,' she gasped. 'Kill it, kill it, the loathsome wretch!'

'It's – it's – too big,' stammered Mr Shute, but he picked up a stone to hurl; the huge fish, as if aware of his intentions, slipped away into the murky depths of the pond, leaving a sluggish ripple on the surface.

Daniel Shute now found his courage.

'Nothing but an old carp,' he repeated. 'I'll have the thing caught.'

Mrs Shute began to weep and wring her hands. Her husband dragged her roughly towards the house, left her there, took a lantern, and accompanied now by Mr Tregaskis returned in search of Paley.

This time they found him sitting in his usual place by the side of the pond. Mr Shute had now changed his mind about sending him away; he had a muddled idea that he would like the pond watched, and who was to do this if not Paley?

'Look here, my man,' he said, 'there's a great carp in this pond – a very big, black old carp.'

'They live for hundreds of years,' said Paley. 'But this isn't a carp.'

'You know about it, then?' demanded Mr Shute.

'I know about it.'

'Well, I want you to catch it – kill it. Watch till you do. I loathe it – ugh!'

'Watch the pond?' protested Mr Tregaskis, who held the lantern and was chilled and irritable. 'Damme, esquire, what can the thing do? It can't leave the water.'

'I wouldn't,' muttered Mr Shute, 'promise you that.'

'You're drunk,' said the other coarsely.

But Mr Shute insisted on his point.

'Watch the pond, Paley, watch it day and night till you get that fish.'

'I'll watch,' answered Paley, never moving from his huddled position.

The two men went back to the desolate house. When Mr Shute at last staggered upstairs he found his wife with half a dozen candles lit, crouching under the tawdry muslin curtains with which she had disfigured the big bed.

She clutched a rosary that she was constantly raising to her lips as she muttered ejaculations.

Mr Shute lurched to the bedside.

'I didn't know that you were a Papist, Flo,' he sneered.

She looked up at him.

'That story's got me,' she whispered, 'the man tied up to the fish god – the curse – and he following her – tracking her down for three hundred years, till she was hounded back to the old place where they'd loved.'

Daniel Shute perceived that she had been drinking, and sank into a chair.

'Goody Chase's gossip,' he answered, yawning, 'and that damned ugly fish. I've set Paley to catch him – to watch the pond till he does.'

She looked at him sharply, and appeared relieved.

'Anyhow, what's it to do with you?' he continued. 'You ain't the jade who left the man on the island!' He laughed crudely.

Mrs Shute sank down on her pillows.

'As long as the pond is watched,' she murmured, 'I don't mind.'

But during the night she tossed and panted in a delirium, talking of great ships with strange merchandise, of lonely islands amid blazing seas, of mighty stone gods rearing up to the heavens, of a man in torture and a curse following a woman who sailed away, till her husband shook her and left her alone, sleeping on a couch in the dreary parlour.

The next day he spoke to Mrs Chase.

'Between your news and your lies you've turned your mistress's head. Good God! she is like a maniac with your parcel of follies!'

But Goody Chase protested that she had told her nothing.

'She told me that story, esquire, and said she had found it in an old book. What did I know of Florence Flannery? Many a time you've asked me about her when you were a child and I've had no answer to give you – what did I know save she was a hussy who disgraced Shute Court?'

At this Daniel Shute vehemently demanded of his wife where she had got the tales which she babbled about, but the woman was sullen and heavy and would tell him nothing; all the day she remained thus, but when the few hours of wintry light were over she fell again into unbridled terror, gibbering like a creature deprived of reason, beating her breast, kissing the rosary, and muttering, '*Mea culpâ, mea culpâ, mea maximâ culpâ!*'

Mr Shute was not himself in any state to endure this; he left his wife to herself and made Tregaskis sleep with him for company in another room.

Winter froze the bleak countryside; Paley kept guard by the pond and the Shutes somehow dragged on an intolerable existence in the deserted house.

In the daytime Mrs Shute revived a little and would even prink herself out in her finery and gossip with Mrs Chase over the vast log fire, but the nights always found her smitten with terror, shivering with cowardly apprehension; and the object of all her nightmare dread was the fish she had seen in the pond.

'It can't leave the water,' they told her, and she always answered:

'The first night I was here I saw wet on the stairs.'

'My God, my God!' Daniel Shute would say, 'this is like living with someone sentenced to death.'

'Get a doctor over from Plymouth,' suggested Mr Tregaskis.

But Mr Shute would not, for fear of being betrayed to his creditors.

'Better rot here than in the Fleet,' he swore.

'Then take her away – and keep her from the bottle.'

The wretched husband could do neither of these things; he had no money and no influence over Mrs Shute. He was indeed indifferent to her sufferings save in so far as they reacted on him and ever accustomed him to the spectacle of her breakdown; he knew it was not really strange that a woman such as she was should collapse under conditions such as these, and his life was already so wretched that he cared little for added horrors.

He began to find a strange comfort in the man Paley, who, taciturn, slow and queer, yet did his work and watched the pond with an admirable diligence.

One night in the blackest time of the year, the bitter dark nights before Christmas, the shrieks of Mrs Shute brought her husband cursing up the stairs.

Her door was unbolted and she sat up in bed, displaying, in the light of his snatched-up taper, some red marks on her arm.

'Let him kill me and done with it,' she jabbered.

Mr Tregaskis came pushing in and caught rudely hold of her arm.

'She's done it herself,' he cried; 'those are the marks of her own teeth.'

But Mrs Shute cried piteously:

'He came flopping up the stairs, he broke the bolts; he jumped on the bed! Oh! oh! oh! Isn't this the bed, the very bed I slept in then – and didn't he used to creep into this room when John Shute was away?'

'Still thinking of that damned fish,' said Mr Tregaskis, 'and it's my belief you neither of you saw it at all, esquire – that man Paley has been watching, and he's seen nothing.'

Mr Shute bit his fingernails, looking down on the writhing figure of his wife.

'Light all the candles, can't you?' he said. 'I'll stay with the poor fool to-night.'

While Mr Tregaskis obeyed he went to the door and looked out, holding his taper high.

There were pools of wet and a long trail of slime down the dusty, neglected stairs.

He called Mr Tregaskis.

'Ugh!' cried the Cornishman, then, 'It's from Goody Chase's water crock.'

On the following windy morning Mr Shute went out, shivering in the nipping air, to the carp pond.

'I don't want another night like last,' he said. 'You'll sleep across my wife's door – she thinks that cursed carp is after her –'

Then, at the gross absurdity of what he said, he laughed miserably.

'This is a pretty pantomime I'm playing,' he muttered.

A horrid curiosity drove him up to look at his wife.

She sat between the draggled muslin curtains hugging her knees in the tumbled bed; a wretched fire flickered wanly in the chill depths of the vast room; a wind blew swift and remote round the window on which was scratched the name of Florence Flannery.

Mr Shute shivered.

'I must get you away,' he said, stirred above his fears for himself; 'this is a damned place – the Fleet would be better, after all.'

She turned lustreless eyes on him.

'I can't get away,' she said dully. 'I've come here to die – don't you see it on that window – "Died 1800"?'

He crossed the floor and peered at the scratching on the glass. Someone had indeed added the word 'died' before the last date.

'These are the tricks of a Bedlamite,' he said nervously. 'Do you think there was only one Florence Flannery?'

'And do you think,' she returned harshly, 'that there were two?'

She looked so awful crouched up in bed with her hanging hair, her once plump face fallen in the cheeks, her soiled satin gown open over her labouring breast, her whole air and expression so agonized, so malevolent, so dreadful, that Daniel Shute passed his hand over his eyes as if to brush away a vision of unsubstantial horror.

He was shaken by an hallucination of light-headedness; he appeared to enter another world, in which many queer things were possible.

'What are you?' he asked uneasily. 'He's been after you for nearly three hundred years? Aren't you punished enough?'

'Oh, oh!' moaned the woman. 'Keep him out! Keep him out!'

'I'll put Paley at the door to-night,' muttered Mr Shute.

He crept out of the horrible chamber; he now detested his wife beyond all reason, yet somehow he felt impelled to save her from the invincible furies who were pursuing her in so gruesome a fashion.

'She's a lunatic,' said Mr Tregaskis brusquely. 'You'll have to keep her shut in that room – it's not difficult to account for – with the life she's led and this place and the coincidence of the names.'

The first snow of the year began to fall that night, sullen flakes struggling in the coils of the leaping wind that circled round Shute Court.

In the last glimmer of daylight Paley came to take up his post.

Drab, silent, with his sloping shoulders and nondescript clothes, he went slowly upstairs and sat down outside Mrs Shute's door.

'He seems to know the way,' remarked Daniel Shute.

'Don't you know he works in the house?' retorted Mr Tregaskis.

The two men slept, as usual, in the parlour, on stiff horsehair couches bundled up with pillows and blankets; the litter of their supper was left on the table and they piled the fire up with logs before going to sleep. Mr Shute's nerves were in no state to permit him to risk waking up in the dark.

The wind dropped and the steady downdrift of the soft snow filled the blackness of the bitter night.

As the grandfather clock struck three Daniel Shute sat up and called to his companion.

'I've been thinking in my dreams,' he said, with chattering teeth. 'Is it Paley, or Daley? You know the name was D'Ailey.'

'Shut up, you fool,' returned the agent fiercely; but he then raised himself on his elbow, for a hoarse, bitter scream, followed by some yelled words in a foreign language tore through the stillness.

'The mad woman,' said Mr Tregaskis; but Daniel Shute dragged the clothes up to his chattering teeth.

'I'm not going up,' he muttered. 'I'm not going up!'

Mr Tregaskis dragged on his trousers and flung a blanket over his shoulders and so, lighting a taper at the big fire, went up the gaunt stairs to Mrs Shute's room. The glimmering beams of the rushlight showed him tracks of wet again on the dirty boards.

'Goody Chase with her crocks and possets,' he murmured; then louder, 'Paley! Paley!'

There was no one outside Mrs Shute's door, which hung open. Mr Tregaskis entered.

She who had been Florence Flannery lay prone on her tawdry couch; the deep wounds that had slain her appeared to have been torn by savage teeth; she looked infinitely old, shrivelled and detestable.

Mr Tregaskis backed on to the stairs, the light lurching round him from the shaking of his taper, when Mr Shute came bustling up out of the darkness.

'Paley's gone,' whispered Mr Tregaskis dully.

'I saw him go,' gibbered Mr Shute, 'as I ventured to the door – by the firelight; a great fish slithering away with blood on his jaws.'

10 Young Magic

BY HELEN SIMPSON (1925)

When Viola was very little she used to play by herself exactly as a cat does. She would fix her eyes upon an invisible adversary, stalk him, and fly from him when her manoeuvres could not take him unawares. It was a very good game to play in a garden, especially in autumn when the taller flowers came out, delphiniums, and a strong kind of white daisy; but curiously enough in the garden it was never a success. Viola used always to hope that one day it would be. She used to run out of the house pretending not to care, not looking behind, and would hide, allowing some part of her dress to show in a most alluring way. It was no use, though sometimes she caught a grown-up, with whom it was no fun to play, for such persons showed a long way off, and trod heavily, and were awkward at dodging. The grown-ups considered her a good child, always amusing herself and not noisy. They thought it was perhaps a little odd, the way in which she talked and nodded to flowers or patches of shadow, and they used to question her.

'Is that a fairy you're playing with? Oh, how nice! What is her name?'

Viola would stare at them, realising that some answer was required if she were not to be rebuked for sulkiness; and when the enquirer asked again, wheedling, for the fairy's name she would contemptuously answer,

'Binns.'

And go on with whatever she was doing. This always caused laughter, and as a rule put the grown-ups to silence. Persistent ones, however, would keep at it.

'And what is Binns like?'

'Thin.'

'Oh! And what does she do?'

At first Viola used to ignore this question, but when she found that it meant being told not to be silly she invented an occupation for Binns. She hated more completely than anything in her experience to be told she was silly. So she would answer,

'Washing.'

And sometimes when people were looking she would pretend to be washing, so that they would believe her when the inevitable question and answer came along. But it was all the purest invention. She did not like the way other people came trampling into her mind, just as they often walked unheeding and made dull marks on a nice-shaped patch of dewy grass she had been treasuring since morning. And they would have said she was silly if she told them truthfully that there was no Binns, only a feeling, and this feeling was not a she, and that he did no washing and was not thin; he was rather soft and big. She did not know what he looked like. He played with her only in the house. Perhaps for that reason Viola lost touch with him in summer. She liked to be a prince in summer, and her throne was a tree that had split in two low down, and was easily to be climbed. In the rounded fork she would sit with a sword tucked into her leather belt, and sometimes other trappings, a piece of gold braid round her head or a few bits of ribbon pinned on for medals. She was not often a prince in the house, and never wore decorations there, because if she did somebody was sure to comment. She was sure to be asked where she had got the braid from, and if she were playing soldiers. She knew when they asked in that voice and smiled in that way that they thought she was being silly, even when they said quite kindly,

'Having a lovely game, darling? Don't get in Annie's way, dear.'

So she was only royal in the garden; in that special part of the garden where nobody ever bothered to come, and where she was not watched. She would make tremendous speeches there, standing up in the fork with her left hand on the cross hilt of the sword to make it stick out; her subjects all adored her, because she was so very noble. Once or twice she allowed herself to die in battle, and lay with her arms stretched out on the daisies, that felt damp but were only cool, listening to the sad things her people said as they passed. They all thought that there could never have been a prince so brave or so good. They said,

'What we'll do now I don't know, I'm sure.'

And Viola listened, every moment inventing new and more splendid things for them to say about her. When she had to go in to her dinner – and she knew, when the shadow of the big branch got as far as the fence, that it was about time to go in – the contrast was too great. It was too big a distance to be bridged in a moment. There had to be a period of readjustment, of coming back, and during this period she was silent and aloof, paying no attention to the small talk of the table; this habit, when she neglected to answer questions immediately addressed to her, sometimes led to trouble, accusations of sulkiness; or nurse would say, from sheer caprice, when she had finished and wanted to go out again,

'Now you don't want to go off by yourself in the garden. Stay about here where I can see you. Don't go running off.'

It made Viola angry to be told she didn't want to go off by herself when she did. Often she wondered if it would count as a lie against nurse when she died, for it was as untrue as possible on the face of it. In her more savage moods she hoped that it would count, and that Jesus would say to nurse when she wanted to get into Heaven,

'What about all those lies you told Viola?' For it was one of nurse's favourite expressions. It cropped up in relation to almost every impulse of Viola's life.

'You don't want to look like those little dirty children. You don't want to be always running wild in the garden. You don't want that old tin soldier in bed with you.'

If nurse had had her way, or what she liked to pretend was her way, Viola would have been very nearly always in the house; but in fact nurse, though she scolded and bullied a little for form's sake, was glad enough not to have Viola underfoot and always permitted the garden in the end, so that during the long days, of which only the sunny hours remained afterwards in her memory, Viola was happy by herself.

But towards the end of October things would begin to happen which she could recognise, and which meant that there was to be no more summer. One day as she sat in her throne a yellow leaf would fall on to her knee, half-a-dozen others following; she would look round her and see that all the trees were losing their green. Then the branches would begin to lash about and sweep the air, making a wind that sent the poor leaves running on the grass, lost and homeless. When they were quiet again the thick shade that had lain like an island under her tree would be pierced with holes when there was sun to show them; looking up, the sky showed clearly in a hundred places. At last no leaves would be left at all, but only the branches, ugly against the sky, like lace without any proper pattern, or cat's-cradle when it came very tight and muddled towards the end. The prince game ended with the green year, and the warm free days gave place to an infinite time without colours, or any outdoor play except the official walk before tea. The house was big, but there was nothing much to do in it except watch cook now and then. Viola could not read, for her mother always thought it so unwise to force children. In the winter which held her ninth birthday she began seriously to play with Binns.

These games were something quite different; not in themselves, for there were still fairy tales to be acted in which she was the prince; but this indoors winter prince was a more romantic figure, dressed like one of the photographs in the drawing-room, with a shining breastplate and a long-tailed helmet. People did not weep over him; he had no people, and no need of them with all his magic things, the table that was covered with food each time he rapped on it, and the sword that could kill twenty enemies at a blow. He was less real than the other prince, but he went better with an audience she could not see or touch, and which did not interfere. She knew Binns was there by the sounds he made, and by the feeling he brought with him, which nurse always said was a draught. At first he could only make very little noises, like the cracks that furniture makes in the night. Viola knew that it was not the furniture because the sounds came from the air, quite near her; as they increased in strength she began to understand what he said; and at the end of a month of rain, when she had had to stay in the house nearly all the time, she knew all his meanings. His noises did not make sense if you thought of them as words; he could not give a plain answer to a question, yes or no, so many cracks for each. One sort of crack meant that he was pleased, another sort meant that he wanted her to go on playing, and after a time he learnt to make four or five cracks close together, like a laugh.

The first time he did this she was frightened. Nurse was quite near, just at the door, and the cracks were so deliberate, not like anything that furniture could do. Nurse heard, for she turned her head suddenly, and said that it was time they had somebody to see to those loose boards. Then she went out, and Viola told Binns not to do it again, but he was proud of his achievement and would not keep quiet. Fortunately nurse had gone. Viola tried all sorts of ways of making that sound, so that she could pretend, if anyone else heard, that it was her own. She tried bending a nice round stick that she had found and peeled, but it had gone dry and soon it broke. She tried with a cotton-reel against the leg of a chair, but that made a dull, woolly sound. The problem was not solved until the afternoon of her birthday party, when she found in a cracker a black piece of tin shaped like a beetle, which, if its wings were pressed down towards its stomach, gave out a sound exactly like Binns' laugh. The grown-up who had pulled the cracker with her said,

'Oh! It's only a nasty old locust. Never mind, I'll find you one with something pretty in it.'

While she was away Viola dropped the locust right inside her clothes, where it felt cold for a moment before her skin warmed it. She was afraid that Binns might come to the party and crack at the grown-ups. However, he stayed away, and she went to sleep with it under her pillow, relieved from the fear that they might be discovered and somehow not allowed to play any more.

The locust answered its purpose well for a day or two, until the morning when nurse kept her in the sewing-room trying on dresses and underclothes. There was no need for her to stay. Most of the time nurse was occupied with the sewing-machine, a reluctant thing that always clucked angrily before it began to make its regular thudding buzz. Viola was interested in the almost human unwillingness of the machine; it had one or two tricks, such as refusing to swallow the stuff, and holding it fast in one place while it stabbed the needle down a dozen times, savagely, that pleased her for a few repetitions. But soon nurse got what she called the knack and the machine obeyed her, and roamed over Viola's clothes-to-be just as nurse wanted it to go. Still Viola was not allowed to put on her dress and go away. She stood by the fire, trying to see how the flames grew, hoping that soon they would turn the coal into bright pinky hills; but the fire was new, the lumps of coal were hardly red even underneath, the thin yellow flames did not look as if they would burn if she were to put her finger into them. She thought that it would be fun if flames could be picked like flowers. They would be alive, snaky, all twisting about in the hand that held them; much nicer than flowers, that stayed still, and never cared for being in a house, but died soon. Fire didn't mind houses, it was used to them; it wouldn't need water in its vases; it would always be twisting and straining and doubling back; nice bunches of flames; and her mother would say, as she often did about flowers,

'Wonderful how a vase or two will brighten a room.'

Viola watched the hot flame-flowers growing, and would have liked to put her hand into their funny black garden, but nurse saw and said,

'Come away from that fire at once. You'll be getting chilblains.'

Viola would have liked to say that nurse was wrong, and that only servants got chilblains; but she knew that such answers annoyed nurse, who called them arguing. 'Don't you argue with me,' was one of nurse's speeches that Viola feared. There was temper behind it. So she moved away from the fire and went slowly over to the window, to breathe on it, and make patterns in the breath that got caught on the panes. Nurse said at once that she was in the light and told her to move out of it. She obeyed, feeling sulky and impotent, and wishing with all her strength that something would happen to nurse, that she would get very ill, or go away to some other child as she had often threatened to do. She wished the scissors would stand up on their round ends where the holes were for fingers, and snap at nurse's hands as they flattened the stuff under the quick needle. Viola looked very hard at the scissors, wanting them to get up and walk on those round feet towards nurse's hands. She put herself on her honour not to blink, which would break the strength of the wish, and she stared at the scissors, lying with their blades a little open on a pile of stuff. She stared so long that her eyes began to draw towards each other and to feel watery; to drive away the feeling she moved them up and down, following the white line that shone on one of the blades; the other was dull, shadowed by the stuff on which it lay. She thought that she would make her eyes like magnets; she could almost think that they were becoming that shape, like a thin round horseshoe. She had to keep herself from winking by bits at a time. 'Not until I've counted twenty very slowly; another twenty; ten.' Just as she finished the last second of the ten she forgot why she was counting. She could see the scissors beginning to move, twitching themselves up in little jerks, and she thought with triumph, 'I can do magic.' She could see the dent the weight of them was making in the stuff, the little movements in the stuff as they twitched themselves upright on it. Nurse did not see, busily making the machine slave for her, but she was warned of something by the child's silence. She stopped the wheel with her right hand and turned round to see what Viola was doing. When she found her standing quite still, very white, with eyes, as nurse said afterwards, that put her in mind of a maniac, she turned back again to find out what the trouble was, and saw the scissors standing upright, but unsteadily, like a man walking a rope, and moving with timorous jerky steps towards the hand that still held the wheel. Nurse gave a scream that made Viola start and cover her face, a scream so loud that she could not have heard the double crack that sounded close beside her. The scissors dropped, and lay innocently on the stuff again; but now the line of the light showed along a different blade.

Nurse looked then as Viola had never thought any grown-up could ever look. She was ugly with terror, more frightening than the happening that had surprised her. She made a scrambling movement towards the door, but halted, and came back to catch Viola by the arm and push her first out of the room. The key was on the outside, and nurse turned it before she let Viola go; then she seemed to forget her, and ran down the back stairs to the shelter of the kitchen.

Viola waited while the stairs hid nurse bit by bit, until even her head was gone, and went back into the room which, now that nurse with her ugly fear was out of it, was calm. The fire still climbed, the scissors had not moved. Viola went to the window, feeling happy. She blew on the glass and started to draw in the grey vapour that began to shrink at the edges almost as soon as it was there. She drew a face, and her own name, and nurse's name, and then another face in a big piece of breath that was the size of a whole pane. This last face was not very like anyone. It was more like an animal, a slug or a fish. It was different from anything Viola had ever seen, and she was proud of it. She watched it for a long time with her face close to it so that she could breath it back again as soon as it began to fade. Then she could hear voices in the passage, Annie's scornful voice, and nurse protesting. She heard Annie say,

'I thought it must be a fire or something. You want to be ashamed, yelling like that.'

'I take my God to witness –' said nurse.

But Annie interrupted,

'You ought to take something for your nerves; not what you do take, neither.'

'I never –' said nurse.

'Oh, get on with you,' Annie interrupted again. 'Well, let's see into the room. Whatever it is can't have got out.'

Viola could hear the dry refusing sound a key makes when it is turned back as far as it can go. Annie shook the door.

'Oh, don't,' said nurse, 'No. What's the good?'

'Whatever have you done to this lock?' Annie asked, paying no attention.

Viola turned away from the window, unable to attend to her drawing while they disputed. At the sound her feet made nurse screamed again, and the horrible noise angered Viola. She ran to the door and opened it, but before she could say a word nurse caught her by the arm and roughly shook her, so that everything she had meant to say went out of her head.

'What do you mean by going back in there, you naughty girl?' said nurse.

Viola did not answer because she was still being shaken. She had felt proud, contemptuous of nurse and able to shame her; now she was silly again only because nurse, though a coward, was strong. She began to cry. The shaking continued, and nurse's voice went scolding on in the full vengeful flood of her relief from fear. Then she saw Annie put her fingers and thumb on nurse's arm and give it a good wringing pinch. The noise and the shaking stopped. Viola could hear her own sobs, which were bigger and more uncontrollable than any she could remember. Annie said,

'Let that child alone. She's got more sense than what you have. Let her go, now, or someone'll know about it.'

Annie waited for a moment, looking very hard at nurse, and went on in a different voice, to Viola,

'It's all right, lovey. Don't cry. Where's your dress?'

She advanced into the sewing-room, picked up the dress and called, 'Come while I put it on for you.'

'You bring that dress here,' said nurse, holding Viola.

Annie laughed and brought it. Nurse snatched it from her and hurried it over Viola's head, not caring how it caught one of her ears and almost pulled it away.

'You be off,' said nurse. 'And you're not to say anything to Mummy; mind what I tell you, now. Go along to the nursery, and don't you move till I come.'

Viola went along to the nursery, where she sat doubled up on the floor near the fire. After a moment she went to sleep, quite unexpectedly, and when she woke it was dinner-time. The morning seemed almost not to have happened. Nurse said nothing. She did not repeat her warning. In any case Viola would not have told, lest her mother might find some way of putting a stop to the magic, but the knowledge lay in her, golden as a treasure, with all her senses on guard about it.

After this the games became great fun, when they could be played; they needed secrecy because of the cracking, whip-lash noises which grew louder the more they played together. She tried to put him through all the fairy tricks, one after another, but he was as obstinate and as unteachable as a cat. There was no magically spread table for Viola, no walnut shells with dresses inside, not even a leaf of the cabbage that could turn people into donkeys. In the mornings, at the forlorn hour when nurse brought her two uninteresting biscuits and a cup of milk covered with wrinkled white skin, she used to wish that he had never come. Before, it had been fun to pretend; the things she imagined she was eating used to taste as distinct as the food at dinner, so that she had once asked her mother if thinking you were eating would do instead of really eating. Now, somehow, the fun had gone out of pretending. She could not build those steep fairy castles in her head, nor ride through those forests. She had made her inside world as a place to slip into when the green ordinary world was dull; now it could never be dull, because she never knew when it might suddenly flare up into magic, and flames might begin to lift and curl instead of flowers in the vases. And a great sword swinging in a castle gateway was less marvellous than a pair of ordinary scissors walking across the sewing-room table on their round heels.

It was disappointing to realise how little Binns could actually do. He could move things and he could make noises, and that was all. And the only improvement Viola could notice after a month's training was that he could lift heavier weights and the noises were louder. He spoilt things for her. He had taken the keen edge off the old games, and would not help with the new ones. She could not think of anything that she really wanted to do, and used to stand by the nursery window watching the sky go past, wondering how the trees could make, with their bare winter arms, enough wind to drive the heavy clouds at such a rate. At the end of such stormy vacant days there was nothing to go to bed for.

Six weeks after her birthday her godfather came, a little man in spectacles so large that she thought he must be a diver. She was taken down to the drawing-room after tea to see him, and her mother said,

'Here's Uncle Godfrey, darling, who gave you that nice fork and spoon. You've never seen him before, have you? At least, you don't remember.'

'Don't be so sure of that,' the little man answered, shaking hands politely with Viola.

'Oh, my dear,' said her mother, 'at the font!'

'Well, why not?' asked the little man. 'You have no right to assume that people forget certain events merely because they happen at a time when the mind has no pigeon-holes ready for them.'

'But you haven't seen Uncle Godfrey before, have you, Viola?' said her mother.

Viola stared at him.

'Of course the child can't in one moment bring to the surface of her mind a thing which happened before the crust of consciousness formed. But I dare say she has the appropriate dreams.'

'She doesn't have dreams, do you? Not at night, anyhow.'

'No,' said Viola, very shortly. She knew the question about Binns was coming.

'Very wise,' said Uncle Godfrey, 'they're a great waste of good sleeping-time.'

'I'm afraid they waste a lot of play-time too,' Viola's mother said; and rather wistfully added,

'It's difficult down here. They're all octogenarians; no children at all on this side of the county. It's difficult with only one.'

'Parents always suppose that children must be lonely by themselves. It's the sentimental instinct of creatures that live in a herd, but it's quite false. How is a child to develop an imagination if you crowd it up with half-a-dozen others and give it elaborate toys, and illustrate its books to the last scale on the dragon's tail?'

'I'm not listening to you,' said Viola's mother, pulling Viola's sash straight.

'I know you're not. But sense is sense even if nobody hears it, as a table left solitary on the top of Everest at the end of the world continues to be a table after all consciousness has perished; though there are people who dispute that.'

'People with a great deal of time on their hands.'

'Possibly, though that's not relevant. A wise man knows that time on the hands is worth eternity on the clock. But the point at issue is this. You suppose that your daughter must be lonely and dull if she is left alone with her imagination, because, similarly left, you would yourself be lonely and dull. And why? Because you, in common with most fully developed persons, physically, are in the habit of restraining your imagination.'

'I'm sure I don't.'

'You're not listening. I say you do. You permit it to depict for you only such happenings as are strictly possible.'

'I often imagine quite impossible things; you behaving like an ordinary person, for instance.'

'I repeat, the most you allow your imagination, which is

your power of creation, to do for you is to provide ropes of real pearls or an admirer like a young Greek god. Both lie conceivably within your power of attainment; utterly dull, utterly remote from the fantastic. Sky-scrapers limit your empyrean. Now the child –'

'You're too absurd. Do you talk this nonsense to your undergraduates?'

'I can't understand how women who are not good listeners ever get married. No, of course I don't. What is the use of talking nonsense to undergraduates or fairies to children? They both know more about it than I do.'

'Oh, you have some limitations?'

'Certainly. My only claim to distinction is that I recognise them.'

'Viola knows all about fairies,' said her mother, bringing her into the conversation.

'I've no doubt she does,' said Uncle Godfrey.

'She has a fairy who comes and plays with her, and helps with the doll's washing.'

'Not she,' said Uncle Godfrey, 'that's not the sort of thing a fairy worth its salt would do.'

'But Viola sees her, don't you? She really plays in the most uncanny way sometimes, just as if somebody was with her. Tell Uncle Godfrey what Binns does.'

Viola did not answer. She felt that Uncle Godfrey would see through the usual answer. Her mother went on.

'Binns comes and helps her to be a queen when they're not busy with the washing. She's very thin, isn't she, Viola? And they have a lovely kingdom down in the far corner of the garden where we burn the rubbish.'

Viola wanted to explain that her mother had got it all wrong, every single word of it; but that would have meant giving up her secret. She stood very square on her feet and kept quiet.

'It can't be much of a fairy,' said Uncle Godfrey. 'What's

the use of setting an elemental power to do menial jobs like washing, or running a kingdom? I reject Viola's domestic fairy as I reject your Greek gods. You fail, both of you. You bind fire with chains; for two pins you'd set Pegasus to pull the municipal dustcart.'

'What is the matter with you? You scold me first because I'd rather she had other children than these funny plays of her own; and then you scold her and say her fairies are no good. Of course they're good. Why shouldn't her Binns be a nice friendly person?'

'Because in that case she might as well have been given an undersized body and sent out into the world, with a reference from Lady Stick-in-the-Mud, to replace your kitchen-maid.'

'He's very unkind, isn't he, Viola? Well, we're quite happy about Binns. We know she's real.'

Viola's mind was in a tangle. She could see that it was Uncle Godfrey who really understood, and that her mother, who defended her on the surface, inwardly, deep down, thought the invention of Binns rather silly. She wanted to do something to show them both the meaning of the unseen companion, and it was her mother's attitude which made her want to come out into the open, abandoning her secret place; the tone, not exactly condescending, but affectionately tolerant and bland. While the decision hung in the balance her mother added something which snapped, like a spider's thread, Viola's resolution to hold back. She said to Uncle Godfrey,

'We won't let you play with us. You can't pretend.'

Viola had no words with which to answer this. It was too wrong, more wrong even than her mother's account of the fairy games that were Viola's own property, and of which her mother, unasked, ignorant, assumed control and patronage. Viola smiled, and a hot misty feeling mounted from her stomach to where her throat began. There was a loud crack just by her right hand, a crack more arresting than any she had yet heard.

'What's that?' asked her mother, startled.

'My locust,' Viola answered, keeping her hand shut tight.

'What a hateful noise! Don't do it again.'

'I'll try not,' Viola answered, with unusual meekness.

But she knew very well that she had no control over Binns in these proud fits; almost immediately he cracked again.

'Viola!' said her mother, 'I asked you not to do that.'

'I know,' Viola answered; a third crack sounded in the middle of her words. Her mother got up from her chair.

'Give me that thing at once,' her mother commanded.

Viola withdrew the hand and held it behind her back. She could not afford to have it examined, for it was empty. Uncle Godfrey stood looking on with interest, as though they were acting a play for him. Her mother repeated,

'Give it to me, Viola.'

Viola took a step backwards, not answering. Her mother made a sudden movement, intending to become possessed by force of the clenched hand which her strength would be able to open. To Viola, frightened already, it seemed the most important thing of all that nobody should open that hand. She had somehow to distract her mother, and make her abandon her intention. She stretched out her left arm with a jerk, pointing at a jar of heavy painted poppy-heads that served for flowers in winter; the jar was a foot distant from the longest of her pointing fingers, and much higher. The odd, stiff gesture surprised her mother, who stopped, looking at the outstretched hand, expecting to see in it the scrap of black tin; instead, she saw one of the poppy-heads begin to lean towards it. It leant out at an impossible angle, and when it was free of the jar it seemed to fall very slowly towards

Viola, as though it were sliding down a solid invisible slope, and it hung in the air just short of her fingers for a definite moment before they closed on it.

Viola could not remember what happened after that. She had an illness almost at once that lasted for weeks and obliged her to forget; then, as soon as she got well her mother took her away to a village in the south-west of France. They stayed there for two years in a whitish villa roofed with curved red tiles; at the end of those years Viola could speak French with a savage facility which she had acquired in self-defence. She was never, for more than ten minutes at a time, left by herself; not even to sleep. At first she was inclined to shut herself up in her silent castles, but they were no longer the same. They would not build themselves easily in France, within a bee's flight of a real castle, to which she could climb. And the village people were different, more vivid, and they were always singing; the songs were queer, like pictures drawn in sound. Viola could not learn them; there were no words on which to hang the slow, balancing phrases; but she loved to listen, and during the second year, because in French it was something of an adventure, she learned to read. Overtaken by that immense new interest as by an enveloping sea the castles disappeared, and the princedoms, and the memory faded of solitary games played in an empty room.

When she could read pretty well, and after a serious French doctor had examined her, she was sent to school at an establishment on the south coast of England where her mother had been assured that a healthy tone prevailed. At first she was not homesick, but after a year or two a longing grew up in her, not for the villa backed by mountains and the dark cheerful people with their unhappy songs; some unreasonable fraction of her wanted, and saw clearly in dreams, the house where she had played alone. She crowded the stupid longing out of her waking thoughts, and did not speak of it to anyone. When she was seventeen they went back to the house.

She had looked forward so long and so eagerly to being there that the actual arrival felt a little flat, as though the house, which for years had been busy with strangers and their affairs, had forgotten her. She came as an acquaintance into the brown hall, looking about her, unrecognised. She remembered everything, the positions of the furniture, the way the light came in from the autumn afternoon outside. Forlorn and restless, with the vacant feeling of a person newly arrived in a new place, cheated of habits and at a loss for occupation, she wandered about, while her mother dealt with the servants and the unpacking. She went into the nursery, where she was no longer to sleep; the patterned birds on its walls had scarcely faded at all. Going down the passage from the nursery she came to the sewing-room, and thought with a pang of wonder, 'Could I have been that child?' She could see the child as though she had been someone else, one of the children who used to come to tea; sulky and secret, and very sure of the worlds she had created. The child had been safe, her strong imaginings had protected her; the invisible thing had been no more and no less real than they. Now it was as though one of those imagined creatures had escaped, taking body and power apart from her; huge, towering above the dwarfish company her grown mind could picture for her. It would be dangerous now. And she had a feeling of courage and elation, like a moment before battle.

She had been given a different bedroom. Grown Viola could not make for herself a golden hall in an attic, nor conjure a pattern of parrots and cherries into a tropical forest at night. She had been robbed by the years of these splendours, and instead was given the room which before had been kept for the most important guest. It was on the first floor, very light, and there were flowers on a small table in the window. The nursery had never been given flowers, except the frail things that Viola used to pick from the hedges and put in a doll's teacup with the water forgotten. There were writing things, as for a guest, and cupboards for clothes. But when she had unpacked and put her own belongings about it still felt empty; and she thought, 'Hiding.'

At dinner her mother said that it was delightful to be home again, not to be nomads any more. She said the house gave one such a friendly feeling, as though it were making one welcome. She said she had almost forgotten what it looked like, and supposed that Viola had, too. She was civil about the departed tenants, except that they had let the garden get into a dreadful state. Viola agreed with it all.

Next day she announced that she would like to have the sewing-room as her own room, to sit in.

'But there are plenty of places for you to sit,' said her mother, astonished, 'and your own room is quite nice. There's a comfy chair. What are we to do if a woman comes in to sew?'

'She can have the old nursery.'

'But that little room is so inconvenient, right at the top of the house. Dark –'

'Oh, please. Really I'd like it.'

'Well, of course – But I can't give you any more furniture. I really can't have anything taken out of the other rooms.'

'I didn't ask for anything. I don't want anything.'

'But you can't leave it like that, without any proper things. I don't see why you want it; you've got all the rest of the house –'

In the end Viola was allowed to keep the sewing-room just as it had been. A fire was lighted there each morning, and this was the only sign that the room expected anyone. It had always been a room that lived by fits and starts. Its guests were the shadows cast by some passing emergency, sewing women, monthly nurses, housemaids in quarantine. It was unaccustomed to people, and during the first weeks of Viola's tenancy it continued to have an air of awkwardness, like a person who is willing to be friendly but has not the habit of civility. Then it began to respond to her continued presence; and although its furniture remained austere, although there were no flowers on its table, it began to look, as her mother said, quite habitable; quite human.

Viola used to sit there for hours, doing nothing, trying to make her mind empty, a long bare attic such as children love to play in. She was sure that if she could succeed in doing this he would be tempted out of hiding, but she could not banish altogether the furnishings that the years had collected and stored there. And there were people, too. There had been a great many of them in the nine years of absence, and they kept coming in, without warning, to the bare room of her mind; people she thought she had forgotten, or had hardly known, shop-assistants, schoolgirls, gardeners. While they were there he did not come. At night she would sit in the dark, staring at some glowing promontory of coal; the red ashes moved as though they breathed light, and the running white glow sketched for her hills and cities she had known; real places always, not the steep, thin towers of her childhood with bridges curved like scimitars leading to their gates. He was obstinate, but she was more patient than Viola the child had been. She tried other ways. Once or twice she spoke aloud, on windy evenings when nobody could have heard.

'You're afraid. You won't come because you know I'm stronger than you. Can you hear me? You're afraid.'

'Do come. I can't remember you, it was so long ago. We used to have such good games. I want to find you again. Oh, do come on. I know you're there – aren't you? – listening. You needn't be frightened of me. I won't ask you to do anything.'

Silence; then, in a burst of temper.

'All right, you silly beast; you coward; you ugly dirty beast. I'm sick of you. Good riddance.'

Between the sudden thrusts of the wind she could hear silence waiting in the room, full of tiny prickling sounds, unguessed movements, and knew that he was there. She wondered if there could be anything in herself that shut him out; sought, but could find nothing, except that she no longer had entry to her invisible, obedient world.

Then James happened. He was an ordinary young man but for one or two engaging tricks which made him more adorable to Viola than the Greek god of her uncle's taunt. His hair grew very close to his head in the shape of a wig; he had large feet and large limbs that contrived to arrange themselves in soft puppy-attitudes. He had a mark like a little arrow-head near each corner of his mouth from smiling so often. Viola sat in the sewing-room more than ever, thinking; but now every part of her thought was concerned with James. She even brought him up once to see it, and gave him tea. He thought it an odd room for her to have chosen, and said so; he was not to know how she felt about him, nor why she was allowing him to see the place where her very self lived. At first he temporised.

'I suppose you feel more on your own up here, out of everybody's way?'

'No, I just like it.'

'Well, you're high enough up. Is there a view?'

But the sewing-room looked on to a couple of nondescript trees and the shed where the servants kept their bicycles.

'No. I hate views. I've had to live with too many of them.'

'What do you do up here, then?'

'Nothing. I don't read or sew or play the violin or cat's-cradle or learn anything or make anything.'

'Just one of the idle rich.'

She laughed because he did; and when he tried to lean back in the unyielding chair and fold his legs comfortably together in their usual way she laughed again because it was so obvious that he would have been happier on the sofa downstairs. She did not mind when he said that women could not understand comfort, for she knew it was true, and when he said that she was a Spartan and he must give her a little fox she was delighted with him for being so funny and so dear as to talk, even in joke, of giving her anything. She fussed over his tea, wanting it to be just right, and made one or two of the little faces she had noticed in her glass and hoped that he would like. While he coaxed a pipe she looked hard at him so as to be able to remember the shape of his head as it bent forward, and his face, serious for once, the arrow-heads quite smoothed out with the pursing of his lips. She thought he would look like that kissing someone; kissing her; serious and intent, thinking only of one thing at a time. She was friendly and natural, not herself exactly, but the sort of self he probably liked, and which she played for love of him so that it almost became the real Viola. She let him laugh at her chairs, and her unattractive view, and the complete absence of what he called the woman's touch.

'I know just the sort of house you'll have when you're married. You'll go to the firm that does station waiting-rooms and give them a free hand. And you'll say to your husband, "There's a sale at the Office of Works tomorrow, dear; they're selling off a lovely lot of iron seats from the parks".'

'I'll marry someone who won't notice. Or someone that's never at home.'

'A commercial traveller.'

'Or a policeman. Or one of those men that sit all night with a street when it's up, with buckets full of charcoal.'

'Good idea. He might let you have the bucket to put an aspidistra in by day. I'll give you one for a wedding present.'

'Thanks, but it's to be a very quiet wedding. The bride and bridegroom will leave by Tube for the Edgware Road, which will be their address for the season.'

'It's funny about you. You've really got a sense of humour.'

'I had the three permanent jokes in *Punch* carefully explained to me when I was little. Since then I have used no others.'

'You are an ass. But nice.'

'Thanks. Your old-world courtesy is charming.'

When they came downstairs and were under observation once more she was casual and normal, and there was not a word to be got from her that was amusing. She interested and stimulated him, so that he found himself that night writing a marvellously good letter to the lady in Ebury Street who had taken charge of his sentimental education. While he wrote and admired Viola sat in her room, or walked irrepressibly about it, with her arms lifted above her head. The room of her mind was to be bare no longer; it should be hung with tapestries and have a thousand candles in gold sconces alive on the walls. She stared into the fire, smiling, trying to see it there as the red and white heats shifted. She thought,

'I wish I had lots of things that I could give him. I wish I was rich and most frightfully beautiful, and that he was poor. I'd ask him to marry me and he'd be surprised and would hate not having anything of his own. But I'd make him and we'd be together. Happy.'

She could see herself, dressed in silver and much taller than at present, standing with him on some balcony, some terrace which looked out on to water. There was no moon, and no light except that which came from a long window open behind them. He would be looking at her, dreadfully in love; and then she would put her hand on his and say,

'We love each other. What does it matter who says it first?'

She did this scene over several times, improving it here and there, changing the *décor*. At the end it went beautifully, with several admiring people looking on, unseen, of course; but she heard their comments afterwards.

After this her own bedroom, with white lights everywhere and incorruptible mirrors, was an anticlimax, and she went to sleep at once, in a prosaic attitude.

She saw him often, for a time. He had a car and would call for her at odd hours, just after breakfast, just before luncheon. They would race through sixty or eighty miles of country while he tried to draw her out and make her say the things which tempted him to wit. She knew what he expected and gave it, thinking that even to make him laugh was something; but compared with the other gifts she wanted to put into his hands it was rather pitiful.

Upstairs in her room she tried to send messages to him, patiently imagining him as he might be at any given moment, sitting with his legs crossed and one foot twisted under the other ankle; reading a newspaper; bending over the shining body of the car. She made herself see these pictures of him so clearly; even the grain of his skin and the way his eyebrows grew were visible to her as though she were in the room with him. And holding him like this in her company she would talk to him, and give him those other things. Now and then his head would lift as if he listened, and tilt on one side as though he could not hear all her nonsense, or her passionate boasting.

'You don't know all the things I can do. I can make ordinary things not be the same. You feel that when I'm with you. I'm a kind of witch. I could do all the magic, godmother things for you. Can you feel me now, standing beside you? I've gone out of myself, I've left myself quite empty, to visit you and talk to you. I'm strong, aren't I? That's why I can come to you like this. When I go back I shall be weak, because I'll have left part of my strength with you. We'll share. I love you when you laugh at me.'

At the end of three weeks he said that he was going back

to London. It was dreadful. She was shocked by the thought of not having him near her, and by another thought, that perhaps it would not take him long to forget her. Only one thing could have made it bearable, if she could have been sure that the night messages reached him. She was almost sure – the pictures were very real – but she was afraid to ask him, lest, to tease her, or because he would not admit he was sensitive, he might deny it. The day before his departure she begged him to come. He refused, lightly, offering some very reasonable and acceptable excuse. She insisted, with a curious force that surprised him.

'I want you to come, please.'

'But I've got ten thousand things to do.'

'One more won't matter, then.'

'No, seriously –'

'Seriously, I want you to come.'

'Any particular reason?'

'One.'

'Tell me now.'

She lifted her left shoulder, and the hand that held the receiver, in a shrug.

'It's far too indelicate.'

'What's that?'

'Nothing. Will you come?'

'Only for a minute, then, and probably cross. About six-thirty.'

'Right.'

She spent the day waiting, and wondering if the whole thing were madness, or a kind of primal sanity. She had not the energy even to smoke. She was utterly listless, surprised at the outgoing of her strength. It could not, she thought, disappear like a blown candle-flame; it must go somewhere, touch something. It was satisfying to imagine those waves of strength beating continuously against the strong wall of his mind. It was worth being tired to have that going on, but she had to keep away from mirrors in order to believe it. Her square child's face and body made an incredible shrine. If she could hardly believe, seeing herself, how should he?

When he came he found her sitting by a fire that was red and low, with only a candle beside her to light the room.

'Well, Cinderella,' said he.

'The light's fused. Can you put up with a candle?'

'I'll fix it.'

'No, don't. Let it alone. You're going back to marble halls tomorrow.'

'So I am, and not a thing packed. What's this indelicate secret?'

'It's not, really.'

'You said it was. Why do you tell such appalling lies?'

'I thought you probably wouldn't come if I didn't.'

'Perfectly correct, I wouldn't have.'

'I thought not.'

'Well, what? Are you going to make an offer for my hand?'

'Not quite. It's something that's been worrying me. I want to ask you something.'

'Don't make it too difficult.'

'I – you see, when I was little I could do all sorts of funny things. Make things move just by willing, and so on.'

'Things? What?'

'Oh, well; a pair of scissors, once. Flowers.'

'Move?'

'Yes. I know it sounds silly, but other people saw them too. This hasn't anything to do with it really, only it sort of leads up. I used to do it for spite, chiefly, then. It was something in the house – oh, I don't know. At least, I do, but it's no use my explaining that part of it. Anyhow, these last few weeks I've been trying something else.'

She leant forward. The light, placed a little behind her,

showed her round head and thick shoulders; her voice was that of a child, and all the candle did was to make her outline correspond to the voice. But already she had forgotten why she had arranged the candle. He felt that he must say something.

'All sounds pretty necromantic.'

'Yes, that was; the first part. This is different, what I'm trying to do now. I'm thinking how to put it. Well, I've been trying to communicate with people. I get out of myself somehow and go to them.'

'Good lord, who?'

'You, for one. And I'm sure I've got you once or twice.'

'Viola, look here –'

'No, let me tell you. Two nights ago did you go out at ten minutes to six to look at the car? Pat was with you. He put his paws on the mudguard and you knocked him off because he scratched the paint. Did you?'

'I don't know what I was doing at ten minutes to six on Tuesday. I think all this is a trifle far-fetched.'

'Well, last night, then. Did you go to bed about eleven and take two books up with you, and drop one on the stairs?'

'No.'

'Don't just say that. I mean, don't tell lies just to snub me. I'm frightfully serious about this. Did you?'

'No.'

'But you must have felt something. Did you hear me saying I was strong?'

'No.'

'Have you ever thought you could hear me talking to you? You mightn't have known what I was saying. Did you ever think I was sort of there?'

'No.'

'Honour?'

'Yes.'

'But where's it gone, then?'

He was alarmed by the change in her voice; it cut through his indifference and his impatience. He tried to cover it up, talking loudly, even advancing to pat her shoulder.

'Of course I often think about you. Look here, don't you think this sort of thing is rather unhealthy? You're only a kid. Eighteen is only a kid, after all. I don't like to think of you taking it out of yourself over a silly thing like this.'

She was not listening to him. She was leaning sideways and back, behind the candle, watching a shadow that was beginning to take shape on the forget-me-not patterned wall of the sewing-room. It was a shadow without definite edges, almost formless, but certainly there. It was a sleek shadow, not angular; like a fish, perhaps, or a slug. She began to laugh when she saw how it was growing, and James, who had his back to it but was frightened, ran to the switch by the door and pressed it down. Instantly light flooded into the room, overwhelming the candle and its shadows, and he was brave again, so that he could even bear to kneel by her and hold his arms round her while she fought with her laughter.

11 The House Party at Smoky Island

BY LUCY MAUD MONTGOMERY (1935)

When Madeline Stanwyck asked me to join her house party at Smoky Island I was not at first disposed to do so. It was too early in the season, and there would be mosquitoes. One mosquito can keep me more awake than a bad conscience: and there are millions of mosquitoes in Muskoka.

'No, no, the season for them is over,' Madeline assured me. Madeline would say anything to get her way.

'The mosquito season is never over in Muskoka,' I said, as grumpily as anyone could speak to Madeline. 'They thrive up there at zero. And even if by some miracle there are no mosquitoes, I've no hankering to be chewed to pieces by black flies.'

Even Madeline did not dare to say there would be no black flies, so she wisely fell back on her Madelinity.

'Please come, for my sake,' she said wistfully. 'It wouldn't be a real party for me if you weren't there, Jim darling.'

I am Madeline's favourite cousin, twenty years her senior, and she calls everybody darling when she wants to get something out of him. Not but that Madeline ... but this story is not about Madeline. It is about an occurrence which took place at Smoky Island. None of us pretends to understand it, except the Judge, who pretends to understand everything. But he really understands it no better than the rest of us. His latest explanation is that we were all hypnotized and in the state of hypnosis saw and remembered things we couldn't otherwise have seen or remembered. But even he cannot explain who or what hypnotized us.

I decided to yield, but not all at once.

'Has your Smoky Island housekeeper still got that detestable white parrot?' I asked.

'Yes, but it is much better-mannered than it used to be,' assured Madeline. 'And you know you have always liked her cat.'

'Who'll be in your party? I'm rather finicky as to the company I keep.'

Madeline grinned.

'You know I never invite anyone but interesting people to my parties' – I bowed to the implied compliment – 'with a dull one or two to show off the sparkle of the rest of us' – I did not bow this time – 'Consuelo Anderson ... Aunt Alma ... Professor Tennant and his wife ... Dick Lane ... Tod Newman ... Senator Malcolm and Mrs Senator ... Old Nosey ... Min Ingram ... Judge Warden ... Mary Harland ... and a few Bright Young Things to amuse *me*.'

I ran over the list in my mind, not disapprovingly. Consuelo was a very fat girl with a BA degree. I liked her because she could sit still for a longer time than any woman I know. Tennant was professor of something he called the New Pathology – an insignificant little man with a gigantic intellect. Dick Lane was one of those coming men who never seem to arrive, but a frank, friendly, charming fellow enough. Mary Harland was a comfortable spinster, Tod an amusing little fop, Aunt Alma a sweet, silvery-haired thing like a Whistler mother. Old Nosey – whose real name was Miss Alexander and who never let anyone forget that she had nearly sailed on the *Lusitania* – and the Malcolms had no terrors for me, although the Senator always called his wife 'Kittens'. And Judge Warden was an old crony of mine. I did not like Min Ingram, who had a rapier-like tongue, but she could be ignored, along with the Bright Young Things.

'Is that all?' I asked cautiously.

'Well … Doctor Armstrong and Brenda, of course,' said Madeline, eyeing me as if it were not at all of course.

'Is that – wise?' I said slowly.

Madeline crumpled.

'Of course not,' she said miserably. 'It will likely spoil everything. But John insists on it … you know he and Anthony Armstrong have been pals all their lives. And Brenda and I have always been chummy. It would look so funny if we didn't have them. I don't know what has got into her. We all *know* Anthony never poisoned Susette.'

'Brenda doesn't know it, apparently,' I said.

'Well, she ought to!' snapped Madeline. 'As if Anthony could have poisoned anyone! But that's one of the reasons I particularly want you to come.'

'Ah, now we're getting at it. But why *me*?'

'Because you've more influence over Brenda than anyone else … oh, yes, you have. If you could get her to open up … talk to her … you might help her. Because … if something doesn't help her soon she'll be beyond help. You know that.'

I knew it well enough. The case of the Anthony Armstrongs was worrying us all. We saw a tragedy being enacted before our eyes and we could not lift a finger to help. For Brenda would not talk and Anthony had never talked.

The story, now five years old, was known to all of us, of course. Anthony's first wife had been Susette Wilder. Of the dead nothing but good; so I will say of Susette only that she was very beautiful and very rich. Luckily her fortune had come to her unexpectedly by the death of an aunt and cousin after she had married Anthony, so that he could not be accused of fortune-hunting. He had been wildly in love with Susette at first, but after they had been married a few years I don't think he had much affection left for her. None of the rest of us had ever had any to begin with. When word came back from California – where Anthony had taken her one winter for her nerves – that she was dead I don't suppose anyone felt any regret, nor any suspicion when we heard that she had died from an overdose of chloral; rather mysteriously, to be sure, for Susette was neither careless nor suicidally inclined. There were some ugly rumors, especially when it became known that Anthony had inherited her entire fortune under her will; but nobody ever dared say much openly. We, who knew and loved Anthony, never paid any heed to the hints. And when, two years later, he married Brenda Young, we were all glad. Anthony, we said, would have some real happiness now.

For a time he did have it. Nobody could doubt that he and Brenda were ecstatically happy. Brenda was a sincere, spiritual creature, lovely after a fashion totally different from Susette. Susette had had golden hair and eyes as cool and green as fluorspar. Brenda had slim, dark distinction, hair that blended with the dusk, and eyes so full of twilight that it was hard to say whether they were blue or gray. She loved Anthony so terribly that sometimes I thought she was tempting the gods.

Then – slowly, subtly, remorselessly – the change set in. We began to feel that there was something wrong – very wrong – between the Armstrongs. They were no longer quite so happy … they were not happy at all … they were wretched. Brenda's old delightful laugh was never heard, and Anthony went about his work with an air of abstraction that didn't please his patients. His practice had fallen off awhile before Susette's death, but it had picked up and grown wonderfully. Now it began dropping again. And the worst of it was that Anthony didn't seem to care. Of course he didn't need it from a financial point of view, but he had always been so keenly interested in his work.

I don't know whether it was merely surmise or whether Brenda had let a word slip, but we all knew or felt that a horrible suspicion possessed her. There was some whisper of an anonymous letter, full of vile innuendoes, that had started the trouble. I never knew the rights of that, but I did know that Brenda had become a haunted woman.

Had Anthony given Susette that overdose of chloral – given it purposely?

If she had been the kind of woman who talks things out, some of us might have saved her. But she wasn't. It's my belief that she never said one word to Anthony of the cold horror of distrust that was poisoning her life. But he must have felt she suspected him, and between them was the chill and shadow of a thing that must not be spoken of.

At the time of Madeline's house party the state of affairs between the Armstrongs was such that Brenda had almost reached the breaking-point. Anthony's nerves were tense, too, and his eyes were almost as tragic as hers. We were all ready to hear that Brenda had left him or done something more desperate still. And nobody could do a thing to help, not even I, in spite of Madeline's foolish hopes. I couldn't go to Brenda and say, 'Look here, you know, Anthony never thought of such a thing as poisoning Susette.' After all, in spite of our surmises, the trouble might be something else altogether. And if she did suspect him, what proof could I offer her that would root the obsession out of her mind?

I hardly thought the Armstrongs would go to Smoky Island, but they did. When Anthony turned on the wharf and held out his hand to assist Brenda from the motor-boat, she ignored it, stepping swiftly off without any assistance and running up through the rock garden and the pointed firs. I saw Anthony go very white. I felt a little sick myself. If matters had come to such a pass that she shrank from his mere touch, disaster was near.

Smoky Island was in a little blue Muskoka lake and the house was called the Wigwam … probably because nothing on earth could be less like a wigwam. The Stanwyck money had made a wonderful place of it, but even the Stanwyck money could not buy fine weather. Madeline's party was a flop. It rained every day more or less for the week, and though we all tried heroically to make the best of things I don't think I ever spent a more unpleasant time. The parrot's manners were no better, in spite of Madeline's assurances. Min Ingram had brought an aloof, disdainful dog with her that everyone hated because he despised us all. Min herself kept passing out needle-like insults when she saw anyone in danger of being comfortable. I thought the Bright Young Things seemed to hold *me* responsible for the weather. All our nerves got edgy except Aunt Alma's. Nothing ever upset Aunt Alma. She prided herself a bit on that.

On Saturday the weather wound up with a regular downpour and a wind that rushed out of the black-green pines to lash the Wigwam and then rushed back like a maddened animal. The air was as full of torn, flying leaves as of rain, and the lake was a splutter of tossing waves. This charming day ended in a dank, streaming night.

And yet things had seemed a bit better than any day yet. Anthony was away. He had got some mysterious telegram just after breakfast, had taken the small motor-boat, and gone to the mainland. I was thankful, for I felt I could no longer endure seeing a man's soul tortured as his was. Brenda had kept her room all day on the good old plea of a headache. I won't say it wasn't a relief. We all felt the strain between her and Anthony like a tangible thing.

'Something – *something* – is going to happen,' Madeline kept saying to me. She was really worse than the parrot.

After dinner we all gathered around the fireplace in the hall, where a cheerful fire of white birchwood was glowing; for although it was June the evening was cold. I settled back with a sigh of relief. After all, nothing lasted for ever, and this infernal house party would be over on Monday. Besides, it was really quite comfortable and cheerful here, despite rattling windows and wailing winds and rain-swept panes. Madeline turned out the electric lights, and the firelight was kind to the women, who all looked quite charming. Some of the Bright Young Things sat cross-legged on the floor with arms around one another quite indiscriminately as far as sex was concerned ... except one languid, sophisticated creature in orange velvet and long amber ear-rings, who sat on a low stool with a lapful of silken housekeeper's cat, giving everyone an excellent view of the bones in her spine. Min's dog posed haughtily on the rug, and the parrot in his cage was quiet – for him – only telling us once in a while that he or someone else was devilish clever. Mrs Howey, the housekeeper, insisted on keeping him in the hall, and Madeline had to wink at it because it was hard to get a housekeeper in Muskoka even for a Wigwam.

The Judge was looking like a chuckle because he had solved a jigsaw puzzle that had baffled everyone, and the Professor and Senator, who had been arguing stormily all day, were basking in each other's regard for a foeman worthy of his steel. Consuelo was sitting still, as usual. Mrs Tennant and Aunt Alma were knitting pullovers. Kittens, her fat hands folded across her satin stomach, was surveying her Senator adoringly, and Miss Nosey was taking everything in. We were, for the time being, a contented, congenial bunch of people and I did not see why Madeline should have suddenly proposed that each of us tell a ghost story, but she did. It was an ideal night for ghost stories, she averred. She hadn't heard any for ages and she understood that everybody had had at least one supernatural occurrence in his or her life.

'I haven't,' growled the Judge contemptuously.

'I suppose,' said Professor Tennant a little belligerently, 'that you would call anyone an ass who believed in ghosts?'

The Judge carefully fitted his fingertips together before he replied.

'Oh, dear, no. I would not so insult asses.'

'Of course if you don't *believe* in ghosts they can't happen,' said Consuelo.

'Some people are able to see ghosts and some are not,' announced Dick Lane. 'It's simply a gift.'

'A gift I was not dowered with,' said Kittens complacently.

Mary Harland shuddered. 'What a dreadful thing it would be if the dead really came back!'

"From ghoulies and ghaisties and lang-legged beasties

And things that go bump in the night

Good Lord, deliver us," quoted Ted flippantly.

But Madeline was not to be side-tracked. Her little elfish face, under its crown of russet hair, was alive with determination.

'We're going to spook a bit,' she said resolutely. 'This is just the sort of night for ghosts to walk. Only of course they can't walk here because the Wigwam isn't haunted, I'm sorry to say. Wouldn't it be heavenly to live in a haunted house? Come now, everyone must tell a ghost story. Professor Tennant, you lead off. Something nice and creepy, please.'

To my surprise, the Professor did lead off, although Mrs Tennant's expression plainly informed us that she didn't approve of juggling with ghosts. He told a very good story, too – punctuated with snorts from the Judge – about a house he knew which had been haunted by the voice of a dead child who joined in every conversation bitterly and vindictively. The child had, of course, been ill-treated and murdered, and its body was eventually found under the hearthstone of the library. Then Dick told a tale about a dead dog that avenged its master, and Consuelo amazed me by spinning a really gruesome yarn of a ghost who came to the wedding of her lover with her rival ... Consuelo said she knew the people.

Ted knew a house in which you heard voices and footfalls where no voices or footfalls could be, and even Aunt Alma told of 'a white lady with a cold hand' who asked you to dance with her. If you were reckless enough to accept the invitation you never lost the feeling of her cold hand in yours. This chilly apparition was always garbed in the costume of the Seventies.

'Fancy a ghost in a crinoline,' giggled a Bright Young Thing.

Min Ingram, of all people, had seen a ghost and took it quite seriously.

'Well, show me a ghost and I'll believe in it,' said the Judge, with another snort.

'Isn't he devilish clever?' croaked the parrot.

Just at this point Brenda drifted downstairs and sat down behind us all, her tragic eyes burning out of her white face. I had a feeling that there, in that calm, untroubled scene, full of good-humored, tolerably amused, commonplace people, a human heart was burning at the stake in agony.

Something fell over us with Brenda's coming. Min Ingram's dog suddenly whined and flattened himself out on the rug. It occurred to me that it was the first time I had ever seen him looking like a real dog. I wondered idly what had frightened him. The housekeeper's cat sat up, its back bristling, slid from the orange velvet lap and slunk out of the hall. I had a queer sensation in the roots of what hair I had left, so I turned hastily to the slim, dark girl on the oak settle at my right.

'You haven't told us a ghost story yet, Christine. It's your turn.'

Christine smiled. I saw the Judge looking admiringly at her ankles, sheathed in chiffon hose. The Judge always had an eye for a pretty ankle. As for me, I was wondering why I couldn't recall Christine's last name and why I felt as if I had been impelled in some odd way to make that commonplace remark to her.

'Do you remember how firmly Aunt Elizabeth believed in ghosts?' said Christine. 'And how angry it used to make her when I laughed at the idea? I am … wiser now.'

'I remember,' said the Senator in a dreamy way.

'It was your Aunt Elizabeth's money that went to the first Mrs Armstrong, wasn't it?' said one of the Bright Young Things, nicknamed Tweezers. It was an abominable thing for anyone to say, right there before Brenda. But nobody seemed horrified. I had another odd feeling that it *had* to be said and who but Tweezers would say it? I had another feeling … that ever since Brenda's entrance every trifle was important, every tone was of profound significance, every word had a hidden meaning. Was I developing nerves?

'Yes,' said Christine evenly.

'Do you suppose Susette Armstrong really took that overdose of chloral on purpose?' went on Tweezers unbelievably.

Not being near enough to Tweezers to assassinate her, I looked at Brenda. But Brenda gave no sign of having heard. She was staring fixedly at Christine.

'No,' said Christine. I wondered how she knew, but there was no question whatsoever in my mind that she did know it. She spoke as one having authority. 'Susette had no intention of dying. And yet she was doomed, although she never suspected it. She had an incurable disease which would have killed her in a few months. Nobody knew that except Anthony and me. And she had come to hate Anthony so. She was going to change her will the very next day – leave everything away from him. She told me so. I was furious. Anthony, who had spent his life doing good to suffering creatures, was to be left poor and struggling again, after his practice had been all shot to pieces by Susette's goings-on. I had loved Anthony ever since I had known him. He didn't know it – but Susette did. Trust her for that. She used to twit me with it. Not that it mattered … I knew he would never care for me. But I saw my chance to do something for him and I took it. *I gave Susette that overdose of chloral.* I loved him enough for that … and for *this*.'

Somebody screamed. I have never known whether it was Brenda or not. Aunt Alma – who was never upset over anything – was huddled in her chair in hysterics. Kittens, her fat figure shaking, was clinging to her Senator, whose foolish, amiable face was grey – absolutely grey. Min Ingram was on her knees and the Judge was trying to keep his hands from shaking by clenching them together. His lips were moving and I know I caught the word, 'God.' As for Tweezers and all the rest of her gang, they were no longer Bright Young Things but simply shivering, terrified children.

I felt sick – very, very sick. *Because there was no one on the oak settle and none of us had ever known or heard of the girl I had called Christine.*

At that moment the hall door opened and a dripping Anthony entered. Brenda flung herself hungrily against him, wet as he was.

'Anthony … Anthony, forgive me,' she sobbed.

Something good to see came into Anthony's worn face.

'Have you been frightened, darling?' he said tenderly. 'I'm sorry I was so late. There was really no danger. I waited to get an answer to my wire to Los Angeles. You see I got word this morning that Christine Latham had been killed in a motor accident yesterday evening. She was Susette's second cousin and nurse … a dear, loyal little thing. I was very fond of her. I'm sorry you've had such an anxious evening, sweetheart.'

12 The Black Stone Statue

BY MARY ELIZABETH COUNSELMAN (1937)

Directors,
Museum of Fine Arts,
Boston, Mass.

Gentlemen:

Today I have just received aboard the SS *Madrigal* your most kind cable, praising my work and asking – humbly, as one might ask it of a true genius! – if I would do a statue of myself to be placed among the great in your illustrious museum. Ah, gentlemen, that cablegram was to me the last turn of the screw!

I despise myself for what I have done in the name of art. Greed for money and acclaim, weariness with poverty and the contempt of my inferiors, hatred for a world that refused to see any merit in my work: these things have driven me to commit a series of strange and terrible crimes.

In these days I have thought often of suicide as a way out – a coward's way, leaving me the fame I do not deserve. But since receiving your cablegram, lauding me for what I am not and never could be, I am determined to write this letter for the world to read. It will explain everything. And having written it, I shall then atone for my sin in (to you, perhaps) a horribly ironic manner but (to me) one that is most fitting.

Let me go back to that miserable sleet-lashed afternoon as I came into the hall of Mrs Bates's rooming-house – a crawling, filthy hovel for the poverty-stricken, like myself, who were too proud to go on relief. When I stumbled in, drenched and dizzy with hunger, our landlady's ample figure was blocking the hallway. She was arguing with a tall, shabbily dressed young man whose face I was certain I had seen somewhere before.

'Just a week,' his deep, pleasant voice was beseeching the old harridan. 'I'll pay you double at the end of that time, just as soon as I can put over a deal I have in mind.'

I paused, staring at him covertly while I shook the sleet from my hat-brim. Fine gray eyes met mine across the landlady's head – haggard now, and over-bright with suppressed excitement. There was strength, character, in that face under its stubble of mahogany-brown beard. There was, too, a firm set to the man's shoulders and beautifully formed head. Here, I told myself, was someone who had lived all his life with dangerous adventure, someone whose clean-cut features, even under that growth of beard, seemed vaguely familiar to my sculptor's-eye for detail.

'Not one day, no sirree!' Mrs Bates had folded her arms stubbornly. 'A week's rent in advance, or ye don't step foot into one o' *my* rooms!'

On impulse I moved forward, digging into my pocket. I smiled at the young man and thrust almost my last two dollars into the landlady's hand. Smirking, she bobbed off and left me alone with the stranger.

'You shouldn't have done that,' he sighed, and gripped my hand hard. 'Thanks, old man. I'll repay you next week, though. Next week,' he whispered, and his eyes took on a glow of anticipation, 'I'll write you a check for a thousand dollars. Two thousand!'

He laughed delightedly at my quizzical expression and plunged out into the storm again, whistling.

In that moment his identity struck me like a blow. Paul Kennicott – the young aviator whose picture had been on the front page of every newspaper in the country a few months ago! His plane had crashed somewhere in the Brazilian wilds, and the nation mourned him and his co-pilot for dead. Why was he sneaking back into New York like a criminal – penniless, almost hysterical with excitement, with an air of secrecy about him – to hide himself here in the slum district?

I climbed the rickety stairs to my shabby room and was plying the chisel half-heartedly on my *Dancing Group*, when suddenly I became aware of a peculiar buzzing sound, like an angry bee shut up in a jar. I slapped my ears several times, annoyed, believing the noise to be in my own head. But it kept on, growing louder by the moment.

It seemed to come from the hall; and simultaneously I heard the stair-steps creak just outside my room.

Striding to the door, I jerked it open – to see Paul Kennicott tiptoeing up the stairs in stealthy haste. He started violently at sight of me and attempted to hide under his coat an odd black box he was carrying.

But it was too large: almost two feet square, roughly fashioned of wood and the canvas off an airplane wing. But this was not immediately apparent, for the whole thing seemed to be covered with a coat of shiny black enamel. When it bumped against the balustrade, however, it gave a solid metallic sound, unlike cloth-covered wood. That humming noise, I was sharply aware, came from inside the box.

I stepped out into the hall and stood blocking the passage rather grimly.

'Look here,' I snapped. 'I know who you are, Kennicott, but I don't know why you're hiding out like this. What's it all about? You'll tell me, or I'll turn you over to the police!'

Panic leaped into his eyes. They pleaded with me silently for an instant, and then we heard the plodding footsteps of Mrs Bates come upstairs.

'Who's got that raddio?' her querulous voice preceded her. 'I hear it hummin'! Get it right out of here if you don't wanta pay me extry for the 'lectricity it's burnin'.'

'Oh, ye gods!' Kennicott groaned frantically. 'Stall her! Don't let that gabby old fool find out about this – it'll ruin everything! Help me, and I'll tell you the whole story.'

He darted past me without waiting for my answer and slammed the door after him. The droning noise subsided and then was swiftly muffled so that it was no longer audible.

Mrs Bates puffed up the stairs and eyed me accusingly. 'So it's you that's got that raddio? I told you the day you come –'

'All right,' I said, pretending annoyance. 'I've turned it off, and anyhow it goes out tomorrow. I was just keeping it for a friend.'

'Eh? Well –' She eyed me sourly, then sniffed and went on back downstairs, muttering under her breath.

I strode to Kennicott's door and rapped softly. A key grated in the lock and I was admitted by my wild-eyed neighbour. On the bed, muffled by pillows, lay the black box humming softly on a shrill note.

'I n – n n – ng – ng!' it went, exactly like a radio tuned to a station that is temporarily off the air.

Curiosity was gnawing at my vitals. Impatiently I watched Kennicott striding up and down the little attic room, striking one fist against the other palm.

'Well?' I demanded.

And with obvious reluctance, in a voice jerky with excitement, he began to unfold the secret of the thing inside that onyx-like box. I sat on the bed beside it, my eyes riveted on Kennicott's face, spellbound by what he was saying.

'Our plane,' he began, 'was demolished. We made a forced landing in the centre of a dense jungle. If you know Brazil at all, you'll know what it was like. Trees, trees, trees! Crawling insects as big as your fist. A hot sickening smell of rotting vegetation, and now and then the screech of some animal or bird eery enough to make your hair stand on end. We cracked up right in the middle of nowhere.

'I crawled out of the wreckage with only a sprained wrist and a few minor cuts, but McCrea – my co-pilot, you know – got a broken leg and a couple of bashed ribs. He was in a bad way, poor devil! Fat little guy, bald, scared of women, and always cracking wise about something. A swell sport.'

The aviator's face convulsed briefly, and he stared at the box on the bed beside me with a peculiar expression of loathing.

'McCrea's dead, then?' I prompted.

Kennicott nodded his head dully, and shrugged. 'God only knows! I guess you'd call it death. But let me get on with it.

'We slashed and sweated our way through an almost impenetrable wall of undergrowth for two days, carrying what food and cigarettes we had in that make-shift box there.'

A thumb-jerk indicated the square black thing beside me, droning softly without a break on the same high note.

'McCrea was running a fever, though, so we made camp and I struck out to find water. When I came back –'

Kennicott choked. I stared at him, waiting until his hoarse voice went on doggedly:

'When I came back, McCrea was gone. I called and called. No answer. Then, thinking he might have wandered away delirious, I picked out his trail and followed it into the jungle. It wasn't hard to do, because he had to break a path through that wall of undergrowth, and now and then I'd find blood on a bramble or maybe a scrap of torn cloth from his khaki shirt.

'Not more than a hundred yards south of our camp I suddenly became aware of a queer humming sound in my ears. Positive that this had drawn McCrea, I followed it. It got louder and louder, like the drone of a powerful dynamo. It seemed to fill the air and set all the trees to quivering. My teeth were on edge with the monotony of it, but I kept on, and unexpectedly found myself walking into a patch of jungle that was *all black!* Not burnt in a forest fire, as I first thought, but dead-black in every detail. Not a spot of colour anywhere; and in that jungle with all its vivid foliage, the effect really slapped you in the face! It was as though somebody had turned out the lights and yet you could still distinguish the formation of every object around you. It was uncanny!

'There was black sand on the ground as far as I could see. Not soft jungle-soil, damp and fertile. This stuff was as hard and dry as emery, and it glittered like soft coal. All the trees were black and shiny like anthracite, and not a leaf stirred anywhere, not an insect crawled. I almost fainted as I realized why.

'It was a petrified forest!

'Those trees, leaves and all, had turned into a shiny black kind of stone that looked like coal but was much harder. It wouldn't chip when I struck it with a fallen limb of the same stuff. It wouldn't bend; I simply had to squeeze through holes in underbrush more rigid than cast iron. And all black, mind you – a jungle of fuliginous rock like something out of Dante's *Inferno*.

'Once I stumbled over an object and stopped to pick it up. It was McCrea's canteen – the only thing in sight, besides myself, that was not made of that queer black stone. He had come this way, then. Relieved, I started shouting his name again, but the sound of my voice frightened me. The silence of that place fairly pressed against my eardrums, broken only by that steady droning sound. But, you see, I'd become so used to it, like the constant ticking of a clock, that I hardly heard it.

'Panic swept over me all at once, an unreasonable fear, as the sound of my own voice banged against the trees and came back in a thousand echoes, borne on that humming sound that never changed its tone. I don't know why; maybe it was the grinding monotony of it and the unrelieved black of that stone forest. But my nerve snapped and I bolted back along the way I had come, sobbing like a kid.

'I must have run in a circle, though, tripping and cutting myself on that rock-underbrush. In my terror I forgot the direction of our camp. I was lost – abruptly I realized it – lost in that hell of coal-black stone, without food or any chance of getting it, with McCrea's empty canteen in my hand and no idea where he had wandered in his fever.

'For hours I plunged on, forgetting to back-track, and cursing aloud because McCrea wouldn't answer me. That humming noise had got on my nerves now, droning on that one shrill note until I thought I would go mad. Exhausted, I sank down on that emery-sand, crouched against the trunk of a black stone tree. McCrea had deserted me, I thought crazily. Someone had rescued him and he had left me here to die – which should give you an idea of my state of mind.

'I huddled there, letting my eyes rove in a sort of helpless stupor. On the sand beside me was a tiny rock that resembled a butterfly delicately carved out of onyx. I picked it up dazedly, staring at its hard little legs and feelers like wire that would neither bend nor break off. And then my gaze started wandering again.

'It fastened on something a few dozen paces to my right – and I was sure then that I had gone mad. At first it seemed to be a stump of that same dark mineral. But it wasn't a stump. I crawled over to it and sat there, gaping at it with my senses reeling, while that humming noise rang louder and louder in my ears.

'*It was a black stone statue of McCrea, perfect in every detail!*

'He was depicted stooping over, with one hand holding out his automatic gripped by the barrel. His stocky figure, aviator's helmet, his makeshift crutch, and even the splints on his broken leg were shiny black stone. And his face, to the last hair of his eyelashes, was a perfect mask of black rock set in an expression of puzzled curiosity.

'I got to my feet and walked around the figure, then gave it a push. It toppled over, just like a statue, and the sound of its fall was deafening in that silent forest. Hefting it, I was amazed to find that it weighed less than twenty pounds. I hacked at it with a file we had brought from the plane in lieu of a machete, but only succeeded in snapping the tool in half. Not a chip flew off the statue. Not a dent appeared in its polished surface.

'The thing was so unspeakably weird that I did not even try to explain it to myself, but started calling McCrea again. If it was a gag of some kind, he could explain it. But there was no answer to my shouts other than the monotonous hum of that unseen dynamo.

'Instead of frightening me more, this weird discovery seemed to jerk me up short. Collecting my scattered wits, I started back-trailing myself to the camp, thinking McCrea might have returned in my absence. The droning noise was so loud now, it pained my eardrums unless I kept my hands over my ears. This I did, stumbling along with my eyes glued to my own footprints in the hard dry sand.

'And suddenly I brought up short. Directly ahead of me, under a black stone bush, lay something that made me gape with my mouth ajar.

'I can't describe it – no one could. It resembled nothing so much as a star-shaped blob of transparent jelly that shimmered and changed color like an opal. It appeared to be some lower form of animal, one-celled, not large, only about a foot in circumference when it stretched those feelers out to full length. It oozed along over the sand like a snail, groping its way with those star-points – *and it hummed!*

'The droning noise ringing in my ears issued from this nightmare creature!

'It was nauseating to watch, and yet beautiful, too, with all those iridescent colors gleaming against that setting of dead-black stone. I approached within a pace of it, started to nudge it with my foot, but couldn't quite bring myself to touch the squashy thing. And I've thanked my stars ever since for being so squeamish!

'Instead, I took off my flying-helmet and tossed the goggles directly in the path of the creature. It did not pause or turn aside, but merely reached out one of those sickening feelers and brushed the goggles very lightly.

'And they turned to stone!

'Just that! God be my witness that those leather and glass goggles grew black before my starting eyes. In less than a minute they were petrified into hard fuliginous rock like everything else around me.

'In one hideous moment I realized the meaning of that weirdly life-like statue of McCrea. I knew what he had done. He had prodded this jelly-like Thing with his automatic, and it had turned him – and everything in contact with him – into shiny dark stone.

'Nausea overcame me. I wanted to run, to escape the sight of that oozing horror, but reason came to my rescue. I reminded myself that I was Paul Kennicott, intrepid explorer. Through a horrible experience McCrea and I had stumbled upon something in the Brazilian wilds which would revolutionise the civilized world. McCrea was dead, or in some ghastly suspended form of life, through his efforts to solve the mystery. I owed it to him and to myself not to lose my head now.

'For the practical possibilities of the Thing struck me like a blow. That black stone the creature's touch created from any earth-substance – by rays from its body, by a secretion of its glands, by God knows what strange metamorphosis – was indestructible! Bridges, houses, buildings, roads, could be built of ordinary material and then petrified by the touch of this jelly-like Thing which had surely tumbled from some planet with life-forces diametrically opposed to our own.

'Millions of dollars squandered on construction each year could be diverted to other phases of life, for no cyclone or flood could damage a city built of this hard black rock.

'I said a little prayer for my martyred co-pilot, and then and there resolved to take the creature back to civilization with me.

'It could be trapped, I was sure – though the prospect appealed to me far less than that of caging a hungry leopard! I did not venture to try it until I had studied the problem from every angle, however, and made certain deductions through experiment.

'I found that any substance already petrified was insulated against the thing's power. I tossed my belt on it, saw it freeze into black rock, then put my wrist-watch in contact with the rock belt. My watch remained as it was. Another phenomenon I discovered was that petrifaction also occurred in things in *direct contact* with something the creature touched, if that something was not already petrified.

'Dropping my glove fastened to my signet ring, I let the creature touch only the glove. But both objects were petrified. I tried it again with a chain of three objects, and discovered that the touched object and the one in contact with it turned into black rock, while the third on the chain remained unaffected.

'It took me about three days to trap the thing, although it gave no more actual resistance, of course, than a large snail. McCrea, poor devil, had blundered into the business; but

I went at it in a scientific manner, knowing what danger I faced from the creature. I found my way again to our camp and brought back our provision box – yes, the one there on the bed beside you. When the thing's touch had turned it into a perfect stone cage for itself, I scooped it inside with petrified branches. But, Lord! How the sweat stood out on my face at the prospect of a slip that might make me touch the horrible little organism!

'The trip out of that jungle was a nightmare. I spent almost all I had, hiring scared natives to guide me a mile or so before they'd bolt with terror of my humming box. On board a tramp steamer bound for the States, I nearly lost my captive. The first mate thought it was an infernal machine and tried to throw it overboard. My last cent went to shut him up; so I landed in New York flat broke.'

Paul Kennicott laughed and spread his hands. 'But here I am. I don't dare go to anyone I know just yet. Reporters will run me ragged, and I want plenty of time to make the right contacts. Do you realize what's in that box?' He grinned with boyish delight. 'Fame and fortune, that's what! McCrea's family will never know want again. Science will remember our names along with Edison and Bell and all the rest. We've discovered a new force that will rock the world with its possibilities. That's why,' he explained, 'I've sneaked into the country like an alien. If the wrong people heard of this first, my life wouldn't be worth a dime, understand? There are millions involved in this thing. Billions! Don't you see?'

He stopped, eyeing me anxiously. I stared at him and rose slowly from the bed. Thoughts were seething in my mind – dark ugly thoughts, ebbing and flowing to the sound of that 'I – n n – n n g – n n g!' that filled the shabby room.

For, I did see the possibilities of that jelly-like thing's power to turn any object into black stone. But I was thinking as a sculptor. What do I care for roads or buildings? Sculpture is my whole life! To my mind's eye rose the picture of co-pilot McCrea as Kennicott had described him – a figure, perfect to the last detail, done in black stone.

Kennicott was still eyeing me anxiously – perhaps reading the ugly thoughts that flitted like shadows behind my eyes.

'You'll keep mum?' he begged. 'Do that for me, old boy, and I'll set you up in a studio beyond your wildest dreams. I'll build up your fame as – what are you?'

His gray eyes fastened on my dirty smock.

'Some kind of an artist? I'll show you how much I appreciate your help. Are you with me?'

Some kind of an artist! Perhaps if he had not said that, flaying my crushed pride and ambition to the quick, I would never have done the awful thing I did. But black jealousy rose in my soul – jealousy of this eager young man who could walk out into the streets now with his achievement and make the world bow at his feet, while I in my own field was no more to the public than what he had called me: 'some kind of an artist'. At that moment I knew precisely what I wanted to do.

I did not meet his frank gray eyes. Instead, I pinned my gaze on that droning black box as my voice rasped harshly:

'No! Do you really imagine that I believe this idiotic story of yours? You're insane! I'm going to call the police – they'll find out what really happened to McCrea out there in the jungle! There's nothing in that box. It's just a trick.'

Kennicott's mouth fell open, then closed in an angry line. The next moment he shrugged and laughed.

'Of course you don't believe me,' he nodded. 'Who could? – unless they had seen what I've seen with my own eyes. Here,' he said briskly, 'I'll take this book and drop it in the box for you. You'll see the creature, and you'll see this book turned into black stone.'

I stepped back, heart pounding, eyes narrowed. Kennicott leaned over the bed, unfastened the box gingerly with a wary expression on his face, and motioned me to approach. Briefly I glanced over his shoulder as he dropped the book inside the open box.

I saw horror – a jelly-like, opalescent thing like a five-pointed star. It pulsed and quivered for an instant, and the room fairly rocked to the unmuffled sound of that vibrant humming.

I also saw the small cloth-bound book Kennicott had dropped inside. It lay half on top of the squirming creature – a book carved out of black stone.

'There! You see?' Kennicott pointed. And those were the last words he ever uttered.

Remembering what he had said about the power of the creature being unable to penetrate to a third object, I snatched at Kennicott's sleeve-covered arm, gave him a violent shove, and saw his muscular hand plunge for an instant deep into the black box. The sleeve hardened beneath my fingers.

I cowered back, sickened at what I had done.

Paul Kennicott, his arms thrown out and horror stamped on his fine young face, had frozen into a statue of black shiny stone!

Then footsteps were clumping up the stairs again. I realized that Mrs Bates would surely have heard the violent droning that issued from the open box. I shut it swiftly, muffled it, and shoved it under the bed.

I was at my own doorway when the landlady came puffing up the stairs. My face was calm, my voice contained, and no one but me could hear the furious pounding of my heart.

'Now, you look a-here!' Mrs Bates burst out. 'I told you to turn that raddio off. You take it right out of my room this minute! Runnin' up my bill for 'lectricity!'

I apologized meekly and with a great show carried out a tool-case of mine, saying it was the portable radio I had been testing for a friend. It satisfied her for the moment, but later, as I was carrying the black stone figure of Paul Kennicott to my own room, she caught me at it.

'Why,' the old snoop exclaimed. 'If that ain't the spittin' image of our new roomer! Friend of yours, is he?'

I thought swiftly and lied jauntily. 'A model of mine. I've been working on this statue at night, the reason you haven't seen him going in and out. I thought I would have to rent a room for him here, but as the statue is finished now, it won't be necessary after all. You may keep the rent money, though,' I added. 'And get me a taxi to haul my masterpiece to the express station. I am ready to submit it to the Museum of Fine Arts.'

And that is my story, gentlemen. The black stone statue which, ironically, I chose to call *Fear of the Unknown*, is not a product of my skill. (Small wonder several people have noticed its resemblance to the 'lost explorer', Paul Kennicott!) Nor did I do the group of soldiers commissioned by the Anti-War Association. None of my so-called *Symphonies in Black* were wrought by my hand – but I can tell you what became of the models who were unfortunate enough to pose for me!

My real work is perhaps no better than that of a rank novice, although up to that fatal afternoon I had honestly believed myself capable of great work as a sculptor some day.

But I am an impostor. You want a statue of me, you say in your cablegram, done in the mysterious black stone which has made me so famous? Ah, gentlemen, you shall have that statue!

I am writing this confession aboard the *SS Madrigal*, and I shall leave it with a steward to be mailed to you at our next port of call.

Tonight I shall take out of my stateroom the hideous thing in its black box which has never left my side. Such a creature, contrary to all nature on this earth of ours, should be exterminated. As soon as darkness falls I shall stand on deck and balance the box on the rail so that it will fall into the sea after my hand has touched what is inside.

I wonder if the process of being turned into that black rock is painful, or if it is accompanied only by a feeling of lethargy? And McCrea, Paul Kennicott, and those unfortunate models whom I have passed off as 'my work' – are they dead, as we know death, or are their statues sentient and possessed of nerves? How does that jelly creature feel to the touch? Does it impart a violent electrical shock or a subtle emanation of some force beyond our ken, changing the atom-structure of the flesh it turns into stone?

Many such questions have occurred to me often in the small hours when I lie awake, tortured by remorse for what I have done.

But tonight, gentlemen, I shall know all the answers.

13 Roaring Tower

BY STELLA GIBBONS (1937)

My father bent his head to kiss me, but I turned my face away and his lips brushed the edge of my veil instead. Over his shoulder I met my mother's grieved eyes, and my own filled with tears.

I lowered my veil, with trembling fingers, murmured some words which I have now forgotten, and stepped into the compartment, my father holding open the door for me. On the seat in the corner lay a bunch of white roses, a copy of a ladies' journal, and a basket packed with my refreshment for the journey.

My heart was like stone. The roses, picked from the garden of our house in Islington, softened it not a whit. I moved them aside carefully and sank into my corner seat. I said not a word; and my father and mother stood in silence too; how I wished they would go away!

'You will write tomorrow, my child, and tell us what your journey was like and how your Aunt Julia is?' said my mother.

'Yes, Mamma.' My lips felt stiff and cold.

'Remember, Clara, we shall expect you to take full advantage of the Cornish air, and to return to us in a very different frame of mind and quite restored to health.' My father's voice was a warning.

'Yes, Papa.'

I folded my black-gloved hands on my lap, and stared out of the window, avoiding my mother's eyes.

The passions which invade a heart at nineteen, like a beautiful menacing army, seem faded and small enough if one looks back on them after a lapse of fifty years, as I am doing now, but on the late summer morning I describe, as I waited with my parents under the dome of the railway station, no heart could have been fiercer, and yet colder, than mine. One voice, which I should never hear again, sounded in my ears, and one face, which I had promised to forget, filled my eyes.

'All else' (as that German philosopher wrote) 'was folly.'

Well, my parents had parted us; and my heart was broken; and there was no more to be said. I wished the train would start, so that I could be alone.

The journey was uneventful. My Aunt Julia was not wealthy enough to afford a carriage, and when, on the evening of the same day, I got out of the train at the Cornish town of N – I found that I must take a fly to the village two miles hence where she lived, which was near the sea.

I found an ancient carriage, driven by a surly-looking old man in a great cape, and the porter, with this old fellow's help, hoisted my trunk into the driver's seat, gave me a gallant arm into the carriage with a wink at the cabby, and we were off.

We left the town behind; and at last, in twilight, we came to the end of the last lane, and faced a little sandy bay in which broke the waves of the open sea. On the other side of the bay stood the village where my aunt lived.

The horse slackened his pace almost to a walk and the wheels slid in the fine sand as we crossed the bay; the soft sound of the falling waves and the lights shining in the village windows were a balm to me.

Suddenly I saw something which – even then – startled and impressed me so much that I leaned forward and plucked at the driver's cape.

'What is that – what are those ruins there, on the left?' I asked, pointing.

He did not turn his head in the direction in which I pointed and I had some difficulty in hearing his surly, indistinct reply, which came after a pause:

'That be the Roaring Tower,' he said at last, curling his whip round his horse's ribs.

I looked, with a livelier interest than I had looked at any object for months past, at the indistinct outline of the ruined circular tower, which faced the breaking waves, and which was almost covered by a fine bush of wild roses. It was no more than a circular rim of stone, higher at some points than at others, but the circle was unbroken. It stood by itself, in the lowest curve of the low cliff encircling the bay.

I remember that I sat upright in the swaying carriage, as we drew nearer to the village, and eagerly studied the tower until a curve in the cliff hid it from sight; and even when it had disappeared, I saw it plainly in my mind's eye, like the dazzling memory of a light after it has gone out.

My Aunt Julia's greeting was kindly but reserved, as befitted a welcome to a troublesome and headstrong niece who had been so imprudent as to bestow her affections on an unsuitable wooer. I was given to understand that my month's stay with her was not to be a time of idle repining – 'mooning', I remember she called my listless air. I was to help her with hemming sheets, with her fowls, and with her garden.

But after I had made my bed in the mornings, tidied my room, and helped Bessie to feed the fowls my time was my own until midday dinner; and this was the time I liked best of all – as much, that is, as I liked any 'time' in those unhappy days.

I clambered from rock to rock, waited through pools in a bitter dream, and saw with unseeing, unhappy eyes the conservatories and hothouses of the sea, green fronds and purple and red, swaying below me in innocent beauty.

But I only grieved the more to see them. Was I not alone in the midst of beauty, and would be so forever? And my heart grew harder, my tongue less apt to exclaim or praise, and my thoughts turned every day more and more inward upon myself.

The Roaring Tower, which, you may be sure, was the first place I visited on the first day of my stay, became my favourite haunt. Its rose-bush was in fullest flower, and no matter at what time of the day I visited it, the first sound I heard as I flung myself down on the parching grass, breathless with my climb up the cliffside, was the sustained, slumberous drone of the wild bees, ravaging the open chalices of the roses.

I have written 'the first sound I heard'.

But there was another sound.

I learned, before I had been staying with Aunt Julia a week, whence the Tower got its strange name.

It was the noon of a burning and cloudless day. I was returning languidly along the cliff-edge from a walk to a village which lay inland, swinging my hat in my hand, my eyes half closed against the waving glitter of the grass and the smiting glitter of the sea.

I was not thinking of anything in particular, not even of my sorrow, my mind lay like a black marsh under the sun – flowerless, stagnant. If there was a thought hovering at the back of my head (I can write it now with a smile) it was a hopeful surmise that there might be fresh fish for dinner. But had I been taxed with this I should have denied it with anger. I hugged my grief; it was all I had. Nothing could heal it; it was a deathless wound.

Alas! the bitterest lesson I have since learned is how gently and remorselessly Time steals even our dearest wounds from us.

As I drew near the Tower I glanced, as usual, in its direction. A little group of village people stood about it, the women clustering together at some distance, the men scattered round it in a broken circle, like a doubtful advanced guard.

As I drew near I heard an indescribable sound which seemed to come from no particular spot but from the whole surrounding air, which I thought at first (for lack of better knowledge) to be the drone of bees in swarm.

It was a soft, hollow, furious roaring, such a sound as a giant distant waterfall might make; the sound I have heard that great hunter, my Uncle Max, describe when he told us how his heart would shake in his body to hear, in the dead of night, the solemn far-off voices of lions at their wooing and hunting in the starlit desert.

The sound rose and fell in waves, exactly as the roaring of an animal rises and falls.

As I advanced over the grass, intending to ask one of the women what was amiss, I saw my own inward uneasiness reflected in the sly, downward glances of the village people.

'What is it? What's the matter?' I asked sharply of a woman near me. 'What is that strange noise?'

She hesitated, glancing appealingly at the man by her side, but he avoided her eyes. I repeated my question imperiously.

'It's only the Roaring Tower,' she said at last, reluctantly. 'When the rose-bush is all out, and on sweltering hot days, miss, the Tower roars, like you can hear.'

'But what is it? What makes that awful sound?'

Again there was silence. The other villagers were looking curiously at me; a few of them drew slowly near to our little group, but no one attempted to answer me.

At length, from the back of the group, a man's doubtful voice volunteered:

'They say it's the water under the Tower, miss. There's a great cave under the Tower, so they say, and when the tide gets into it it makes that noise.'

There were one or two half-hearted assents to this.

But I was not satisfied; the explanation was plausible and yet unconvincing. But the uneasy manner of the villagers and their inquisitive eyes repelled me, and I hastened to leave the spot.

✕

I had been with Aunt Julia a week when one morning I went out into the kitchen to give Bessie some linen which she had promised to wash for me.

She was not there, but at a corner of the kitchen table sat a little fair-haired girl, busy with paper and pencils, which she used from a painted box at her elbow. This was Jennie, Bessie's niece, whom my aunt allowed to play in the kitchen as she was a good, quiet child.

'Good morning, Miss Clara,' she whispered, looking shyly at me.

'Where is your aunt, Jennie?' I asked, impatiently; I wanted to be off to the seashore. 'She must wash these ruffles for me today, I shall need them for church tomorrow.'

'She's gone to market, Miss Clara, and won't be back for an hour or more.'

'Then it's very forgetful and careless of her. They will never be dry and pressed in time for tomorrow. Give them to her as soon as she comes in, Jennie, and say I must have them by this evening.'

But just as I was flouncing out of the kitchen, my annoyance increased by Jennie's solemn, timid stare, I stopped suddenly and picked up her pencil-box from the table.

'Why – there's the Roaring Tower!' I said, half to myself in a new voice, full of the pleasure I felt at the sight of the picture painted on the lid of the box. 'Where did you get this, Jennie? Who painted it? And what's this queer creature with the snout, close to the Tower?'

'Davy gave me that,' drawled Jennie. 'Daft Davy, they call him. He's not right in his head. He painted the box for me with that queer beast. And Davy said he's seen it.'

I stared at her, and back at the box, wondering where the weak-minded old man could have found his model for the gross, long-snouted monster with four brown paws which he had painted squatting close to the Tower.

'You mustn't tell lies, Jennie. It's wicked,' I said, primly.

'But Davy *has* seen it, Miss Clara,' Jennie persisted. 'Long ago, when he was a little boy. That's the noise we hears, coming out of the Tower, when the rose-bush is all out. That's why it's called the Roaring Tower. It's that poor bear-thing, shut up in there, and he can't get away, Davy says.'

I continued to stare at her. She did not seem at all frightened; one little hand was posed over her drawing, as though she was about to go on with her game.

'Well – ' I said it last, drawing a deep breath, 'you are a very wicked little girl to repeat Davy's lies, Jennie. You ought to be ashamed of yourself.' But my voice did not sound so severe as I should have liked.

'Yes, Miss Clara. I'm sorry,' whispered Jennie, anxiously, and then I went towards the door. But at the door I paused, and called back to her, curiously:

'Weren't you frightened, Jennie, when Davy told you about it?'

'Oh, no, Miss Clara,' she replied, sedately. 'He don't hurt people, that bear-thing don't. Everyone's afeard of him round here, and no one's sorry for him a bit, but he don't hurt people. He only wants to get away home, Davy says.'

Well after such a talk between us, where should my steps go but towards the Tower, that afternoon, when my aunt was taking her nap in the garden?

I crossed the sands, and climbed the gentle slope towards it. There it was, half-mantled with its rose-bush, its very stones steeped in quivering heat and silence. Bees droned in the flowers and butterflies reeled about the higher branches.

I crossed the grass and mounted the fallen stone which I

always used as a step whenever I wanted to look down on to the circle of grass inside the Tower.

In the early morning the rose-bush and the wall cast a lop-sided shadow half-way across the grass, and at sunset the shadow reappeared on the other side, but now, at high noon, when I looked down on the grass, it was shadowless, clear and deep as emeralds.

I leaned my elbows on the broken stone rim and stared downwards. My thoughts were vague. Certainly, I was not afraid, and this now seems strange to me, for Daft Davy's drawing depicted a beast that was enough to put queer thoughts into the mind of a better-balanced girl than I was.

But all I felt, idling there in the heat and drowsy silence, was a kind of mischievous curiosity, and a return of the inexplicable pity I had experienced when I heard the Tower at its roaring.

As I lingered, more asleep than awake, an infinitely soft tremor began to jar in the air, scarce distinguishable from the far-off rumour of the sea, and it grew in volume, rising above the sound of the waves and the bees until it dominated them entirely, and I realized that the Tower was roaring, and that I stood, like a swimmer on a sea-girt spit of sand, in the full tide of its sound.

Then, indeed, my heart began to beat a little faster. I glanced quickly over my shoulder, and took my elbows from the wall, and prepared for flight.

But I did not go – I stayed, and no one was more surprised than myself. For pity had come back into my heart; that astonishing, irrational pity for a mere sound which I had felt before.

I hesitated on my stone pedestal, gripping the wall with one hand, and peering down into the silent pit of green. There was nothing there, of course. The grass burned coolly in the sunlight, the bees hung among the roses. And the soft, piteous sound roared about me in waves, abandoned, despairing.

Frightened and moved as I was, I did a strange thing. I hung over that empty pit, calling softly:

'Can you hear me? Poor soul! Poor tormented creature! Can I help you? I would if I could.'

The foolish words, banal and human, faltered back from the airy but impassable wall of beauty presented by rose-bush and glimmering grass. I called again, over the ominous hollow:

'Listen! I am here. I would pray for you, if prayers would help you. You poor, lost thing, you! You have a friend left on earth, if you care to have her. I will do what I can ...'

My eyes streamed with the first unselfish tears I had shed for months. Scarce knowing what I did, I put my hands firmly on the wall, and vaulted the low drop into the hollow. Heaven alone knows what purpose I thought that would serve!

I landed with a jarring shock, staggered forward, and fell on my hands and knees in the grass. I was conscious that all I could see of the familiar world I had left was a rough circle of bluest sky, against which the rose-bush moved in the wind.

All about me, stunning the ears with soft reiteration, rose and fell the voice of Roaring Tower.

'Well!' I said aloud, shakily, scrambling to my feet, and standing with my back almost touching the wall as though I were at bay. 'Here I am, in the middle of things, with a vengeance. I must go through with it now.'

But the words were unnecessarily bold. Nothing happened, not even the catastrophe expected. These feelings, relieved by my shower of tears, slowly grew calmer. The roaring seemed to be dying down in long exhausted peals of sound, or else my ears were growing used to it.

'Of course. The tide is going out,' I murmured, walking

slowly round the circle of grass, brushing the wall with the tips of my fingers. 'How silly of me.' I blushed for my tears and pity of a few moments ago.

My prison was not really a prison. I knew I could get out the moment I wanted to by scrambling up the six feet or so of rough wall, which provided more footholds than I needed. But I liked to linger there, shut away from the world in the sunshine and silence. I sat down on the grass, under the overhanging mass of the rose-bush, and leaned back against the wall with a tired sigh.

How deep the quiet was! For now the roaring had ceased. Not a bee droned, not a butterfly stirred. The air of summer, cooled in this pit of silence, smelled sweet.

It would be easy for me to write at this point, 'I must have fallen asleep.'

But I know, as I know that my body must soon die, that I did not sleep, even for a few seconds. I was awake, wide awake. And I saw what I saw.

A shadow rose from the emerald grass.

It was brown, and large, larger by many times than I was, and at first it seemed like a thickening of the air immediately above the grass, and I blinked my eyes once or twice, thinking they were still dim from my recent tears. But the shadow persisted. It grew darker and thicker, and began to take shape. It was squat, obese, crouching, with a small head sunk between its shoulders, a long snout, and four paws drawn up ratlike against its furred sides.

I bent forward, blinking my eyes again; I even rubbed them with my fists, but the shadow did not move. And as I watched it, the faint sound jarred again on the still air, rose to a rumour of noise, fell to a whisper, and rose again.

The Tower was roaring, and the sound came from the throat of the monster before me, with its head flung back. The creature – vision, spectre, whatever it may have been

– turned its head from side to side as it roared, as though in extremity of anguish; I caught the glint of its oblique eyes as the head swayed.

Did the monster look at me? Strange question, with more than a hint of ludicrousness! How can one speak, in sober earnest, of looks exchanged between a dweller in this world and a visitor from some world at which I cannot even guess? But it seems to me, remembering, that the beast recognized my presence there, for soon it made a blundering, circular movement and turned its head towards me, still roaring piteously, as though entreating my help.

So we faced each other, I and the Voice of Roaring Tower, and as I looked, every feeling driven from my heart suddenly flooded back in a huge wave of pity.

I held out my hands, I spoke to the monstrosity before me as though it could understand:

'Is there anything I can do?' I whispered. 'Shall I fetch a clergyman?'

But even as the foolish words left my dry lips the brown shadow changed.

I cannot describe what followed. I am only a human being; the pen of one of Milton's archangels would be needed for that.

The shadow streamed upwards, melting as it streamed. It seemed to be drawn straight into the zenith, sucked by some invisible strength.

I had, for a terrifying flash of time, a glimpse of huge wings, feathered with copper plumes from tip to tip, of a face crowned with hair like springing rays of gold, a wild face, smiling down on me in ecstasy, of a sexless body, veined again with gold as a leaf is veined. A blinding shock passed through my frame, which may have been (may the creature's God forgive me if I blaspheme) an embrace of gratitude.

Then it had gone. It had gone as though I had never seen it.

There was nothing left. The Roaring Tower was empty as a sun-dried bone; I could feel that, as I sat with my eyes now closed. Virtue had gone out of the very roses; they were mysterious only with the mystery of all growing things.

Presently I roused myself, and after several attempts climbed out of the Roaring Tower.

Weak as a kitten, I sauntered home by the sea's margin. The crisping foam ran to my feet; I could trace its snow under my tired, lowered lids. The slow, strong sea wind, blowing along the evening clouds, smoothed my cheeks. I thought of nothing. My mind was calm as the sands stretched before me.

I was not unhappy anymore. I looked at the great sky, the sand, the darkening sea, the flower-fringed cliffs, and thought, with tired pleasure, how rich I was in having many, many years before me in which to love their beauty.

For now they belonged to me, as all beauty did. This was the gift of that terrible spirit I had pitied in the Tower. My pity, I believed, had released it, and in return it had swept personal sorrow out of my heart, and made me free of all beauty.

I felt strangely impersonal, as (with our human limitations) we imagine a grain of sand or a clover-flower must feel. Light-footed, unthinking, calm, I idled homewards with the homing light.

✳

That was fifty years ago.

During the rest of the time I stayed there, I asked cautious questions of my aunt, Daft Davy, and in the village, but never a shred of a legend could I find that might explain (if explanation were possible) what had happened in Roaring Tower. Davy was terrified, and refused to answer me; and my aunt stared at me as though I had gone mad.

But the gift of Roaring Tower has never left me throughout

my long life filled to the brim with sorrow and happiness. Part of me is untouchable; part of me can always escape into the watching, surrounding beauty of the natural world, and be free.

Is it to be wondered at, now I am too old a woman to make concessions to those who believe that this world is the only world we shall ever inhabit, that I am not afraid to die?

Unhaunted, voiceless, a mere ruin of stones, the Roaring Tower may stand to this day. But I have never returned there to see.

Notes on the stories

BY KATE MACDONALD

1 A Twin-Identity

shocked: police officers, especially female ones, were not held in high regard socially at this period.

agent-de-police: French, a police officer.

salon: French, drawing room.

sergent-de-police: French, police sergeant.

sub-rosa: Latin for 'under the rose', commonly used as a metaphor for secrecy.

chef: French, chief or boss.

confrères: French, colleagues.

bal masque: French, masked ball, probably a public ball with entry by ticket, so one would be dancing with strangers.

blue domino: a domino was a hood and cloak commonly used at masked social events, covering the eyes and hair and obscuring the figure with a dramatic swirl of fabric.

mad escapade: for an unmarried young woman to attend a public ball, at night, alone, and wearing a mask, was the height of impropriety for this period, and was not the behaviour of a lady who did not seek attention from stray men.

voilà tout: French, there it all is.

ma parole: French, my word, on my honour.

qui vive: French, literally 'who lives', used more commonly to mean 'on the lookout'.

Ciel: French, literally 'sky', but meaning here 'Good Heavens'.

'hell': an eighteenth-century term for a gambling den.

en garçon: French, as a boy, in disguise as a man.

at the Antipodes: on the other side of the planet, or at the ends of the Earth.

toque: a turban-like woman's hat, indicating that Marie is now wearing women's clothing.

omnibus: a horse-drawn double-decker public conveyance, with the upper level open to the weather.

Gray's Inn Road: about a mile west of Tottenham Court Road, on the edge of Clerkenwell, then a slum area of London near King's Cross.

on the latch all night: locked all night.

mise-en-scène: French, theatrical term for the set against which the drama will be played out.

valise: a small suitcase.

Que Diable: French, 'What the Devil'.

Bow Street: headquarters then of the British police.

mandat d'arrêt: French, arrest warrant.

fiacre: French, a horse-drawn cab.

trammelled: bound up, hindered by.

2 The Blue Room

gentle or simple: gentlefolk, or gentry, and simple or common folk.

gayest: liveliest, most attracted to parties and revels.

all slipping off her shoulders: she is dressed in Restoration Court fashion.

lych-gate: the gate allowing entry to the churchyard.

shooting-season: the period in early autumn when game birds are shot by country-house parties.

covert-side: beside the places arranged for the shooting to take place, on the moor or on high ground.

Cambridge: Miss Erristoun is part of the first generations of women students permitted to study at the University of Cambridge, indicating her capacity for learning and her desire for understanding.

in my room: tea in the housekeeper's room is a privilege not often extended to guests.

Mrs Marris: it was conventional for an unmarried senior woman servant to be given the courtesy title of 'Mrs'.

salts: smelling salts, made with ammonia to produce a powerful smell that induces deep breaths, to raise the level of oxygen in the blood, and revive faintness.

cinque cento: Italian, short for *millecinquecento*, denoting the fifteenth century, which in Italy was the peak of Renaissance art.

Scott: Reginald Scot (1538–1599), an English Member of Parliament and country gentleman, who wrote *The Discoverie of Witchcraft* (1584) which, in arguing against the existence of witches, lists all his sources and all the evidence he had examined.

Glanvil: Joseph Glanvill (1636–80), a clergyman and philosopher, and a leading exponent of rational investigation that a later generation would call science. His work *A Blow At Modern Sadducism In Some Philosophical Considerations About Witchcraft* (1681) discusses poltergeists and visiting spirits.

Sprenger: Jacob Sprenger (1436/38–1495), a German theologian and inquisitor, who has been associated with the republication of *Malleus Maleficarum*, the fifteenth-century treatise on witchcraft and how to get rid of it. Sprenger is now thought not to have been one of its authors, but was more likely an early sponsor.

3 The Green Bowl

reproach: a lady travelling in this period without attendants (which is what 'alone' meant to Mrs Crosdyck) was unusual, and risked social disapproval.

shirt-waist: a woman's bodice or blouse that ended at or a little below the waist. It would have been considerably easier to wash while travelling than an entire dress.

tea-gown: a long, loose and decorative gown for lounging in, notoriously associated with not needing corsets, and with illicit visits from men friends.

'the key of the fields': this may refer to a recent short story of the same name by Mary Tappan Wright (1898), which relates the indecision of a teacher over whether or not to travel out into the wider world.

bicycling: bicycle clubs had been popular in the US from the 1870s, and the invention of a reliable pneumatic tyre and brakes in the 1880s made independent travel possible at relatively low cost, especially for women.

lap-robe: a large cover to draw up from the buggy floor to shelter the feet, legs and lap, which would have been unprotected from rain by the buggy's hood and back.

hemlock woods: the crushed leaves of this species of conifer apparently smell like the poisonous hemlock, though they are unrelated. Jewett undoubtedly chose this description to suggest that the woods could be dangerous.

triumphant: the (unnamed) hostess is relieved that Mrs Crosdyck has forgotten to be disapproving, which would have put a blight on the gathering.

wainscotting: skirting boards, the boarding that runs along the edge of the walls where they meet the floor.

check rein: an extra rein running from the bit in the horse's mouth, to prevent it from lowering its head while working.

meeting-house: used here as a synonym for a church, suggesting the ubiquity of Quakers, Shakers or other nonconformist populations in the county.

Marion Crawford: Francis Marion Crawford (1854–1909) was an American novelist and short story writer. *The Tale of a Lonely Parish* was published in 1886.

hoarhound: hoarhound (or horehound) drops were made from sugar and a herb from the mint family, tasting of menthol, and used as a folk remedy for coughs.

to pick over: remove rotten beans, leaves, insects and other detritus, to make the crop ready for selling.

Not on Sunday: banning the reading of fortunes on Sundays in this New England nonconformist Protestant community is appropriate for its frivolity and for its ungodliness.

4 A Dreamer

up-country: Australian, for rural, distant from towns.

hand: Australian, worker or employee.

she-oaks: causarina tree, widespread in Australia, whose fallen leaves carpet the ground in a sound-absorbing layer.

swift tapping: the carpenters are making a coffin.

banker: the creek was overflowing and in danger of breaking its banks.

5 The Hall Bedroom

chromos: chromolithographs, an early form of colour printing.

balked: prevented, opposed or obstructed by someone or something.

pricks: 'to kick against the pricks' is an ancient proverb, meaning to lash out at the thing which oppresses you.

transom: the beam forming the top part of the door frame.

Sweeter than honey or the honeycomb: from Psalm 19, verse 10.

6 The House

'spotted': hats made of soft materials like suede or felt show the spots of rain long after the hat has dried.

madeira cake: a soft sponge cake that disintegrates in water.

rubbers: rubber galoshes, overshoes worn in wet weather. (But recall that when she first sat down on the basket chair that she looked ruefully at her split shoe.)

the door open: in upper- and middle-class households the master of the house had his own dressing-room where his clothes were kept.

pomegranate trees: a symbol of fruitfulness appropriate to a bedroom. The luxury this couple live in is both a dream of financial security and aesthetic taste.

Roger ... Virginia: these names are clearly intended to suggest an intimate acquaintance with Roger Fry and Virginia Woolf of Bloomsbury.

Crane: possibly Walter Crane (1845–1915), a great turn of the century British artist, designer and illustrator.

H'Eros and 'Yman: Eros, god of love, and Hymen, god of the marriage ceremony.

7 The Red Bungalow

Kulu: Kullu is a town in Himachal Pradesh, one of the mountainous states in Northern India, formerly the Punjab Province and a social and military centre for British Imperial colonisation.

the station: a colonial term meaning where the military forces and their civilian support networks were located.

John Company: the informal name for the East India Company, the commercial precursor to British Imperial rule in India.

pig-sticking: hunting wild boar on horseback.

Gazette: a government newspaper or other periodical printed to announce official appointments, arrivals and departures to and from an area.

the billet: he has been billeted, ie given this posting by his superiors, which will include a place to live for the duration: this will be his billet, as well as his official role.

wired: sent a telegram, the fastest possible means of communication, sent through a state-sponsored system.

coquette: Victorian term for a flirt, here used to suggest that Baba is a very feminine little girl.

ayah: a nurse-maid for children, in this case from Madras, a large city on the western coast of south India. An ayah could also work as a lady's maid, as the narrator mentions later.

Fort William: an eighteenth-century military garrison and army headquarters built by Clive of India.

Dirzee: a tailor.

going home: moving back to Britain.

chokedar: a watchman or caretaker.

verandahs: colonial-era Indian bungalows tended to follow the same plan of a single open-sided verandah around the central rooms, which all opened on to the verandah, thus allowing a good flow of air to cool the inner rooms which would not necessarily all have had windows.

coolie person: a porter or messenger.

staff-tenant: a tenant on the General Staff, that is a senior army officer.

on its honour: untethered, trusting that it will not stray.

baboo: more familiarly styled 'babu' by Kipling, a university-educated native Indian, employed in administrative positions. While their idiosyncratic English was often presented as a joke in anglophone writing of the period, their educational standards were very high. 'Babu' itself is a synonym for 'Mr', a term of respect.

en suite: French, meaning the drawing-room, dining-room and nursery all connect with each other without any intervening corridors.

go-downs: storage areas.

Highlander: people from the Highlands of Scotland are reputed to have the Second Sight, or be sensitive to the supernatural.

mallees: gardeners.

AQMG: Assistant Quartermaster-General. It is ironic that Netta herself has demonstrated the qualities of a quartermaster in fitting out and supplying her new home in record time.

Chotah Hazra: an early morning meal.

topee: a moulded hard hat with a separate, ventilated interior to keep the head both cool and shielded from the sun.

bran pie: also called a lucky dip, in a which a tub of something innocuous (here, bran) hides small presents for people to dig into to find.

took Baba home: took Baba back to Britain.

hoo-poos: hoopoes, a colourful and raucous bird with a dramatic appearance.

8 Outside the House

Blighty: British army slang for Britain, in the context of safety, and as a refuge from war service.

game: permanently damaged, probably with a limp and unable to take much weight or strain.

my lines had fallen: from Psalm 16, verse 6: 'The lines are fallen unto me in pleasant places'.

livery: uniform of the servants of the family, suggesting that Elsie's family have money if not position.

O P: Observation Post, standing sentry listening for signs of enemy activity in their trenches.

mum's the word: from 'to keep mum', meaning to be silent.

Mater: Latin for mother, indicating that this schoolboy routinely uses Latin tags in his speech as a reflection of his public-school education.

a purple and white ribbon: the ribbon of the Military Cross, a third-level medal awarded to servicemen from 1914.

funk-hole: slang for a sheltered spot away from the trenches where a man could rest in comparative safety.

war scones: food was rationed in the First World War, and butter and sugar, both ingredients for scones, would have been in short supply, so the scones would have been tough.

limelight: the lights set at the front of a Victorian stage, named after the quicklime used to create them. They had largely been replaced with electric lighting by 1900, so John's reference is quite old-fashioned.

cleared: the servants have cleared the food away.

have a slate off: have something missing in his head, as a roof might have a missing slate, suggesting some kind of disconnection in the butler's intelligence.

done: exhausted.

ripping: period slang for really splendid, admirable.

clock golf: a garden game like putting, played around a central hole into which players 'putt' the ball from each of the twelve numbers of a clock face arranged in a circle.

rag-time: popular music from the very early twentieth century with a choppy, syncopated rhythm.

'**Long, long trail**': 'There's a long, long trail', a 1914 song by Stoddard King and Alonzo Elliott. The lyrics make a point of emphasizing the loneliness of nights without the singer's best girl.

of a war kind: like the scones, these would not have been as nice as pre-war toffees.

Possess my soul: from Luke 21, verse 19.

your traps: your bags.

rotter: in this content, someone who is trying to get something he ought not to have.

sport: someone who will accept the conditions that have been set.

old shop: old house, estate.

Gelert: a legendary Welsh hound who was killed by his master for apparently killing a baby, when in fact Gelert had killed the attacking wolf, protecting the child. The name is synonymous with faithfulness.

Angels of Mons: in August 1914 a story began to be circulated that during the Battle of Mons the British forces were supported and encouraged by ghostly figures of long-dead soldiers. It was popularized by Arthur Machen, whose 'false document' short story 'The Bowmen of Mons' attributed the ghosts to soldiers from the 14th-century Battle of Agincourt. This was soon read as fact rather than fiction, and the legend grew rapidly out of control.

tubbed: had a bath in the standalone bathtub that would have been in his room.

seven sleepers: the Seven Sleepers of Ephesus escaped persecution for their faith by hiding in a cave, and were discovered alive hundreds of years later, having slept for what they thought was only a day.

9 Florence Flannery

gimcrack: a cheap and shoddy ornament or decorative device.

poppy: poppies often are in strong colours, but after weeks of blooming their tough petals become ragged, stained, and faded, eventually falling off the seed head.

nankeen: a thick, durable cotton fabric, originally from Nanjin (Nanking) in China, usually in pale grey, yellow or beige, and often used in the eighteenth century for children's clothes and men's trousers.

leaded: the small squares of glass are held in place with strips of lead between them.

corybante: a chorus girl of the period, the term deriving from Corybant, a worshipper of the goddess Cybele, with all its connotations of wild drunken dancing and promiscuity.

duns: creditors, those to whom he owes money, or their representatives.

past her meridian: past her noon, or too old for contemporary expectations of when a woman should marry.

holland: a coarse linen cloth used in household furnishings, originally made in Holland.

cabriolet: a small two-wheeled horse-drawn carriage with a hood, to carry two people.

the park: this would be Hyde Park in London, where fashionable society went for outdoor exercise and to be seen.

quarterings: they came from families with the coats of arms. The more divisions in each quarter that a coat of arms had, its quarterings, the more ancient, and impressive, its owner's ancestry.

Bartholomew Fair: an ancient public fair that had been held from 1133 near Smithfield in the City of London. It would be suppressed in 1855 for debauchery and public disorder. Shute implies that Florence is putting on an act of gentility, since the Fair would have held many performances.

water the horses: give their carriage horses a drink and a rest before driving on.

cordial: an alcoholic fruit drink.

fenced by strangers: he has let his fields to other farmers for their rent, and they have brought in new agricultural improvements, signified by fences.

trumpery: this normally means a useless object, so here it probably suggests merely vegetable rubbish.

Oporto: port.

deserted sailor: a sailor who had deserted his ship.

wattled: a hut made from woven branches.

nabob: a merchant who has made a fortune from trading in the Indies.

beldam: an old woman.

pretty: in the sense of not at all pretty, ugly.

posset: a warm drink of milk and eggs.

Prater: a public park in Vienna, used for amusements.

Saxe: the French name for Meissen porcelain much prized for its fine quality.

Lunéville: French faience earthenware used to make decorative china figurines.

opopanax: a strong-smelling gum resin used in perfume.

frangipane: the sweet-smelling Frangipani flower.

must: a smell of mustiness, unaired and damp.

docks: the juice from dock leaves neutralises nettle stings; the two plants often grow together.

tricked out: dressed up elaborately.

pelisse: a long fitted woman's coat with frogging, buttons and other military details, modelled on a Hussar officer's cape.

bezique: a card game for two players.

Bow Street Runner: the first organized police force in Britain, named after their headquarters in Bow Street, London.

greatcoat with the capes: this is a heavy late-eighteenth-century riding coat with several capes sewn across the shoulders to keep the rain off.

disfigured: muslin is too thin and easily crushed a fabric to be suitable for bed curtains on a massive wooden four-poster bed. But 'disfigured' seems a little harsh.

Papist: in this period Roman Catholics were barred in Britain from the legal and medical professions and from political office, as well as experiencing other, more subtle prejudices dating from the Reformation.

jade: treacherous woman.

***Mea culpâ, mea culpâ, mea maximâ culpâ*:** Latin, for 'It is my fault, my fault, my most grievous fault.'

sleep with him: share the room, but not in the sexual sense.

taper: a strip of waxed paper used to light candles with.

Bedlamite: someone incarcerated in Bedlam, a notorious London hospital for the mentally deranged.

10 Young Magic

white daisy: a Michaelmas daisy, which can grow to four feet high.

cats' cradle: a game played with string or elastic held and twisted around the fingers of both hands.

chilblains: chilblains are an inflammation of the skin and underlying tissues on finger and toes, usually caused by too much exposure to cold temperatures; it used to be a sign of poverty. Warming these up too quickly beside a fire can also produce a similar reddening of the skin.

monthly nurses: nurses to care for a newborn baby and the mother.

temporised: played for time, said things of little importance.

Spartan, little fox: Plutarch's *The Life of Lycurgus* tells the story of a Spartan boy who stole a fox, and then seeing his trainer approaching, hid the illicit prize under his cloak. The fox began to scratch and tear at the boy's flesh, to get free, but the boy refused to give away the fact that he been stealing, or to acknowledge his own suffering, and died from his wounds.

coaxed a pipe: sucking on a lit pipe to make the tobacco draw properly, which requires concentration.

Edgeware Road: they are joking about lifestyles below their class.

Punch: *Punch* was a humorous weekly magazine from the Victorian period, still going strong in the early twentieth century, famous for its cartoons and comic sketches, which were, as is referred to here, often repeated over the years.

Ebury Street: a pleasant street in Belgravia, west London, in easy reach of the richer area of Mayfair but with lower rents.

sentimental education: this lady has been flirting with James in a semi-maternal way.

marble halls: a quotation from the popular song 'I Dreamt I Dwelt in Marble Halls' from the 1843 opera *The Bohemian Girl*.

11 The House Party at Smoky Island

Muskoka: a town in Ontario off the eastern shore of Lake Huron, north of Toronto.

Whistler mother: referring to the famous painting of an old lady sitting in a chair with her hands folded wearing a black dress and a white lace cap, by James McNeill Whistler, which he called 'Arrangement in Grey and Black 1', but which is more commonly known as 'Whistler's Mother'.

Lusitania: a British ocean liner sunk by Germany on 7 May 1915, which precipitated the entry of the USA into the First World War on the side of the Allies. Miss Alexander is using a twenty-year old tragedy she was not part of as part of her personal story, which does not say much for her character.

chloral: a commonly-used sedative in the nineteenth and twentieth centuries.

fluorspar: an emerald-green crystal.

bones in her spine: she is wearing a fashionable backless evening dress.

twit me: tease maliciously.

12 The Black Stone Statue

on relief: accept a government subsidy during the Depression.

fuliginous: the colour of soot.

13 Roaring Tower

fly: a one-person horse-drawn carriage, commonly used as a taxi.

More Handheld Classics

Rediscover some of our other Classics about
fantasy, darkness and Gothic peril.

British Weird

Selected Short Fiction, 1893–1937

Edited by James Machin

British Weird
Selected Short Fiction,
1893–1937
Edited by James Machin

James Machin presents ten classic British short stories by Weird writers, showing the preoccupation of British writers in this period with the things that are only just out of sight, and which should not exist.

- Edith Nesbit, 'Man-Size in Marble' (1893): immense statues walk by night.
- John Buchan, 'No-Man's Land' (1900): a prehistoric tribe in the Scottish Highlands.
- Algernon Blackwood, 'The Willows' (1907): a canoeing holiday on a haunted river.
- E F Benson, 'Caterpillars' (1912): crawling country house hallucinations.
- John Metcalfe, 'The Bad Lands' (1920): obsessive outdoor hallucinations.
- Eleanor Scott, 'Randalls Round' (1927): a deadly folk tune.
- L A Lewis, 'Lost Keep' (1934): a terrifying trap.
- Arthur Machen, 'N' (1934): a lost London street.
- Mary Butts, 'Mappa Mundi' (1937): an American student gets lost in medieval Paris.

Also includes 'Ghosties and Ghoulies' by Mary Butts (1933), her influential essay on supernatural writing.

Women's Weird

Strange Stories by Women, 1890–1940

Edited by Melissa Edmundson

Women's Weird
Strange Stories by Women, 1890–1940
Edited by Melissa Edmundson

Early Weird fiction embraces the supernatural, horror, science fiction, fantasy and the Gothic, and was explored with enthusiasm by many women writers in the United Kingdom and in the USA. Melissa Edmundson has brought together a compelling collection of the best Weird short stories by women from the late nineteenth and early twentieth centuries, to thrill new readers and delight these authors' fans.

- Louise Baldwin, 'The Weird of the Walfords' (1889): a gruesomely haunted bed.
- Mary Cholmondely, 'Let Loose' (1890): an inhabited crypt.
- Charlotte Perkins Gilman, 'The Giant Wistaria' (1891): what lies beneath?
- Edith Nesbit, 'The Shadow' (1910): it creeps.
- Edith Wharton, 'Kerfol' (1916): dogs and a jealous husband.
- Francis Stevens, 'Unseen – Unfeared' (1919): things seen in the lab.
- Elinor Mordaunt, 'Hodge' (1921): prehistory can climb.
- May Sinclair, 'Where Their Fire Is Not Quenched' (1922): a love that will never, ever die.
- Margery Lawrence, 'The Haunted Saucepan' (1922): it rattles.
- Eleanor Scott, 'The Twelve Apostles' (1929): something in the wainscot.
- Margaret Irwin, 'The Book' (1930): whose was it?
- D K Broster, 'Crouching At The Door' (1933): feathery revenge
- Mary Butts, 'With and Without Buttons' (1938): wandering, haunted gloves.

Kingdoms of Elfin
by Sylvia Townsend Warner

Sylvia Townsend Warner

Kingdoms
of Elfin

'Sylvia Townsend Warner wrote one great fantasy novel, *Lolly Willowes*, at the beginning of her remarkable writing career, and one great book of linked short stories, *Kingdoms of Elfin*, at the very end. It's a glorious sequence of stories, in which the courts of Elfin existed through history in our world, with their own customs and manners, attendants and events. History and comedy, romance and tragedy interlace. A book for anyone who has heard the horns of Elfin in the distance at twilight, as much as it is for readers who crave fine literature and are certain that elves and their kingdoms are fairytale bosh.'
— Neil Gaiman

Sylvia Townsend Warner's final collection of short stories was originally published in *The New Yorker*, and appeared in book form in 1977. This reprint brings these sixteen sly and enchanting stories of Elfindom to a new readership, and shows Warner's mastery of realist fantasy that recalls the success of her first novel, the witchcraft classic *Lolly Willowes* (1926).

Warner explores the morals, domestic practices, politics and passions of the Kingdoms of Elfin by following their affairs with mortals, and their daring flights across the North Sea. The Kingdoms of Brocéliande in France, Zuy in the Low Countries, Gedanken in Austria and Blokula in Lappland entertain Ambassadors, hunt with wolves and rear changelings for the courtiers' amusement. But love and hate strike at fairies of all ranks, as do poverty and the passions of the heart. Enter Elfindom with care.

The Foreword is by the noted US fantasy author Greer Gilman, and the Introduction is by Ingrid Hotz-Davies.

Of Cats and Elfins
Short Tales and Fantasies
by Sylvia Townsend Warner

Sylvia Townsend Warner

Of Cats
and Elfins

Short Tales and Fantasies

'Sylvia Townsend Warner was one of our finest writers. I'm thrilled that Handheld Press are bringing some of her uncollected fantasy stories back into print to delight and amaze a new generation.'
— Neil Gaiman

Warner's remaining four Elfin stories are gathered together with her essay on Elfins, a strange story about a dryad, and the remarkable forgotten tales of *The Cat's Cradle Book* (1940), eighty years after its first publication. This is a new selection of Warner's remaining fantasy short stories, collected for a new generation of fantasy enthusiasts and Warner fans.

The Cat's Cradle Book reflects Warner's preoccupation with the dark forces at large in Europe in the later 1930s. It opens with a story about the talking cats that die of a murrain in a manor based on Warner's own Norfolk home with Valentine Ackland. 'Bluebeard's Daughter' narrates the adventures of Bluebeard's daughter by his third wife, and her propensity for locked doors. Warner mixes fables and myths with storytelling traditions old and new to express her unease with modern society, and its cruelties and injustices.